NOTICE

For information about the author, translations and content guidance, please refer to the back of this book.

D1601226

THE ASSASSIN THIEF

MADELINE TE WHIU

First published in 2022 by New Dawn Publishing Pty Ltd
www.newdawnpublishing.com.au

@newdawnpub

A catalogue record for this
work is available from the
National Library of Australia

Typeset in 11/15pt Adobe Garamond Pro

ISBN: 978-0-6454899-0-3

Printed and bound in Australia by Griffin Press, part of Ovato

—

New Dawn acknowledges the Elders and Traditonal Owners of country throughout
Australia and their connection to lands, waters and communities. We acknowledge
the Noongar people whose lands on which we operate. We pay our respect to Elders
past, present and emerging, and extend that respect to all Aboriginal and Torres
Strait Islander peoples today.

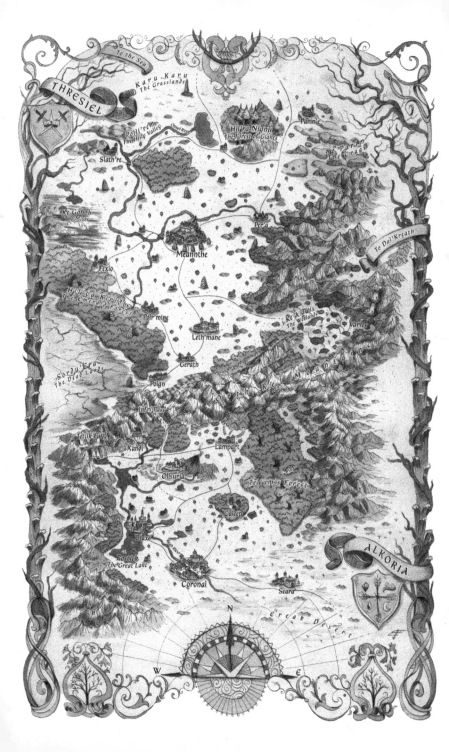

PROLOGUE

SELENIA

She knows their time will pass, that one day, they will fade into the ashes of memory. All the Gifts they wield will become lost to legend. She wonders how skewed the story will become in time; what whispers will be shared over meals and fires about the might of the Thieves? She snorts at the name given to her kind. Far across the seas, they are given different names. Each are feared and hated in their own way. Yet that does not stop people from bowing to their greatness or paying for the use of their Gifts.

Laying back in a huge copper tub, she props her long legs up on the rim where they sit gleaming with the oils infused in the water. Steam rises in a steady curl as she trails her fingers across the surface, watching the ripples.

Tipping her head back, she sighs. She had not thought it would come to this, to these sorts of pleas and bargains to keep her people safe.

A tentative knock pulls her from her musings. A young girl peers her head around the door to let her know the guests have arrived, before scurrying away. Water sloshes to the marble floor as the woman climbs out of the bath. Wrapping a robe around herself, she pads into her bedroom.

Presentation is everything tonight; her guest will seek out any flaws she might possess. Her handmaidens carefully prepare her, creating the mask of a woman with no cracks or footholds with which to bargain. Powder and curls, glittering gems, an elegant sea-blue gown – all to hide the power in her veins; a sleight of hand to distract those who wish to destroy her and those she stands to protect.

She must appear strong and in control, but not too powerful, lest she be seen as a threat to those she hopes to charm.

Once she is ready, the servants file out in silence, leaving her staring at her reflection in the gilded mirror. She runs a critical eye over her appearance, then, satisfied with what she sees, takes a bracing breath before sweeping out of the room in a rustle of silk and winking stones. The time has come.

☙

She lies in the darkness of her room, swamped by the massive plush bed and exhausted to the bone from her dealings over dinner. She has put her plans in place and yet she fears what is to come next. The night has pushed her Gifts to the limit and she fights the pull of sleep as she strains her ears.

The moon moves across the sky as the bells crawl by. Though she is expecting it, though she had planted the seed for it to happen at dinner, the soft click of the latch on her door makes her heart surge into her throat. Her heart begins to race and she squeezes her eyes shut against the sudden prickle of tears. She sits up as the door gently thumps closed and forces a sultry smile to her lips as she gazes at the male across her bedchamber.

He approaches without a word, his stride across the carpet lithe and predatory like that of a falkir. He stands looking down at her. When he reaches to tug back the satin, she has to fight the urge to cover herself, despite the slip clothing her. Instead, she shifts over to make space, inviting him to join her.

For a moment, her fingers twitch towards the dagger hidden between the mattress and the headboard. Her eyes dance across his features, watching for any sign that he knows what she is doing. That he knows she is indulging in the thought of driving a blade between his ribs.

Sliding her hand under the pillow, her fingers barely graze the cool steel. She can do it. Rip the dagger from its hiding place and leap on him. Slide the sharp blade across his throat, leaving behind a ruby necklace that would run down his chest and stain her sheets.

The moment stretches out, like taffy pulled too thin. Her heart thumps in her chest, so loudly she is sure her visitor can hear it. The steel is a cool caress against her fingertips.

But such luxuries would be an act of war. One she, nor her people, are prepared for. Instead, she adjusts her position, propping her arm up behind her head. The picture of prideful sensuality.

His gaze rakes over her body possessively. He reaches up to unbutton his shirt front. The look on his face makes bile rise in her throat. She forces herself to hold his gaze, keeping her mask firmly in place, as he pulls the fabric over his head and leans down toward her.

CHAPTER 1

BEFORE THE WAR

The heavy clip of boots down the winding stone corridor precedes the guards, making Telium's heart leap up into her throat.

Shit, shit, shit.

The stone under her fingers is cool and rough as she tries to pry it from its place in the floor. It shifts slightly under the pressure. Her pulse beats in her throat in time to the guards' footsteps. Her wrists, bruised from the constant rubbing of her cuffs, cry at the abuse.

Her fingernails strain as she forces them into the small lip of the stone, jiggling it back and forth. Desperately trying to pull it free.

Telium swears under her breath, jaw flexing.

Her tiny, dank cell lightens in small degrees as her three captors come closer. The torchlight dances on the damp stone walls. She keeps her back turned to them, cuffed hands hidden in the shadow of her body.

Thirst rakes its claws up her throat. The noise cuts off abruptly as the guards come to a stop. The only sound is the crackling of flame.

'Come to make sure I haven't died?' Telium rasps, her voice gritty from disuse.

Her starved muscles tremble from holding her crouched position. Fingers stinging from where she has scraped them raw, Telium cringes at the whisper of stone against stone as she works the small slab free.

'Or come to make sure I haven't escaped and come to kill you in your sleep?'

Her voice bounces strangely off the walls. She knows who stands behind her. Has watched the guards who come to check on her through the bars of her cell. The red-haired one occasionally rubs his shoulder; an old injury flaring up in the cold of the prison. The others are twins in every aspect bar their hair. One keeps it cropped close to his scalp. The other, a length of blond braid disappears under his black uniform.

The red-haired guard snorts. 'As if you could escape here anyway.'

'Don't speak to her, Adam.' That was the short-haired guard.

Telium's brain latches onto that piece of information. *Adam.*

'Shut up.' Adam hisses, as if he too realises his friend's mistake. 'What can she do, anyway?'

There is the sound of boots on stone and Telium knows he has moved closer to the bars. Telium grits her teeth against the pain in her hands as she works the stone. She is very rapidly running out of time.

'Life-Thief's comin' to get you.'

Telium twitches, chains around her wrists jingling. Ice-cold dread sloshes through her. For a moment, fear reaches for her, hooking its talons into her chest; freezing her in place.

Flexing her jaw, Telium shakes them off. Attacking the stone with renewed fervour, the mortar around the edge has begun to crack. She just needs a few more moments.

'Must'a been something awful,' that is the twin with the braid, his voice soft, 'for the Queen to throw her most trusted assassin 'n here. Greybane ain't exactly for swindlers and bread thieves.'

Adam hums a noncommittal response. Telium hears the whistle of his club before it bashes into the iron bars. The clang dances down the corridor before echoing back. She doesn't flinch hearing the ire in his voice when he speaks.

'I remember you walking around the palace, all high and mighty – the Queen's pet. Like you really had the blood of Tenebris in you.' A rustle of fabric and the click of his ring on the bars. 'Yet here you are. Caged and beat. You're just a girl.'

'Just a girl,' the short-haired twin repeats, his voice an octave too high. 'And t'morrow you'll die like one.'

Telium's ears prick up. 'Tomorrow?'

'Aye, an' when that Life-Thief arrives, I bet you scream like one too.'

Though her back is turned, Telium keeps her face blank. Empty. Even as a sliver of fear spikes through her. A Life-Thief.

How could she?

'Doesn't sound so bad,' Telium croaks as the mortar around the stone starts to crumble.

'Liar. Your tune will change when your soul is being sucked from your body. Rippin' out everything that makes you, you.' The squeak is gone from the twin's voice now.

'When I get out of here,' she breathes, loud enough for the guards to hear, 'you'll be the first to die.'

'Let's see how long that cocky facade lasts when a

Life-Thief is feastin' on every horrible moment and memory,' Adam spits. 'Prolonging it to make the experience as painful as possib—'

He cuts off with a sharp intake of breath that makes Telium's pulse spike.

'What are you doin'?' Adam snaps, voice heavy with suspicion.

Telium doesn't respond this time. The scrape of stone against stone is deafening in the sudden silence.

'Hey!' Adam's shout is accompanied by his club cracking against the bars. 'Turn around.'

Telium curses under her breath as the stone lifts up a finger's-width then catches again.

'Stop that.' The jingle of keys and the sound of a second guard moving closer. 'Turn around!'

A hiss of pain escapes as her nails split and crack. Telium's pulse flutters in her throat. She doesn't bother with stealth now as she reefs on the stone. Her manacles clatter and ring like a death bell. She hears the clunk of the cell door unlocking.

Time's up.

'Turn around! I swear to Tenebris I'll bash your head in.'

As if in slow motion, Telium hears the creak of the cell door swinging open. The rasp of a blade being drawn from its scabbard from the short-haired guard. Her fingers scramble for purchase on the stone as Adam strides towards her.

It is a small cell; barely wider than her outstretched arms. The clip of his boots sounds once. Twice. Then Telium throws herself to the side. Adam's massive club slams into the floor, missing her by a hair's-breadth.

Flipping onto her back, Telium uses her momentum to kick out at him. Having put all his weight behind his blow, Adam is bent over and Telium's foot catches him square in the face. The guard's head snaps back, blood splattering the blue embroidery on his uniform.

Telium lunges forward, grasping for the stone; at the same time, Adam's hand comes away from his face, red with blood from his split lip. Her cuffs scrape against the stone floor. Pain flares as her bare knees skid across the rough surface.

'You little *bitch*.' He lunges at her, club raised. With a final tug that pulls the skin off the ends of some fingers, Telium gets the stone loose. Ducking in close, she swings.

The stone connects with Adam's elbow with a satisfying crunch. But the move costs her, and Telium catches part of the club on her shoulder. The blow sends her skidding across the cell floor to fetch up against the wall. Stars dance across the backs of her eyes. Pain and wet warmth bloom across her elbows from where the stone floor takes off skin. The taste of copper fills her mouth.

With a grunt, Telium pushes herself to her feet. With a speed that defies her weeks in captivity, she steps inside Adam's reach before he can recover. Her fingers cramp around the stone as it arcs towards his head. It finds its mark with an oddly muffled thump. Like a marionette with its strings cut, Adam topples to the ground.

Telium staggers back to avoid being taken down by the man. She has barely sucked in a breath when she is forced to throw her arms up to defect a blow from the short-haired twin. His blade slices towards her neck. Sparks jump to life as the sword connects with the granite in Telium's hand.

The edge of the blade misses her fingers by a whisper. Telium kicks out at the inside of his knee. Despite being barefoot, the joint yields with a pop. As the man's weight buckles, Telium grips the wrist that holds his sword. She spins in close, putting her back to his front.

Using the momentum of her turn, she pitches the stone at the second twin with the braid. The movement is hindered by the chains linking her wrists. Still, the projectile catches the man in the face just as he steps over the threshold of her cell. Blood spurts from his nose. He falls back with a muffled cry.

Completing her spin, Telium brings her elbow up and over her shoulder. Her grazed skin stings as it collides with the short-haired twin's jaw. He staggers from the blow. Bringing her elbow down, she grips the pommel of the sword. With her other hand she reefs on the man's wrist. Twisting it savagely until he screeches and drops the blade.

Telium twirls the sword in her grip as she turns to face him. He is cradling his wrist, doubled over the arm. His face is flushed red, eyes flashing as he looks up at her. The blood rapidly drains from his face as he spots his blade in Telium's shackled grasp.

He throws out his good hand and staggers back a step. As if he could ward her off with sheer will alone.

'Now let's see who's going to scream like a girl.' Telium's voice grates out of her as she stalks towards the twin. Over his shoulder, the brother has staggered to his feet. Blood runs down his neck, staining his uniform a deep purple.

He blanches as he sees Telium with a weapon. Turning on his heels, he flees. Cursing his brother, the short-haired twin throws himself at Telium in vain.

'Always knew there was somethin' about you,' the remaining twin pants, 'with your queer looks and your penchant for death.'

A blow to the temple with the pommel of the sword sends him crashing to the ground. With the air of someone picking flowers, Telium grips a fistful of blond hair. Her chains bounce and ring like church bells. Yanking his head back, she bares his throat to her steel. His life-blood paints a scarlet arc across the floor.

Her blade clatters to the ground as she takes a steadying breath. It shudders into her lungs. Grunting with the effort, she launches into a sprint after the final guard.

She can feel her lip beginning to swell from her collision with the wall. But the hurt pales in comparison to the pain shredding her heart.

Gritting her teeth, Telium forces her mind back to the present; away from the screaming echoes and blood-stained floor.

Spitting blood, Telium races through the damp corridors, fleeing the prison of the Queen she had sworn to serve with her life. Her bare feet slap the cool, grey stone, racing the rhythm of her heart as it pounds in her chest. Her breath scrapes in and out of her lungs. The once-pristine court gown she wears is now dirty and torn. Fresh blood splatters the skirts and soaks one sleeve cuff. None of it hers.

⁀

Telium's muscles tremble as her body hangs precariously from the side of the prison. She has overestimated her strength to scale the wall from one of the few windows three storeys up.

She hisses in pain as she jams her fingers into another tiny crevice. Her nails are cracked and bloody. Her muscles twitch and spasm. Willing her mind to blankness, she struggles to distance herself from the pain in her body as she slowly, painfully, makes her way down the wall.

Easing her weight down, Telium carefully curls her toes around a slight ledge in the stone.

Then gasps as it gives way beneath her. As if in slow motion, she feels the mortar crumble out from beneath her foot. Her heart flies up into her throat as a breathless cry escapes her.

Her skin rips as her fingers scramble desperately for purchase as she skids down the wall. Green flashes in the corner of her vision seconds before she hits the ground. But it is enough for her to know she wasn't as high as she thought.

The impact forces the air out of her lungs in a *whoosh,* and she rolls to save her ankles.

Years of training has her body pushing itself up before she can register her aches. She is staggering to the cover of the gardens before she manages to draw a gasping breath.

Ducking under the cover of a large hedge, Telium makes her way to the outer wall. Staying hidden between the generous greenery, she heads towards the border of the prison. Staggering like a drunkard all the while.

I have to get into the city, disappear into the streets, she thinks. *I can't fight in this condition. If I'm caught—*

She won't finish the thought. Telium's legs shake with every step, her fingers twitching with cramps. Panting gently, she takes stock of her injuries. With how weak she is, that climb should have killed her. It was a miracle she hadn't fallen to her death.

One of her nails is nearly completely ripped off; her feet are black and bloody. The red of her dress is stained an even deeper crimson in spots. When the guards had dumped her in her cell, they had searched her thoroughly, even going so far as to yank the leather tie from her hair. Now it blows wildly about her face.

She looks a mess.

Reaching the far edge of the prison grounds, Telium searches for the patrolling guards. Scraping together her dwindling energy, she readies for her final dash to freedom.

Without warning, an odd tickling sensation brushes up against the back of her mind. Something cold and harsh slams into her side, knocking the breath from her with a grunt.

Caught by surprise and too weak to fight gravity, Telium goes crashing to the dirt.

She spits as the metallic taste of blood fills her mouth. Her heart kicks into a gallop. Someone has caught her. Gritting her teeth through exhaustion, Telium flips onto her back.

'That was a coward's blow,' she growls, just as a silky voice sounds behind her.

'My, my. What a state for the Siren Queen's assassin to be in.'

From a gap between the dense leaves a man appears. His gaudy purple robes cover him from neck to toe. They rustle quietly as he strolls towards her. His amulet catches Telium's eye; orange and suspended around his neck from a length of gold chain, the gem is the size of a duck's egg. He steeples his fingers in front of him, causing his multitude of rings to glint in the twilight.

The Thief looks vaguely familiar, but Telium's exhausted brain will not supply her with a name. She wipes her mouth on her shoulder, eyes not leaving him as he comes to a stop a few feet from her. The man looks at her with a mixture of triumph and expectation, his narrow face pulled into a smirk.

'Am I meant to know who you are?' she asks wearily.

The Thief's lips thin. 'Tenebris Kin; always so arrogant. You know you met me multiple times in court. I was just on my way to help prepare the summoning.' When Telium stays silent, red stains the man's cheeks. 'Faustus,' he grinds out.

Telium doesn't reply and Faustus curls his lip at her.

'How far you have fallen; your tumble from grace not sitting well with you? The cell's a far cry from your lavish palace chambers?' There is something slimy about his silken tone.

Telium only pays half a mind to his taunting, shakily forcing herself to her feet. She knows what the robes and jewels mean. Power-Thief, born with the ability to draw raw power from other Thieves and store it in precious gems to be shaped at will.

Just five gems? she notes. *Such rabble my Queen has surrounded herself with. I would have thought Faustus would have amassed more power by now.*

The more gems a Power-Thief has, the more power they have stored. One of the most powerful Thieves in her Queen's court has no less than fifteen glittering, precious gems on his person.

Reaching out a hand, Faustus makes a fist. Telium's breath is forced out of her as her arms are cinched to her sides. Invisible bands holding them in place.

'I wonder what the Queen will give me for thwarting your pathetic attempt at escape?' Faustus muses, turning his head as he scans for a guard.

'Tenebris claim you.' Telium spits viciously, even as her heart stumbles into a sprint.

She bares her blood-coated teeth at him in defiance. Sweat prickles her palms. Her pulse beats in her throat as she struggles weakly.

You are going to die, she realises, *weak as you are, you can't even break the restraints of a low-level Power-Thief.*

Telium's body makes small, jerky movements as she attempts to twist free from her invisible restraints. Her teeth grind together in frustration. Pain lashes up her arms from where they are bound.

It can't end like this.

The faintest pressure like a whispered breeze in her ear, so low and faint she nearly misses it, captures her attention. Trepidation prickles her skin. She fights against the bonds holding her.

Desperate, Telium strains her mind, chasing the odd feeling. The effort causes a slow ache to form by her temples. She continues to struggle. Heart in her throat. Sweat slips down her spine and she tastes blood as she bites the inside of her cheek.

Tenebris curse me. I will not die like this!

Telium thrashes in the bonds, letting out a sound that is part growl, part shriek.

NO.

There is a dull pop in her ears, like the cracking of knuckles, before her mind *shifts,* stretching beyond the limits of her skull and pushing out feelers.

Telium's heart races. Her palms become slick with sweat. The odd feeling solidifies into what she can only describe as a *presence.* Like standing in a pitch-dark room and knowing someone else is there.

It hovers around the Thief like a shroud. *Power,* her instincts whisper in her mind. *Strength.*

Faustus had continued talking while Telium's attention was turned inward. Turning back to face her fully, he seems annoyed by her lack of response.

'You,' Faustus says, looking down his nose at her. 'What are you?'

Telium eyes the man and chuckles darkly. Defiant to the end. 'You know who I am.'

The Thief watches her intently. 'Oh, I know *who* you are, Telium – assassin, Bloodless Maiden, *Tenebris Kin.*'

She bristles at the titles, not the least because she has earned every single one of them.

Faustus tilts his head to the side, studying her. 'What manner of beast must you be, for your Queen to lock you in the deepest depths of her prison?' the Thief sneers at her. 'Pity, if she did not fear your kind so; you could have gone to learn from their most powerful teachers. Oh, what a weapon you would have become then, Tenebris Kin.'

Telium's anger flares. She would be darkness-claimed if she let this man mock her. He would fear her if nothing else, he would ... that odd feeling in her mind again, like her consciousness spooling out. Reaching. Searching. It creeps across the grass like the tentacles of a deep-sea beast.

She concentrates on the strands, compelling them towards the Thief. To her endless shock, they comply. The threads crawl up his legs, snaking toward his gems of power like reaching fingers. Faustus' eyes dart downwards as if he can feel her mind slithering over him.

'I don't answer to you, Power-Thief. Keep your riddles to yourself,' Telium hisses at him with as much contempt as she can muster.

The distraction works. Faustus' eyes snap back to her, lips curling into a snarl. 'Mind your tongue, you're in no position to antagonise me. One shout and the guards will come running.'

Arrogant, cocky bastard. Any other time, Telium would have broken his nose. As it is, her concentration is divided. The snaking tendrils of her mind reach the Thief's gems. They brush up against the stolen power there. It tickles the edge of her mind and makes her gasp.

Confusion flits across Faustus' face. He glances down, his gaze travelling between his amulet and rings, before sliding slowly back to Telium. Her face set in concentration.

'Fascinating,' he muses. 'It seems the Queen's pet has outgrown her. Such a shame! I would love to have seen what power you could have possessed. I did a bit of digging ...'

Telium's pulse spikes. With it, the threads of her mind seem to contract as if reacting to her distress. Faustus gives a startled cry, hand flying to his chest. The distraction causes the invisible force binding her to loosen.

Not giving it a second thought, Telium thrashes. She is freed from the binds so abruptly she stumbles. With a grunt, she throws herself at Faustus, knocking him bodily to the ground.

She is so weak that her arms are unable to soften her fall and she crashes down on top of Faustus. They are a tangle of limbs and Telium's head smacks against the Thief's collarbone as they hit the dirt. Huffing with the effort, she shoves away from him.

Throwing a punch, she struggles to pin Faustus' arms under her legs. Planning to beat him into unconsciousness. But Telium is starved, weak. And though her punch is hard enough to make him spit blood, he is determined – desperate to win the Queen's favour.

He throws up his hand. The Thief's weak Gift hits her square in the chest. Forcing the breath from her lungs in a rush as she goes careening backwards. Telium lands on her back hard enough to see stars. Faustus stands, panting as he wipes his mouth with the back of his hand.

'Tenebris-cursed *witch*,' he spits.

He raises his hands, and the invisible bonds clamp down on her again. They are so tight, Telium can barely draw air. Her breath comes in shallow gasps and her mouth gapes open as she fights to get enough oxygen.

She blinks hard, her vision flashing white. Head lolling, Telium watches as Faustus flicks blood from his hand, lips twisting to the side. Telium tries to force herself towards him as he brushes dirt from his robes. Her eyes roll in her head as she fights against the unconsciousness starting to blacken the edge of her sight.

Faustus turns, his face lighting up as his eyes catch on some-thing. Or someone. Just as he raises his hand, Telium *pushes* again. This time, the threads of her mind snap out, fast as a sand viper. They twist around him like vicious, dense vines.

With a twitch of her head, Telium wrenches the threads back toward herself, jaw clenched. The Power-Thief jerks forward with a startled look. Branches snag on his robe as he collapses to his knees, crying out. The sound rips from his body painfully and bounces around the shabby gardens.

Telium barely notices. Power floods her senses. A feeling of pleasure so intense it borders on pain bursts through her. Stars flash in front of her eyes as her head spins. She groans and puts her head in her hands, heaving gulps of air as the world tips about her like the rolling deck of a ship. Her mind feels as though it is splintering apart and reforming in a new, different way. She pants through gritted teeth.

Slowly, the flood of power recedes from her limbs but does not disappear entirely. Instead, it seems to condense in on itself and tuck into an empty corner of her skull, like it had been there all along. The bizarre feeling causes a headache to spike behind her eyes.

Once her scattered thoughts return to a semblance of order, Telium snaps her head up, searching for the Thief. She braces herself for a fight but finds him slumped forward on the grass, skin waxen and eyes glassy.

Telium creeps forward on silent feet. Cautiously, she reaches down to place a hand on the man. Dead. The gems on his fingers are dull. The inner fire that had lit them before is gone. The stones are as lifeless as his body. Not a crack or splinter mar the multifaceted surfaces.

Strange, she notes, brushing her fingers over the amulet. Without the will of the Thief's mind to bind the power to those gems, they should have shattered.

It doesn't matter! Shaking herself, Telium disregards the dead man and flees. Heading for the safety of the city, and beyond.

CHAPTER
2

AFTER THE WAR

Branches creak overhead. The wind making them clack together like old bones. The breeze does nothing to ease the stifling heat. Summer continues to keep the land in her harsh grip – wilting crops, killing stock and fanning wildfires. Those smaller trees and shrubs without deep, ancient roots and arching branches hang limp in the heat, hanging onto life by a thread while they wait for the autumn rains.

The wood of the bow is smooth in Telium's hand as she creeps through the trees. Her feet barely make any sound.

Her breathing is controlled and even as she scans the undergrowth for her prey. All around her the forest shows signs of the long hard summer: sparse undergrowth and the ground baked solid. Even the air itself is without the telltale smell of damp. Each breath feels dry, like the very air is trying to steal moisture from her body.

She winds through the colossal trees. They stand like giant sentinels, silently watching her progress. Between them stand briar bushes, odd herbs and massive plants with vibrant, heart-shaped leaves the size of a man. A seemingly innocent plant that got its name 'silent rain' from the miniscule toxic needles it produces, killing anything that gets close to it and feeding its roots with the corpse.

Telium weaves through them without a backwards glance. With feline grace, she steps out from behind a tree. In front of her, a small stream winds lazy. Its gurgles cheerful and clear, the sound at odds with the atmosphere of the forest.

With its back turned, her prey doesn't see her coming. Telium's bowstring groans as she pulls the arrow back until the fletched feather brushes her cheek. Aiming for the heart. Her breath whooshes gently out of her pursed lips. Her prey bends to drink from the water and—

A bird bursts from the trees close by. Down the length of her arrow, Telium watches the deer start and bolt. She tracks it for a moment, the metal tip of her arrow marking its flight. But she isn't willing to waste one of her precious arrows by missing.

With a sigh, she lowers her bow, watching the deer disappear between the trees. It is limping slightly, something she picked up from its tracks. It won't get far without needing to rest. Telium takes a long exhale through her nose, praying for peace.

Dropping her bow and quiver, she pads to the water's edge. A shadowy presence hovers over her shoulder, stroking her restlessness with ebony-tipped talons. As she has for the last moon, Telium studiously ignores it as she stoops down to fill her waterskin.

The water is cool against the heat of the day and Telium splashes the sweat from her face. Rocking back on her heels, she looks up at the sunlight flickering through the canopy of her forest. A light breeze dances through the trees, making the leaves shiver and licking Telium's wet skin.

A crash sounds behind her. Something explodes out of the trees hard and fast. Adrenaline spikes through Telium's body, putting all her senses on high alert. Sharpening the smell of damp earth and greenery.

Without hesitation, she spins, pulling a dagger from her bandolier. The beast rushing for her stops its charge. Huge talons dig into the dirt as it comes to an abrupt halt. Yellow, feline eyes watch her obsessively as the beast settles into a crouch; cautious but not dissuaded.

Telium knows what the creature is. A falkir. A towering, panther-like creature that looks like something Tenebris has dragged up from the Underrealm, morphed with a dragon and hunger-made flesh. Its dappled grey and black coat ripples with muscle, but its legs and belly are sheathed in motley scales.

The hind legs are particularly grotesque. Bending at an odd angle like that of a goat. But they give the animal a powerful burst of speed.

Readjusting her grip on the dagger, Telium eyes the towering antlers protruding from the beast's head – a male, then. They could easily gut her with a swipe. So could the talons that end the scaled feet, deadly sharp and black as night.

Not to mention the set of canines protruding over its lower jaw that are as long as her dagger.

Slowly, so slowly, she reaches for the blade at her hip. The falkir's eyes gleam with predatory intent. Behind it, its armoured tail swishes back and forth like a house cat. The deadly tip scraping in the dirt.

The creature pounces again, lightning quick. Telium throws herself out of the way, swiping at it as she goes. The claws of the falkir miss gutting her by a hair's-breadth. Her blade, however, hits its mark, leaving a long, stinging line in its wake.

Telium slips slightly, ankles straining as she fights to keep upright on the mud edging the stream. She can hear her heartbeat in her ears, taste the warm forest air on her tongue.

The falkir hisses at her, sounding like the dragons of old. Telium screams a wordless challenge at the creature in front of her. Throwing her arms wide, brandishing her weapon.

Black talons knead the mud. The falkir snarls, the sound rumbling in Telium's chest. But she holds her ground, keeping her arms spread and weapon at the ready. After another strained moment, its eyes drop that intense, predatory look. Turning to the water, it crouches down and laps at the stream.

Telium backs away slowly, panting with exertion. The threads of her mind thrash in time with her pounding heart. After a beat, the falkir prowls off between the trees, hissing with frustration.

For long moments, she stands there, allowing her racing heart to calm. Still not believing her luck held.

Glancing around, Telium half expects to see Tenebris, the Dark Goddess, watching over her. With a heaving sigh, she allows her muscles to relax. She gathers up her bow and quiver, and sets off at a jog, letting the ancient trees swallow her whole.

చన

The heat of the day has reached its peak when Telium arrives at the enormous hollow tree that makes up her home. Her fingers brush the black scorch marks as she passes through the makeshift door.

The burn marks zigzagging across the tree's side tell the story of its demise at the hands of a lightning storm. The door creaks as she closes it behind her, shutting out the view of her little garden full of vegetables and poisonous herbs.

Sighing, she tips her head back and rolls her neck to ease

some of the tension there. Tiny pinpricks of light filter down through the mottled roof. Telium frowns.

That had been the hardest trick to master: creating a roof to block out the elements. Even now, years later, a wild thunderstorm could pull away branches and dried mud, letting the rain in like a miniature waterfall.

Telium lets her breath out gently between pursed lips. In the dim light her eyes shine like a wolf, reflecting what little sun reaches the floor level of her home. Above, a small loft-like space holds her bed of furs and more weapons. She barely uses it though, preferring to sleep on the ground floor. It is warmer in winter with the fire and at least moderately cooler during the scorching summers.

Moving around the small, open room she lights shoddily made candles – she has gotten used to the smell of animal fat by now. Her progression slowly reveals the rest of the space. The candlelight dances along the curved walls of the inside of the tree, oiled and polished to a gentle gleam.

The majority of the space is pockmarked with small nooks and hollows, all of which are filled with different items – mostly a startling assortment of weapons. All pilfered from the corpses of the soldiers who have hunted her. But also cured furs, bunches of dried herbs, even a small collection of interestingly shaped stones.

It is a far cry from the lavish palace chambers of the Siren Queen's assassin, her most trusted advisor.

She plops down on her furs with a huff. Drawing a dagger from her bandolier, she holds it up for inspection. Turning it this way and that in the dappled lighting. Telium catches a flash of her odd, mismatched eyes in the reflection before she bends her head and begins cleaning out her nails.

Despite the adrenaline rush from the scuffle with the falkir, she is in a particularly foul mood today. Her sleep was interrupted by haunting dreams of her past. *Again.*

After the first one, she woke up dizzy and disorientated. The repressed memories of her old life like a bucket of ice water to the face, heart aching with long-forgotten pain. After that, it was like a dam in her mind had broken, memories and people crowding into her dreams after so many long winters of silence.

For years, she has worked to put her past behind her, to make peace with herself. And she has, or as close to as she will ever get. It is good enough, she told herself. That is, until these goddess-damned *dreams.* Dragging up memories and emotions she thought long since lost back in her time of madness.

Unable to sit still, Telium pushes herself to her feet. Wandering around the room, she runs her hands over items stashed in various hollows. Her bow. A carved wooden bowl. The small cache of herbs hanging to dry in one corner. She picks up her haladie; a beautiful, curved weapon. The blade is double-ended and can be detached in the middle to form two long, deadly blades. Without conscious thought, she straps it to her hip.

She pulls a battered leather bag down from another hollow, shaking it free of dust. In it goes some extra blades, dried fruits, balms, salves. Telium realises what she is doing as her hand closes about a worn wooden box.

The red ink stains on the edges of the wood seem to taunt her. She has not used the contents of the box since she arrived here. The shadowy presence sits heavy on her shoulders. Eyes watching in the dark.

With a curse, she spins on her heels and stalks out the door of her hollow tree home. She strides past her rudimentary garden of herbs and plants. Her deft fingers scratch along her scalp as she walks, untying the intricate braids that keep her hair back from her face. She sighs as the tension eases.

A bad omen, ladies in the court would whisper about the bone-white colour when she was a child, *for someone so young to have hair of the dead.*

Reaching the dwindling stream not far from her home, Telium dumps her pack at her feet and begins shedding her belts and clothes in a heap. Her blades glint in the light as they leave the bandolier strapped across her chest. The tinkling of steel echoes through the forest. This stream is safer than the one she hunted beside mere hours ago. The water barely reaches her waist.

Keep moving – change, change is coming. The feelings pulse in time with her heartbeat.

Telium stubbornly ignores them and wades into the shallows, the cold water causing goosebumps to break out all over her body.

Sunlight glistens on her wet skin, showing off a thick band of blood-red tattoos inked down her spine. The markings curl and twist like smoke. Similar ink patterns track from her hip to the outside of her left knee.

As she scrubs her skin, Telium swears she can feel the presence hovering over her shoulder. One that threatens to upset the delicate balance of peace she has found under the leafy shelter of her forest. Even bathing, the hounding sense gives her no peace, stroking her restlessness with ebony-tipped claws.

Telium tenses up, head snapping to the side as a laugh echoes through the trees. Barely breathing, she scans the forest. She swears she can feel eyes raking her body. She glances over her shoulder, half expecting to see someone standing on the bank. Finding it empty, she cautiously calls on the darkness inside her. It enhances her eyesight and hearing. The wind whistles quietly through the trees, rustling leaves.

Nothing.

'You really need to get some sleep,' she groans, rubbing her eyes. *Or do you need to find what is haunting you?*

Strange that she has found a semblance of peace in the quiet dark of her forest, and now, something seems Tenebris-bent on chasing her out of it. She has buried her lust for revenge, her bitterness, the sense of betrayal, so deep in her soul that not even her own personal demons could reach them. Telium has told herself she is content with her life here now. Over and over again, until she began to believe it.

Now, she sloshes up the bank. Dripping wet, Telium stands a moment, indecision gnawing at her. She steps in the direction of her discarded pack, hesitating again. Her fingers drum out an irritated rhythm on her thigh. She swears she can feel dark eyes on her, watching, waiting.

Her frustrated growl splits the silence, 'For the love of Tenebris, leave off.' She rolls her eyes with a huff.

She stoops to gather her clothes and weapons, getting dressed in quick succession. Pursing her lips, she rubs her thumb over the leather starting to wear thin on her bandolier. Her knives clink together softly as she buckles on the rest of her belts.

She curses and seizes her bag before she stuffs her feet into boots and jams her pack over her shoulder with an annoyed jerk. A soft thump makes her look down. Telium stills at the dust-covered box that has fallen at her feet.

I thought I had left that behind. The red stains stand out harshly in the dappled sunlight. The skin along her spine tingles. *Are you really going to leave the sanctuary of your forest after all this time? Because of some feeling you've been having?*

Without giving herself time to second-guess the decision, she snatches the box up and stuffs it down the bottom of her pack.

She prowls off, stalking between the trees.

CHAPTER
3

As her long strides eat up the distance, Telium's mind wanders. The idea of possibly leaving the forest after so long sets her slightly on edge, loathe though she is to admit it. There was a period of time here that she doesn't recall; time she spent succumbed to her darkness.

Praying the journey will quiet her sense of unease, she forces herself to keep moving. Besides, how long has she been secluded in here? Half-a-dozen winters, at least. The memory of the first time she entered, and why she stayed, surfaces.

Telium shakes her head, banishing the images of those days. They were long ago, and nobody with malice has set foot in her forest for more winters than she can recall. Still, her time in madness is always shifting, the memories like smoke, twisting and gauzy. How long had the darkness ruled her mind and body?

Despite the small semblance of peace she found here, the forest has changed her. In the palace halls, she had been sly, cunning. The darkness of the forest and the draw of that beast inside her has sharpened her edge into something else; something crueler and more feral than before, hidden though it is beneath her serene surface.

Dappled sunlight tracks over Telium's face as she walks, meandering along, still not convinced she should leave. Out of habit, she throws her mind out like a net. The trait is not linked to any Thief she has ever known.

Still, it's one she has built and honed over years of practise. Fighting for dominance over her darkness with black determination, refusing to allow it to control her. It allows her to *feel* her surroundings – sense the life-force of everything within her net, from the tiny pinpoints of strength belonging to small mammals, to the colossal trees she wanders through. They feel like the warmth radiating off a hearth fire: controlled and comforting, yet still something that can roar out of control and destroy.

She pauses by a rather plain-looking plant but for the dark purple on the underside of its leaves and strong lavender scent. Telium knows it tastes of orange, and if dried, crushed and mixed with wine, it puts a person into a death-like trance – useful for smuggling people, but if the antidote is not administered within half a bell, a person will die in earnest.

At the palace, she'd had an affinity for poisons, and the fascination remained. A low form of assassination perhaps, but Telium did not play for honour. She played to win, whatever the cost. This brutal efficiency quickly gave her a reputation at court.

Tutting at the direction her thoughts have wandered, Telium draws up the Gifts of a Blood-Thief, infusing her limbs with strength and speed. She pushes into a sprint and flies across the ground as if she can outrun her memories.

She hears their whispered words. *Different, demon … Other.*

As an orphan child, Telium had been hurt by their cruel words. But as she inched towards womanhood, whatever lurked under her skin began to surface. Talents she should not have begun to manifest, she became exactly what those vapid courtiers called her. *Tenebris Kin*.

The old slur makes Telium's heart ache with emotion so strong it forces the air from her lungs. Sorrow, betrayal and rage rake her senses.

She flexes her fingers, banishing the phantom pain, her throat burning as if she has screamed herself hoarse.

What are you doing, Telium? Where are you going?

Her eyes drift to where the Orth Rel slashes along the north of Alkoria like a great scar. The ranges act like a natural wall, curving from north to west, shielding the Alkorians from the Fae lands to the north and the Sordu'era dead lands to the west.

Her eyes catch on strange little notches in a tree trunk just off the path. Her feet skid to a stop, freezing as her brain takes a moment to understand what she is seeing. With a frown, she steps up to the tree, running her fingers over the cuts in the bark. She cocks her head.

'Target practise,' Telium murmurs, recognising the holes left by a blade.

Turning her head, she spots an area of dirt and leaf litter that has been disturbed. But not by the usual beasts that roam her forest. There are boot marks.

With her enhanced speed, she has travelled a great distance, running all day and late into the evening. She is closer to the border of her forest than she has been in years.

Someone was here, she realises.

The last people she came across under these ancient trees were after her blood. Stupidly persistent soldiers, and a few mercenaries greedy for the reward her head offered.

At the possibility of threat, the darkness within her snaps

and snarls to the surface. *Who dares?* Telium grits her teeth as she struggles to restrain it, grappling with the storm internally. With a growl, she shoves them down, locking them in cages of iron will. There they sit, hissing and spitting like feral animals inside her chest.

The violent reaction brings a rush of ecstasy and anticipation. Telium does not fear much, but she fears losing herself to her darkness again. Fears the hunger and want that comes with it; the tickling at the edge of her mind that tells her if she is not careful, she will lose herself to it again.

'Must have come from one of the bordering villages,' she says out loud to distract herself from the roiling in her chest. But who would be bold enough to wander so far into her forest? And why?

Her eyes scour the area, but finding no other sign of passing, she shrugs her shoulders and begins walking north again.

This can't be a coincidence.

Her sanctuary has been breached, right at the time she has folded to the dark sense of foreboding and entertained the idea of searching for the cause. Though she can't say if the intruder has ill intentions, the discovery shakes her, and she feels a burning need to find out *why*.

Lampart it is, then, she decides, naming one of the small towns huddled between the elbow of mountain and forest in the northern reaches of her domain.

Long moments pass before the darkness settles completely.

After she had returned to sanity, Telium was able to comprehend the allure of the things inside her – how they drew her in. Seducing her mind with black, whispered promises. Telium refused to be owned by them, refused to allow them to rule her again. So, she trained. And trained. Hoping that with time and experience she would learn to manage them. That her control over them would be absolute.

It is just like learning to wield a knife or a bow, she had told herself, *just another weapon.* But while her mastery over her darkness grew rapidly, learning new skills and tricks, her control over them did not.

If I lost myself to madness again, would it keep me in the forest? Or would it roam? With her dreams of her old life haunting her, she does not want to find out.

∾

Early morning light spreads across the canopy of the forest; it causes all manner of beast to crawl back to whatever hole they had come from, as they attempt to escape the rising sun's reach. On the ground, the ancient trees do their best to hold onto the dwindling darkness; their towering branches cling to the receding shadows, keeping them alive when the sun should have long since banished them.

In her chest, her darkness snarls and hisses. It stretches under her skin, filling her. Running ebony-tipped talons over her muscles as their growls skitter along her bones.

Telium hurls a dagger at the target with a frustrated snarl. The blade hits dead centre, quivering in the trunk of the tree.

Sweat drips down her spine and beads at her brow as her bone-white braid whips about her. Boulders, rocks and weapons litter the small clearing of hard-packed earth, making for precarious footing. But she weaves through the obstacles with lethal grace, booted feet finding the areas between that provide a sure foothold.

With the fluid grace of a Freedom-Thief, Telium spins, loosing a small throwing dagger at a target far across the clearing. Without hesitating to see if the weapon has reached its mark, she draws another knife from the belt at her chest to hurl at a new target.

The restless feeling chases her around the clearing as she trains, ghosts of her past lurking in the corner of her eye or standing in front of a target. Telium grits her teeth and ignores the memories. That life is long gone now – no longer is she the Siren Queen's assassin.

As the final throwing blade leaves her hand, she stills, gulping down the sticky summer air, the dust settling around her. Slowly, Telium straightens from her crouch. Her gaze narrows on the target as she approaches, panting gently. She purses her lips and frowns down at the blade, an inch off the mark.

She blames the sleepless night before, visions of screaming queens and stone cells haunting her. This morning, phantom chains were still chafing her wrists as she woke.

I wonder if she has forgiven me; what would happen if I returned?

The thought stings.

Her gaze is drawn once more to where she knows the Orth Rel tower stands, guarding them from the lands beyond.

Telium travelled all through the night, catching a few bells' sleep in the quiet before dawn.

Every time I wake, I feel restless; hounded by some sense of premonition I can't quite grasp.

Telium fingers the smooth stone of green that has hung around her neck since birth; next to it lays a claw of the deepest shade.

Like it's telling me everything is about to change, that I've been secluded here long enough.

Something stirs in Telium, and she tightens her grip on their chains. They may be a useful tool but still she fears that she may fall back into madness, knowing that it stems from her darkness. The loss of control frightened Telium almost as much as her enjoyment of them. If she revels in the darkest parts of her soul, is she any better than the Mad Fae King across the border?

A sudden flare of life in the net of her mind catches her attention. Fast and fluid as a feline, she sidesteps from the small patch of dirt and drops to her haunches.

Telium crouches in the shadows, her gaze sweeping the forest. She senses all the creatures that slink and crawl and slither through the undergrowth. But there is something else there too. Something that feels more like her. The coils of her mind sweep out, creeping over the soil and rocks, only to rebound off a wall of pure, dominating power. *Danger,* the darkness whispers. *Power.* Emotions flash through her, so convoluted her mind cannot rest on one. *How in the Dark Goddess' name …?* A devilish grin splits her face. *Oh, this will be fun.*

Spooling the threads of her mind back into herself, Telium calls upon her darkness, keeping it close at hand should she need it. She allows it to sharpen her reflexes and senses. She pulls her cloak from her pack and drapes it around her body, obscuring her arsenal of weapons from view. She draws up her hood to conceal her face, then stands and begins meandering along in the direction of whoever is crouching in her forest.

Not wanting to give herself away, unsure if they can sense such power, she keeps the threads of her consciousness coiled tight inside her mind.

She follows a worn animal track as it curves around a large tree trunk. Her hand dips into the folds of her cloak, fingers wrapping around a throwing dagger.

Her feet come to an abrupt halt and her eyes widen as she gazes at the man across from her. That incessant restlessness that has been haunting her flees before him, not the slightest whisper of an itch left behind. The shadowy presence that haunted her for more than a moon: gone.

As he turns his head towards her, she notes the slightly tapered ears.

Fae.

CHAPTER
4

The Fae goes motionless as death when he notices her. He holds himself with an unnatural stillness that sparks Telium's unease.

She remembers the tales of the Fae's inhuman strength, their reputation for being both cunning and wise. During her time at the palace, Telium heard many quiet speakings about Thresiel, the Fae lands to the north. But the subject was not discussed openly by anyone wishing to keep their organs *inside* their body.

The male stands in the middle of the path, hands turned out to show they are empty. He towers over her, despite Telium not being short herself. A plain shirt stretches over broad shoulders and across a sculpted chest. His lightly tan skin sets off his startling blue eyes and deep golden hair.

She had a secret fascination with the Fae as a child, something which had brought her no small amount of shame. Yet she had been enthralled by the texts that told of a race far different from the one her Queen spoke about. The books had described their other-worldly beauty.

Telium is cautiously curious to see this Fae's face better;

wants to know if they really stay unmarred by age despite living hundreds of years.

Other words spring to Telium's mind, describing things other than their looks. All tainted with the bitterness of the Siren Queen's voice. *Greedy, sadistic, arrogant, selfish, powerful.*

Telium had been a young girl at the time. But she still clearly remembers how after the Fae King's visit, the Siren Queen had forbidden all passage between the two lands. No-one in Alkoria has seen a Fae since.

Even the smudge of dirt across his cheek does nothing to dull this one's beauty. If anything, it enhances his high cheekbones and strong jawline. His travelling clothes – dark trousers tucked into sturdy leather boots – are dirty, but well made.

Telium wiggles her toes inside her own self-made boots. The Fae is lucky his feet are too large, else she would rob him blind simply for some new shoes.

Completing the male's look is a hooded cloak, clasped across his chest by an ornate broach, but it does not hide the sword strapped to his side. He holds his hands out, palms up in supplication. Dappled sunlight falls on him, highlighting the dark rings of ink circling his muscular forearm.

Shit.

Even with her limited knowledge, Telium knows what the tattoos represent – warrior. What in the name of the Goddess is a *Fae warrior* doing in her forest?

'Who in Tenebris' name are you?' she snaps.

Her voice is raspy from disuse and her volume too quiet. Too long has it been since she spoke to another being.

When he speaks, his voice is like honey: smooth and seductive. It brings to mind silken sheets and whispered promises. 'My name is Mallux. I mean you no harm.'

Looking at the male across from her, she cannot help but

think that the old scholars have never seen a Fae for themselves; he looks like some long-lost god, standing in the shadows of her forest.

Telium does not reply; shifting her feet into a more grounded position, she eyes him from under her hood. Wrestling the snarl building in her chest as her fingers twitch towards her haladie.

He takes a tentative step forward, as if afraid he will startle her. 'Are you from the village?'

'Yes,' she replies, the word sharp on her tongue. Not knowing any other answer to give him.

It is a blatant lie. They must still be a day's travel from the edge of her forest and the closest town. Unwilling to say anything further, she falls into silence.

Mallux pauses as if waiting for her to say more, perhaps explain what she is doing out here alone. When she doesn't, he takes a few more steps toward her, close enough that Telium could reach out and brush a hand across his chest. His scent reaches her, warm and dominating. Like citrus, and fresh bread baked over embers. Her Gifts hiss.

His nearness makes her uncomfortable in a way she cannot explain. *You have been too long out of human company, Telium,* she tells herself. Shifting slightly, she moves her weight onto the balls of her feet – in anticipation of what, she doesn't know.

Mallux glances around like he is expecting someone else to appear from behind a tree. 'I have a question for you.' His voice is low and soothing. It irritates her.

That is not what she had expected him to say. Curiosity piqued, Telium cocks her head to the side. 'Well? What sort of question?' she growls, having the unnerving feeling she is walking into a trap.

His smile is disarming and too perfect – flashing white,

even in the shadows of her forest. 'A question about your legends,' he says. 'In my country, we have heard rumours about a powerful being that haunts this forest – a dark queen with even darker powers. She rules over all the beasts within, haunting the land like a ghost.'

Telium frowns in confusion. *I have never heard my Queen described so.*

She remains silent as she studies the Fae warrior's face, looking for signs of deceit. Her lips twitch as she fights a snarl. Her fingers itch to wrap around the hilt of her haladie.

'Do your legends say anything of this?' he prompts when she does not immediately respond.

'A dark queen?' Telium scoffs. 'You must be mistaken, we only have one Queen in Alkoria, and she is not exactly "dark".' She smiles at him with venom, hoping to disarm him so he wouldn't notice the way her voice choked on the words.

A slight frown creases his brow, and he narrows his eyes as she continues speaking. Telium is struggling to keep her voice pleasant.

'Perhaps your rumours speak of one of our gods or goddesses, for we have many—'

'No,' he cuts her off. 'I have heard of your Goddess of Death who rules the Underrealm. I am told *she* has hair of obsidian and oil. Not her – the one I speak of has the hair of the dead, her power a black storm. When the great army came to raid her forest, she turned the beasts within against them and wore a crown of bones as those still alive retreated in defeat.'

CHAPTER 5

The Fae's voice floats by her. He looks at her expectantly, waiting for an answer.

'What did you say?' she asks, her voice croaky. The shadow of blood lingers on her tongue.

'I said,' Mallux replies, giving her a strange look, 'your kingdom has not had a queen in near fifty winters.'

Not for the first time, Telium wonders how long ago she fell out of the Queen's favour and found sanctuary in the forest. When she bothered to look in the mirror of a stream, the reflection staring back at her never changed and so she told herself perhaps a handful of winters had passed. Still, she is not sure how long she spent lost in her madness – never wanted to seek out that truth.

Her heart begins to thud in her ears as she teeters on the edge of understanding. Perhaps she has been here longer than she thought. Much longer.

She lifts one shoulder in a casual shrug, forcing nonchalance even as she bares her teeth at him. Under her skin, her Gifts hiss and snarl, twisting in and around each other.

'Yes, well.' Her voice has grown stronger and now it cracks

like a whip. 'The Siren Queen was the last *real* monarch to grace our lands.'

She tries to keep her words flat, keeping the familiarity out of her voice when she speaks of her Queen. He is standing so close to her now that she has to tip her head back to look at him. Careful to keep her damning eyes hidden in the shadow of her hood.

Mallux's eyes narrow and his gaze rakes her up and down. The look has her Gifts rumbling in her chest. A snarl pulls back her lips. Again, his brilliant smile lights up his face, the shadow of suspicion gone as swiftly as it arrived. If it were not for her training, she would have missed it.

'And what is a pretty young thing, such as yourself, doing out here in these woods?' he asks.

When Telium hesitates, deciding what to tell him, his smile turns predatory. Triumphantly, he reaches for her, pressing close.

She brushes his reaching hand aside and steps out of range, discarding her pack in the dirt. She bares her teeth in a snarl as her Gifts snap under her skin and skip along her bones. Telium's fingers tingle as talons try and fail to take form.

Mallux retracts his arm and leans back on his heels, watching her with a contemplative gaze.

She keeps her breathing slow and even, returning his stare without flinching. In her mind she takes note of every blade she has strapped to her body but hidden from view.

With blinding speed, Mallux lunges forward before she has time to react and grabs her roughly by the cloak. Goddess, he is fast. This close, his scent envelops her again, all warm fires and citrus. Pain spikes up her skull as he twists her hood and yanks the fabric away, exposing her stark white hair and startling eyes.

She glares up at him in defiance, ignoring the painful pull of her hair. His grin has the effect of grabbing a cat by the tail and rubbing its fur the wrong way. If she had hackles, they would all be standing on end by now.

'You're—'

Telium's hand shoots out, palm up, cracking him in the face.

With a cry somewhere between surprise and pain, he lets her go and takes a step back, hand flying to his now broken nose to stem the bleeding.

'Try that again, *Fae,* I dare you.' The words rumble out of her with quiet menace.

Telium pulls out a blade, not the throwing daggers she usually favours, but the haladie hanging from her hip. While small compared to the monster weapon on the Fae's belt, the naked steel is still the length of her arm, its edges deadly sharp.

Double-edged blades poke out from each end of the wooden handle, both pieces of steel curving in a gentle wave. Traditionally a weapon carried by roving bands of traders of the Ereak Desert, Telium had fallen in love with it due to the way even the most seasoned soldiers struggled to fight against the exotic blade.

Her weapon has been modified – the blades longer so it is effective against both swords and poleaxes, as well as daggers. The hilt has been specially crafted to unlatch and fold in half, so the weapon can be easily sheathed. Over the years, Telium has modified it further so the handle can separate and form two curved gleaming blades as long as her forearm.

Mallux eyes her in irritation as he tilts his head back, pinching his nose to try and staunch the flow of blood. When he feels the break in his nose, he growls in annoyance. The muscles in his jaw clench at Telium's answering smirk.

The warrior's face is a mask of stone, giving away nothing of his thoughts. Mallux stays silent, working his jaw back and forth as if considering. Then suddenly, his eyes soften. 'Your Highness,' he says, speaking slowly to draw out the title. His broken nose does nothing to dampen his silken voice. 'I have come to sway you to our cause. To beg the help of one with such powerful and ... unique gifts.'

Telium snorts, levelling her haladie at him. 'You can drop the "Your Highness" crap,' she snaps, 'and what do you mean "your cause"?'

She feels her Gifts rise to the surface; the air becomes charged with them. When she bares her teeth at Mallux, she notes his gaze snags on the teeth that are now tipped in fangs.

Mallux grins and answers with a courtly bow, dripping with equal parts charm and disdain. It makes Telium want to break something else – a leg, perhaps. Even with a hand to his bloody nose he still somehow manages to make the action look graceful and dashing.

'Are you not her?' Mallux asks. 'She who holds the forest, has defeated armies? Bloodless Maiden? Kin to your Dark Goddess?'

'Do not speak in riddles,' she growls, stabbing her blade at him, making him concede a step. 'You seem to know very well who I am. The question is, who are you?'

'I am Mallux—'

'Yes, you said that.'

He carries on, undaunted by her attitude. 'I represent a certain group of Fae who ... do not agree with our monarch.'

Agree seems too weak a word for what Mallux was trying to express. The tip of her blade doesn't waver as she keeps it pointed at his heart.

'A rebellion?' Telium barks a laugh.

'Of a sort. If you must call it so.'

'Don't agree?' she asks slowly. 'How so?'

'He has, let's say, a very *keen* interest in Alkoria. Especially your Thieves.'

A spike of fear – not for herself – flares in her chest; a hazy memory fights for recognition. But it disappears the moment she looks directly at it.

'Why?' Telium barks out the word.

'I do not know.'

'But?' she presses.

The male's lips press into a thin line.

'We have discovered that the King is amassing an army, plans for what we believe are to attack Alkoria again.'

Again? Telium picks up on the word. Her haladie glints as she lowers it to her side, even as her brain automatically goes to Alkoria's defences: what towns would be evacuated, how many could be called to arms. Such a war would be devastating, the loss of life immense. She imagines countless Alkorians, human and Thief alike, cut down by Fae blades.

'We cannot abide by the loss of life again for such selfish endeavours,' Mallux continues. 'I have come to recruit you. We are gathering an army. If you are as powerful as they say, you can help us stop this madness and save the loss of many lives.'

Something snarls within her mind at the word *recruit*, as if she were some common soldier or farmer's son to be trained up and placed in the ranks.

Another memory swims to the surface; the Queen telling Telium of a mad and twisted King who ruled over the Fae lands. Who stole Gifted children away from their families, never to be seen again. The whispered stories of what he did to those children haunted a young Telium's nightmares.

Telium's arm snaps back up as Mallux makes to step towards her again. She bares her teeth at him in feral challenge.

'Why would I help you?'

'Because,' Mallux replies, 'with your help, we could stop this war before it even reaches the border. You have the skills we need. We need an assassin, not an army. You are a wild card. Stories of your power reach the furthest ends of Thresiel. You could prevent both Fae and mortal casualties. You will, of course, be paid handsomely for your troubles.'

Though she is startled by his words, she keeps her face blank. Thresiel, the Fae lands, is across Orth Rel, the gigantic mountain ranges. How word of her has gotten that far, she cannot fathom.

Telium takes in Mallux's muscular form and the sword hanging from his side. He looks like he has walked right out of one of the books she secretly studied as a child. Her brow furrows as she tries to recall the writings on Fae warriors and their armies. *He must be quite the warrior*, she thinks.

The bleeding from his nose has already stopped thanks to his accelerated Fae healing. When he grips his shirt front and tugs it up to clean the blood from his face, she catches a glimpse of defined stomach muscles and her heart flutters briefly.

It is possible, she supposes. As a young girl, she remembers the castle being all abuzz because the Fae King was coming to meet with the Siren Queen. A treaty, they called it, when the Fae King left. The Siren Queen had made a pact with the King and the coming war that people whispered about never came.

'Why can you and your rebels not have your own assassin kill him? Even here in Alkoria, we hear of the Fae's skills. Surely one of your own can manage?'

'We could,' Mallux growls, 'if the coward did not hide

behind a battalion of powerful Fae. He has amassed a personal guard, each touched by the All-Mother: *Ka'hine Lei'kah*. That male does not deserve to wear the Ivory Crown. To attack him head-on would require a huge sacrifice – numbers we do not have – without any guarantee of success. What we need is a weapon of our own, something no-one would expect, to combat their powers and give us a chance to get to him. It's a long shot, but if we take him by surprise, we just might pull it off.'

'What you speak of is treason,' Telium says softly. 'How can I believe you? And what would I gain from helping you, anyway? Money is worthless to me.'

Mallux rubs his jaw as he ponders. Again, that calculating look. Telium's mind sings with a hundred questions but she brushes them aside, for now, preferring to focus on finding out whether this Fae is speaking the truth. Let her decide whether she can trust this Fae warrior who mysteriously turns up in her forest the one day she is thinking of leaving it.

Telium's heart begins to race. Maybe being among the Gifted Fae would help her control her own black powers. Perhaps she could stay on to train as part of her payment?

Pushing itself to the forefront of her mind, the memory of her escape demands to be recognised. The Power-Thief who mocked her had said something about her kind and what they could offer her.

You could have gone to learn from their most powerful teachers.

'If our gold is no good to you, name your price, Queen Assassin. What can this Fae offer you to sway you to our cause?'

'*No*. I …' Telium trails of after her knee-jerk refusal.

Mallux is Fae, he is from … enemy territory. Isn't he? Telium looks across at Mallux in contemplation. With her restlessness and her strange dreams, it is almost like the Dark Goddess had whispered of his coming. As if Tenebris herself has nudged her onto this path, forcing her to come across this Fae warrior and his offer. He could give her answers. He could give her *control*.

What a coincidence that she would dream of that night and the Power-Thief's words less than a moon before their meeting.

'You need to leave,' Telium barks, when Mallux opens his mouth to speak.

The Fae's face remains stoic; he rubs his hand along his jaw. When he speaks, his voice is tight.

'I would consider my offer, Queen Assassin. The fate of your people may rest on your decision.'

In her mind, she curses her Dark Goddess, convinced her meddling has a hand in this. But the irritation is half-hearted. Her mind buzzes with questions and possibilities; after all this time, here is someone who could help her.

She should refuse him. She knows she should. But the real-isation that this male could hold the key to helping her control her Gifts makes her feel oddly exposed. She feels like moths are fluttering around in her stomach.

Albeit unintentionally, Mallux has just laid bare all her deepest desires, offering her up hope on a blood-lined plat-ter, leaving her terrifyingly vulnerable. She could not have felt barer if she were stripped naked before him.

This was what I have been looking for since my powers manifested.

Without her realising it, Mallux has moved closer to her again. His scent reaches her on the breeze.

'No.' Telium says, her voice flat. *Tenebris claim me if I work with my Queen's enemy.*

'Name your price, I swear on a blade to my heart that I will endeavour to fulfil it.' He pauses, as if allowing her a moment to change her mind.

'I will consider,' she allows, though her tone makes it obvious she will not.

Mallux nods. 'I will be travelling north-west for a day and a night if you should change your mind.'

Then he is gone, stalking through the trees in the direction of her forest border.

Beneath the chaos in her mind, a black voice whispers, calling her to seek her vengeance, to come find her fate at the point of a blade, take revenge and end the life that ruined hers.

She draws a breath into her lungs. Citrus mixed with the smell of pines blowing down from the mountains.

'I swear on a blade to my heart,' she murmurs, 'what an odd way to say "I promise".'

Blade … heart.

CHAPTER
6

The darkness of the night is absolute. The moon a mere sliver of white against the blackness. Telium wanders out onto the balcony, wanting to look at the stars blanketed across the sky. How she loves looking at the galaxy overhead.

Tonight is a perfect night for it: still and clear. She knows if she stands looking long enough, more colours will start to form – midnight purples and deep blues. A tapestry thrown into the heavens by Tenebris herself.

'Oh … Telli.'

Telium turns her head and sees the Siren Queen further down the balcony. She hadn't spotted her when she stepped outside. Trigg would scold Telium for such a lack of awareness. At seven winters, her assassin training had begun, and Trigg had high expectations of her.

As Telium approaches the Queen, the tears on her face become apparent. They track down her cheeks and drip off her chin, the streaks reflecting the silvery starlight. Concern spikes though Telium's chest, and she goes to the Queen's outstretched arms. Crawling into her embrace from where the Siren Queen sits on the stone floor in a very un-queenly billow of skirts.

'I had to,' the Queen murmurs to herself, so quietly Telium strains to hear. 'I could not let him take one more Thief child.'

With one hand, the Queen tucks Telium close to her side. The other stays holding her abdomen, fingers curled into the fabric of her dress as if she would tear it from her body. She smiles softly when Telium reaches up to wipe the tears from her cheeks, only to have fresh ones fall a moment later.

Telium does not know what to say, so she wraps her little arms around the Queen and squeezes her tight. The Queen has been out of sorts since the Mad Fae King left the palace a moon ago. None of her court seem to notice the change, but Telium sees it. How her usually stunning blue eyes are muted with hidden pain. How the Queen's mind drifts, jaw flexing as her thoughts turn inwards.

'Did he make you sad?' Telium breathes the words, partially scared to ask them.

The feeling of soft hands on her hair makes Telium look up at the Queen's face. Her eyes are hard as she nods, and though her jaw seems to be locked tight, a ghost of a smile touches her lips as she looks down at Telium.

'If you are ever presented with the opportunity, my dear Telli,' the Queen whispers, 'drive a blade through his heart.'

CHAPTER

7

Telium blinks as the world comes back into focus. She has to put a hand out to steady herself. The bark rough and warm under her fingers.

Drive a blade through his heart.

The words echo through her heart and soul. Clanging around like the tolling of a great bell.

Drive a blade through his heart.

Telium was considering going with Mallux for even the slightest chance she may be able to control her Gifts. Maybe even for her people; for that old sense of responsibility she felt.

But now there is a darker part of her mind whispering to her. It speaks about the atrocities she knows the Mad Fae King committed. And not just in his own lands, but in the halls of the castle she had once called home. *Vengeance,* it whispers. *Kill.*

Hot, unfiltered rage sweeps over her. The strong thirst for revenge surges inside her chest. She cannot forget the grave offence to her Queen.

Drive a blade through his heart.

The words whispered fervently to Telium when she was just seven winters old reverberate through the years.

At the time, she had not understood the assault on her Queen. It was not until she was older that she heard of how the guards had seen the Fae King creeping into the Queen's bedchamber, how the handmaids had found the Queen in the tub, skin scrubbed raw and tears drying on her face. She had ordered the bed to be burned, and a moon later, her rooms had been trashed. Anything the Queen could get her hands on, she shredded or smashed.

After all these winters, the desire for revenge rushes back: bitter and sharp on her tongue. She allows the feeling to fill her, swelling inside her chest as she turns in the direction Mallux had left.

If you let him leave, he takes with him your only chance of revenge and hope of controlling your powers.

She couldn't forget the sneered words of the Power-Thief.

You could have gone to learn from their most powerful teachers … the full extent of your Gifts revealed and harnessed.

Abruptly making up her mind, Telium tosses her shock of white hair over her shoulder. Picking up her pack, she adjusts it and sets off at a brisk jog. Mallux can't have gone far.

❧

Telium catches up to the Fae far faster than she would have thought. As if he were loitering around, considering doubling back.

His head snaps up when he hears her approach, turning to meet her. Telium slows her pace a healthy distance from the Fae, walking the remainder of the way. She pants gently from the exertion of her un-Gifted run; hesitant to use her Gifts so close to Mallux.

She stops before him, crossing her arms. She has to grit her teeth and force her expression into something other than outright disdain. When she speaks, it is without greeting, her voice brisk.

'You have Fae who tutor those with Gifts. Teachers, of sorts.' She makes the remark with confidence, but her bravado is false, knowing near nothing about these teachers that the Power-Thief spoke of that night long ago.

Mallux cocks an eyebrow at her bluntness but nods.

'I would have them teach me, in all aspects of your training. Battle, history ... Gifted combat. All of it.' The finality in her voice brokers no room for argument.

Despite her calm exterior, butterflies dance in her stomach. There is no way this Fae male could know how much Telium's powers frighten her, how desperate she is to control them and shine a light on her past. How she lusts for the thrill her dark powers give her but also fears the lack of control that comes with them.

Her Gifts are like the ocean on a stormy night. Rough, endless, powerful. Without fear or conscience, whatever it comes across, it devours.

Mallux stares at her as if he can read her inner thoughts. Reflexively, she tightens the coils of her consciousness around her mind. Whatever Mallux sees must be the answer he is looking for because he casually shrugs his massive shoulders.

That was it. No comment of how she had turned him away a little more than a bell ago. No questions about what made her change her mind.

For so long she has wished to better understand her powers, for she is not like any Thief in Alkoria. She is completely *Other*. Alkorians have no word for her Gifts or what she has become. To be able to leash her Gifts, to control them without fear of them controlling her. It is a tantalising prize.

She *could* refuse to help him and find out on her own if he speaks the truth about this imminent war. It has been some time since she skulked in the shadows of taverns and halls to gather information. Surely someone has heard of this amassing army. But what then? Can her countrymen really hold against the might of the Fae? Can she control her Gifts in such a conflict and not fall to madness again? Chills skitter across her skin at the thought.

Something about this Fae piques her curiosity, loathe though she was to admit it when she ran after him. The last time she had felt the guiding ebony touch of Tenebris, she directed Telium to flee to this forest; her intervention saved Telium's life.

Besides, Fae are well-known for their great powers. Their teachers must be greatly skilled if they are able to train such fearsome and powerful warriors, and not have them go mad or power-drunk. The spark of hope the thought causes is difficult to contain.

'So that is a yes, then?' She knows how Fae can twist promises. 'In exchange for helping you assassinate your King, you will ensure I am tutored by the best of your teachers, in everything from Gifts to tactics to history?'

The Fae nods his head solemnly. 'If you aid us in killing the Fae King, this, I do promise, Queen Assassin.' The deep timbre of his voice is like a caress. 'And I will keep you safe from any repercussions of our endeavour.'

'Ah.' Telium taps her chin, pretending to mull over the offer, unwilling to reveal her weakness to this Fae. Despite the fact she has just chased after him to accept his offer. She steps closer, angling her head to look up at him.

'So, let me see if I have this right. You need me to come help you defeat your evil King and his big, bad army? And you came all this way on rumour and speculation that some assassin with Thief-like Gifts lives in this forest?' Telium hopes to push him onto the defence with her tone. 'And you just planned on, what, *wandering* around the forest, hoping to bump into me?'

Mallux hesitates, as if unsure how to take her sarcasm. Telium can practically hear the gears turning in his mind, trying to work out if her questions are genuine.

'Yes.'

'Huh.' Telium searches his face. The Fae shifts uncomfortably under her piercing gaze.

Drive a blade through his heart.

The whispered words buzz around her head again. The pain fresh in her chest.

With pleasure, she snarls in reply.

This is her best chance to get within striking distance of him.

'If you understood the severity of our situation, the threat the King poses to Alkoria, you would not be so hesitant to believe me. You will be our trump card – our surprise weapon nobody will see coming,' Mallux adds.

Telium's answering grin is both beautiful and feral. 'Well then, it seems I have a king to kill.' She takes a few steps past Mallux before turning towards him and sweeping her arm out in an exaggerated gesture.

'After you.'

CHAPTER
8

Insects whizz and click in the warm summer air; leaves rustle gently in the wind as they pass under the colossal trees. The day is at its hottest point, the sun having reached its zenith. They are still heading in a westerly direction, so Telium does not question Mallux on their destination. Instead, she uses the time to reorder her thoughts around the recent events. She studies her new travelling companion as he walks. He moves with confidence; there is no hitch in his stride, no sign of weakness or injury that she could exploit.

They will have to fix that. Her training will not allow her to be lax, she needs to know how to beat him if the situation required it, she—

'We will travel to Lampart. Where we will stay at an inn and purchase some horses before making for the Infri Pass,' Mallux says.

'Oh, *will* we?' Telium drawls.

Mallux, apparently, misses her sarcastic tone. 'Yes, we must make haste to Meannthe at once.'

'Maybe you missed it on your way through,' Telium replies, voice scathing, 'but getting horses through this side of the Pass is near impossible.' She reaches out and plucks a bunch of small orange flowers from a vine as she passes. She pops them in her mouth. 'Unless Fae horses have wings, which would be spectacular indeed.'

Telium could nearly *see* the male fighting the roll of his eyes.

'The best way would be to take the horses to Xandi,' she continues, savouring the sweet nectar. 'Sell them off there and make the last league on foot. You'd make some coin back that way too.'

'Very well,' is all Mallux says.

From her guess, they would have to travel all through the day and part of the night before they hit Lampart, especially if Mallux insisted on walking the whole way.

'What will you do if the inn has no rooms left?' Telium makes an effort to keep her tone neutral this time.

From the look Mallux throws over his shoulder, she fails miserably.

'I have already secured a room. But had I not, I would simply pick another inn.'

Lampart is a tiny village that ekes out its living by trading leather and furs caught by poachers who hunt the slopes. The last time Telium was there, there was only one inn, and even calling the glorified tavern such was a stretch.

Misinterpreting her silence, Mallux adds, 'There are a handful of well-kept taverns in your mining town – Lampart – I am sure we will find one that is acceptable.'

A mining town. That explains it. If someone had found precious materials in the mountains, the town would have swelled as the need for tanners, blacksmiths, farmers and lumberjacks, as well as miners, grew.

Telium's eyes skip across the canopy as she chews on her

handful of honeysuckles. The patches of sky between the leaves are blue and cloudless.

How long have I been here?

A memory echoes up through the winters, blurry with time, but the emotion is still there. She remembers sitting on the floor with the Queen, a topaz stone glinting at her throat, who placed her crown upon Telium's small head. It slipped down over her eyes and the Queen's laughter rang off the chamber walls.

Ahh, my Telli, the Queen had said. *I will miss these times with you, but I must prepare us for what is to come.*

Unexpected tears prickle behind Telium's eyes. The Siren Queen may not have always been kind to her, but she is the closest thing to a mother figure she has ever had, bar Trigg.

The memory leaves her tongue-tied and conflicted; neither feeling is one she appreciates. Besides Trigg, the Queen was the only one who seemed to look past Telium's otherness, who she didn't feel so alone around.

With a twitch of her head, Telium forcibly pushes the memory away. She rips the next bunch of flowers from the vine with a little more force than necessary. Part of the plant comes away with it.

Mallux glances over his shoulder at her with a raised brow. As their eyes lock, an image flashes into her mind, of her pressed up against a tree, wedged between the rough bark and his body, his hands in her hair and his lips on her neck.

A flush rises to Telium's cheeks and she flings a fistful of bright orange flowers at him. For goddess' sake, what is wrong with her? Mallux catches them with ease, watching her stuff another two flowers in her mouth. Turning back, he sniffs the plant curiously. With a shrug he takes a bite.

Telium watches him chew once, twice.

'The leaves are poisonous.'

When Mallux gags and hacks up his mouthful, Telium snickers. She answers his glare with a smirk.

Forcing her mind back to the task at hand, Telium spends the next hour grilling Mallux about the Fae King. Using the opportunity to mould her voice into something … well, not *pleasant,* but at least not a snarling demand. Telium catalogues everything Mallux knows about the King's habits and the Fae who are protecting him. *Lei'kah,* Mallux had called them; from what she understood, it was an elite group of soldiers – apparently all female and hand-picked by the King.

'I hear your people have great Gifts and are fearsome warriors,' she says, trying to feel out her new travelling companion.

'It is true that we are warriors of some renown,' he replies. 'We pride ourselves on being skilled in feats of strength and arms. Those chosen to be warriors train from a young age to master their skills, but every Fae strives to be unbeatable regardless.'

'And your Gifts?' Telium prompts, not willing to let him off that easy. 'Our writings say that your people have powerful Gifts, far surpassing that of our Thieves.'

The Fae warrior frowns as if the question makes him uncomfortable. 'Some of our race have powerful Gifts, yes. Yet they are far fewer than your so-called Thieves. When a young Fae shows signs of Power, she is sent to our temples to learn how to master her skills and taught the responsibility of her power, so that she will not misuse them against our people. It is for this reason that a Fae cherishes his daughters above all else, for they are a gift from the All-Mother.'

'Why not his sons?' Telium asks, although she has already pieced the answer together.

'You misunderstand. All our young are treasured. But only

our females receive gifts of Power.' His firm tone indicates the conversation is finished.

'Oh, *that's* why all the King's guards are women,' she quips, testing him.

Mallux raises an eyebrow at her. 'Females. And yes. Why else?'

She shrugs her shoulders, faking nonchalance and looks up at the branches of the towering trees. 'I've heard of the Fae King's ...' she waves a hand in the air, 'habits.'

Cocking an eyebrow, Mallux searches her face intently, before turning around and picking up the pace without responding. His booted feet crunch over dried leaves that litter the worn animal path.

Only their women carry Power. Telium muses over this bit of information. She's unsure of its significance but tucks it away for later. Then her mind snags on another piece of information. 'Females?' she asks. 'Not women?'

Mallux shakes his head. 'No, a woman is a human female. As men are human. These are mortal words; Fae do not use them.'

'So, you are a male, then, not a man?'

'Yes,' Mallux says, flashing a bedroom smile her way.

His slightly pointed canines gleam in the dappled sunlight. Telium swears his voice has dropped an octave. She forces herself to hold his gaze a moment longer, fighting a blush, refusing to let him cow her, before turning away. They walk in silence for a while after that. By now, the sun has begun to creep towards the horizon. It will be dark in another bell.

Remembering the way her Gifts reacted to Mallux before, Telium cautiously pushes her consciousness out. The threads creep right up to his mind ... only to rebound off walls erected around his thoughts like a shield. Her green-and-amber gaze flicks over the warrior as she draws the coils back. This time, she casts her mind out as she would a net; the way she does when keeping her senses open to her surroundings. Again, her magik is rebuffed by the walls of his mind.

When Mallux shows no signs of noticing her experiment, she pushes harder. Her power parts around the walled shield of his mind like a river about stone and reunites once it has passed the boundaries of his defence. Once her consciousness settles, Mallux's mind sits like a void in her net, a small hole of nothingness that shifts when he does. Telium hums to herself as she mulls over what this means. The Fae warrior seems unable to detect her Gifts when she uses them, but he can certainly deflect them.

They travel for another bell in silence. Telium's throat is sore from their conversations after not speaking in so long. Mallux abruptly changes course, veering off the animal path they have been following.

When she hesitates, Mallux looks over his shoulder at her. 'I noticed this place earlier today when I passed by. It will be a suitable camp for the night.'

Telium looks over him with new-found appreciation, raising an eyebrow. 'You spent the night in my forest?'

The Fae shakes his head. 'I travelled much faster on my search for you, Queen Assassin.'

'Telium,' she corrects. The title chafes. 'I am Queen of Nothing.' She is surprised he has not asked her name, more surprised that she has only just realised.

'Telium.' He repeats her name like a promise on his lips.

She strides after him, wanting to see this place that he deems safe to spend the night. It is a small cave-like structure, standing out amongst the trees. Created by jutting slabs of stone that have been forced from the earth long before humans populated Alkoria. The narrow mouth opens into a space with a low ceiling – just large enough for both of them to sleep stretched out without touching.

Mallux begins to crawl in but Telium stops him. 'Wait until after dark to see what crawls out of there before you go caging yourself in with it.'

Mallux looks over his shoulder, one eyebrow raised in question. 'There is nothing in here, Telium.' His lyrical Fae accent hugs her name.

'Not now, but some of the night creatures here come up from the ground and they prefer to do so in sheltered places.'

'Up from the ground?' the Fae asks. He looks into the stone hollow once more, his sharp blue eyes scouring the cave.

Anticipating his next words, she sighs heavily through her nose before explaining. 'You won't be able to see them,' she growls. 'Even if you dig through the dirt, you will find no trace. They just …' she sweeps her hand out in front of her, 'materialise.'

Mallux folds his legs under him and sits smoothly with his back leaning against the flat wall of stone. 'Very well,' he says, his voice smooth. 'We will wait for these … creatures you speak of.'

He unstraps his blade from around his waist and lays it across his lap, settling in to wait for the sun to fall. Telium keeps her consciousness spread about her. She moves across from Mallux and leans against a tree before drawing one of her small throwing daggers which she uses to clean the dirt from under her nails.

Every so often, she notices Mallux stealing a peek at her. Telium's hands itch with the need to run her hands over his broad shoulders and down his chest. She wonders what the fabric of his shirt would feel like under her—

With a jerk, she reins in her thoughts. Her lustful ponderings evaporate like mist in the sun. *What in Tenebris' name was that?*

Telium sheathes her blade with an agitated movement before dumping her pack on the ground and rummaging through it. She produces a strange assortment of berries, roots and dried meat which she hands to Mallux before retreating to her tree where she studiously keeps her eyes downcast and mind on her food. She can feel the Fae watching her still.

As they eat, the light rapidly fades. She knows the sun has gone down because the forest begins to stir. The shadows lengthen and darken, becoming true night as the nocturnal beasts wake. It begins as a lone screech winding between the trees.

Then the howls start up, and within moments, the entire forest becomes a cacophony of screeches, howls and hisses. One of those sounds echoes out from their little cave. Mallux's eyes widen in surprise at the sound. He starts to his feet with unnatural speed and faces the opening with sword drawn.

'No,' Telium's voice is like a whip crack. 'You will not kill whatever creature comes out of there unless we must. Stand aside.'

Mallux opens his mouth to argue, but a hiss from the mouth of the cavern cuts him off.

'Stand aside,' the words grind out of her, her tone that of someone who expects to be obeyed.

A scowl crosses the Fae's face. For a moment it seems like he will defy her, and Telium's hand itches for her haladie. But he sheathes his blade and moves away to stand beside her.

Just inside the cave, mist pools and condenses. One moment it is a swirling mass, the next, it solidifies into a creature. Long and sinuous, it has scales the colour of tilled earth covering its reptilian body and a mouth full of pointed teeth in a dog-like head.

Beside her, Telium feels Mallux tense as the thing slithers out from the cave, smelling like mud and decay. Upon seeing them, the creature stills and lets out a long, threatening hiss. Its head sways hypnotically like a sand viper.

In reaction to the threat, Telium's Gifts flare. She pulls back her lips in a snarl of challenge. Her teeth, now tipped with fangs, gleam in the dim light. Under her skin, her Gifts swell and push against their constraints, suffusing the air with power. The beast goes deathly still, able to feel the strength Telium possesses and registering her as a threat. They stand, unmoving, eyes locked in silent combat.

A long, metallic scrape breaks the deafening silence as Mallux draws his broadsword, the sound echoing amongst the trees. The creature hisses again, eyeing its two opponents. The beast must realise it's outmatched because, with a frustrated shriek, it backs away from them quickly before turning tail and disappearing into the dark between the trees.

Telium stands still a moment more before spooling the threads of her mind back into itself and banishing her fangs. Straightening, she turns to Mallux who is standing close and watching her with a look she cannot place.

'What?' she barks, leaning away a bit. Unused to the feeling of closeness.

The Fae shakes his head and sheathes his blade. 'Nothing. Will it now be safe to rest here?' He gestures to the jumble of rocks that makes up their camp for the night.

Telium nods, fighting the 'I told you so' and instead saying tightly, 'We will just shift that stone over the entrance behind us. It will not enclose us completely, but it will save us from prying eyes.'

Telium ducks into the space, hunching to avoid smacking her skull on the stone. She throws her pack down and removes her cloak, spreading it out on the ground, then sits cross-legged on it, facing the entrance. She readies her Power-Thief Gifts to pull the stone shut behind Mallux, only to watch him haul it into place with a grunt. Telium snaps her mouth shut with an audible click. *That rock must weigh as much as me seven times over! Tenebris curse me.*

Mallux mimics her makeshift bed, throwing down his cloak and settling on it. With nothing else to do, Telium lies back, arms behind her head, as she waits for sleep to claim her. The silence stretches out for so long she thinks Mallux must have drifted off already, so when he speaks, she nearly jumps in surprise.

'Would it not also be prudent to light a fire by the entrance, to deter the beasts outside?'

The sound of fabric shifting over stone whispers as he shifts to get comfortable. She shakes her head, thinking of how to answer. 'The fire would just draw them like moths to flame. Better to hide with them among the shadows than light a beacon announcing our presence.'

The Fae seems satisfied with this answer and settles back into silence. The moon has risen high in the sky before Telium feels the gentle tug of sleep. Mallux's snores began bells ago. She reaches across to her pack, feeling the hard edges of the box she had hastily shoved in before setting out on her journey.

The box contains the needles and ink she will need for her *Ta Vir* – her tattoos – all sourced from the forest and made over her long winters here. She added the curling red tattoos to her flesh every time she took a life. Why had she brought them? Did it mean she was willing to kill? That she *wanted* to?

CHAPTER
9

The border of the forest creeps up on them. One moment they are walking through densely packed trees that seemingly stretch on for miles; the next, they spy a vast field peeking through the trees.

Telium's heart stutters a moment, skipping a beat before thundering into a gallop. The reaction surprises her. She had not realised how used to the forest she had become. Something in her hesitates as if a string inside her soul is tethered to these looming goliaths that have stood watch over her for many winters.

Telium has the oddest sensation of her body being pulled forward by puppet strings; her legs keep moving forward, lungs continuing to draw in oxygen with no conscious thought from her. While her soul hesitates amongst the trees.

The dappled sunlight dances as a gust of wind blows down from the mountains making the branches overhead sway. It carries the scent of distant rain clouds.

It's as if the tie in her has been cut. Her soul snaps back forward into her body. Her limbs are her own again. Just as her feet reach the border of all that she knew, and all that she was.

Telium steels herself as she passes out from under the last

shadow; she has not set foot outside of her forest since she ran into it for refuge. She feels exposed, the hairs on the back of her neck standing up. Now she has to force her legs to keep moving; it is a conscious effort to get her lungs to keep drawing breaths into her body.

The heat of the midday sun beats down, hitting her like a slap. Telium feels her breath leave in an odd huff. Then return in a steady inhale. *Breathe.* Her lungs contract as her next breath leaves her. *Again.* In. Out. Her breath keeps coming. Her legs keep moving. Nothing changes.

Her fluttering heart steadies into its regular rhythm. She refuses to glance over her shoulder. To look at the trees that were both her prison and her haven all these winters past.

Within minutes, the heat becomes unbearable. Telium shrugs off her pack so she can remove her cloak which she stuffs in her bag. She taps her fingers on her dagger, trying to dispel the odd feeling of open space, so used to the forest of trees standing watch over her.

Her assortment of weapons catches Mallux's eye and he rakes his gaze up and down her body. He raises an eyebrow but says nothing. *And that's just what you can see*, Telium thinks. Still, she knows the bandolier would attract attention in the town.

While she can claim to be a travelling mercenary, she does not want to risk her cover being blown thanks to her damning eyes and hair that make her so recognisable. So she rolls up her bandolier, blades clinking, and removes the sheath and knife strapped to her thigh and the one at her hip, and places them in her pack.

Next, she removes her haladie from where it hangs at her side and straps it to her bulging bag. Nothing she can do to hide that; she does not want to sheathe it along her spine while carrying her pack.

Telium rolls her shoulders, unused to the feeling of being free of her belts and steel. She still has blades within easy reach, but not the bristling arsenal she is used to. If the situation demands, it will only take her a moment to draw her haladie.

She stifles a yawn as they walk. Farms spread out on either side of them, the meadows dominated by crops or livestock. The sweet smell of hay mingles with the salt of animal sweat and dust. The looming shadows of the mountains are a sage and constant presence, rising like a gigantic wall cutting across the landscape.

They reach the road, a hard-packed strip of earth that leads south to the logging town of Calcep and eventually the capital – Coronal. The western branch of the road leads all the way to Diaxe. The fishing town sits on the shores of Rostick, the great lake.

Their pace picks up once on the main thoroughfare, and soon the town comes into view. The road is busy with people going into town for wares, leaving it to travel to other cities or farmers going to tend their fields.

Without warning, the approaching people reach the outer edge of Telium's consciousness with an intense mental slap. She gasps at the sudden assault of so many life-forces and nearly stumbles under the onslaught. Mallux glances at her from the corner of his eye but says nothing. He leans closer to her, their arms nearly brushing. Telium twitches away a moment before their skin touches, as if he would burn her.

Squeezing the bridge of her nose, Telium inhales deeply. She had been unprepared for that many consciousnesses all at once. The last time she had felt the brush of multiple minds was when she was stalking her forest, barefoot, power-drunk and mad.

Mustering all her self-control, she keeps walking and with a slight grimace, snaps her mind back into itself. The lights of the people's minds wink out. The sensation was like walking from a quiet night into a room packed full of people and music. The shock to her senses has brought on a headache.

Gingerly, Telium spreads out her net again, more slowly this time, keeping it a few feet from her body. To her right, she can sense the void that is Mallux's mind and a brief flash of life-forces as people walk by and cross through her net.

As they pass, she begins to pick up on the *feelings* of people. She cannot read their thoughts or sense anything deeper than the basest emotion. From the corner of her eyes, she notes the faces of people as they pass by, matching them to their different feelings. Fatigue. Hunger. Desire.

The last one makes her head shoot up and her eyes lock with a boy passing by. His skin pales as he looks at her fearsome face, then splashes of red warm his cheeks. He flinches away from her gaze and Telium snorts gently in amusement.

Ducking her head and hunching her shoulders, she tries to look as inconspicuous as possible. She need not have worried; next to the towering wall of muscle that is Mallux, the townsfolk barely give her a second glance. With his broad shoulders and slightly tapered ears poking out from his golden-blond hair, he cuts quite the figure moving through town.

'Mallux,' she murmurs, 'where are you staying?'

Seemingly unperturbed by the attention he is getting, especially from ladies whose gazes linger on him, Mallux points toward the centre of town.

'The Kinsman. The one with the large oak door, across from the bakers.'

'Fine. I'll meet you back there for lunch. I need to get some things.' She begins to drift into the crowd.

'But it is only a few bells until sunset!' he calls after her.

'Dinner, then!' she growls over her shoulder.

She watches him huff out a frustrated sigh before carrying on in the opposite direction. She needs supplies. *Maybe something for my hair,* Telium thinks, adding to her mental list as she ducks her head to avoid the curious gaze of a passing man. She's seen a few of the local women wearing soft, pretty wraps made of cotton, light enough to keep the wearer cool while shielding them from the harsh midday sun. The nights would be fine this close to the mountain, the temperature drops enough for her to wear her hooded cloak. But while in towns, she needs to cover her hair to avoid being recognised.

Walking through the streets, Telium marvels at how the town has grown. Once barely worth a mark on the map, Lampart has now blossomed into a small city, with stalls, vendors and shops of every kind. Older, smaller stores now stand next to larger, more modern shops whose polished wood gleams gently.

The main thoroughfare has been lined with cobblestones, but the smaller streets and alleyways remain hard-packed dirt. Most of the buildings are made with a patchwork of stone quarried from the mountainside, pine and a mud-mortar mix.

Telium wanders down the road until she finds the square set up with vendors hawking their wares. Bright colours and a variety of smells assault her senses, and Telium, so used to the calming smell of her forest, draws the scents into her lungs, savouring the smells of bread and cooking meats, leather and iron. Colourful cloth has been hung over stalls to provide shade, and people hurry to and fro. Her eyes dart from place to place, drinking in the sights and sounds of the busy square after so long in isolation.

She lurks in the shadows until she spots what she is looking for – a middle-aged man, soft around the middle and wearing gaudy rings that flash in the sun. He looks down his nose at the townsfolk and kicks a young street urchin who gets underfoot.

As he walks among the stalls, Telium tracks him with her gaze. Once she is confident he is alone, she makes her move.

Looping around, she walks towards him, pretending to examine the wares of the young woman he is currently ogling over the makeshift counter. Using perhaps a bit more force than necessary, she crashes into the man hard enough to make him stumble a step backwards. Telium's hand flies out to steady him, crying an apology.

'Idiot fool!' the man bellows, grabbing her by the wrist. He roughly twists her hand around, palm up, revealing her empty hands.

'I—I'm sorry!' She drops into an awkward curtsy while the man still grips her hand in his meaty fists. She keeps her eyes on his belt and he gives her wrist a sharp jerk. 'Apologies, milord,' she gasps, breathless. 'I was so taken by this beautiful lady's wares; I did not see you!'

The woman behind the stall shirks backwards as the man turns his attention back to her. Telium feels a swell of pity for the poor woman. The pig will not stop hounding her until she gives in to his advances, and here she is using her as a distraction.

The man pats his purse hanging at his hip. With one more look at her empty hands, he lets Telium's wrist go. 'Mind your step next time, girl,' he says, before brushing past roughly, shoving her aside and storming away.

Telium watches him go, giving a mocking two-fingered salute to his back. 'Sure thing, mister,' she drawls sarcastically. Her fingers drift to her pocket, brushing the soft leather of the man's purse now hidden there.

A startled snort to her left causes her to glance over at the young woman who is biting her lip to stop her laugh escaping.

'Too heavy on the sarcasm?' Telium asks, before winking at the woman and flipping a gold dath onto her countertop.

The woman's eyes go wide as saucers, glancing up from the coin to Telium in surprise, before fearfully looking after the man who has disappeared from sight. She slaps her hand over the coin.

A few feet away, Telium chuckles to herself as she slips in and out of the crowd, the man's purse weighing heavily in her pocket. While she could have just stolen the items she needs, it was too much fun not to pickpocket the man. She knows his type: arrogant and spiteful. He is probably the town's tax collector, banker or self-elected leader. He would not miss the coins and they were better off with Telium, being spent on the townsfolk's trades.

The first thing she buys is a shawl for her head. Once she has the tan fabric covering her stark white hair, she feels less exposed. She keeps the wrap loose, so that if she tilts her head just so, her eyes are hidden in the shadow of the cowl. Next is a trip to the blacksmith, who looks at her weapons belt and sends her across town to a leathermaker, who, after some convincing of the monetary sort, promises to have a new bandolier ready for Telium by the morning.

She also adds a new pack to her purchases, along with some good travelling boots – sturdy things made of soft, supple leather that hugs her calves. Back in the square, she buys another set of clothes, lest hers be ruined on their travels. All that is left is to prepare some food for the journey, a task that can be left with the cook at The Kinsman, where Telium now heads.

While completing her purchases, she listens to the gossip of the people she passes, breathing in the smell of dust and wares. She crunches an apple as she listens, the sweet, tangy juice bursting in her mouth, delighting her with the simple pleasure. They talk of Mallux, of course, not knowing much about him other than he is Fae. Rumours and stories buzz around the townsfolk like flies, each more outlandish than the last. But it is not the stories people speak about in the open that interest her, so she skulks in the shadows, listening for scraps of whispered conversations.

... a bad omen, to have a Fae in our town ...

... Where are the rest of them? You know, it's the ones you don't see that get you ...

... should not be allowed here at all. These youngsters have learnt nothing from the Great War ...

... I heard another Thief child went missing – from Xandi – probably the Mad Fae King up to his tricks again ...

... cannot reach far enough to protect a little town at the furthest edges of Alkoria ...

... Da told us stories, ones that his Da told him. Of a great war between the Siren Queen and the Mad Fae King ...

Telium latches on to all this information, gobbling it up like a starved man. Mallux had mentioned that his King had tried to invade Alkoria before – perhaps that is the Great War people speak of. She catches one of the young children weaving between the crowd, the one she heard talking about the stories his father used to tell him.

'Child,' she murmurs, 'I hear your father is a great storyteller.'

The child looks cautiously up into her face hidden in the shadow of her wrap. Telium produces a small silver chet from her pocket, dancing the coin back and forth over the back of her knuckles, before placing it in the child's hand. His dirt-streaked face lights up as he clenches his fist around the money.

'Yes, miss,' he replies shyly. 'He tells stories while he works to entertain guests. People say he has the knack for it.' The boy puffs his chest out with pride. 'When I am older, I'm going to be a bard.'

Telium grins. 'Ah, I see. And where does your father work?'

'At The Greenleaf Inn.' He points down the road. 'The one with the green roof.'

Telium commits the name to memory. She is about to leave, but hesitates, looking down at the child turning the chet over in his hands. 'A bard, you say?' When the young boy nods, she continues. 'Well, how about I be your first customer?' She taps the coin in his hands and angles her head so he can see the smile on her face. 'What stories do you know about the Siren Queen's assassin – Telium?'

The boy's mouth forms a small 'o' and he glances up and down the street. 'Ma used to tell me those stories,' he murmurs. 'Telium; they called her Bloodless Maiden on account she could fight a *hundred* soldiers and leave without a single scratch. They called her Tenebris Kin. Ma said she had powers that no other Thief had, so she must have come from the Underrealm. And that she was part Life-Thief, 'cos only a demon could have the powers to take someone's soul. But Lance says that Ma is wrong because Life-Thieves don't have that power. An' it is just a story that mothers tell their kids to get them to behave. Ma doesn't like Lance; says I can't play with him anymore.'

When he frowns, Telium nods in understanding, prompting the young boy to stay on track. 'And Telium?'

'Oh, well. She used to be the best assassin the Siren Queen had, *ages* ago. Ma said grandpapa was one of the soldiers who had to go into the forest looking for Telium. So, it must have been like a hundred, hundred winters. Anyway, she was the best assassin *ever*, and nobody would cross the Siren Queen without having Telium come after them – she would open her mouth so wide an' swallow you whole! Then one day, the Fae King came, and Ma said he did something awful to the Queen, and it kinda broke her, you know? Like the way little

Lacey down the road is broken. Ma said the Fae King planted something in the Queen that night and as it grew, she became really horrid. Then she found out one day Telium was in … what's the word? *Caa? Caahoie?'*

'Cahoots,' Telium whispers.

'Yeah, that's it! Cahoots. She was in *cahoots* with the Fae King and so the Queen locked Telium up. But she escaped! And Ma said she got away from a *whole* army! Then she ended up in the forest and she didn't have to hide from the Queen anymore. But that's Tenebris' forest, and it turned Telium all inside out … pulled the Life-Thief right from her. She used her powers to kill anyone who went there, pullin' down the night sky and smotherin' armies. That's why Ma says not to wander. Because if you do, Telium will come out of the forest and get you! When her Da was little, they used to leave naughty children in the forest for Telium to eat! Ma says she would have died long ago now though; that even Thieves can't stop old age, not like the Fae … Lance says there's a Fae here in town!'

The boy stops, cheeks flushed with excitement from being caught up in the story. He looks up at her, face expectant.

Her head is spinning so violently, it takes a moment for her to realise the boy is waiting on a response from her. Telium clears her throat. 'That's a very good story. I think you will make a fine bard.'

The young boy swells with pride before giving her a nod and running off.

Telium watches him go as conflicting emotions war inside her. While she is sure some of the boy's story has been fabricated by people trying to make it more fantastic as it passes from mouth to ear, some parts ring true.

More pieces of the puzzle click into place and Telium

struggles to get her head around it all. 'Great,' she grumbles to herself, 'I have become a child's hearth-tale.'

Another thought follows closely on its heels. The boy had said his grandfather was one of the men who chased Telium into her forest. No, perhaps the child was exaggerating. But despite her efforts to push it away, Mallux's words from before force the truth on her.

Your country has not seen a queen in near fifty winters.

Telium's breath rushes out of her in shock and she leans back against the wall to steady herself. *Impossible.* There is no way she was there that long. She is human ... mortal, with a mortal lifespan. The time she spent in madness cannot have been longer than six cycles of the sun. But in the back of her mind, a memory fights to be recognised of the last time she saw her Queen and the horrible words she had thrown at her.

Phantom screams ring in her ears. A shadow of shock and pain whispers over Telium's heart. She pushes off the wall, heading back towards the main thoroughfare at a brisk pace, trying to distance herself from the memory. She shoves her denial and shock deep down, she can examine them later. As she walks, she sifts through the information she has collected. Sidestepping a cart laden with barrels of ale, the bitter smell tickling her nose, Telium comes up with a plan to get the confirmation she needs.

CHAPTER
10

Telium approaches The Kinsman and eyes it with suspicion. It is a grand building for town standards; the walls and roof clean, the sign out the front dusted and the porch swept. Even the little filigree hugging the edge of the roof has been well looked after. Of course, the Fae would choose the nicest, and likely most expensive, tavern in town. While she can appreciate such comforts, it will not hold the type of patrons Telium likes – hardworking townsfolk, likely drunk after a tough day's work, easy to ply with more alcohol to loosen their tongues.

She sighs, resigning herself to a late night out skulking the back-alley taverns. She tries *not* to think of how amazing the beds here will be: big, soft, down filled and covered by thick fluffy rugs.

The warmth and chatter of conversation greet her as she passes through the doors. A middle-aged man behind the bar is taking orders from his patrons, his greasy jet-black hair shining in the candlelight. Telium perches on a stool in front of the bar, ignoring the sidelong glances from men.

When the bartender turns to her, she flashes him a smile, making sure to keep the top half of her face in shadow. It's a habit she just cannot shake, despite suspecting those who knew her have long since made the journey to the Gardens of Opimare.

'What can I get you?' he asks.

'Rum.' She attempts to soften her voice but fails miserably.

The man raises an eyebrow at her choice but pours a cup without comment.

'I am also looking for the Fae, Mallux. Is he here?'

The man's face darkens but he is wise enough to keep his mouth shut. He nods tightly, and points over her shoulder. Telium turns, following the man's meaty finger to find Mallux descending the stairs.

'Thank you,' she replies, throwing him a dazzling smile. Slapping a chet on the wooden bar, she takes her drink and weaves between the tables towards Mallux.

Halfway across the room, he looks up and spots her. He dips his head to an empty table in the corner. Something tells her he has laid claim to the spot since he has been here and nobody is fool enough to challenge that.

They sit on the hard wooden chairs, and Mallux leans back to study her intently. In response, Telium flicks her eyes up and down his form. He has changed and washed since she saw him last. His slightly damp hair curls at the ends. Quickly, she casts her gaze away, lest her thoughts get carried away as she imagines the Fae bathing.

She casually surveys the room, then turns back to see he is still watching her. She opens her mouth, ready to ask him what in Tenebris' name he is staring at when a serving girl arrives with two plates of food: bread, vegetables cooked in oil and herbs, a whole roast potato and some cut of meat that Telium identifies as beef as soon as it is put under her nose. The rich, hearty smell of the dish instantly makes her mouth water. Before the girl can scurry away, Telium catches her attention and rattles of a list of items. She tells her to pass it on to the cook and that they will be down to pay and collect the items at sunrise.

Mallux raises an eyebrow at her with unspoken question.

'Supplies,' is all she says, before stuffing a spoonful of food into her mouth.

She groans at the taste. While she rarely went hungry in her forest, she has not had food like beef or salt or *gravy* since she left the palace. She sets about devouring every morsel, while Mallux eats his food with the air of a prince. When he licks his lips, her adulterous eyes flick towards them, before her traitorous mind joins in. She wonders what it would be like if he put his tongue …

'I have a room for you for the night.' A ghost of a smirk hovers around his mouth.

What in Tenebris' name was that?

His words catch her off guard, likely because of the direction in which her wayward thoughts are wandering. She nearly chokes on her food. She leans back, mirroring his casual bearing and sips her rum as she looks around the room, enjoying the burn as it warms her stomach. Her eyes land on a young man, well dressed and with an air of arrogance about him. His clothes are fine, gaudily coloured in the fashion of nobles who have nothing better to spend their money on. A rapier hangs at his hip. She had noticed him stealing glances at her when she first arrived. He does so again, catching her watching him. Telium turns back to Mallux, dismissing the young noble.

'I have somewhere to sleep,' she says, smirking into her drink.

Mallux frowns. Shrugging, he finishes off the last of his meal. Afterwards, the serving girl clears away their plates, Telium's all but licked clean.

'Have you heard the rumours about you in town?' Telium watches Mallux over the rim of her cup.

The Fae raises an eyebrow at her. 'Yes,' he says, 'though they take care with their words around me, I hear them.'

It seems the people forget Fae have heightened hearing. *So Mallux knows of the dissent his presence has caused in the town.*

'What about the Great War? Have the townsfolk been whispering about that?'

Mallux pins her with his piercing blue gaze. It is Telium's turn to raise an eyebrow; she hadn't thought it was a difficult question.

'No,' Mallux says, finally looking away to scan the room. Telium taps her nail on her cup as the Fae turns back to her. 'We leave at dawn. Travel west to your holy city of Xandi where we can check our supplies and … trade in the horses. Then we will head north, back through the Infri Pass.'

Telium nods in agreement, listening to his plans as she sips her rum.

The Infri Pass is an ancient stone path that switches back and forth across the cliff face. The journey is rough and perilous but it is the shortest route to Thresiel. The alternative route is to travel all the way via the Tetilk Falls. Besides being a longer way, the plains beyond the falls are home to roaming bands of outcasts – robbers and bandits banished from both Alkoria and Thresiel. The barren landscape is known as Sordu'era – the Dead Lands. Combined with the deadly giant sand vipers and other monstrosities that lurk in the dunes, the Sordu'era is rarely considered as a travel option.

'In Thresiel, we must take a roundabout route to the capital. Spread the word of my return to those loyal to the cause.'

'How will that work?' Telium asks, genuinely curious.

'In nearly every city I have a network of contacts. They will help up spread the word and have our army ready to mobilise.'

Army?

'I was lucky to find you when I did. In less than two moons, the *Ramaeris* festival will be held in Meannthe. We can move a greater number of Fae much quicker under the guise of attending.' Excitement lights his eyes. 'We will have to move quickly. We cannot afford to miss this opportunity and the journey is long.'

Telium nods, a savage grin slashing across her face. She silently thanks Tenebris for hounding her out of the forest when she did.

'*Ramaeris,*' she says, trying out the Fae word on her tongue. 'What is the festival for?'

'It is a … celebration of sorts, for the King.'

'And when we reach your capital. What then?' she prompts.

Mallux returns her grin. 'Once at the capital, we strike at the peak of the festivities. The King will host a feast that night. It is grand event, food and wine will be free flowing. Their guard will be down, too busy revelling.'

A group of people sit down at the table closest to them. Mallux leans back, glancing at them from under lowered brows. The tavern is filling up. There will be no more talk of rebellion and mad kings tonight. Telium's questions will have to wait.

It seems so simple. But so loaded with risk. There are so many ways this plan could fall apart. Moving so many Fae without being noticed is risky, and even the journey through the mountains could kill them. Everything gambles on this element of surprise.

Telium leans back, smothering a yawn. 'It seems that everything is in order. If it all runs to plan, this should be easy.'

Mallux frowns at her, indicating he does not appreciate the

sarcasm. She swears she can *feel* his blue eyes trace a path across her cheeks and lips, before trailing down her throat. She swallows and forces a sleepy look on her face, which is not hard considering her belly is full and warm. She yawns, loudly this time.

Taking the hint, Mallux says, 'It is getting late; we should retire. We leave early tomorrow.'

Telium waves her half-empty cup in the air, the dark liquid swirling around it. 'I am not far behind you,' she replies, bringing the drink to her lips.

Mallux nods and with a silken 'goodnight' heads off towards the stairwell.

Once he is out of sight, Telium leans back in her chair before looking over at the young noble again. Now that Mallux has gone, his eyes focus on her openly. *Bold.* She returns his gaze, holding it for a moment longer and downing the contents of her cup. She smacks her lips together before rising and slowly winding her way through the tables, swaying her hips as she goes. At the door, she tosses a look over her shoulder, smiling at the man before slipping out into the night.

Telium strides into the narrow alley outside the tavern. After only a few moments, the young man appears at the doors, looking up and down the street. She snorts before stepping out from the shadows. *Really, that was nearly too easy.*

When he spots her, he grins and walks towards her.

'You flatter me with your attention, milord.'

'What is your name?' he asks boldly.

'Alice,' Telium lies, bobbing into a quick curtsy.

He runs his eyes up and down her body, probably noting her pants in place of a skirt or dress and how they hug her thighs. His eyes turn hungry. 'You're not from around here, are you?' His question is more of a statement, but she answers anyway.

'No,' a secretive smirk curves her lips. 'Are you staying here … at The Kinsman?'

Her brazenness causes a warm flush to rise on the noble's cheeks and he nods.

She hums in contemplation, stepping up to the man to look closely at his face. Plain, but handsome, he has soft hazel eyes and a shadow of a beard along his jaw. He smells pleasantly of peppermint. Attractive, in a simple way. Not the dazzling handsomeness of Mallux, but still … he will suffice for the task she has in mind.

Telium smiles again and leans forward. She hesitates a moment, fighting a grin as she hears his breath hitch. 'Good,' she whispers, before turning and stepping away.

'Wait,' the young man calls after her.

Telium does no such thing but favours him by slowing her pace and glancing over her shoulder. When he fumbles with his words, she quirks up the corner of her mouth. *Goddess, he is wriggling like a fish on a hook.* She has really picked a sucker. 'I will see you later,' is all she offers, continuing on her way with a final peek over her shoulder as she turns the corner.

The young noble watches her go. His mouth hangs open slightly. He snaps it shut before shaking his head in bemusement and returning to the inn.

Telium bets he makes a note to ask the innkeeper for another candle to keep burning, just in case.

CHAPTER
11

Striding off down the street, Telium heads towards The Greenleaf Inn that the young boy had mentioned earlier. As she nears, she can hear the muffled sound of a band playing. She unslings her pack, draws out her hooded cloak and replaces her shawl. She skulks along in the shadows and slips in the door of the inn behind a band of merry revellers.

Telium finds an empty chair in a dim area of the inn where she is far enough away from the huge hearth that a light chill mars the air. She orders a rum and sits back, letting the ebb and flow of conversations wash over her. She listens for bells, mostly hearing the stories and rumours she already knows, albeit with more of a flourish on some of the details. Alcohol turns even dull men into the most fantastic of storytellers.

On a table set in the middle of the room, a raucous game of Bones is being played. From the small pile off to the side, the players are betting on their win. Silver chets shine in the firelight, along with a pretty dagger and a small talisman of Opimare; the leaf carved in silver probably the most valuable item in the pile.

The five bones, likely harvested from the ankles of a sheep, have been painted a deep green. Telium's eyes track the bones as they are tossed and caught on the backs of hands. Each player progresses through as many tricks as they can before they drop a bone and the set is passed on to the next person.

Every so often, the music halts and one of the workers stops what he's doing to tell a story. The stories he tells are full of passion and vigour with noble heroes and amazing beasts, where the light always triumphs over the dark.

When a young girl comes to collect her second empty cup, Telium stops her with a hand on her arm. The girl bends her head so she can hear Telium over the chatter of voices.

'I would ask a favour of you,' Telium says in a hushed voice as she pushes a dath into the girl's palm.

Gold glints in the soft light and the young girl gasps at the sight of the coin that is likely worth a week's wages. She grips it tightly and nurses it close to her chest. She nods.

'I want you to ask the storyteller to tell the tale of how the Great War came.'

Another dath appears between Telium's fingers and she tilts it towards the man across the room, before placing it in the girl's free hand and tapping her nail against the metal.

'The *real* tale,' she adds, tapping the coin again, before jerking her chin at the man.

With a nod, the girl stashes her coin down her dress front. Telium watches the girl disappear into the kitchen, before returning empty-handed and heading towards the storyteller. She beckons the man closer, their heads bent together as the girl murmurs something to him.

The man shrugs and the serving girl shakes her head before leaning forward, reaching for his hand. She says something else and mimics Telium's tap on the dath that she presses into his palm. The man looks at the money for a moment before nodding warily and pocketing it. The serving girl scurries off to continue her work.

As the man stands, those gathered fall silent and the band peters out. The storyteller looks at the floor and chews on his lip, deep in thought. When he looks up, his eyes are far away; he is already in his story.

'I am Derik, Heath Kin. Storyteller of Lampart. You all know this to be true. Part of being a "teller" is to record our history by passing it down through the generations, through song and story and rhyme, so that our children and their children may know the path we have walked and learn from it.'

Derik's voice is deep and carries throughout the room with ease. The only other sound is the gentle crackling of the fire in the hearth. 'This tale is one of woe and ruin, but listen well, for it is our predecessors' path. They do not wish us to walk it again.'

The teller pauses and scans the faces in the crowd. Telium leans back, chair digging into her shoulder blades, as Derik begins his story.

'The Great War came in the time of the Siren Queen. When she heard whispers that the Mad Fae King was amassing an army, planning to attack our borders, she called for a peace meeting.

'You must remember, friends, that before this time, Fae and all manner of beings were free to cross in and out of our borders. Alkoria was rich with trade; our black stones from Ollsuria, fish from Diaxe, even the sands from the Ereak Desert, all sought out by foreigners. In return, they brought new delicacies, silk and grain, new crafts.

'The Mad Fae King saw all this and more. He was jealous, greedy. He believed Fae to be above all others and thought that they should rule over Alkoria. The Mad King and his delegation travelled to Coronal, where they met with our Queen.

They say the Siren Queen was as beautiful as the mountain wind on a hot summer's day. But she was also cunning and she knew what the Mad Fae King wanted. So, the night of the dinner, she draped herself in silks and jewels. She powdered her face and painted her lips a seductive red.

'As she sat through negotiations, she threw all her Thief powers into seducing the King. Planning to bend him to her will with her charms. Though a Freedom-Thief's Gifts were never known to sway the Fae. I see you frowning, but listen …

'Our Queen was so powerful that she was able to influence the Fae King's emotions, just the tiniest bit. Just enough to stop him declaring all-out war, because of the stirring in his loins. Instead, they reached an agreement. They would mix the bloodlines of the royals; the Mad King would choose a suitor who would marry our Siren Queen and rule beside her as King. Their children would be something never heard of: half-Fae, half-Thief.

'The terms were agreed upon, and with one last almighty push of her Song, the Siren Queen declared the dinner over. So became the Treaty Dinner.

'Late that night, hounded by the whisper of the Queen's Gifts, the Mad Fae King changed his mind about a suitor and visited the rooms of the Siren Queen.'

Telium grits her teeth but forces herself into stillness as the teller continues.

'He passed through without hindrance from the guards and left mere hours later. The King and his retinue left the next morning. Leaving behind a single Fae emissary to confirm the Queen fell with child.'

Telium's Gifts rumble in her chest. Their growls skitter through her blood. She crosses her arms, stuffing her hands under her biceps as her fingers tingle. Mind-Thief Gifts struggle to take form in the shape of deadly talons, despite the white-knuckled grip she keeps on her restraint.

'The Siren Queen must have known all along what was to come; that by seducing the King, allowing him into her bed and promising their heir to be ruler, she bought Alkoria the time it needed to prepare for war.

'A moon later, whispers began among the servants; the Queen had missed her bleeding – she was pregnant. But other whispers travelled the halls and chambers of the castle too. The Mad Fae King had requested the child be sent to him at twenty-one winters of age. The Mad Fae King would raise the child under his wing, teach them how to rule, before sending them back to Alkoria to take over once the King felt the child was ready.'

The memory of coming across the Siren Queen on the balcony is still fresh in Telium's mind.

Telium knows what happened the night the Fae King visited her Queen, and it was not as consensual as the teller makes it sound. The Siren Queen had offered up her body as a sacrifice for her country. Telium is the only one who understands what the Queen had done to protect her people.

Drive a blade through his heart.

Her rage spikes; angered by the way the story turned out, as if her Queen is the seductress and the Fae King completely helpless to her wiles, as though he is not a tyrant, darkness-bent on consuming Alkoria whole.

She focuses again on the teller's words.

'The moons went by, and her belly grew. It seemed that the Siren Queen would produce a happy, healthy baby. Then the worst happened – a horrific accident, and her unborn child could not be saved.'

The teller hangs his head, pausing a moment in respect for

the lost life. The silence is so thick it could have been cut with a blade.

'Time went on, as it does, and things began to change. The trade routes started to close, checks at the border became sterner and more frequent. People began to notice it was always the Fae who were taxed the most or turned away entirely. As the date of her unborn child's twenty-first winter neared, the Queen became more and more agitated and paranoid. The word "Fae" became a curse. To even speak to one stank of traitorous intent. Old friendships between Alkorian and Fae strained and broke under the weight of the Queen's prejudice. It is said that the guilt of losing her child drove her mad and the fear of the Mad Fae King's looming return made her paranoid. So much so that she imprisoned her most trusted assassin and sentenced her death – Telium Tenebris Kin. Yes ...'

Derik nods at the glances exchanged between his listeners.

'*That* Telium – the very dark being who haunts the forest at our doorstep. Not quite Thief, but something else entirely, terrorising our grandfathers, stealing children and livestock.'

Telium snorts softly at that. If anyone was stealing live-stock, it would have been the falkir. Reaching up to touch the claw on her necklace, she fiddles with the smooth, cool piece as the teller continues his story.

'The Siren Queen sent her forces after Telium. She feared her former assassin would turn on her and make an alliance with the Fae King. Telium had found refuge within the dark forest, and mad with betrayal and despair, unleashed the might of her dark powers on the army that hunted her.

'It was while the Queen was distracted that the Fae King struck. His army had come through the trade route between our countries, overwhelming the border guard before they could raise the alarm.

'That first battle was devastating. Alkorians were pushed into a desperate fight for survival while reinforcements rallied. The war that followed was long and bloody. Thief Gifts were pitted against Fae Powers, with many mortals trapped in-between.

'The war raged on for years, both sides evenly matched. First, the Fae army would advance, then they would be pushed back in an endless game of tug of war. In desperation, the Siren Queen called for any man, woman or child strong enough to hold a sword to join her ranks. In the final push, the Siren Queen was captured and the Fae King took her as a prisoner of war and retreated to the Fae land of Thresiel.

'Using the last dregs of their power, the Fae caved in much of the route, nearly sealing the mountains shut behind them. The Siren Queen was never heard from again. Cruel is the fate that allows a monarch to die in lands not of her own. Alkoria was in chaos. With no immediate heir, there was nobody to claim the throne. Some of the soldiers and Thieves banded together and attempted to breach the Fae border to rescue their Queen, but the Fae King was ready for them. The bones of those brave souls now litter the passage between the mountains. Tenebris willing, they will guard us against the return of the Fae.

'The ensuing chaos would have been an ideal time for the Fae King to raid, but mad as he was, he was distracted by his new prisoner and the opportunity slunk by unnoticed.

'Alkoria milled in confusion. The remaining army dispersed; villagers back to their homes and soldiers back to the castle, only to find those remaining lost and listless. People mourned their dead. Mothers had lost children, siblings never returned, orphans showed up at the Temples of Opimare in every village and city.

'From this, the Sixth Council, the Queen's committee of advisors, stepped up – a group of men and women, one from each of the main cities in Alkoria: Scara, City of Sand; Diaxe, City of Water; Ollsuria, City of Stone and Fire; Calcep, City of Trees; Xandi, the Holy City; and Coronal, the capital. Each city voted a representative; someone of honour, skill and knowledge. Each of these representatives made up the Sixth Council who will rule until a royal line can be found to retake the throne of Alkoria. It has been said that the Siren Queen had a brother and that if he can be found, he and his heirs are the rightful rulers of Alkoria ...'

The teller trails off. The silence of his listeners is so complete the fire crackling in the hearth sounds like the roar of a wildfire.

It seems to Telium that very few, if any, of the villagers have heard the tale told with such stark truth before. Likely, the story was passed down by their grandfathers who made the war sound like some great adventure. The reality is far more brutal.

Derik nods at the crowd before taking a seat, and the band starts up a jaunty tune. The merry noise is harsh and grating against the stillness left in the wake of the teller's tale. As the conversation at the surrounding tables stumbles back to life, Telium shoves back her chair with a screech and storms out the door.

CHAPTER 12

'All this time,' she hisses. 'All this time I cared for you. Fed you, clothed you, trained *you*.'

She swipes her hands through the air in a cutting motion. Telium has never seen the Queen like this; her hair a mess, like she had been pulling at it, and her dress crumpled, the hem stained with mud. The only jewel she wears is the turquoise stone that hangs about her neck on its thin gold chain. Her Queen is usually the master of masks, using her gowns and gems to hide her true power beneath.

'And *you*,' she whips around, pointing an accusatory finger at Telium, her hand quivering with rage. 'You go and fraternise with the very beasts that try to destroy me!' Her sentence ends in a screech.

Telium's mouth hangs open with shock. Never has her Queen been so unhinged, not even after the riding accident that caused her to lose the child in her womb. There has been speculation in the palace. The Queen's powerful Freedom-Thief abilities extends to animals too; she had never fallen from her mount before. The few staff who whisper those ugly words usually find themselves at the end of Telium's knife or at the bottom of Rostick – the Great Lake.

The whispers started after the Fae King and his council left and continued after the Queen's accident. Murderer. Rapist. Half-breed. Fae. *The words are the tolling of a death-bell for whomever speaks them. Only those who are completely loyal to their Queen remain working in the castle.*

*Telium tries to reason with her now. Tries to convince her Queen that she is loyal to her and her only. But Telium's arguments are hindered by her confusion. After returning from a trip to Scara, Telium had immediately been summoned to the throne room, only to find the Siren Queen in a rage, screaming half-*finished *accusations at her and rambling on about her betrayal.*

Again and again, Telium tries to reason with the Queen, trying in vain to make sense of the situation that is rapidly spiralling out of control. Her pleas send the Queen pacing back and forth, her steps twitchy and agitated, as Telium explains that she really has carried out the mission she'd been assigned. No, she did not go anywhere else but to the desert city of Scara. No, she did not secretly meet with an outsider while there.

'Lies,' the Queen hisses at Telium's attempts to make peace. 'Your father may have been Alkorian, but your mother was nothing but a whore.'

The words hit Telium like a slap in the face. Her heart drops to her stomach and her mouth opens and closes, working hard to find words that will not come.

The sneer on the Siren Queen's face is fearsome to behold. 'Do not act so shocked,' she says. 'I know it all. I know that you and your beloved Trigg were planning to let the King's soldiers into the castle. I know that you have been plotting with your mother's people. That you were with them this whole time! Treason!' she screeches.

She looks down her nose at Telium, quite a feat considering she is shorter than her. The Queen's eyes are glazed and her cheeks flushed as if she has a fever. She bares her teeth in a macabre imitation of a smile. 'Well, that stops right here.'

She spins, calling for her guards. Two, from the many lining the marble walls of the room, break off and open the heavy wooden doors. After a moment, prison guards appear, dragging Trigg by the arms between them.

Telium's teacher is bruised and battered; both eyes swollen shut, her lip split and bleeding, her mahogany skin coated in a sheen of sweat. Her head hangs between her shoulders as though she does not have the will to hold it up.

Telium's gasp echoes through the throne room. All that can be heard are Trigg's rasping breaths. Shocked beyond words, Telium can do nothing but look between her fallen teacher and her Queen.

The guards dump Trigg unceremoniously at the Queen's feet. Trigg, who usually looks intimidating in her tailored red uniform, lays crumpled in a heap, not having the strength to stand. Her dark curls are a wild mess around her face that is pinched in pain. Telium wants to run to her side but shock roots her to the spot.

The Siren Queen looks at the woman with cold eyes, lips curling in disgust before turning her icy gaze on Telium.

Telium looks into those staggering blue eyes; there is nothing of her Queen in them, this woman who's turned mad with rage and hate. Gone is the cunning, competent Queen Telium has known and loved.

'Trigg of Scara, you have been accused of conspiring with the enemy, knowingly housing a half-breed and defying your Queen. How do you plead?'

Even some of the guards shift in surprise at that, the fabric of their uniforms rustling quietly. The Queen's words carry the weight of the charges – a death sentence, for that is what the punishment is for such crimes. Trigg raises her head, staring defiantly into the eyes of her would-be executioner.

'Selenia, you are not yourself. I have been your friend and your confidante all these long years; you know I would never betray you. Do not let your hatred and paranoia blind you. Telli loves you. She is ignorant of her heritage. I never told her! You cannot hold the sins of her mother's race against her.'

Shock jolts Telium's senses when her teacher doesn't deny the Queen's claims. The Queen scoffs in disgust, ignoring the blatant use of her name, a sneer twisting her beautiful features.

Spinning away from Trigg, the Queen stalks to her throne, the echo of her steps mimicking the pounding in Telium's ears. When she turns to sit on the overstuffed cushions, her face is eerily calm, all emotion wiped from her features. The sudden change is terrifying, making the hair on the back of Telium's neck prickle.

'What wolves I have kept in my house.' Her stunning blue eyes travel between Trigg and Telium. 'What traitorous, conniving wolves.'

She nods her head at the guards standing over Trigg and one of them kicks her savagely in the side. Trigg coughs and spits blood on the marble floor, crying out in pain. The sound snaps something in Telium. Never has she heard her teacher cry in hurt, not when Telium accidentally sliced her thigh open in sparring practice, nor when her arm broke saving a young boy from a runaway horse. Rushing forward, Telium throws herself at the bottom of the steps, knees barking against the cold stone. But the pain is muffled by the rising panic in her mind.

'Please, my Queen,' Telium pleads. 'We are innocent of these crimes. I owe you my life and more. I have dedicated my existence to protecting you. I would never ... we would never ...'

She trails off as she looks up into the Queen's face, flinching at the venomous look of hate in the other woman's eyes. Unable to face her, Telium stares hard at the marble floor beneath her knees. She turns her palms up, the back of her neck exposed, hands held out in supplication.

'Please,' Telium whispers, voice breaking on the word, not knowing what else to say. Fear like she has never felt before coats her tongue with a sharp, metallic taste. Her chest aches as her heart breaks and her breathing turns ragged. 'Please.'

Behind her, Telium hears Trigg spit again. She turns her head so she can see her teacher from the corner of her eye.

Trigg struggles to her knees, a hand pressed to her ribs. 'You are letting your fear guide you,' she rasps. 'You have an army amassing across the border; you cannot afford to lose your greatest weapon. Do not let him get to you, Selenia. Do not let the Fae King have that power over you!' As soon as the words pass Trigg's lips, she pales under her russet skin.

Telium cringes at Trigg's poor choice of words. Her emotions swing so fast between confusion and fear she feels sick, sweat slicks her palms. She whirls back to the Queen whose face is like a thundercloud. The Siren Queen stands slowly and waves forward another guard. As he approaches, he draws his blade from his hip, the steel glinting in the light from the window. Dread curls in Telium's stomach and her mouth goes dry. There has to be a way to stop this, to get through to the Queen.

'You have been found guilty, Trigg of Scara, and I sentence you to death.'

The air catches in Telium's throat and everything seems to happen in slow motion, the scene before her fuzzy and out of focus.

Trigg hangs her head in defeat as the guard approaches with a raised sword. One moment he has the blade above his head, ready to sever flesh, the next, one of Telium's throwing knives is embedded in his chest. He looks down, his face a picture of surprise, mouth forming a small 'o'.

The world snaps back into focus. Telium is on her feet with her arm outstretched and hand empty. Her lips part in a silent gasp as the guard falls to the floor, dead. His blade clatters to the polished *marble as the coppery scent of blood slides through the room. There is a rustle of fabric as the Siren Queen steps forward. Telium's spine goes ramrod straight and she slowly lowers her arm back to her side. For the first time in her life, Telium is too afraid to face her monarch.*

'Guards,' the Queen says, her voice thick and melodic with her Freedom-Thief Gift. 'Restrain Telium by any means necessary; your life is no object.'

Telium whirls to the Queen in shock. Never, never does she use her Gift on her guards or court. She never layers her voice with Song to get her soldiers to do her bidding by taking away their freedom to choose.

Unexpected tears prickle her eyes and Telium's throat closes up as half-a-dozen guards surround her. She does not fight back, even though she could have dispatched them easily. She would not harm men unable to make a conscious choice, and the Queen knew that.

All she can do is look up at the Siren Queen, betrayal squeezing her chest like a vice. 'Please.' Telium's voice is a pained whisper, thick with unshed tears. The plea sounds pathetic, even to her own ears.

The Queen does not even spare her a glance but nods to another guard who picks up his comrade's fallen sword, face blank, and positions himself beside Trigg.

Telium's breath comes in pants. She cannot look away from the face of her Queen, cold and expressionless. Selenia might as well be carved from marble.

'Your mother loved you, Telli.' Trigg's whisper bounces off the walls and floor of the chamber. The quiet words pierce Telium's heart.

Nobody ever speaks of her parents. The one time she had asked her teacher about them, Trigg struck her so hard she never asked again. Telium's chest feels like it is being hollowed out.

Telium spins to face her, a question on her lips, only to see the sword glint in the light as it begins its descent. A scream cuts through the room as the blade sinks into the back of her teacher's neck. It takes Telium a moment to realise the sound has come from her. She shoves her fist against her mouth to muffle the noise that warps into a sob, before sinking to her knees. Grief hits her like a wave, washing over her in a great, crashing blow. It forms a hard lump in her throat that she struggles to get any air around, her breathing coming out in jagged, gasping pants.

The Queen is an anchor in the storm. She turns to see her descending the last few steps. 'As for you, half-breed,' her voice is cold and hard, lined with disgust.

'Trigg knew my mother?' The question slips out, the only thing her confused mind is able to grasp onto in the chaotic mess of the past hour. A phantom hand squeezes her heart.

The Queen scoffs again. Whatever she sees in Telium's face makes her eyes flash with anger. 'Such a clever assassin,' she hisses. 'Trying to find out what I know, are you?' She reaches down to grip Telium's chin, nails digging into her skin and sending sparks of pain across her face. She leans in close enough that Telium can smell the sea salt of her skin. 'What does it matter? You're a dead woman walking.' She releases her hold, all but tossing Telium away in contempt. 'Yes, she knew her. She knew that Fae whore and never told me; never told me what you were.' She spits her next words at Telium. 'Your father may have been Alkorian, but your mother was Fae. Trigg knew what you were – a freak, an aberration. Half-Breed.'

CHAPTER
13

Telium jolts awake, screams ringing in her ears.

Wooden walls, a soft bed and a warm body next to her. She is not in the cold prison that was Greybane, nor the hollow tree of her forest. The events of the last two days come rushing back. Mallux. Right. Impending doom, evil King and all that. Then she had found out that she must be over *fifty winters old.* And just because bad things come in threes, she listened to a storyteller spin a tale about a war that ravaged the country and her Queen being taken prisoner by the very same male who had raped her and sent her mad. The one person Telium had sworn to protect with her life had died alone.

After storming out of The Greenleaf Inn last night, she wandered the streets looking for trouble. Shoving her shock and rage and sorrow down, down, down. But apart from a few loitering drunks pissing on someone's barn, she encountered no-one.

In frustration, Telium had stalked to the edge of town, needing space to clear her mind. After bells skimming stones along the hard-packed earth and watching the moon and stars overhead, she had only managed to slightly cool her temper.

She was tempted to storm back into town, wake Mallux and demand they leave immediately. But the thought of barging into Mallux's room led to wayward thoughts of the Fae male sleep rumpled and shirtless. Then she would reprimand herself for such thoughts, which made her frustrated all over again.

'That's it!' she had growled as she cast aside her handful of stones savagely. She had then stalked back into town with single-minded intent – to scratch a rather specific itch.

That is how she ended up here, waking up from night terrors in the quiet moments before dawn with the young noble asleep next to her. Muscles that had not been used in many winters twinge and ache satisfyingly as she stretches.

It had not taken much for her to find out which room he was in. When she knocked on the door he had answered in an instant. The candle still burned, lighting the room behind him. He had been shy, yet made up for it with plenty of passion, pleasantly shocked by her forwardness. She let him have his way with her for a while before she flipped him on his back and rode him until she found her completion. Afterwards, as they lay there catching their breath, the young noble had asked where she was from. The awe in his voice was unmistakable.

Telium gave a husky laugh. 'Scara,' she said, naming the desert city to the south.

The city had a reputation for its skilled chamber dancers, so he did not question her further. She had gotten up to wipe the sweat from her limbs and get a drink. By the time she returned, he was fast asleep. Telium had thought it a shame to waste such a large, comfortable bed, and so she had clambered in beside him, muscles aching, and promptly fell asleep.

Now, she lies for a moment more, savouring the softness of the bed, knowing it is unlikely she will have such luxury again any time soon. With a resigned sigh, she gets up, ignoring the twinge of sore muscles, and dons her clothing and weapons in silence.

Outside the night sky is turning from black to a deep blue, signalling the coming dawn. She quietly pads from the room, planning to wake the stable master and use the last of her coins to buy horses to get them to Xandi swiftly. The man's stolen purse had been surprisingly full.

As she reaches the common room, she gazes through the front windows at the brightening sky. To her surprise, Mallux stands out in the road, looking up at the retreating silhouette of a hawk. She makes her way to the front door, floorboards creaking under her feet, catching Mallux just as he comes through.

He starts when he sees her, but quickly recovers. 'Telium,' he says, nodding in greeting. 'I trust you slept well.'

'Good morning,' she replies awkwardly, unused to such formal company. Or any company, for that matter. She stands a moment more under his gaze, before breaking the silence. 'I was just about to get the stable master up, to ready some horses so we can make better time between here and Xandi.'

Mallux nods. The scent of citrus and embers brushes her senses as he moves past her.

'Just give me a moment to gather my things,' he replies. 'I will meet you down at the stables shortly. Be ready to leave within the hour.'

His commanding tone rubs Telium the wrong way. She watches him stride towards the stairwell before calling after him, 'On your way back, be a gem and get our supplies from the kitchen?'

Mallux turns. A frown creases his face. He is obviously unused to taking orders. He opens his mouth to reply, but Telium does not give him the chance. She flashes a sharp smile before slipping out the door.

They leave town just as the sun is cresting the horizon, making a quick stop to the leathermaker so she can collect her new bandolier.

⌘

The ride to Xandi will take six days. Six days of scorching heat, sticky saddles and the musky smell of horse sweat. Telium keeps her new shawl wrapped loosely around her head to help protect her face from the sun. Still, by the end of the first day, her cheeks and nose are burnt red.

She finds Mallux to be an easy travelling companion. They share many interests; their effortless discussions ranging from favoured weapons to battle tactics. Telium is grateful Mallux does not ask about her upbringing, as she doesn't know how she should answer. She extends the same courtesy and refrains from asking probing questions about his life. The silent pact serves Telium well; she has no desire to air her history to this stranger.

They stop many times throughout the day to rest the horses, cautious not to overexert them. The first time they dismount, Telium nearly falls flat on her ass, only her quick reflexes allowing her to grip the saddle, saving her from mortification. Rarely used muscles quiver as she takes a shaky breath. Relief washes over her when she glances at Mallux and sees his back is turned.

Telium slowly becomes used to the feeling of being in open spaces again. By the time the sun disappears on the first night, she has settled completely. Warmth still lingers in the air so they forgo a fire – simply throwing down their thin bed-rolls and cloaks. After picketing the horses a short distance away to graze, they sit down to a cold meal of dried meats and bread.

When Mallux shifts to sit, his knee knocks hers and their

shoulders brush. Telium stubbornly ignores the goosebumps that chase across her skin. As if his touch still resonates there.

She silently chastises herself. *One roll in the sheets isn't enough for you? What in Tenebris' name has possessed you?*

Mallux merely finishes his meal and mumbles a goodnight, before lying down on his bed-roll and closing his eyes. The barest cool breeze licks across the camp towards them, smelling of night jasmine and dry earth. Telium lies back on her bed-roll to gaze up at the stars, picking out the blue and purple of distant galaxies. Taking comfort in their beauty against the dark, before closing her eyes and letting unconsciousness take her.

Late in the night, Telium rips herself from another dream, heart racing as her eyes fly open. Stars whirl above her. Beside her, Mallux breathes deeply. *Tenebris curse me.* She sighs in relief, even as insults echo in her ears. *Aberration. Freak. Half-Breed. Fae.* Throwing an arm over her eyes, Telium wills herself back to sleep.

The next morning sees them skirting around a small village. Telium is tired and irritable, her eyes gritty from lack of sleep. The harsh sun beats down on them and the constant smell of horse sweat does nothing to improve her mood.

As they travel, Telium notes the odd behaviour of the workers in the fields. None wave and offer a kind word or a shady place to rest their feet.

Have things changed so much?

In small farming communities like this, the people are usually warm and welcoming. A traveller brought with them news, stories, gold and other such things to trade. *Perhaps it is Mallux,* she thinks, watching a young girl run to her father's side as they go by the field a family is tending. She knows that people have been cautious, even fearful, of the Fae since the Siren Queen's paranoia took her.

'These people are full of mistrust,' Mallux murmurs to her after they pass a farmer who turns a hard eye on them.

'Did they treat you this way on your passage through?'

The Fae gives her a look as if her question is odd. He shakes his head before nodding toward the Orth Rel towering over them in the distance to their right. 'I stayed close to the base of the mountains until I came across the forest. However,' he adds, 'while the humans in the town of Lampart were cautious of my presence, they were not so hostile as these.'

Telium is about to argue his use of the word hostile, but when she looks back, she observes the firm grip the farmer keeps on his tool. The way he pushes his daughter behind him and plants his feet apart in a wide stance.

'What could have caused these people to become so hard?' Telium wonders aloud.

She gets her answer later that afternoon. After leaving Mallux behind on the road, she treks up the path to a farmer's door to beg for water to fill their waterskins.

Knocking on the door, Telium stands impatiently waiting for it to be answered. The wooden shutters on the window creak as they are pushed open an inch, and a few moments later the door cracks open. A face appears in the gap. A middle-aged woman with brown curls peers at her with narrowed hazel eyes.

'What do you want?' she demands roughly. Her voice sounds stern, but the hand that grips the doorframe is white-knuckled in fear.

Telium holds the waterskins out. 'Apologies for the intrusion, miss. But we are running low. I came to ask for some water for us and our horses.' At the woman's hesitation, she adds. 'I can pay.'

Digging through her small pouch, Telium pulls out a few

chets. The silver has the desired effect. The woman opens the door further and glances about to confirm they are alone. She nods and shouts to someone inside. A boy, likely her son, arrives. Before she lets him pass, the woman glares around again. Her hard gaze falls on Telium. 'You take the water and you go, understand?'

'Of course.'

'Charlie, help this woman fetch enough from the well to fill her waterskins.'

The boy nods and runs to the well a short distance from the house. He heaves on the rope to pull up the bucket.

As she turns to follow, Telium catches the glint of a dagger hidden in the woman's skirt. The woman follows closely behind and they stand in silence as the boy works to fill the waterskins. The mother seems unable to stop herself glancing around as if waiting for someone to appear.

'Forgive me,' Telium says, 'for it has been many winters since I last travelled this way. But has something happened here? The townsfolk are … not as I remember.'

'It's those bleeding bandits!' the boy exclaims.

'Charlie,' his mother admonishes. 'Mind your tongue!'

'Bandits?' Telium enquires, curiosity piqued. The next question jumps off her tongue before she can stop it, goaded by the whispers she heard in Lampart. 'Are they Fae? Have Thief children gone missing?'

The woman eyes her, frowning. 'No.' She drags out the 'o', making it sound like a question.

'They be human, an' only after coin. A group of them.' Her lips tighten into a thin line before she shrugs. 'Been sacking farms an' homes up an' down this way. Even fool enough to raid houses on the outer edge of town last moon.'

'Raids?' Telium repeats, surprised. 'Has anyone been hurt?'

The woman's eyes dart between Telium and her son, nodding hesitantly. Her unwillingness to give Telium any more details tells her all she needs to know.

'What about the town's guards? Have they done nothing?'

The mother barks a harsh laugh. 'Oh yes, the last time the guard in Gladshire tried to intervene, he came away with a bandaged arm an' a limp.' When Telium frowns, the woman adds, 'Small towns like these only warrant one guard.'

'Why have the people done nothing?'

The woman looks Telium up and down, eyes lingering on her practical clothing and the dagger at her hip. 'We are simple people here: farmers, smiths, bakers … not fighters.' She eyes the blade peeking over Telium's shoulder.

Telium bites the inside of her cheek. She has offended the woman by questioning their lack of action.

The boy completes his task and runs back to the house. As the woman turns to follow, Telium calls after her. 'Why has the Qu—… the capital not sent help? Soldiers to aid the town's guards. How long have these attacks been going on?'

The woman pauses, looking over her shoulder. 'There are no soldiers to spare on such small towns. The Sixth Council keep what they have in the major towns an' cities. Times have been hard. With no rain on the horizon, people have turned to robbery to get by, leaving their fields barren. Who can say if it has always been the same people, who are now growing too bold by half?' She shrugs her shoulders. 'Five moons at least an' still no help in sight.'

Five moons, Telium thinks as she watches the woman hustle back to the house and close the door firmly behind her. *Nearly half a winter.* No wonder the people in the area have become so mistrustful; they live in constant fear of being targeted by these criminals.

More concerning was the woman's interpretation of the Alkorian army. If there were not enough soldiers to protect the outlying towns, there were certainly not enough to stand against the might of the Fae, should the King attack. The thought shoots a spike of urgency through Telium.

When she reaches Mallux, she hands him a waterskin, relaying what she has learned from the woman. 'These people are being terrorised.'

'So it would seem.'

As they mount up and move on, Mallux's reaction hounds her. He is Fae, Telium reminds herself, not human, and therefore does not react the way humans would. With their long lives, mastery over emotions becomes an art for the Fae; they are not so quick to passion as mortals.

The thought of a band of miscreants wandering around unchallenged makes Telium grind her teeth. The fact that the capital has sent no help either infuriates her. If her Queen had still been in power, she would have sent her own guards to protect the townsfolk.

The bandits would have to be few enough in numbers so they could travel and hide without much notice, but large enough to sack a farmhouse and retreat unscathed. *Four or five*, Telium thinks, *certainly no more than six.* Fair enough odds.

Once the notion appears, she is unable to let it go. That old sense of responsibility, drummed into her by years of training with Trigg, reawakens. If she has the ability to help but stands by and does nothing, then she is no better than the male she is hunting. She will not dishonour her teacher's memory by standing idly by.

When they stop that night, Telium has made up her mind. She will head back into town and see what she can find out about these so-called bandits. If Tenebris favours her, she will easily be able to track them down and dispose of them.

While they may be causing havoc, it is unlikely they are more than petty criminals, so will leave traces that are easy for a skilled tracker, like herself, to follow. At the thought of a hunt, her Gifts stir under her skin.

CHAPTER
14

Telium peers through the trees at the innocent-looking derelict barn. A brutish man lounges back in the sparse early morning shade, chatting to a woman as she sifts through the last of their loot. Long blond hair hangs in greasy curtains around his shoulders and a forest-green shirt is tucked into a belt that holds an ugly looking cudgel. The woman is plain with brown hair tied back from her pale face. Wispy strands have sprung free and are plastered to her head with sweat.

Telium has tracked the group through the bells of dawn twilight, from an inn close by that was broken into in the dead of night less than a week ago. The horses have been left behind with Mallux; it was far easier to track her prey on foot. Last night before she drifted off, Mallux had argued with her when she announced that she would be heading into town in the morning, saying that they do not have the time to spare. Obviously, he had thought that he won the argument and went to sleep. His mistake.

Telium's response was to snort at his sleeping form when she left the camp. If they are to travel together, he must quickly learn that she will not be commanded like a common soldier or dog. That once she has made a decision, she will not be dissuaded.

Telium returns her attention to the barn and pushes out her consciousness, picking up a third person inside and a fourth travelling towards them a short distance away. Slowly, she begins to circle the fields around the barn, testing the area for others. Finding none, she concentrates harder on the mind she senses inside the barn. A bright point of power marks the consciousness inside. It has been many moons since she last felt such a thing. It takes her a moment to register what she is sensing – Blood-Thief. She hesitates, frowning slightly. Strange, that one would be out here; perhaps he is an outcast, or feels no need to sell off his Gifts to make his way.

Telium watches the man and woman joke as they rifle through their loot. Now and then, the woman holds up an item for inspection. She finds an empty jar, and smirking, she digs around in her pockets, producing something small and white. She holds it up triumphantly before dropping it into the jar with a clink and then rattles it around. A tooth. A *human* tooth. Disgust and anger war inside Telium. Her Gifts unfurl, stretching under her skin.

She spends a few minutes idling around the barn impatiently. When the fourth and final member of their merry band of miscreants arrives, Telium stalks out of the trees, doing nothing to hide her approach.

Time to test your control, she thinks, mentally checking on her Gifts.

The newcomer – another man – reaches his companions and speaks in undertones to them. The woman holds up the jar with her grisly trophy and the man laughs harshly before producing an item from his breast pocket and dropping it into the jar with a flourish. He is tall and wiry, but where the first with the cudgel is all fat and muscle, this man is all lean willowy strength. He has a cruel gleam in his eyes, which light up when he spots Telium.

He slaps his male companion on the shoulder and nods in Telium's direction. All three turn to watch her stalk through the swaying wheat surrounding the barn, stopping a few feet from them.

The brute's eyes sweep up and down her body greedily. The woman's face is empty, but the wiry man leers at her. Now that she is closer, Telium can see what the lean man had put in the jar – the end of a finger.

Rage explodes in her chest, swift and savage. With effort, she keeps her Gifts caged, not allowing any of them to seep through. She is no stranger to violence. Growing up as the Queen's pet assassin left little room for soft thoughts.

Asshole, she snarls in her head. *To kill without cause.*

'*Coward,*' she hisses at the man.

Her Gifts stretch, pushing against their confines. Telium lets them slip the smallest bit, testing her restraint.

Hypocrite. The words that echo in her mind are not hers. They cause a stab of guilt to flash through her. *Tenebris only knows what you did when you lost control of your Gifts.*

Then another. This time, a voice she recognises.

To hurt or kill and forget is the way of a monster, Trigg's gentle admonishment whispers. Telium recalls how her teacher, who hated torture as much as Telium, had taught her the best way to get information from a man. She had drawn a firm line and Telium agreed with her wholeheartedly – they did not torture for sport. *Ever.*

'What's this then? A visitor?' the lean man says and laughs harshly.

'Too pretty for you, Dale,' the brutish one says, licking his lips. 'Come to join the fun, love?'

Telium shakes her head; a gentle breeze lifts the ends of her hair. Her fingers itch to draw her sword from her side, but as much as she would like to run these cowards through, she knows the justice the townspeople will mete out is a much more fitting punishment. Better they rot in cells for the rest of their miserable lives than give them the honour of a quick death. Though their smell alone might kill the other prisoners. Telium wrinkles her nose at the stink of unwashed bodies under the merciless sun.

'Tempting, but no,' she says. 'Instead, I thought I might beat you bloody and drag you back to one of the many towns you are terrorising,' she replies in a dead voice, shrugging a shoulder. She lets her Gifts surge under her skin, power flaring in her eyes.

The two men exchange a glance and bark out a laugh, while the woman smirks nastily. Either they are too stupid or too arrogant to recognise the threat Telium poses.

'Is that so?' the lean one – Dale – says as he sneers at her. 'You and what army?'

With a grin, Telium reaches out her hand, and calling on her Gifts, smashes the jar in the woman's hand with a small explosion of glass.

The woman flinches away with a yelp but Dale's grin spreads even wider. 'Oh, Preath is going to *love* you.'

Without warning, he lunges forward, hands outstretched as if to grab her. Telium dodges lightly to the side, slapping the man's hands away casually. The woman comes at her next, dagger drawn from the sheath at her hip. The dance continues; Telium skips out of reach and kicks out, tripping the woman. She continues dodging away from her attackers, closing in only to deliver smarting slaps to hands or ears.

Nothing she is doing hurts them much, but it is driving

the two into a frenzy. She wants to do more than break a few bones; she wants to break their pride and their spirit. She smiles savagely to herself as she sidesteps a clumsy slash from the woman.

The entire time, Telium is acutely aware of the Blood-Thief residing in the barn who has failed to appear, despite the commotion outside. So when the brute finally rises from his sitting position and reaches out, Telium allows herself to be captured in his grip. His meaty hands encircle her body and he presses her against him. The sour smell of his breath makes her stomach turn.

Dale rises from his crouch and smiles cruelly. 'Take her in to Preath,' he commands, gesturing to the barn.

The brute pulls her even closer to his body, somewhat possessively. Dale's grin turns hard. 'Come now, Gerald, there will still be some of her left for you to have your fun with.'

'As long as he leaves her with some fight; the others had none left,' Gerald grumbles.

The wet sound of Gerald licking his lips makes Telium cringe before she is lifted off her feet and hauled into the barn. After Dale barks an order to the woman to stand watch in case Telium has any friends looking for her, he follows closely on their heels.

Inside the barn, Gerald tosses Telium to the floor. She can feel the Blood-Thief in her mind lurking in the shadows, watching her closely. Lithely rolling to her feet, she turns to face her attackers with a snarl on her lips. In the enclosed space, the smell of hay, leather and unwashed bodies fills her nose. At least it is marginally cooler in here. Now that she has located the Blood-Thief and is sure he will not be able to get away, the fight can begin in earnest.

Telium lashes out, striking with her fists and feet. She hits

Dale hard enough in the face that his head snaps back and he spits blood. A kick to Gerald's leg sends him stumbling before he can grab her again. Using her own Blood-Thief Gifts to enhance her reflexes, she keeps out of their reach. Still, she has to throw herself backwards to avoid a blow from the cudgel that Gerald draws.

The two men follow her retreat, herding her towards the wall. She grabs and throws a small crate with a Power-Thief push. It crashes into Gerald, the wood smashing across his shoulders. He cries out in rage and pain, throwing his hands up to protect his face. The attack stops Dale's advance. He hesitates a moment before drawing a blade from his side.

'Stop.' The Blood-Thief's voice cracks through the room.

Dale's jaw tightens but he obeys the command. Beside him, Gerald lowers his hands slowly, hatred glittering in his eyes. Telium smirks at them, arching a brow at the pair, half hoping to goad them into another fight. But the two stand like sentinels. From behind them, the Blood-Thief emerges, pushing the sleeves of his robe back from his hands. He keeps the hood of his robe up so that his face is hidden in shadow, but the end of a telltale scarlet braid pokes out one side.

Telium rolls her eyes. *So dramatic.*

'Don't let her get away,' he says to the other two. 'Now, my pet, what do you taste like?' He reaches a hand out. 'I hear Power-Thieves' blood is like the sweetest sparkling wine.'

She is momentarily distracted by the way he draws out his 's's. With a start, she realises why Dale said this Blood-Thief – Preath – would love her. He was going to try to *drink* from her. Distantly, Telium wonders what would happen if the Blood-Thief drained her. Generally, there are no side effects when a Blood-Thief feasts on another Thief. *Knowing my luck, I'll be the exception to that rule.*

The thugs part to let Preath pass and he lashes out, gripping her wrists with bruising force. She allows him to believe she is cowed by his grip. He leans in, uncomfortably close. Telium feels his nose brush the spot between her shoulder and neck. Closing his eyes, he takes in a deep breath through his nose, inhaling her scent.

Pulling back, Telium snaps her head forward, forehead colliding with his nose ... hard. With a startled cry, the Thief stumbles backwards, hand flying to his face.

Dale lunges at her and she swipes out at him with a hand suddenly ending in claws. His efforts earn him a burning set of lines across his chest and bicep. Falling back, he clutches his wounded arm to his body. Blood has already begun to seep through his fingers and his shirt hangs open in tatters. The sight makes Telium's Gifts undulate as they pace the confines of their cages, waiting to be set free in earnest.

'Mind-Thief,' Gerald snarls. Despite his bravado, his words lilt up at the end, betraying his uncertainty. He swings the cudgel at her head violently, as if to cover up his question.

She ducks under it with ease and kicks him violently in the knee. A sickening crunch, followed by a scream, brings the brute to the ground. With a snarl, Telium slams her booted foot down on his fingers, the thin bones snapping like twigs. Gerald screams again, the noise petering off into whimpers as Telium takes the crude weapon out of his now-limp grasp.

'Mercy,' he whispers, glancing up at her fearfully.

A wave of rage makes Telium's head spin and she snarls down at him. How many have said the same thing to him? How many pleaded to him in vain? Her face is completely devoid of mercy as she gazes down at him; a dark goddess handing out judgement. If her Gifts could take form, they would be sparking about her right now.

A whisper of fabric alerts her as Dale launches himself at her. She dodges to the side and his swing goes wide, throwing him off balance. Before he can right himself, Telium steps in close, throwing up her elbow to catch him across the temple, knocking him out cold. He falls to the floor without a sound.

Behind them, the Blood-Thief is cursing and wiping at his face. When he sees his sleeve come away red with blood he hisses at Telium, needle-like canines gleaming in the dim light of the barn. She quickly turns back to Gerald who is struggling to rise on his injured knee. She steps forward, deliberately pressing the toe of her boot on his crushed fingers. His shriek makes her Gifts howl in pleasure and he sways slightly, pain pushing him into unconsciousness. Grabbing him roughly by the shirt front, Telium shakes him until his glazed, pain-fogged eyes meet hers. She swallows back the ashy taste of rage on her tongue.

Drive a blade through his heart.

Thunder rumbles and lightning cracks in Telium's mind as the words are whispered in her ear. Past and present momentarily blur together, before snapping back into focus. 'May this serve as a reminder to keep your hands to yourself. Tenebris claim you, should you forget.'

She grinds her foot down, cutting short the man's cries with a sharp blow to the head. The strike is not hard enough to kill him, but it will leave him with a splitting headache for days, not to mention his broken hand. And his knee. There is a fluttering of fabric behind her.

An impact hits her hard from the side. The Blood-Thief crashes into her, sending them both toppling to the ground. Telium twists, planning to lock his arm. But the Thief twitches out of the way and she only succeeds in clipping him across the ribs with her elbow. His resulting hiss reminds her of a viper.

Preath attempts to grip her wrists and subdue her. Surging up, Telium headbutts him before shoving him hard. A sharp line of pain lances across the back of her hand as the Blood-Thief stumbles away.

Telium springs to her feet. Facing the Thief, she glances down at her hand to see a crescent moon cut into the flesh across her knuckles. The wound is already beginning to drip blood down her fingers.

Did that bastard just bite *me?*

Preath flashes towards her, dodging to the side at the last second and twisting, kicking out at her knees. He is lightning fast. But Telium has the Gifts of a Blood-Thief too. She is faster.

She deflects his flurry of blows before returning a kick of her own. Preath has left his guard wide open with the ferociousness of his attacks.

Telium's boot lands square on his chest. With the combined strength of a Blood- and Mind-Thief running through her veins, she knocks him flying. Preath's feet leave the floor and he goes skidding across the dirt to fetch up against an old haybale.

He lands hard enough that the air is knocked from his lungs. The invisible threads of Telium's mind are already upon him, curling around him like snakes and constricting slowly. The Thief's eyes go wide in panic, unable to comprehend what is happening or how to stop it. The threads of her mind tighten viciously and rip before he can even open his mouth to scream. His body jerks once suddenly, then lies still, head lolling to the side and eyes glazing over as his life-force leaves his body.

Her voice is rough as the pain of her bite registers. 'Yeah, I can move that fast too, asshole.'

CHAPTER
15

As the coils of her mind ravel in on themselves, the Thief's life-force soothes her aching body. Even after all this time, she cannot stop the soft gasp that passes her lips as her body envelops and soaks up the strength of the life she has stolen. The sensation is equal parts pain and pleasure, like climbing into a hot bath when one's body is ice cold.

The Gifts that come along with it curl up alongside the others, fitting into place seamlessly.

Still sane. Telium acknowledges her control thus far with a sort of grim satisfaction.

A sharp gasp draws her attention away from the lifeless body of the Blood-Thief. The woman stands at the door, obviously drawn by the commotion. Her hair is pushed back from her face to reveal bloodless lips bracketed by deep wrinkles. When the woman raises her eyes to look at Telium, she pales and takes off running like a bolt from an archer's bow. Telium sighs in exasperation, quickly binding the two men with a rope she finds hanging on the wall. She starts counting backwards from ten slowly as she walks towards the door. When she reaches it, she watches the woman flee across the field, her dark shirt a stain against the cheerful yellow of the crops.

'Three …'

The woman stumbles in her haste, nearing the edge of the field. Telium's Gifts howl in glee.

'Two …'

Glancing over her shoulder, the woman sees Telium framed by the doorway of the barn.

'One.'

Despite the woman's head start, Telium reaches her in a few short moments and catches her on the border of the field. Telium grips her by the forearm and drags her to a stop like one would a disobedient child. The woman spins to face her, the dagger in her hand flashing in the bright morning light. Telium strikes the woman across the face with the back of her hand. The slap resounds through the trees.

The dagger goes flying as the woman loses her grip and sprawls to the ground. She spits blood and glares up at Telium whose rage has calmed into a glittering wall of ice. Though her Gifts still sigh and pace under her skin, her mind is deadly calm. She looks down on the woman with an expressionless face. 'How could you?' she asks, spitting at her feet.

The woman pushes herself up onto her hands. 'Had children to feed, y'know!' The words, meant to be threatening, fall short.

'So did the people you robbed blind and left bleeding and broken in the dirt. Goddess, the one from last week had *grandchildren*.' The last word ends on a snarl. Telium crouches down next to the woman who shies away from her but keeps her eyes on Telium's. She sees no compassion or remorse in the bandit's gaze. 'I was referring to the women you let that brute abuse.' Her voice cracks like a whip. 'I am not stupid; I can see it.'

'Bett'r them than me,' the woman replies.

Telium curls back her lips and snarls in the bandit's face. 'Better no-one!' Gripping her by the shirt front, Telium hauls the woman roughly to her feet and begins to drag her back the way they had come.

When the woman realises they are heading back in the direction of the town, she flies into a frenzy, thrashing and struggling like a wild thing. She lashes out at Telium, catching her a glancing blow across the ear.

Telium growls and shakes her so hard that her teeth click together. She binds the woman's arms in invisible Power-Thief chains before fisting her hand in the fabric of her shirt and towing the woman behind her like an unruly toddler.

There is a moment of peace. The stalks of wheat sway in the breeze and the sweet, dry smell of them mixes with the coppery scent of crusted blood under Telium's nails. Then the woman starts up again. She issues a steady stream of curses, raging against her fate, cursing Telium, her poor luck and her children for getting her into this mess. She does not, Telium notes, ever blame herself for her downfall.

'If that damn Council 'ad bothered to send aid. They sit there, fat an' content, gorging over the results of farmers' toil. But they 'ave nay lifted a finger to help when the fields dried up an' the rain nev'r came! An' why should I not take from those people? They'r stupid, simple fools. Not strong 'nough to defend their money, their property or their family ...' The tirade carries on and on.

Telium ignores it, hoping she will run out of things to say. She can feel her temper fraying.

'Besides, I am convinced 'alf of those girls were not averse to Gerald's ministrations.' The woman's voice is pitchy. Telium closes her eyes and breathes deeply, praying for peace as the woman continues on. 'Two of 'em were bathing *naked* in the stream! Anyone could'a come 'cross them. Whores. An' then—'

'You will be silent.' Telium's voice is deathly calm, though her rage rises with startling ferocity. When she whirls to the woman, the hand that grips her jaw is tipped in claws. Fangs gleam as Telium's lips draw back in a vicious snarl. 'If you utter but another word, I am going to rip every tooth from your head and wear them as a necklace. Then feed you salt.'

To emphasise her point, she squeezes the woman's jaw so hard that her teeth grind together and bright, ruby-red spots of blood pool under Telium's claws where they have pierced the skin. When the woman whimpers in pain, she releases her, only to grab another handful of her shirt, her claws ripping through the fabric. Telium does not bother to dismiss them, even when she knows they are digging into the woman. She may not hurt people for sport, but she has no qualms doing it to teach a lesson.

A black wind swirls through her mind. Her Gifts prowl the confines of their cages, pushing against the bars. *Kill her,* they whisper. *Eat her heart, eat her soul.* Telium grits her teeth and shoves down on her Gifts, silencing them. As much as she would enjoy leaving this filth for dead in the woods, she wants to take her back to the townspeople. They deserve justice – to put a face to the criminal who has been haunting them. They could pick up the two unconscious men from the barn later.

They march back towards the town, the sun beating down on their heads. Telium takes a circular route, hoping to enter the town without attracting too many onlookers. She wants to hand the woman to the guardhouse and be done with it.

Unfortunately, Mallux has other ideas. A few minutes from the town, he appears through the trees. His face is blank, which Telium guesses means he is furious with her for sneaking off.

As he stalks towards her, she trails to a stop. She can feel the consciousnesses of the horses picketed deeper in the woods.

Her prisoner can do nothing but gape open-mouthed at Mallux in awe and fear. When he opens his mouth, Telium cuts him off, yanking the woman forward to face Mallux.

'I found them. This is the last. She will face the town's justice … no, do not speak,' she says as the woman opens her mouth, no doubt to sprout more complaints upon hearing she is to be handed over to the mercy of the townsfolk.

A muscle feathers in Mallux's jaw as he and Telium glare at each other. The woman struggles wildly in Telium's grip. Vainly trying to break free. After a moment, Mallux's eyes soften and he nods before turning to the thrashing woman.

He gazes at her intently as he steps towards the bandit, his citrus and ember scent brushing by Telium.

'You and your ilk have greatly inconvenienced me. Telium feels you deserve to live. I do not share the sentiment. You will walk to the guard in this town. You will not try to run. I swear on the Ivory Crown you will regret it if you do.'

Mallux's voice rumbles, laced heavy with threat. The woman stills, paling considerably. Her gaze jumps between Telium and Mallux as if trying to decide who is the more dangerous of the two. Telium grins, exposing her fangs in a macabre smile. She twirls her finger at the woman, indicating she should turn and start walking into town. The woman does so without complaint.

As she and Mallux follow behind, a spark of appreciation for the Fae lights Telium's chest. Not only has he scared her captive into submission, he also seems to understand her need for going after this band of undesirables, or if he does not understand, he has at least accepted it.

She peeks sideways at him from under lowered lashes, only

to find him glaring at the woman's back. His look reminds Telium of a panther watching its prey, waiting for it to bolt so it can begin the chase. Telium chuckles under her breath and Mallux meets her eyes, flashing her a savage smile before turning back to lay his predatory gaze between the woman's shoulder blades. As if feeling the Fae's gaze on her, the woman picks up her pace, her stride erratic and jerky, like she is forcing herself to walk when, really, she wants to flee.

When they reach the town, their procession draws the attention of the people they pass. Some watch them curiously, while others trail behind them, doing their best to seem inconspicuous. The road running through the centre of town smells like dust and paint. *Maybe we will actually make it to the guardhouse without a fuss*, Telium thinks.

They pass a solemn-faced woman who is sweeping the steps of her home. When she sees their prisoner, a flurry of emotions cross her face. Fear, sorrow, denial, rage. It is the last one that sticks. She spits in the direction of the woman. 'You! Thieving, murderous FILTH!' she screeches.

That gets the attention of the townsfolk. By the time they reach the guardhouse, there's already a guard outside. He starts as he sees Telium and Mallux with their quarry, along with half the town at their heels.

'Stand still,' Mallux rumbles at the bandit woman.

To Telium's surprise, the woman complies.

The guard is middle-aged, his hair sports streaks of grey and he is a little soft around the middle. Telium would not be surprised if he doubled as the town's judge and mediator as well.

'What's all this then?' the guard asks, gripping the hilt of his sword.

The woman who had spat at the bandit shoulders her way

to the front of the crowd but keeps a healthy distance from Mallux and Telium. She throws an accusatory finger at the criminal, who has come to a stop and is now glancing around like a cornered rabbit. 'That's her! That's the woman who's been roaming around with those *bandits!* Thieving, cowardly, murderous, mongrel bitch!'

The woman's language causes Telium to raise her eyebrows in approval – while she would have described the criminal in much the same manner, she does not expect the obscenities to come from such a woman.

A further chorus of accusations and threats spill out from the crowd. The guard holds up his hand, calling for silence. When it falls, broken occasionally by a disgruntled murmur, he addresses Telium. 'You. Who is this? Why have you brought her here?'

Telium shrugs. 'What the woman says is true. You will find the Blood-Thief and the other two men in the barn less than a bell's travel from here.'

'I see,' the guard replies. 'And these men, will we find them alive?'

Telium only smirks in response.

'She's a bloody Life-Thief!' the captured woman screeches. 'Saw it with my own eyes! She killed Gerald!'

'I did *not* kill him,' Telium says. 'I merely knocked him unconscious.'

'And Preath? You sucked the life right from him!' The woman looks around, brown locks flying, trying to find an ally.

Telium dismisses her with a blank look before turning back to the guard and answering his earlier question. 'I left the two men alive.'

'And the Blood-Thief?' the guard prompts.

'You did not have the means to hold a Thief anyway.'

The guard gives Telium a long look before nodding slowly. He turns to address the crowd, shouting for some men. 'Take your boys and get out to that barn. You there, go with them – take your cart. Somehow I do not think those men will be in a state to walk.'

Telium says nothing, keeping her face blank.

The guard calls forward another two men, 'Take this woman to the cell. The rest of you, go home. The elders will organise a trial.'

As the crowd disperses, grumbling amongst themselves and throwing daggered looks at the woman, two men come forward and haul the screeching prisoner away. Telium pretends not to notice when they flinch away from her.

The guard approaches Telium and Mallux, his eyes lingering on Mallux's pointed ears and the blood on Telium's clothes. 'You have my thanks, friends,' he says. He hesitates before continuing. 'The people here; they are hardworking, but they have little. Whatever they did have was decimated by this drought and people like her.' He waves his hand to the detained woman.

'We do not ask for payment,' Telium says, saving the man from trying to explain further.

The guard relaxes visibly but a cautious gleam enters his eye. 'Then surely you wish to decide the bandits' fate?'

'No.' Telium shakes her head. *I do not care what this town decides to do with them.* 'They admitted to robbery. I would suggest you consult the other towns close by.'

The guard nods his head and rubs his jaw as he looks at their dusty clothes. 'Well then, it seems the least we can do is provide you with a hot meal and a place to stay the night … before you move on.'

Telium nods in understanding; it would not do to linger for more than a night, especially since she all but admitted to murder in front of the entire town. She had noted the sidelong glances from some of the villagers as they left.

The guard introduces himself and offers to walk them to the town's inn. 'It's not much,' he says. 'Really just a place for the farmers to drink, with a few rooms for the odd traveller who blows through.'

Mallux stays silent during the exchange but Telium can feel his presence like a caress as if his ember and citrus essence is sighing across her skin.

CHAPTER
16

Arriving at the inn, the guard pulls aside a girl with a halo of brown curls tied back into a bun. He speaks quietly in her ear, gesturing to Mallux and Telium. The girl runs off and he turns to them, rubbing his sweaty hands on his pants as he shifts his weight from foot to foot.

Telium can feel the silent, looming presence of Mallux at her side. That alone is enough to make anyone nervous, let alone a feral young woman who has just confessed to killing a Blood-Thief and beating another two men senseless. *With blood coating her hands,* Telium thinks with a wry twist of her lips, trying to ignore the sticky substance between her fingers and under her nails. No wonder the poor man is nervous. They probably look like a pair of wild things.

The scraping of a door announces the return of the serving girl, along with the inn's owner. The guard nods his head at the man and turns back to Telium, seeing his chance for escape. 'Is there … uh … anything else you need?'

'Thank you, no,' Telium replies, putting on her best sweet tone. 'Your hospitality is appreciated.'

The guard strides to the door before he hesitates and turns

back. 'I don't know how you … what you must have done …
but thank you. My father-in-law owned one of the farms that
got ransacked by those people. Left him with a broken arm
and a burning house … and he was one of the lucky ones. So,
thank you. This town appreciates what you did today.' With a
final nod, he disappears through the door.

The young serving girl, who introduces herself as Kya,
shows Mallux and Telium to a room. Glancing at Telium's
hands, she tells her she will draw a bath for her and disappears
down the hall.

The small room is just large enough for a bed, a small writing desk and an overstuffed armchair in the corner. Telium
fingers the stone around her neck, noting the lack of a second
bed, and glances over at Mallux. He is watching her with a
strange intensity.

'You've been awfully quiet,' Telium says to fill the awkward
silence.

'I am not a fool, Telium. I know your people distrust the
Fae. I do not think my opinion would have been appreciated,
nor wanted.'

'And what *is* your opinion?' she replies tartly.

Mallux's eyes flash as he takes a step towards her. 'That
you should not have gone cavorting across the countryside to
dispose of petty criminals – or perhaps you do not understand
the urgency of our situation?'

His sarcasm rankles. 'I would hardly call burning people's
livelihoods and abusing them for fun a *petty* crime.' She fights
hard to keep the anger from her voice.

When Mallux does not reply, she pokes him in the chest.
His lack of response infuriates her even more. 'They were *killing* people, Mallux. Either intentionally or by robbing them
of their homes and incomes, it does not matter. Defenseless

people. One of them took a finger as a trophy.' *I had to make sure, had to know how far I could push myself.* She leaves the last part unsaid.

He tilts his head towards her. She had not realised how close she had moved to him in her anger. As if they were constantly drawn to each other against their will. His brow furrows slightly in a frown. 'Do you not kill people?' His words whisper across her skin.

Telium tries desperately to hold onto her ire, which is getting more difficult by the moment in this tiny room with a Fae whose body heat radiates off him like the sun. 'Not like that. Not without provocation, not for greed.'

The words feel like a lie on her tongue. She has little memory of what she did in her madness. Her eyes dip to Mallux's mouth and her anger drains away as quickly as it had come. Suddenly, it feels like there is not enough air in the room. She becomes hyper-aware of where every part of her body is in relation to his. Her shoulders tighten as she fights the startling urge to reach for him. Her lips part on a silent gasp. Eyes roaming over the column of his neck and the strong line of his jaw.

She feels his gaze on her face as he watches her just as intently. The moment stretches out for an eternity. Her stomach flutters as he lays a callused hand on her elbow and ducks his head. With a smile curving the corner of his mouth he—

A knock at the door makes her jump and step back guiltily, caught up as she was in the spell that seems to surround Mallux. The tension in the room shatters and she frowns as her lust-fogged thoughts clear. She is *never* caught by surprise.

'Miss?' Kya pokes her head around the door as Mallux smoothly takes a step back. 'Miss, I have a bath drawn ready for you.'

With a nod, Telium picks up her pack from where Mallux dropped it and flees, following the girl to the bathing chamber. It is surprisingly large and smells of rose oil. A deep, stone-lined tub is set into the floor, and folded neatly beside it are towels, along with bottles of oil, soap and a hairbrush. Such fine things seem out of place for so small a town.

As if reading Telium's thoughts, the girl goes to a corner of the room and lifts a wooden hatch. Steam billows up from the space beneath, heating the already warm room.

'Da says he found this when digging out his cellar. It's a hot spring. We bucket the water from here into the tubs. Guard Damien has one in his house too, and the spring comes up to the surface down by Karmots Farm, so people walk down there for a bath. It doesn't get used much anymore on account of the heat.' Kya shuts the hatch with a thump. 'We usually charge guests for the use, but I figured you would need hot water to clean yourself anyway.' She gestures at Telium's blood-splattered hands.

Telium murmurs her thanks and begins to strip her weapons, looking forward to soaking in the deep tub. The last time she was in a tub was before her world fell apart. She hesitates when she finds the girl has not moved from her spot and is watching Telium with rapt attention as she handles her blades.

Kya opens her mouth as if to ask a question but snaps it closed. Her eyes burn with curiosity.

Telium sighs. 'Out with it,' she says, planting her hands on her hips.

Flags of red colour the girl's cheeks, partially hidden by the spirals of hair escaping her bun. She looks at her feet. When she speaks, her voice is quiet but firm. 'Did … did you really do those things they say? Kill that Blood-Thief and capture those men?'

Telium merely nods, hands still on her hips.

Kya sets her jaw and nods her head once sharply in approval. 'Good,' she says. 'And the big brute?'

The question catches Telium off guard. 'The one who …?' she ventures, unwilling to say the word.

Kya nods again.

Something about the burning intensity of her gaze gives Telium pause. 'I broke his knee … and his hand. Then I knocked him unconsciousness, after reminding him to keep his hands to himself.'

The hard smile from Kya forms a question in Telium's mind.

'Were you one of them?' Telium whispers. Part of her does not want to hear the answer. She can slay armies of men and promise to kill a Fae King without remorse. But this – looking at this young girl before her, wondering if she was one of Gerald's victims, imagining the bruises on her – this is a different kind of battle. One she cannot win with steel and Gift. The image of the Siren Queen sitting in the moonlight, fist clenched over her abdomen, flashes in Telium's mind.

When the girl shakes her head, Telium slumps in guilty relief. She would not know what to say to this young woman if she had said yes. Yet there is something about the girl's stance – the way she crosses her arms over her chest and stares hard at the floor – that tells her there is more to the story.

'Who?' Telium's words are barely a whisper.

A tear trickles down Kya's cheek. When she answers, Telium has to strain her ears to hear her.

'Lucy.' The name sounds like a prayer on the girl's lips. 'They raided her father's farm. Her mother tried to protect her and they …' Kya takes a shaky breath and swallows hard before continuing with more strength, 'struck her down; killed her. Her father did not raise a finger to help and now his grief is eating him alive. They have moved to Diaxe to live with his sister. Said Lucy couldn't possibly stay here. What hope would we have – two women living alone? Who would protect us? When she left, I swore to her I would find a way for us to be together and keep us safe.'

Her words leave her in a rush as if once she starts, she cannot contain the torrent. 'I thought if I could find a kind man to marry, maybe he would not mind if Lucy lived with us. Maybe he wouldn't notice if we ... But then you came into town with that bandit. You killed that Thief all on your own. Beat two grown men in a fight.'

She takes another deep inhale and looks Telium square in the eyes. 'Teach me,' she says, voice steady despite her eyes being bright with tears. 'Teach me to fight.' Kya's chest rises and falls with the force of her emotion. Muscles feather in her jaw as she fights back tears.

Telium feels as if she is standing at the crossroads of this girl's life; if she refuses her, tells her to let go of this foolish dream and forget her lover, she would likely do so. She would probably marry a nice village boy, have a house and a family. Be safe. *Wouldn't she?*

Leaning down, Telium draws a short dagger from her boot and approaches Kya.

Fear flashes in the girl's eyes but she stands firm as Telium approaches her and points the blade towards her face. Kya eyes it and swallows. Yet she does not retreat.

Telium flips the blade in her hand and lowers it back down to her side with Kya tracking it before raising her eyes to Telium's face. Her Gifts sit silent under her skin.

'I will not teach you.' Telium gives a lopsided grin at the

girl's crestfallen look and continues before she can argue. 'I do not have the time nor inclination to do so. I am not a teacher – but I will tell you how to find those who are.'

Kya's face lights up.

Telium raises a hand to forestall her thanks. 'Do not thank me yet. Know that if this is a path you choose to walk, it is dangerous and full of hardship. The people who teach you will push you to your breaking point, then push you some more. When you shatter, you will not be put back together the same. You will experience pain you cannot even comprehend. You will take oaths that you must uphold. You will have to leave this life behind you.'

Sweat beads on Kya's brow from the humidity of the room and a range of emotions cross her face as she considers Telium's advice. Then her eyes harden, decision made. 'I understand.' Her voice holds the weight of her resolve.

Telium nods and holds up the dagger again, this time with the hilt towards the girl. It is a simple blade, plain but well made, a white symbol etched into the hilt. 'You have a long way to go. Take this to Scara. Seek out the trader they call King Assassin. Tell him that Trigg's final apprentice sent you. That you will earn your salt and ink.'

The girl takes the weapon reverentially and looks up at Telium with wide brown eyes.

Digging into her pouch, Telium produces the last of her coins and passes them across to the young woman. 'Blessings on your journey, Kya. May the goddesses walk beside you on your path. Tell no-one of what we have spoken,' Telium intones, turning away.

'Thank you,' Kya whispers, before disappearing out the door with Telium's dagger hidden in the folds of her skirt.

'Tenebris curse me,' she sighs to herself. What was she

thinking, pushing a young girl down the path of an assassin? There was something about the girl, though – it was rare that anyone looked at her with such open curiosity instead of distance or fear.

Reaching for the coarse bar of soap, Telium casts the girl from her mind. The likelihood of her following through and leaving all that she knows behind to travel to the Ereak Desert is little to none. The soap makes her skin tingle, but she washes herself from head to toes regardless. She dunks her head under the water and scrubs her scalp vigorously.

Now I know I can get through a conflict without completely losing myself, she thinks of her Gifts with dark satisfaction. Once clean, she relaxes back in the tub, enjoying the simple luxury and the smell of roses around her as her mind wanders through the events of the day.

Eventually, the cooling water chases her from the tub, and using the soap, she quickly washes the dust and blood from her clothes before combing her fingers through her hair and drying herself off. Digging through her pack, she dons clean clothes before heading back to the room – the room with only one bed. Apprehension, along with another emotion she refuses to identify, swirls in her stomach as she approaches the door and knocks before entering.

Mallux is on the floor, sitting atop his bed-roll and cloak which he has laid out in the narrow space between the bed and the armchair. The ends of his damp hair curl up gently and his blue eyes are startling in his handsome face. He looks up as she enters. Telium swallows as she approaches the bed, but gone is the simmering tension from before.

CHAPTER
17

Up before the sun, Telium and Mallux leave through the window in the dark of the morning while the town is still sleeping. They travel on foot to where Mallux picketed the horses. He had tracked her on foot just as she had tracked the bandits. By the time they reach their mounts, the sun is rising in the sky.

They spend the rest of the day following animal tracks until they reach the road passing from Lampart to Xandi, which is little more than a dusty streak through the plains and copses of trees. Stopping on occasion to rest and water the horses, they continue west for another day.

The land stays much the same; to their right, the hulking presence of the mountains lurk, their snow-capped peaks often wreathed in clouds. Around them, the land is shades of brown, yellow and gold with splashes of green that contrast sharply against the warm palate. A dry wind rustles through the leaves of the trees, and when they veer off the path, the yellowing grass crunches beneath the horses' hooves. All around are signs of the long, harsh summer. Even the air smells hot and dry.

At this pace, they will reach Xandi by the end of the next day. There they will sell off their mounts and head to the pass on foot as horses would be too conspicuous, and they will need to sneak by the border guard to cross between mountains.

Even though they are making good time, their pace chafes Telium, who is aware that every moment they delay brings them closer and closer to the Fae festival, *Ramaeris*. She uses the time wisely, spending the long hours in the saddle exercising her Gifts. Cautiously confident she will be able to use them in open combat.

She pushes her Gifts to their limits; lifting sticks and juggling rocks. Mallux occasionally tosses a pebble her way that she dodges with Thief-fuelled reflexes. She calls on a Mind-Thief to enhance her eyesight and has competitions with Mallux to see who can describe far-off objects in the greatest detail. Much to his disgust, Telium often wins and he claims she must be fabricating some of the specifics.

Telium is quietly impressed with the natural prowess of the Fae. His reflexes are lightning fast, his eyesight and sense of smell as sharp as a falkir. She knows that without her Gifts, she would be hard-pressed to even hold her own against him in a fight, let alone beat him. Telium questions him on Fae skills and senses.

'I have little experience with mortals,' Mallux admits, 'but to my knowledge, our speed and strength far surpass theirs. Fae senses rival those of an *alskmir* wolf and our reflexes are more akin to those of your Blood-Thieves than mortals. Our *Ka'hine*, females of Power, outrank your Thieves, though they are far fewer in number.'

'*Kaa-hin-eh*.' Telium sounds out the strange vowels. 'I thought your Gifted females were *Lei'kah?*'

Mallux shakes his head, 'The *Lei'kah* are the King's personal guard, one such Fae is always picked from the *Kah* – the soldiers. Becoming *Lei'kah* does not require a Fae to be

Ka'hine; males and Powerless females may win the position.' His mouth twists to the side, 'But it seems *this* King hides behind only the skirts of *Ka'hine*.'

Telium closes her mouth against the comment that those 'skirts' could probably beat Mallux into the dirt.

'Could a Thief beat a Fae without Power?' She asks.

Mallux shrugs, 'Possibly, it would depend on how powerful the Thief is, and how skilled the Fae.'

'But, in a fight of Gifts, a *Ka'hine* would defeat a Thief?'

'That is likely the case, yes.' He examines her. 'However, I don't think that would be the case with yourself, Telium. It seems your Gifts are unique to you. I've never heard of your like. A Fae warrior and an Alkorian Thief would be on close-to-equal footing, but it seems you could take on more.'

Of course, I would have to be different, Telium thinks bitterly. She doesn't know what to say to Mallux. She is unprecedented; even amongst Thieves, she seems to hold power that exceeds their limits.

'But a Thief can train their Gifts, strengthen them like any muscle, to improve their skills … to a point,' Telium says. 'Would that put them on par with females of Power?'

Mallux shrugs, hurling another pebble her way without warning. Telium dodges it smoothly.

'Fae are born with abilities that far surpass mortals, even Thieves,' he says. 'Many of us spend our entire lives honing ourselves to a lethal edge – to be the epitome of strength and power. The better the warrior, the better the Fae. Even amongst females, they vie to be the best, the most powerful.'

'And you?' Telium says, lips curling. 'Are you *the epitome of strength and power?*'

'Yes,' Mallux replies, apparently missing her sarcasm. 'Few, if any, can beat me in feats of arms. I could stand against a *Ka'hine* and come out victorious.'

It seems Mallux is to the Fae as Telium is to mortals – trained from a young age to excel in feats of fist and blade. A warrior, a killer. One who represents the pinnacle of lethal grace. They are two sides of the same coin, but where Mallux is all light and valour, Telium is shadows and intrigue. Still, there is a mutual understanding between the two of them, borne from their battle-scarred souls. Telium wonders if it plays on his mind too, how his abilities mean he will always stand a little apart from the crowd.

As they travel, Telium pushes herself to see how fast she can send out the threads of her mind to trap a life-force; birds and small mammals becoming unwilling participants in her training. They squawk in fear as they feel her coils tighten around them, before fleeing in panic the moment she releases them. By the end of the evening, she is attempting to split her mind and capture several life-forces at once. She easily conquers two at a time, then struggles through three. By the time she is attempting four, she has a pounding headache and feels like her mind is going to shatter under the pressure.

She gratefully calls off her efforts when they stop for the evening. Her mind feels gritty and slightly out of focus like she has been reading a book only to look up and realise the entire day has passed by without her noticing. The slighest prickling, like a whispered breeze, brushes her shoulders. Telium looks back to the south, eyes scouring the horizon.

CHAPTER
18

Telium's body feels strange. She watches the Siren Queen and her court riding through the woods. Just like they do every spring, enjoying the sights and smells of wildflowers blooming. All around, the colours are super saturated – the blues too bright, the yellows too harsh.

The faces of the court keep shifting and changing. When Telium tries to look at them directly, she finds she does not recognise a single one of them. The Queen moves her mount a short way from the group, admiring a bunch of electric-blue orchids hanging from a vine as she rests her hands on her round stomach, rubbing it absentmindedly. She pats her mount's neck fondly. Jake: a beautiful, proud creature with a glossy black coat and a tail so long it has to be trimmed lest it trail in the dirt.

Telium watches the Queen lean forward, still stroking Jake's neck and whispering to him. Hisses flit through the air and Telium's heart drops as she realises what her dream is about to show her.

The horse's ears flatten against his head, then all hell breaks loose. Jake launches into a frenzy, writhing and bucking under the saddle. His eyes burn red like the embers of a fire, and the Siren

Queen, who is arguably one of the best riders in the kingdom, hits the dirt hard.

Telium can do nothing as the dream slows, making her relive every sickening second as the huge horse's hooves come crashing down on top of the Queen, trampling her under his great weight. The Siren Queen's screams cut through the air, and between one blink and the next, there is an arrow sticking out of the proud beast's neck. Later, the lords would be chided that a girl of seven winters reacted faster than them.

Telium's limbs feel weak and too small as she pulls back her bowstring for the second time. Dream overwrites memory and black blood pours from her fingers where the string cuts in. Dark as night, the blood runs down her arm to drip off the tip of her elbow like tar. The next arrow flies with deadly accuracy.

The dream skips. Telium is trying to haul Jake's dead body off her Queen's leg. There is blood, so much blood, everywhere, more than there was in reality. The Siren Queen is covered in it. She holds her stomach and moans as tears streak her cheeks. 'My Jake!' she cries. 'My darling Jake. Telli, what have you done?'

Tears prickle Telium's eyes. Even though the words are all part of her dream, they strike her to the core. Dream-Jake now has teeth sharpened to points and red foam leaks from the corner of his mouth. He looks like something dredged up from the depths of the Underrealm. Nothing like the fine, proud creature that he had been in life: sweet-natured and gentle as a lamb.

The grass under the Siren Queen disperses, reforming as plush fur rugs. Jake's dead body has disappeared and huge arching walls form overhead. Telium's head spins as hours blur by and she finds herself standing in the corner of the Queen's chambers, watching the court physician and his assistant bustle around the bed. They flit around the Queen like wraiths.

A tremor runs through the Queen's body and she cries out.

The doctor murmurs to his assistants about the condition of the Queen's unborn child and the early onset of labour. When the Queen's riding pants are cut away, a river of blood flows down the bed. It runs over the edge in little waterfalls, the puddle of ruby-red liquid slowly inching its way towards Telium.

The dream keeps Telium trapped in her young body. She can do nothing as silent prayers fall from her lips to the Goddess of Life, Opimare – as she bargains with Tenebris. The harsh smell of poultice mingles with the coppery tang of blood. In her dream, the river of blood soaks her boots and warms her toes.

The assistant appears at her side. Telium cannot make out her face. It shifts and wavers as though underwater. Leading her gently by the elbow, she takes Telium out to the hallway, calling for a maidservant. Telium follows her numbly, staring at the pile of bloody cloths being carted from the room by one of the castle servants. The Queen's moans fill the air, seemingly coming from everywhere at once.

'Run her a hot bath, black tea with valerian root and honey, then straight to bed.'

Telium snaps out of her shock to hear the assistant's instructions to the maid. 'No,' Telium protests. 'I want to stay.'

The woman puts her hands on her hips and shakes her head. 'No-one wants you here, Half-Breed.'

The words whisper off the walls. Nobody wants you. *The words echo in her mind. An image of a man and a woman cradling a white-haired baby flashes in her mind.*

Without warning, Telium finds herself up to her neck in warm bathwater that shimmers with oils. A steaming pot of tea is set out on a small table beside her and the maid is bustling about her bedchamber, fluffing pillows and turning down her bed. Telium pinches her brows at the sudden wave of dizziness the abrupt change in her dream brings on.

She closes her eyes against sudden tears as a pained scream echoes down the hallway. The maid pauses for a moment, biting her lip, before turning back to her task. There are a few moments of peace before the Siren Queen's cry rings out again, the tortured noise grating on Telium's eardrums.

Attempting to block out the sound, Telium sucks in a deep breath and ducks her head under the water. There she lies, floating in blissful quiet, while in another wing her Queen sobs and screams as her body is racked with contractions and her mind shatters under the weight of her decision.

Bubbles float in front of Telium's face as she exhales. Her chest becomes tight. Still, she stays under the water, unwilling to leave her small sanctuary of peace, even as her lungs cry out for air ...

CHAPTER
19

Telium sits bolt upright, lungs burning. Someone has a hold of her shoulders. A hazy form in front of her is shouting her name. Mallux. She coughs and looks about her. The sun is rising, staining the sky orange. Her heart aches in her chest and a hard lump forms in her throat, tears sting the back of her eyes. Above her, a flock of birds shoot through the sky and a crackling roar fills the air. Still groggy from sleep, she looks about in confusion.

Why is everything fuzzy? She swings her head around, coughing again.

It is hard to see more than a few feet in any direction through all the smoke.

Smoke!

Alarm shoots through Telium and she surges to her feet. Adrenaline races through her veins, throwing off the last dregs of sleep. She jerks her head about to the lightening horizon. *That's not the sun brightening the sky, it's …* 'Fire!' Mallux's words finally reach her. 'Telium! We have to go!'

Hastily, she stuffs belongings into her pack, the effort causing her to cough again. When Mallux spins to face Telium, his eyes go wide at the sight. Behind her, an enormous inferno rages. The night sky is lit up with ghoulish shades of red and orange. Smoke billows up and blots out the stars and a brisk wind pushes some of it towards them, causing them to choke and splutter. The wall of fire has not yet reached them, but judging by the heat and the fleeing creatures rushing past them, it is not far off.

Casting her eyes around confirms that the horses have broken their tethers and bolted; one of them has ripped the stake out of the ground entirely. The noise of them fleeing is likely what woke Mallux, or maybe he heard the crackling roar of the fire with his heightened sense. Which is getting louder by the second. She hopes the horses will escape the fire unscathed and silently thanks Mallux for removing all their tack before they bedded down.

In an instant, they have their belongings packed and thrown over their shoulders. Taking off, they dart away, fleeing like rabbits before a fox. Telium pulls on her Gifts, pushing herself hard with Mallux by her side. The fire is burning parallel with the road to Xandi, so they flee toward the Orth Rel. A huge gust of wind brings the smell of smoke and ash, along with a twinkling display of sparks. Telium curses. The unpredictable wind could easily carry the sparks leagues away and start spot-fires ahead of them.

Wildfires are not uncommon in Alkoria. Their hot, dry summers mean one or two are expected every year. But this year's autumn rains have not come and the sun has kept the land in her merciless grip, baking the ground and drying up trees, turning everything into tinder ripe for burning.

Sweat coats her body, running down her spine and over her brow, stinging her eyes. Her breath comes in harsh gasps, the smoke-filled air burning a track down her lungs.

Mallux seems to be faring no better. His hair is plastered

to the nape of his neck. When he sees Telium tie her headscarf around her mouth, he nods in understanding and pulls his shirt up over the lower half of his face without breaking his stride. For once, Telium is too distracted to admire the sliver of skin the movement reveals.

With their unnatural speed, they are able to put some distance between them and the fire front. The smoke thins somewhat, but not enough to remove their makeshift masks. They flash by a downed deer, the poor beast's leg bent at an ugly angle. It screams in fear and thrashes as it tries to stand on its broken leg. Telium does not even have the time to put the creature out of its misery. She sends a prayer up to Tenebris to guide the animal's soul to the Gardens of Opimare.

The ground becomes treacherous and rocky, forcing them to slow for fear they might end up like the deer, causing them to lose precious time. They pick their way through the hazardous terrain. Despite their slower pace, they still manage to keep ahead of the fire. Out of the corner of her eye, Telium spots an assortment of animals fleeing the blaze as well: deer, rabbits, foxes, even a lone wolf. Overhead, birds escape the raging fire on swift wings.

Telium's legs strain and her head spins from inhaling so much smoke. She puts a hand out to stop their furious pace. 'We have to run west,' she says in-between gasps. 'Try and get out of the fire's path.'

Mallux nods and takes off again. It's a gamble. They don't know how wide the fire front is. But if they keep running in this direction, soon the smoke or the flames will overwhelm them. If they can just reach the edge of the fire, they will be safe. *Hopefully.*

The next few minutes are torture. Hot, smoky air scorches their lungs, their coughing robbing them of what little oxygen they have. Telium's eyes sting from smoke and sweat. Her heart hammers so hard in her chest she thinks it might burst through her ribs.

The heat of the approaching fire billows over them. Soon it feels like they are standing directly in front of the great furnaces of the Siren Queen's castle. The air becomes dry, all the moisture sucked from it. All Telium can hear is her heartbeat in her ears and the fire's crackling roar.

'We should stop,' Mallux yells over the blaze. 'Take shelter on top of that outcrop.' Violent coughs rack his large frame.

Telium looks towards where he points and shakes her head. 'Even if the fire does not kill us, the smoke will.' She has to shout to be heard.

They push on. Telium loses track of time as her entire existence narrows down to her next breath, the next tiny trickle of air that she can drag down into her burning lungs. Her head spins violently. It is a miracle they both manage to stay on their feet.

What may be minutes, or hours, later, the air clears slightly. It's hardly noticeable but gives them enough hope to keep going. They must be close now. They can make it.

Beside her, Mallux stumbles on a loose stone and Telium grips his sleeve, hauling on his arm to keep him upright. Her oxygen-deprived muscles burn and the effort sends her into a coughing fit so hard she must black out for a moment, because when she comes to, Mallux is gripping her arm to keep her standing.

They cling to each other and keep moving forward, their fleet pace slowing to a drunken jog as the heat and smoke take its toll on their bodies. Leaning on and supporting each other in equal measures, they push forward resolutely. Mallux's hand stays on her arm, as if he is afraid if he lets go of her, she will sift into ash.

I have killed us, Telium thinks in an oddly detached manner. *We are going to die here in this fire. At least my soul will reach the afterlife.* Without her and Mallux to stop the Mad Fae King, his army will crush Alkoria, his stain spreading across the land unchallenged. *Maybe all of Alkoria will burn, then he will have nothing to conquer.*

At first, the change in wind direction is barely perceptible, intent as they are on keeping on their feet. Telium carries on, staggering forward, refusing to lie down and die. Beside her, Mallux seems to have the same thought as he pushes on doggedly. Abruptly, the air clears. The fresh wind on her face soothes Telium's parched skin. Her legs collapse under her as she heaves in huge gasps of air. She coughs so violently she leans over and vomits. Valiantly attempting to calm her erratic thoughts, she takes deep steady breaths, filling her painful lungs with life-giving oxygen. The simple feeling of breathing in fresh air nearly brings tears to her eyes. She digs her fingers into the soil, anchoring herself to the earth as her head spins again.

After a moment, Mallux shucks off his pack and rips free his waterskin. He sways slightly, entirely covered in ash. It coats his blond hair and sticks to his face. Small flakes cling to his lashes, making his sea-blue eyes stark against his face. He gulps at the water before handing it over to Telium. Leaning forward, he brushes her sweat-soaked hair from her face.

She swallows a mouthful of water, before glancing over her shoulder. What she sees brings her heart up into her throat. The fire is enormous; the entire night lit up in its hellish glow. Her eyes track the horizon and she notes embers racing ahead of the main blaze on the wind, causing smaller spot-fires.

They are not out of danger yet. Telium can see they are barely on the edge of the inferno. Just the slightest wind change will send the fire racing back in their direction. Now that her head has cleared slightly, she can see they are still surrounded by smoke, albeit thinner than before. The wind changing direction has allowed a trickle of fresh air to be pushed through, but it is not the clear air she originally thought.

'Mallux.' Her voice is practically gone. His name is less than a whisper as it passes her lips. She clears her throat painfully and tries again.

'Mallux,' she croaks. 'Are you okay?'

He seems to take a moment to hear her. When he does, he raises his head, scouring the horizon. 'Let's go,' he says, his voice equally hoarse. 'We have to keep ahead of the blaze.'

He takes back the waterskin and clambers to his feet. Reaching down, he helps Telium to her feet, calluses scraping against her own. For a moment, he leans close, blue eyes searching her face. She distantly notes his hands skimming up and down her arms.

'Are you hurt?' he rasps.

Telium shakes her head, breath stalling in her lungs. With visible effort, he leans away from her. One warm hand slips down into hers. They take off at a somewhat more controlled jog than before. Telium ignores her screaming muscles.

The next few hours make Telium grateful for her training with Trigg as her body screams in pain and her lungs burn, yet she pushes on. They alternate between a jog and a brisk walk, oftentimes leaning against each other just to stay upright. Telium's skin is hot and tight across her body, her mouth dry. Her tongue feels like a thick scrap of old leather.

The ends of Mallux's hair look singed by the heat, the parts of his skin she can see are covered in a high flush, his lips cracked and dry. At one point the wind swirls, turning so that it is blowing into their backs and they break into a panicked sprint, worried the blaze will catch up to them again.

Even when they are far from the fire, they keep walking, their bodies convulsing as their lungs try to expel all the smoke they have inhaled. Behind them, the red glow of the horizon lights up enormous plumes of smoke rising into the sky, so thick and vast it blots out the stars completely. It reminds Telium of the fire mountain at the city of Ollsuria.

Eventually, they come across a stream that trickles down from the mountains and winds its way through the lowlands. The sun is only a few hours from making an appearance when Telium drops Mallux's hand and shucks off her pack and blades, letting them fall to the ground with a thump, before wading into the steam fully clothed. The cool water on her parched skin makes her gasp then moan as she sinks down. Mallux follows suit, sloshing in behind her.

Black soot swirls around her as the current picks it up from her clothes. She splashes her face and scrubs it with her hands which come away black. She takes a long drink of water and sits, swaying slightly, as exhaustion hits her.

Long moments pass until the silence is suddenly broken by a harsh rasping sound. Telium looks over at Mallux – his head is hanging between his shoulders, body shaking. When he raises his head, she realises he is laughing, his burned lungs making the sound rough. With a rueful grin, she scoots back towards the bank as her head begins to spin. He looks so ridiculous, soot stained and sopping wet, kneeling in a stream, that a dry chuckle rasps out of her.

'A fire.' He laughs hoarsely and shakes his head. 'A cursed fire.'

Telium's vision blurs as she sways.

He laughs again. 'Killed by a fire in this damned land.'

The edges of Telium's sight begins to fade. Before she blacks out entirely, she hears Mallux's voice reaching her from the darkness.

'Imagine it, a cursed fire. Mallux *Vortas* burned alive in human lands.'

CHAPTER
20

Telium wakes with a raging headache and a mouth as dry as the Ereak Desert. She shifts slightly and moans before the sloshing of water catches her attention. She sits up slowly, squeezing her eyes together against the throbbing of her head. Wet. Why is she wet?

Cracking her eyes open, she sees that from the knees down, she is lying in water. Looking around, she spots Mallux a short way up the bank. He is dry, obviously having had the presence of mind to get out of the stream – unlike her, who is now sopping wet. She scoots backwards away from the water and slowly removes her waterlogged boots.

The final hours of last night are hazy. She remembers coming across the stream and all but falling into it ... then, nothing. She must have passed out shortly after. Thank the goddesses she managed to get to the bank or she would have drowned.

With the grace of an old crone, Telium climbs to her feet and hobbles over to her pack. The sun has long since risen so she leaves her boots in a patch of sunlight and digs through her pack until she finds her cache of herbs and dried plants.

Unwrapping a small package, she pops the contents in her mouth and chews slowly, cringing. The dried root works as a pain relief but is awfully bitter. She swallows and pulls out some fresh clothes and another cloth-wrapped package containing a large square of soap. She watches Mallux to check he is still soundly asleep before walking a bit further down the stream.

Her skin is raw and stinging as she washes first herself, then her clothes, before tipping her head back and letting the stream's gentle current comb through her hair. The sound of trickling water and gently rustling leaves nearly lulls her to sleep again.

When she hears Mallux beginning to stir, she has a flash of panic as she realises she has nothing to dry herself with. Telium hurries out of the stream, dripping wet and utterly naked before she scoops up her clean clothing and bolts behind a tree. Hopping from foot to foot, she flaps her hands uselessly in an attempt to dry herself. It doesn't take long before she gives up and wrings out her hair of excess water, leaving it down. She hurries to pull her clothes over her damp skin, cursing at the way her pants stick to her legs, thwarting her attempts to pull them up.

Mallux is sitting up rubbing his bleary eyes when she returns to her pack. Without a word, she hands him some of the bitter root to chew on before tossing her wet clothes over a low-hanging branch with a wet slap.

Mallux moans. '*Fe'ta*, my head!'

'The root will help with the pain,' Telium says, pointing to the stone down by the water's edge. 'There's soap down there. You can use it on your clothes as well.'

Something glints in Mallux's eyes and her stomach clenches in response to his heated look. He opens his mouth, but then seems to think better of it and closes it with an audible click.

'Don't worry,' she adds with a smirk at his hesitation. 'I won't watch.'

She makes to move away, but Mallux catches her elbow. She turns to him with an arched eyebrow but her smart retort dies in her throat. His gaze scours her face and he ducks his head to catch her eye. When he speaks, the roughness of his voice sends invisible shivers down her spine.

'Are you hurt, *upa?*'

His thumb brushes back and forth absentmindedly on her arm and Telium forces herself not to lean into the touch. Instead, she pulls her lips to the side in a wry grin. 'Besides my aching chest, no; it's not the worst I've had to endure.'

Mallux says nothing, simply nods and moves away to the stream to bathe.

Telium turns her back on the water, cleaning the grey ash from her blades and bandolier. It is a painstaking process, but one she turns all her concentration on. The sound of splashing water drags heat to her cheeks and she scrubs at the leather even more vigorously. She hums as she works, definitely *not* thinking of Mallux or him bathing.

'Telium.' His voice sounds behind her, low and rough from the smoke last night. His Fae accent curls around the sound of her name.

Turning to look over her shoulder, her mouth goes dry. Mallux stands not three feet from her, wet hair dripping down his bare chest. He is watching her with his clear sapphire eyes and she feels the blush returning to creep up her cheeks. Unable to help herself, she flicks her eyes over his torso, before dipping them lower to the muscles forming a 'v' partially poking above his pants. Realising she is gawking at him, Telium hastily jerks her eyes up to the trees overhead. Mallux's eyes burn with an emotion she can't name and she can smell his familiar scent mixed with the faint lavender of the soap.

'Tenebris curse me, Mallux.' Her voice is a bit breathy. 'Do you not have a spare shirt?' She tries valiantly to keep her eyes trained on the leaves above her head, but they flick back to his face.

He gestures to her pack where he has left the soap sitting on its cloth. 'I just wanted to thank you.' He crosses his arms across his chest, the tips of his ears turning a slight pink. The image is endearing. The male seems suddenly self-conscious at his lack of clothing.

Which, Telium thinks, *is utterly ridiculous. As if he does not always look like some long-lost god carved from marble by skilled artisans.* She only nods in response, feeling a little guilty for making him shy and turns back to her blades. She lets her hair fall between them like a curtain, hiding her flush.

He moves away, only to return with a breakfast of bread and cheese. He sits across from her and hands her some food. She didn't imagine the way his fingers brush hers. He has pulled a shirt on, thank the goddesses, but his damp hair sticking to his neck keeps trying to capture her attention.

'I have never seen a fire such as that,' he remarks after a few mouthfuls. 'Our summers are not so long or fierce as yours.'

'It's the drought,' Telium explains, relieved at the safe topic breaking the tension lingering in the air. 'The rains have not yet come, so it was much worse than it should have been. It may burn for days yet.' She gestures back the way they had fled, the sky still scarred with smoke, causing the light to look faintly orange as the sun's rays pass through.

'Many people may die from this.' He is watching the horizon intently.

'Yes.'

'There would have been farming land, maybe small towns

like the one we were at, in the fire's path. Full of mortals ... and Thieves.'

It is not a question, but still, she replies, 'Yes.'

Mallux turns his blue gaze to her. Whatever he sees makes him close his mouth and eat the rest of his meal in silence. His eyes are continually drawn to the clouds of smoke as if he cannot believe a fire of that size and magnitude is possible. Nor that it is still burning.

'Does it snow here?' Mallux asks suddenly.

Caught by surprise, Telium hesitates a moment. 'Uh, sometimes, in the northern regions, close to the mountains. But it is rare. Not every winter.'

'In Thresiel, it is every year.' Mallux's voice turns far away, as if he were picturing it in his head. 'Some places, just barely, and the ground is turned to frozen slush. But in Meannthe, it snows heavily. Great swaths of white fields.'

Telium hums a noncommittal response, trying to imagine that much snow every year.

'It sounds beautiful,' she says.

'It is,' Mallux replies. 'Maybe you will see it one day.'

Telium resolutely avoids the silent question behind his words. She remembers the horses are missing with a small pang of sadness. She hopes they managed to outrun the fire.

'The horses are gone,' she says. 'Tenebris only knows if they've survived.' She sighs, continuing in a scratchy voice, 'We cannot waste time searching for them and there is little point going to the Holy City now. We may as well bypass the town entirely and head directly for the pass.'

Mallux nods his agreement, eyes still on the plume of smoke. When the last morsel is gone, he brushes his hands on his trousers and looks at her, his eyes softening. 'Do you need to rest longer?' His normally silken voice rough.

Telium shakes her head and clambers to her feet. They do not have time to waste, *Ramaeris* is fast approaching, and with the horses gone, they will have to push themselves to make up for lost time.

The dried root has already helped to ease some of the soreness in her muscles. Mallux seems to be faring much better, likely thanks to his accelerated Fae healing. Her boots and clothes are still wet, but seeing no other option, she shrugs, knots her bootlaces and throws them over her shoulder. Content to walk barefoot until they dry.

Mallux bundles his wet pants up in his shirt and makes to tie them to his pack. He glances at Telium with a grin before lobbing them at her. The playful action is so startling, she doesn't even have the presence of mind to react. The wet bundle hits her in the chest with a *splat*.

She gasps at the sudden cold. Her mouth continues hanging open as Mallux's great, booming laugh bounces around the trees. Telium looks at him in fascination. His whole face changes when he laughs, transforming the stoic, serious warrior into someone gorgeously devious.

Shaking herself from her stupor, Telium tosses the dripping ball of fabric back with a dry chuckle, which Mallux finally ties to the straps of his pack. With the day already heating up, they will dry quickly.

જી

As they walk, Telium's mind travels back over their escape. Her dream from the night before jumps out at her. As if it calls forth the memory, she recalls the moment of the Queen's accident in vivid detail. The reality is no less disturbing for its lack of nightmarish flourishes.

In her mind's eye, Telium sees the Queen lean forward

again, stroking Jake's neck, whispering to him. The Queen was well-renowned for her Gifts, her power such that she could, with great difficulty, influence the will of animals.

The realisation hits her so hard that Telium stumbles to a stop, blood draining from her face. Memories that have long been buried flash in quick succession.

The Queen being trampled under Jakes hooves. Moments after she whispered to him. Hushed concerns from the palace physician about the chances of the baby's survival. Telium overhearing the servants murmuring about the state of the Queen's rooms after she found out she had fallen pregnant. They had been trashed, anything Selenia could get her hands on had been ripped or smashed—

The Queen had been devastated, enraged – but most of all, terrified. Everyone had noted her indifference to the baby growing in her womb, though no-one had said anything out loud.

That's because she … she—

Telium's heart rebels against her train of thought, even as bile rises in her throat. Under her skin, her Gifts snarl and hiss, shifting restlessly. She cannot deny the shadow of truth her memories hold.

The Siren Queen staged her accident.

Selenia never planned to keep the child of the Mad Fae King, never planned to send the babe to him to be trained to take her throne. It was all a diversion. The baby was a pawn, sacrificed to save her people, to give the Queen time to call up an army. She would have twenty-one winters to plan to defend her kingdom against the Fae.

But her grief and heartache sent her mad. She must not have anticipated the toll her actions would take on her mind and heart. She became paranoid and erratic, suspicious of any Fae who entered her kingdom, fearing they would reveal her betrayal to their King before she was ready to face him in battle.

The Queen had ordered that not a word be breathed of her accident. Telium had thought it was because her grief was so great, but it was really to keep word from reaching the ears of the Mad Fae King.

Telium spins away from Mallux, who has turned to her with a raised brow. She clamps a hand to her mouth, trying to muffle the sound of her shaky gasp of breath. The keening howl of her Gifts makes her stomach feel like it is being hollowed out.

Her heart cries out in denial. The Mad Fae King is in the wrong here. He is the bad one, the evil one. But Selenia had killed an innocent. Her own child.

Telium wraps an arm around herself as shock and nausea force the breath from her lungs.

She had thought she was taking revenge on the King for raping her Queen and subsequently pushing her into madness. Forcing the events that led her to hate and fear Telium, ultimately leading to Telium's downfall and her desperate flight into the forest.

Your powers would have manifested regardless. Words whisper in her mind. *And Selenia's breakdown was not entirely the fault of the Mad Fae King.*

Emotions war in Telium's chest – disgust, disbelief, confusion. *What am I even doing?*

Such is the life of a ruler: to make the hard decisions that no-one else would. Selenia had sacrificed her one and only child to save her people. No wonder the accident had affected her so. Her grief and hatred and disgust had eaten away her mind – her soul.

Can Telium honestly say that she would not have considered the same path? One life to save a country. *What of the path you walk now, what are you saving?*

Mallux's words break through her congested thoughts.

'Telium? Are you worried about the towns in the fire's path? They may have escaped, as we did.' He hovers at her side.

She blinks at Mallux. *The towns.* The people that live here in Alkoria …

Under the rule of the Mad Fae King, who can say how many more babes would have died or suffered a fate worse than death, for it is said the King loves to experiment on Gifted children, endlessly fascinated by those with power. Every human child born with Thief abilities would have suffered at the King's hands, had the Siren Queen fallen before him.

'Telium?' Mallux touches her wrist lightly.

If not for her, Telium thinks, unsure how she feels about this discovery about Selenia, *then for the people in those towns. For the Thieves who would suffer under the hand of the King.*

'I'm fine, my head is just fuzzy from the smoke,' she lies, heart hardening with determination. 'Let's keep moving.'

I am their only chance.

Her resolution hardens as they walk. She may not agree with Selenia's methods, but Telium feels a sorrowful pity for her Queen. How many other atrocities has the Fae King committed that she doesn't know about? It must be hundreds. How many other people has he forced to make hard choices that broke them, just to save themselves or their kin from him?

Never again will I let one of my people fall prey to him.

Her rage fuels her and she pushes on through the pain in her chest and muscles, knowing each step brings her closer to the Mad Fae King and the opportunity to run him through with her blade. Deep in her soul, her Gifts snarl in glee at the prospect of a hunt.

Get ready, you bastard. I am coming for you.

CHAPTER
21

Telium's teeth chatter and she braces herself against the freezing wind ripping through the Infri Pass. She crouches behind a jumble of rocks next to Mallux. Together they scan the maze of landslides and rock piles that make up the narrow passage between Alkoria and Thresiel.

The hard-packed dirt is barren, incapable of supporting life. In the distance, they watch the sliver of setting sun between the walls of the pass, and to the side, a towering structure of stone. The watchtower is the outpost of the Fae. Originally used solely to monitor the pass for any signs of Alkorian threat, it is now being prepared as a base for the Fae army.

Mallux could have been carved from stone, he crouches so silently beside her. He scans the pass intently.

'How did you get past last time?' Telium asks in a hushed breath.

'I disguised myself as a foot solider,' Mallux replies, not taking his eyes off the pass. 'It was easy enough. Those here have become lax over the years, so far from the rest of the world.'

The wind tears at his words and Telium leans closer to hear him clearly.

'I snuck out in the dead of night. Nobody was watching for someone trying leave Thresiel.'

Telium taps out a rhythm on her dagger, 'It would be too risky for me to enter the fortress. We will have to avoid the tower completely.'

Mallux nods his agreement.

'Can you not just use your powers to make us invisible, so we can sneak by?' Mallux asks.

Telium fights the urge to roll her eyes. He has asked a similar question three times already. There are disadvantages to her legend preceding her, having Mallux think she can levitate or make people invisible are certainly some of them.

'Mallux, I cannot manipulate light or gravity. Maybe two or three high-ranking Power-Thieves could combine their powers to achieve it, but it is beyond me.'

With a thought, she draws on her Gifts to enhance her eyesight. What she sees is promising – no giant lighthouses illuminate the path and most of the guards are staying near the ramparts. A few lone Fae stand guard on top of giant rocks scattered across the pass.

'Patrols?' Telium asks, mind already mapping out a route to let her slip by the sentries unnoticed.

'Very few, mostly they just have guards standing and watching the path. They stay on top of the larger rocks to give them a better line of sight. On my way here, I switched out with one of the *Kah* on the opposite side of the valley.' Mallux points to the guard furthest away from the tower, nearly leaning against the sharp incline of the mountain face. 'Once the sun had fallen, I slipped away, using the darkness for cover.'

'Well then, we might as well do the same,' Telium replies,

pulling her hood up and leaning back against a rock. She positions herself as comfortably as she can on the hard stone, sitting so she is hidden from the view of even the most sharp-eyed Fae, but so she can occasionally peek around to monitor the guards.

They share a meal of dried meat and bread, saying little. There is an odd sort of companionship about them now, their brush with death bringing them inevitably closer. Mallux intrigues her. She knows little to nothing about the Fae, so is unsure if his magnetism is common amongst his people or unique to Mallux. But she feels ... more at ease around him. As if she does not have to dull her sharp edges quite so much.

Telium studies his profile in the fading light. The deepening shadows throw his features into stark relief. He is handsome, to be sure. But there is something else that compels her to him, like his warrior's heart sings to hers.

Despite their blossoming friendship, Telium will not, cannot, allow anyone to see the fear she holds close to her heart – of how desperate she is to master her Gifts and how she fears the power they give her.

Regardless, Telium sometimes looks up to find his piercing eyes on her and feels like she could drown in his gaze. Mallux has not acted on the quiet moments shared between them, and Telium is too proud to initiate anything. Instead, tension simmers, crackling in the air between them, until one of them manages to look away.

Chewing, she alternates between watching the guard and the Fae across from her. She spends the time tentatively examining her new-found revelation about her Queen and her sacrifice. Her emotions are still convoluted, but thinking about her Queen and how much her decision warped her makes Telium's heart ache.

Mallux leans back against the stone; his gaze has the far-away look of someone lost deep in their memories.

'How old are you?' Her question pops out before the thought has time to solidify.

Mallux looks over at her and smiles, raising an eyebrow. 'I will be one hundred and twenty-nine this summer,' he replies.

Telium's eyes go wide and she chokes on her meal. Her reaction makes Mallux laugh quietly under his breath.

'You are going to be *one hundred and thirty?*' she whispers, conscious of the noise echoing.

'One hundred and twenty-nine, yes.'

'Wait, that means you were alive when the Great War was fought. How old were you? Did you fight?'

Telium knows Fae are long-lived, and even though she understands the Fae King is still alive, it boggles her mind to think that Mallux is over *one hundred winters old.* He looks as though he has seen no more than twenty-five.

Something shutters in Mallux's eyes at the question. 'Yes, I had only seen eighty-five summers when the war raged. My father did not let me fight.' He looks off into the distance and says no more.

The next question hovers on her tongue, but she swallows it back. *How old do you think I am?* She cannot help but wonder at the snippets of truth she has gleaned. Could she believe them?

Fiddling with the falkir claw hanging about her neck, she considers how quickly her lungs recovered from the abuse of inhaling such copious amounts of smoke. Far faster than she had anticipated; by the end of the first day, she was nearly completely healed. Now, two days later, her body shows no signs of her brush with death. She had not drawn on her Gifts to accelerate her healing, so how?

Pushing the question from her mind, she turns back to watch the passage guards. The wind whistles through the pass, sounding cold and lonely. Their plan to sneak by is risky and would be near suicide for anyone else, but Telium is a creature of the dark, both her assassin training and Gifts working to her advantage.

As they wait, Telium checks all her weapons, then checks them again; making sure everything is snug and secure, so none of the blades will clink together and alert the guards to their presence. She tightens the laces on her boots, shakes her hair loose before re-braiding it.

Beside her, Mallux goes about his own preparations. He removes the broadsword from his waist and alters the straps so it can be sheathed along his spine, not wanting it to make a noise if it bangs against his thigh or scrapes along the stone.

All too soon the preparations are complete and they sit in tense silence as the time creeps by. Telium hates these quiet moments; the wait makes her short-tempered and twitchy. To pass the bells, she runs through mental exercises Trigg taught her. It calms her mind and helps her prepare for the task ahead.

'Telium,' Mallux whispers. 'It is time, *upa*.'

Telium ignores the heat in her cheeks. Like twin shadows, they rise from their crouch. Telium whips off her cloak and stuffs it into her pack, not willing to risk even the sound of the fabric snapping in the wind. She grits her teeth against the chill. She calls upon her Gifts, allowing her to see clearly in the dark, keeping her movements swift. Glancing at Mallux, she nods before moving forward. Out of the corner of her eye, she sees him shudder.

The edge of the passage seems a too-obvious place for Telium. It is the place the guards watch the most, so she skulks along between the boulders and darts from one hiding place to another with the swiftness of a fox. Her feet are silent on the earth, her breath a mere whisper.

She keeps her Gifts close to the surface, the mental equivalent of twitching one's finger close to a knife. Still unsure if the Fae can detect her Gifts, she keeps the net of her mind in a tight circle about herself.

After every dash, Telium pauses, straining her eyes and ears for signs that they have been spotted. Across from her, she can't even see Mallux slinking along the wall, though she knows he must be there.

Her next movement brings her right by a guard standing watch. The enormous rock he stands on has a slight overhang. Creeping underneath it, Telium dares not even breathe lest she give herself away to his sharpened senses. Praying he cannot hear her heartbeat.

The scuff of his feet on the stone above her makes her freeze. The hairs on the back of her neck prickle. Under her skin, her Gifts hiss in the iron-fisted grip she keeps them in. Telium counts the beats of her heart as it pulses in the base of her throat.

The Fae drops to the ground so silently it startles her heart into her throat. Without thought her hand twitches to the bandolier at her chest. But the male's back is turned. Her mind takes a second to catch up. He is whistling a merry tune, fumbling with his belt as he positions himself in front of a small pile of rocks.

Telium casts her eyes to the night sky at the sound of liquid hitting stone, sure she will see Tenebris laughing at her. But the heavens are empty. Telium's eyes skip from shadow to outcrop. Too close. The Fae is too close for her to try and run to the next shelter. He would hear her. Or if he didn't, he was sure to turn around and catch her before she made it.

Steadying her heartbeat, Telium slowly lowers herself to a crouch. Trying to make herself as small as possible. She holds her breath as the click of the Fae's belt buckle sounds. She dares not even swallow.

Her eyes never leave the willowy guard as he stares off into the night, as if waiting for someone, before turning around with a sigh. Flexing his knees, he looks up, readying to leap back to his perch atop the boulder.

Telium allows herself to believe she may be able to sneak by.

The erratic wind hurls through, ricocheting off rocks and the cliff walls. With it, tumbles Telium's scent. Right to the nose of the Fae sentry.

His face slackens in shock. Taking advantage of his lapse, Telium lunges. Teeth bared and dagger drawn, she crashes into the Fae, knocking the breath from him.

Her dagger arcs towards him, aiming for his gut—

Telium's head snaps to the side from the impact of the male's blow. The blade that should have killed him merely leaves a bright red score across his abdomen. The landscape tilts wildly as Telium staggers.

She rights herself in time to see a second male round one of the larger boulders. He wears a loose red cotton tunic underneath a thick, fur-lined leather vest.

'*Wai'ta*—' he breaks off with a shout as Telium's dagger embeds itself in his hip.

Shit.

Telium lunges for him, Gifts snapping, determined to shut him up before another one of the sentries hears him.

Less than three feet from him, a hand grips a fistful of her hair. Bringing her to a screeching, painful halt with enough force that her whole body topples backwards.

Tears sting her eyes and her hands automatically come up

to grip the wrist of the male holding her. He twists the white strands savagely as he drags her away. The second sentry yanks the dagger from his hip with gritted teeth, his blood instantly staining the tunic an even deeper red.

Telium snarls at him with teeth tipped in fangs. Her Gifts having partially slipped their leash.

The bleeding male stalks toward Telium with a grimace, brandishing her dagger. Telium kicks out, knocking the blade from his hand. Ignoring the burning pain, Telium twists in the first sentry's grip and boots him in the face. Her Gifts skitter along bones, tingling through her chest as she loosens her hold on them.

Stunned, the male loosens his grip enough for Telium to tear herself free. Some of her snowy strands remained clutched in his fingers as she lunges to her feet and whips around. Ducking under the bleeding male's reaching hands and burying a throwing blade in his ribs.

The first sentry reaches for his companion, putting him off balance. Telium binds his ankles with her Gifts and throws herself at him. He goes down with a startled shout that makes Telium's heart leap into her throat.

Pulling her arm back, she strikes him in the face again. The male's head snaps back and his eyes glaze over, but he doesn't let go of consciousness. Feeling like her mind will split in two, Telium binds the mouth of the bloodied guard shut as she strikes his companion again.

His head lolls back, still pushing feebly at Telium's legs where she has straddled him. Her Gifts howl in wicked delight. Gritting her teeth, ignoring the speckle of blood across her face, Telium strikes yet again. This time, when her blow lands, the sentry's lids flutter as his eyes roll back into his head.

She has barely sucked in a breath before she is tackled

bodily off the sentry. She hits the earth hard, grunting with the impact. Her ribs flare in pain.

Telium blinks away the stars as the bloodied sentry's face swims before her. He rears back as if to strike her. Telium shoots her hands up, fingers ending in talons that punch through the skin of his neck like it is paper.

She curls her fingers inwards, shredding as she goes. The male's gasp is already wet and rattly. Telium isn't sure if it's her or her Gifts that hiss in pleasure at the blood that drips onto her neck and chest. Warm points of life in the cold night. With a grunt, Telium pushes the sentry off her. He collapses into the dirt, hands wrapped around his throat as his mouth opens and closes like a fish.

Pushing herself to her feet, she staggers into a run, heading for the other end of the pass. Praying no-one had heard the commotion.

Where is Mallux?

What feels like a boulder suddenly crashes into her side, knocking the breath from her. She pinwheels her arms as she trips, vainly trying to stay upright. Something warm and rough encompasses the back of her head, shoving downwards.

Telium crashes to the dirt, teething barking with the impact. The skin across her cheek stings and burns where it is scraped off by the force of her tumble. Immediately, she shoves herself to her elbows.

'Tenebris curse me,' she growls, spitting dirt.

A curse in gruff Old Fae causes her to look up. Just in time to throw herself out the way of the boot aiming for her head. She rolls onto her back, scrambling away from the newcomer as the male rains kicks and punches down on her.

Most she manages to avoid. One kick catches a glancing blow to her already bruised ribs. Pain flares across her chest. A gasp escapes her as she feels his hand enclose her ankle. With a jerk, he topples her off balance and begins to drag her bodily backwards.

He looks down on her with eyes as rich as honey as he grinds out something in Old Fae. Telium twists and turns, trying to gain purchase as she is hauled across the uneven ground. Her Gifts rattle in their cages and strain at their chains. Telium gathers herself.

The male frowns down at her, then turns and casts his eyes around. Opening his mouth he— Telium's Gifts clamp down on the male's wrists and *twist*. The delicate bones give way under the pressure, snapping and popping in multiple places.

Surging to her feet, Telium draws her haladie. She doesn't even unclasp the double-ended blade as she drives it into the male's skull. The sentry's mouth falls open as he collapses in a heap.

CHAPTER
22

Telium's pants are harsh in the still air. Her Gifts thrum through her veins, running ebony-tipped claws down her spine. She stills a moment, whipping her head in every direction. Nothing.

Jamming her haladie into its sheath, she takes off at a sprint. Her heart pounds in her throat. She desperately tries to calm it as she listens for pursuers.

She can feel her powers pulsing in time with her heartbeat, waiting for the chance to slip their leash entirely. After a few beats of silence, Telium forces herself to slow. To move as silent as a shadow.

She concentrates on the net of her mind; a consciousness moves steadily towards her, as familiar now as her own. Ignoring the prickles in her legs telling her to run, she sidesteps close to a boulder and waits.

A dozen heartbeats later, Mallux materialises out of the night. Grinning like a fiend when he spots her, he moves over on silent feet. Telium's heart jumps up into her throat as he steps up to her, leaning in close enough that his lips brush her hair.

'Show off,' he whispers with a grin, his voice warming the shell of her ear. 'Did you really just take on *three* Fae sentries and walk away?'

She unconsciously tilts her chin up at the brush of air, suppressing a shudder when he leans away. *From the cold,* she tells herself. His words register; he'd been watching her.

She is about to reply when the soft sound of shuffling feet over stone reaches them.

Ears straining, she spins to the sound. But it isn't a sentry. It is coming from the Thresiel end of the passage. As they stand in dead silence, the sounds become clearer and more defined: footsteps, many of them.

Tenebris curse me.

Mallux's hand is heavy and warm on her shoulder. His lips are in her hair and he speaks so quietly she has to cock her head towards him to hear. 'Too many to be a patrol; it must be a new shipment. We need to move, before they bump into your sentries and circle back to find us.'

A shipment?

The question burns on Telium's tongue, but they don't have the time to stand around and clarify it. She nods and tosses her head forward, raising an eyebrow in question.

'Meet you at the other end,' Mallux breathes, a glint in his eye.

Her lips twitch as she fights a snarl. A test. That's what this is to him – to see if she is capable of the things the legends say.

Fighting the urge to flip him off, Telium pads into the darkness with the grace of a falkir. No sounds emerge from the Alkorian end of the passage. She can hear the approaching 'shipment' but struggles to pinpoint the exact location. The high cliff walls of the pass cause sounds to echo strangely. Up ahead, she sees the wavering light of a torch flame, casting elongated and warped shadows on the walls.

Telium's senses kick into overdrive as she creeps between stone and shadow. At one point, she stops to crouch behind a small jumble of rocks to hide. The smell of dirt and shale carry on the wind.

She can make out words now: people speaking, complaining about sore feet and empty stomachs. Harsh words in response. Telium holds her breath as a few stragglers walk right by the boulder she is hiding behind. A snippet of conversation reaches her.

'Please, we need to relieve ourselves, just a moment.'

'Damn it! Hurry up, and do not bother trying to escape. Do not make me come back and look for you.'

Telium is about to creep away when a phantom touch on her shoulder halts her. At the same time, the man's words register. With a frown, she stays put. Though every other instinct screams at her to move on, her curiosity wins out.

The dragging of feet on dirt becomes louder. Telium's caution quickly escalates into defensive alarm, realising the owner of the first voice must be back-tracking into the dark to go about her business.

From around the corner, a young woman emerges, dressed in a patchwork of different clothes darned together haphazardly. Her brown hair is lank and dirty. Her ears poke out from between the strands: round. Human. And so is the elderly woman following, her hair a jumble of silver and blonde curls.

The shock knocks her, and Telium puts a hand out to steady herself. The movement causes a shower of pebbles to rattle to the ground, the sound enough to draw the attention of the younger woman in the near silence.

A look of utter terror crosses the woman's face. She takes

a frightened step backwards, opening her mouth and looking over her shoulder to shout for help.

Mallux appears out of the shadows a few feet away, blue eyes wide as he takes in the scene in front of him.

Before the woman has a chance to cry out and alert the others to their presence, Telium reacts, throwing out the coils of her mind instinctively and roughly jerking backwards. The stranger's life-force is ripped from her as easily as plucking an apple from a tree. The woman collapses without a sound, dead before she even has a chance to scream.

The rush hits her and Telium gulps in air, instantly horrified at her actions, even as pleasure swamps her senses as the woman's life-force fortifies her. The elder woman stands frozen in shock, all the colour drained from her lined face.

Before she can even form a thought, Mallux is at her side. Distracted as she is, she does not even react to his closeness.

He breathes a single word into her ear before swiftly taking off into the darkness. *'Run.'*

Telium's eyes jump between the lifeless woman and the elder, who has begun shaking. When Telium's bicoloured gaze lands on her, she takes a shaky step backwards.

'No,' Telium hisses at her.

The elder wraps a trembling hand around her throat, glancing between Telium and the path leading back to the Fae.

'No,' Telium whispers, 'come with me.' She curls her fingers at the woman, banishing her talons. 'I'm human. I'm Alkorian.'

Telium steps forward and grips the elder's wrist as gently as she can, tugging her forward.

'Come with me,' Telium repeats. 'I can help you.'

As if in a daze, the older woman moves forward. Her steps are stiff and shuffling. Telium grits her teeth and tugs her along faster, pulling the woman between boulders. *Hurry, hurry, hurry.*

'What are you doing here?' The older woman's voice is high and clear.

Telium glances over her shoulder, noting the position of the torchlight bouncing off the rocks. *We are not going to get away fast enough.* The realisation slices Telium's heart, but she refuses to let go of the elderly woman.

'I'm going to kill the Fae King, in revenge for my Queen,' Telium breathes.

She is beyond caring at this point. Desperate to keep this woman out of the Fae's hands. She tugs the woman along faster, who makes a small sound of pain that rips at Telium's heart.

'What?' the woman wheezes. 'Why? Who are you to think you can do this?'

Telium throws another glance over her shoulder. 'Because I loved her,' she answers truthfully.

Telium's heart stumbles into a gallop as she sees the torchlight beginning to move back in their direction. *We are not going to make it.*

She looks to the elder, who locks eyes with her. The woman's mouth pops open in recognition and she stumbles a step as her eyes go wide.

'*Tenebris Kin,*' she breathes.

Suddenly, the woman digs in her heels. Telium falters, not wanting to hurt her. Hauling herself backwards, the elder looks over her shoulders, face lighting with understanding.

When Telium tries to pull her along again, the woman shakes her wrist vigorously until Telium releases her. Urgency nipping at her heels, Gifts seething, Telium stops and turns to the woman.

'We cannot stop. Here. I will carry yo—' Telium's mouth snaps shut in surprise as the elder reaches up to cup her face tenderly.

Telium's brows pull together as she stares at the woman who searches her face intently, a soft smile on her lips.

'Bring that bastard to his knees.' The old woman's words make Telium start, so at odds with her gentle tone. Her hand leaves Telium's face, fingers trailing lines across her cheek as she takes a step backwards. 'For Alkoria,' the woman whispers. 'Don't leave our people behind.'

Without warning, the elder turns on her heels and breaks into a limping run back towards the Fae. She knocks over a pile of stone as she goes, the sound bouncing off the walls of the pass, magnifying itself.

'No!' Telium's word is lost in the cries from the Fae.

They shout as they realise their 'shipment' is making a run for it. Tears sting Telium's eyes as she watches the elder's grey curls disappear from view. The sound of a dozen thundering boots echoes back at her. Angry, shouting Old Fae. If she goes after the woman now, they will both be caught. She will lose her chance to get close enough to the Fae King to kill him.

Choking on a frustrated sob, Telium spins on her heels. She breaks into a run. The voices turn from angry to shocked as they discover the lifeless body of the younger woman and Telium pushes into an all-out sprint.

With her Thief Gifts fuelling her, together with her newly stolen life-force, Telium flies over the ground. Ahead of her, she can hear the slight scrape of boots hitting stone as Mallux runs on.

Her ragged breaths are not solely from her pace. Her jaw flexes as tears prickle the backs of her eyes. *No, no, no!* She curses at herself and her Gifts, her lapse in control. That she had to leave the elderly woman behind to whatever fate the Fae thought best for her.

Within minutes they reach the mouth of the pass. They explode out of the passage, then turn sharp left and down a path that seems to be formed solely by the crossing of so many feet. Mallux does not stop. The end of the pass opens to a vast stretch of land.

Unlike Alkoria, where the Orth Rel rise up sharply, the landscape here slowly peters out. The huge mountains gentle into rolling hills, leaving the land in-between a strange scene of uneven, sloping ground with patchy snow and rubble.

CHAPTER
23

The descent makes for treacherous footing. Loose stone and shale clatter underfoot but they dare not slow their breakneck pace.

The hairs on the back of Telium's neck stand on end as they scramble down, aware their flight potentially exposes their backs to deadly Fae. With Mallux's Fae speed and Telium drawing on her Gifts, the distance that would have taken them a bell to walk is covered in less than ten minutes.

Once they hit more level ground, they pick up their pace even more. The terrain changes from loose stone and snow to more familiar scenes of natural meadows, rolling hills and copses of small trees. They run in silence for another quarter of a bell, reaching flat land before Mallux slows to a stop beside a strange stone column carved with whirls and patterns.

Telium vaguely remembers passing one as they exited the passage between the mountains but was too preoccupied. The younger woman's face swims before her closed eyes. The elder's words ring in her mind. *Don't leave our people behind.*

It makes no sense. To her knowledge, there are no humans in the Fae lands; the Siren Queen had forbidden travel long before Telium was sentenced to death. Those living here had either returned to Alkoria or moved on to elsewhere.

When they come to a halt, Mallux pulls out his waterskin, panting gently. Telium stalks towards him, her own breathing fast from the run.

'Why in Tenebris' name are there huma—'

'How long can you keep up this pace?' he asks, casting a critical eye over her.

She snaps her mouth shut abruptly and curls her lip up in a sneer. After drawing the life-force from the woman, she has enough reserves to run all night and well into the morning before stopping to rest, but she doesn't see any reason to let him know that.

'As long as *you* can,' she snipes.

'Good,' he replies, handing her the water without meeting her eyes. 'I want to put a few leagues between us and the pass before sunrise.'

'Mallux,' she hisses when he turns away, 'what where those humans doing in there?'

When he doesn't respond, a snarl rasps out of her. She reaches out, gripping his arm and hauling him around to face her.

'Answer me.'

'We do not have time for this.' Mallux shakes her hand off and turns back around.

Her hand flies to the haladie at her waist.

'Unless you want to discuss it once the guards have caught us?' he says over his shoulder.

Telium's mouth shuts with an audible click. Her teeth grind together as she growls. She will not waste either woman's sacrifice.

As much as she craves answers, now is not the time. With the possibility of a scout on their tail and the risk of discovery, her need for answers will have to be put aside. She silently vows to ink both of the women's deaths onto her leg, honouring their sacrifice by ensuring they live on in someone's memory. *I am sorry.*

'Fine,' Telium snaps. Tossing her head back, she swigs the water.

When they set off again, Telium tries to ignore the image of the younger woman's face when she'd laid eyes on Telium crouching in the dark – like she had seen a Life-Thief. *No wonder humans fear you and Thieves despise you.* Pushing the thought aside, she watches the land as they move through it. Both similar and strange in equal measures.

CHAPTER
24

Before the sun rises, they stop at the outskirts of a small farming village, both of them puffing from their pace. While they are sharing the last of their water and food, Telium's anger cools from a boiling rage to a gentle simmer. Questions and accusations swirl around her mind, but she holds her peace for the moment.

They have to go into the town – *Polgn,* she remembers – for supplies. For the first time, Telium wonders how recognisable she will be as a human. If there are not meant to be humans here, she cannot exactly go strolling through the village. It has been too long since she's played the games of assassination and intrigue. She is a little rusty.

She looks over to her pack with her cloak inside. Away from the mountains, the temperature has warmed significantly, more so than even Alkoria. If the weather warms up any more it will be too hot for her to wear her cloak and not look suspicious.

'How sharp are your senses *exactly?*' she asks Mallux. 'Will the townsfolk be able to tell I'm a human or can I simply hide my ears?' *Since there are not meant to be any humans in Thresiel,* she adds mentally.

Mallux shrugs dismissively as if the answer were obvious. 'We will tell people you are my slave.'

Telium stills, rage a rapidly swelling heat in her chest. She cocks her head toward him, thinking she must have heard him incorrectly.

'What?'

The snapped word is not a genuine question. But Mallux repeats himself anyway as he drops to the ground, resting with his back against a tree with peeling bark and odd, bluish-green leaves.

Telium clicks her tongue, the only outward sign of her building ire. Walking in front of him, something snaps into place in her brain and she slowly crouches down in front of him.

He fiddles with his sword sheath, readjusting the straps so it can be hung around his hips again.

'Mallux.' Her voice is tightly controlled, veiling the hot anger lashing through her veins. At her tone, he looks up at her. He seems hesitant to meet her eyes.

With a thought, she banishes her Mind-Thief powers, the animalistic shine of her eyes disappearing with it. Ignoring the sting of hurt as she realises her eyes must have been what was making him uncomfortable as Mallux relaxes slightly.

'What were those humans doing in the pass? The Siren Queen forbade any travel to Thresiel.'

Mallux opens his mouth to reply, but the dangerous tone of her voice appears to give him pause. He studies her face closely. She hopes he can see her anger and disgust.

'They … would have been part of the new shipment,' he replies tentatively.

'What do you mean, new *shipment*?' Telium hisses.

'Every so often, the fort will get a delivery of new supplies:

food, armour, uniforms … slaves, to carry out the upkeep.' He shrugs at the last part, trying to downplay its meaning.

Her Gifts rumble throaty growls as they push up against their confines. She can feel her lips curl back in a snarl. Her anger rises with startling ferocity. Part of her whispers to run a blade across his throat and leave him with his life-blood soaking the earth. With an agitated jerk of her head, she dismisses the thought, pushing it away, fearing it is her old madness whispering to her.

'And I don't suppose,' she says with a sneer, voice heavy with menace, 'that you have any *Fae* slaves, do you?'

Mallux opens and closes his mouth, grasping for an answer as he searches her face.

Telium growls in disgust, spinning on her heels and stalking a few paces away. *I'll kill that bastard King.*

Behind her, Mallux cautiously climbs to his feet. 'Many wealthy Fae have human slaves in their homes or businesses.'

His weak attempt at an explanation only enrages her further. She flicks a hand in his direction dismissively, the motion jerky and agitated. She can feel her fury building inside her like a storm and she struggles to keep it in check as her Gifts thrash.

It is not Mallux who allows these laws, she reasons with herself. Trying to wrangle her emotions. It is the twisted King who rules over these lands. Mallux did not get a say when the decree was made.

But will he now? The thought surfaces, and once it does, Telium cannot let it go. Excitement battles with anger inside of her as a plan forms in her mind – a chance to do some good for the humans here. To help bring hope instead of incite fear. To have a purpose.

She turns abruptly to face Mallux, only to find him

watching her with an inscrutable gaze. The look flits across his face, quickly replaced by concern.

Her determination to aid the human slaves sets her face in a mask of stone. 'You are leading this rebellion.' She says it as a statement rather than a question, though she isn't sure.

Thrown off by the sudden change in subject, Mallux frowns and nods once. 'With others, yes. But they are not warriors. My companions deal with the logistics and politics of the rebellion. I carry out the … physical side.'

'So, once we are successful, will a council be established? And will you be part of it?' Telium crosses her arms over her chest.

'Yes. It will be voted upon, but it is likely I will be given a place … for my efforts.'

'Good.' Telium storms up to him so that they are toe to toe. She has to tilt her head back to look up at him. 'You will abolish these slave laws. You will decree that all humans are free – to stay and live here or to return to Alkoria, or any other land they choose. I do not care what it takes to get the others on the council to agree. You *will* do this. If you refuse, I am going back to Alkoria, and I will finish what you Fae started and bring that entire passage down behind me. Then I will stay in Alkoria and fight for my people. Tenebris claim any Fae who dares step foot in my home with evil intent. I will slaughter them and drag their souls down to the Underrealm.'

Her words are tight with emotion and heavily laced with warning. She grinds her teeth together to stop any more threats or promises spewing forth, lest she vows to burn the Fae lands from here to the King's palace. Her chest rises and falls in the silence that follows.

Mallux looks down at her, a slight frown creasing his brow

and he rubs a hand along his jaw. 'Of course, Telium,' he says, his voice low and rumbling. 'I was … we were … always intending to change the laws. Of course.' He nods and places a hand on her arm, squeezing gently.

At his words, her anger ebbs, replaced by a small blossom of hope in her chest. *That woman's death will not be for naught.* Mallux will help her give the humans here back their freedom.

When she looks up into his face, he smiles gently, nodding at her again as his ember scent twists about her. The sudden urge to stand on her toes and press her lips to his hits her like a slap in the face. Flustered, she steps back hurriedly. She holds her hand out to Mallux, who looks at it for a moment, before shrugging and putting his hand in hers. Shaking, they seal the deal.

Telium sets about stripping her weapons. Those she cannot hide in her boots or under her clothing, she wraps in her spare clothes and packs away in her bag. Even so, she manages to conceal a fair number of weapons on her person.

They move some of Mallux's clothes to Telium's pack to make it look large and bulky. A slave carrying her master's belongings. Even though it is just for show, her skin crawls at the thought and she must fight to keep the snarl off her face.

Before she lifts the bag onto her back, Mallux clears his throat. She thinks he looks decidedly uncomfortable.

'Telium …' he starts, then hesitates.

'What?'

He looks at her, then looks away – at the trees, the ground, anywhere but her. 'Your hair.'

She reaches up to touch her hair and runs her hand over the bumps of her braids, searching for one that has come undone or something caught in them. When she finds nothing, she turns to Mallux in confusion.

'It is ... not how a human would wear it,' he says. 'And the colour ...' He trails off awkwardly.

'*Oh*.' With a shrug, she begins to undo her hair. It falls about her shoulders in uneven waves. She does not know what to do about the colour though. Struck by inspiration, she rummages through her pack. Retrieving the shawl she bought in the village, she ties her hair into a knot and wraps the fabric about her head. 'Good enough?' she asks him.

'It will have to do,' he says, 'but wrap it tight around your head ... No, like this.' He reaches out, taking the piece of fabric from her. With deft hands he wraps it tightly, knotting it at the nape of her neck and tucking in a few loose strands of hair. Her skin tingles from where the calluses on his fingers graze her neck, his fingers lingering.

Mallux steps back and surveys her, nodding in approval at what he sees. 'At least your clothes are plain.' Then he peers closer at her face. 'There is nothing we can do about your eyes. Just keep them downcast. Nobody will notice anything amiss. And do not scowl at anyone.'

At that, Telium feels a scowl twitch across her face. Without replying, she shoulders her pack, schooling her features into blank nothingness. She raises an eyebrow at Mallux, who turns and sets off at a brisk pace towards Polgn.

CHAPTER
25

The sun peeks above the horizon just as they reach the town. Despite her pride screaming at her not to, Telium follows Mallux's advice and keeps her eyes on the ground. However, she cannot help sneaking peeks at the Fae and at the buildings they pass.

Mallux had told her Polgn is a small out-of-the-way town, barely worth a mark on the map. However, that does not stop the townsfolk taking great pride in their homes.

Everything – eaves, beams, rafters, door frames – is carved with exquisite attention to detail. The curving lines depict an array of scenes from nature to battles. Whoever carved the artwork was meticulous and worked with no small amount of skill. It is beautiful. Telium drinks it all in. Surely it must be the home of multiple artists or sculptors for the town to look so.

In Alkoria, such beautiful displays are left to the wealthy; those who can afford to spend their gold on such lavish things. Here, it seems, it is the norm to make every building a work of art. The warrior side of her tells her such extravagance is unnecessary and pointless. But the larger part of her is in awe.

As they reach the centre of town, Telium takes care to stay close to Mallux's side, hunching her shoulders and walking with a dejected step.

Mallux stops a passer-by to get directions to the tavern. Once there, Telium waits outside, hiding in the shadow of the building, while he goes inside to restock their supplies. Humans are not permitted in the tavern. She scowls at the ground. She would bet her blade that if she snuck around the back into the kitchen, she'd find at least one human toiling away.

While they were walking, she had tentatively thrown out the net of her mind, surprised to find that all Fae are a blind spot in her consciousness – just like Mallux. Her mind had moved around them with ease. When nobody seemed to notice her powers running over them, she kept her mind spread out. She will have to train herself to notice these dark spots that are the Fae. They are not like humans – whose intense emotions light up her mind like a blazing torch.

As Mallux approaches, she concentrates on the spot in her net. While she cannot feel his emotions, his mind still feels unique to him. It's as if the fortress of his mind has its own physicality – like cold, hard stone walls. She can almost *feel* the rough edges as her consciousness brushes along them.

Turning her attention to a Fae across the street, Telium concentrates on his mind. The Fae is tall and thin with corded muscles and a shock of chocolate-brown hair tied at the nape. He is speaking to another Fae who is his complete opposite. Broader even than Mallux, his soot-stained clothing and callused hands mark him out as a blacksmith. As she concentrates on the leaner Fae, she feels the prickle of thorns as she pushes up against his mind's defence. *Briar bush*, Telium decides. That is what guards this Fae's mind.

She hums in contemplation at this discovery, then lowers her head again and follows Mallux without a word as he passes. On the way out of town, they pass the local water well where Telium pulls up the bucket and refills their waterskins.

As soon as they are out of sight of the town, Telium tears off the fabric covering her head, pulling free some strands of white hair from her bun in the process. She hates what the wrap represents, does not want to wear it any longer than necessary. *I will not let my Queen's people be slaves for the Fae.*

Anger still burns low and hot in her chest. She tucks it close, nursing it next to the iron will of her revenge.

As they walk, Mallux points in the direction they are heading, explaining their route and naming the towns at which they will stop. He keeps glancing sidelong at her as they travel, a soft frown creasing his brow.

The wind tumbles gently about them, bringing the sweet smell of wheat and wildflowers. When Mallux looks at her for the umpteenth time, she sighs. 'What is it?'

'Are you okay?' His voice is soft and more than a little wary.

Telium sucks in a deep inhale of the late morning air, calming her ire. 'I just found out that my people have been enslaved here for almost half a century, Mallux, and now I have to pretend to be one of them. Excuse me for not dancing with joy.' Her sarcasm hides her sorrow, burning her tongue like acid.

Mallux reaches out as if to run his fingers across her cheek but stops short and drops his hand. 'I am sorry.' His voice is heavy.

A snort escapes her and she drums her fingers on the empty space at her waist where her dagger usually sits. 'What for? It's not your fault your King is a cruel bastard or that your people keep human slaves like dogs. That my Queen is dead and I didn't even get to mourn her. That in the end, it was like I didn't even know her. It's not your fault I killed that woman without even thinking. That I have no place with humans or among Thieves. I can't control my Gifts, or help but be this dark, wicked thing, only good for taking lives.' Telium snaps her mouth shut, warmth suffusing her cheeks at her outburst. The death of the slave woman has put her on edge more than she cares to admit.

She is not usually so lax with her words. She grits her teeth, working her jaw, as her fingers take up their agitated rhythm on her leg again.

Mallux is silent for a long while. Telium is embarrassed by her words. She must seem like a sulking child to him, crying over a life that was forfeited to save theirs. When he speaks at last, his silken voice seems to wrap itself around her heart.

His words are hesitant at first but build as he goes on. 'When I was younger, I was forever trying to win my mother's favour. Next to my brother, I was this unruly, disobedient child, forever getting into fights and mischief. Despite my best attempts, it seemed trouble always found me, and I would settle it myself with wits and fists, much to my mother's endless disappointment.'

He cringes slightly and throws Telium a wry smile. 'It was never enough. I grew up in my brother's shadow, forever feeling like I was not good enough, that perhaps if I were less violent, less curious and adventurous, I would not be so disappointing. And I tried. I avoided troublemakers, I held my temper, tried to be the quiet, obedient, sweet child that she wanted. I acted like I was the same as my brother – all love and light – whereas, in reality, I was all fire and stone. I spent years pretending to be something I was not, losing myself to the fake smiles and masks I wore for her benefit. It never made her love me though. I was never enough.' Mallux swallows hard, eyes on the dirt beneath his feet.

Despite herself, Telium's heart aches for him, for the small child he had been, desperately trying to earn the love his mother should have showered him with as her son. 'Why are you telling me this?' she whispers.

'Because I know what it is to pretend to be something you are not, the strain it puts on your heart. They may shun people like us, frightened of our blades and our violence. But we are the first they come to when trouble arrives. We are the people who step up and do what must be done.'

A muscle feathers in his jaw and Telium reaches out, brushing her fingers across the back of his clenched hand, offering what small comfort she can. One outcast to another. His hand engulfs her smaller one. It is warm and rough.

She had not realised they have trailed to a stop. Around them, the wind continues to skitter through the trees and grass, even as the sun beats down on them.

Telium stands still, barely breathing, as Mallux lifts their entwined hands to his lips, brushing his mouth across her knuckles, sea-blue eyes never leaving her face. Heat scores across the back of her hand and she fights a shiver at the feather-light touch.

'What I am telling you, *upa*,' Mallux says as he leans forward, 'is that your powers do not frighten me. They are exactly what I need.' Abruptly, he drops her hand and steps back.

When his eyes leave her face, Telium's breath rushes out of her. 'I'm sorry about your mother. No child should have to earn their parents' love.'

Mallux shrugs, throwing her a charming smile, and the moment shatters.

CHAPTER
26

'*Kah.*' Mallux's words are a whispered hiss.

He tenses up at the sight of the Fae that march around the corner of the dusty road.

Telium's Gifts prickle, but she concentrates on keeping her head down, her posture unthreatening – a human slave following her master. Still, she is acutely aware of the tramp of boots as the gaurds approach.

They had been travelling for near a week now without trouble. She just hopes they will not notice her pack looks about as heavy as Mallux's. When they are outside towns they distribute the load evenly between them.

As the soldiers approach, Telium hangs back in the shadow of Mallux's body. Keeping the net of her mind spread wide as she tracks them. Beneath the sound of boots crunching, insects form a low chorus of hums in the dry summer air. She feels when the Fae come within reach, the empty pockets of their guarded minds moving along at a steady pace.

As they pass each other, one of the warriors scrutinises Telium. His gaze prickles across her skin, but she refuses to look up. Just as he is about to pass from her periphery he pulls up short.

'Hey! You cannot have—'

His words are cut short as Mallux spins with frightening speed, sinking his blade into the warrior's stomach. The male gasps as if surprised, looking down at the blade. Telium can see the tip protruding from his back.

Another male, who she supposes is the leader, looks Mallux full in the face. Shock and rage cross his features.

'*You*,' he snarls, before Mallux launches himself at the Fae.

The next few minutes are a blur of steel and flesh. Mallux and the captain clash blades. One of the female Fae moves to intervene, and Telium looses a throwing dagger at her. But she misjudges the Fae's quick reflexes and merely delivers her a glancing blow to the shoulder.

With a snarl, the female rounds on her. Two of her companions, also realising that Mallux is not the only threat of the pair, joins her in the attack. They approach Telium with blades drawn. Her Gifts snarl in savage glee, sending a shiver down her spine as they unfurl under her skin.

The battle is short but vicious. Telium pulls out her haladie. The blade's strange shape often gives her an advantage; her opponents used to fighting against swords or poleaxes. This time is no different. The female is dispatched with a slashing blow that flays open her face. Next, a stab pushes Telium's blade through a male's eye, blood spurting as she wrenches it free. Turning on her final opponent, Telium deflects a flurry of blows. His blade tears the fabric at her shoulder before she steps past his guard. Ramming her haladie into his gut, she carves it upwards, opening the Fae from pelvis to sternum.

Dancing back from the male as he collapses, Telium looks around. She stands victorious over the Fae as, a few feet away, Mallux rises from his defensive stance.

Her breaths come in harsh pants, the air scraping up her

throat as she sucks in lungfuls of warm summer air. Beside her, Mallux twists his wrist, flicking his broadsword that is red with blood. It is also splattered across his chest and face, yet he pays it no mind.

Telium concentrates on levelling out her breathing, forcing herself to take long deep inhales. Her heartbeat returns to its normal rhythm and her muscles begin to relax. Her Gifts seethe under her skin as if annoyed they were not a bigger part of the bloodshed.

Looking about the clearing, she counts seven bodies cooling in the dirt, their blood coating the air with its metallic smell. Three slain by her hand and the other four by Mallux. She runs an appreciative eye over him. She knew of his skill, of course, but it is another thing completely to see it in action. Inhuman speed and strength make the Fae formidable opponents.

Wiping her blade on her pants, Telium sheathes her haladie and focuses on Mallux.

As the adrenaline of the battle wears off, a throbbing in her shoulder makes itself apparent. Frowning, she glances down to see a tear through her shirt. A line of blood marks where the final male's blade caught her. She pulls the fabric away from the wound, hissing through her teeth at the sting.

The noise draws Mallux's eyes. He is at her side in an instant. 'You are hurt.'

Telium is about to shoot back a sarcastic retort at his observation skills, still pissy about the situation in the Infri Pass. But when she looks up at him, the words catch in her throat.

Heat radiates off him in waves – primal male aggression at her being hurt, though the male responsible lies dead just a few feet away. A strange feeling hits her low in the gut and she swallows at the sudden rush his nearness brings. Damn it, she had been so busy trying to ensure her Gifts did not rage out of control, that she paid little attention to her emotions, and they are now running wild. Trigg would have scolded her from now until Tenebris came at her lack of control.

I'm still mad at you, she tries to say. Though for what, she isn't sure. He was not to blame for the slave women's sacrifices.

Swallowing, Telium watches Mallux's eyes follow the movement of her throat with razor focus, before lazily tracking up to her lips. Her heart jumps up into her throat and her lips part as her breath rushes out.

She has caught him looking at her like this before but has always managed to pull her gaze away before anything happened. This last week, she has held her ire between them like a shield. Now, it seems invisible hands hold her in place while butterflies dance in her stomach.

Mallux tosses his blade to the side with deliberate slowness and steps towards her. He is so close his breath whispers over her skin. Caught in the moment, she dares not move as his hands graze up her arms to grip her biceps. His massive hands easily encircle her entire arm. He hesitates a moment and looks at her as if asking for permission.

Telium returns his gaze without wavering before her traitorous eyes drop to his lips.

Mallux squeezes her arms in response, before pushing her back and ducking his head so his lips are a hair's-breadth from hers. Desire rages through her. His lips stay there, tantalisingly close, as he walks her back until she fetches up against a tree. The rough wood against her back is a shock. A gasp escapes her lips.

His nose dips to her neck. When it skims across the soft skin there, her toes curl. It sets all her nerve endings on fire. When Mallux licks the place his nose grazed, her eyes roll back in her head. A moan escapes and her hands fist in his shirt front. It is as if his touch has opened the floodgates of her lust.

More, she wants more.

Telium tips her chin up, giving him better access as he grazes his lips up to her jawline. Her lips part on a sigh.

Suddenly, he lets go of her arms. He pushes his body up against her, wedging her between him and the tree. She makes a rather undignified sound as she feels every inch of his hard body press against her and she slips her hands under his shirt, spreading her fingers over the smooth skin of his back. His hands roam up and down her sides as if memorising the feel of her curves.

If it were not for the young lord back in Lampart, Telium would have thought her body is responding this way because it had been so long. But it isn't. It is Mallux. There is something about him that is so intoxicating, she is unable to resist his call.

With his body crushed against her, she cannot think straight. She stands on her toes, searching for his lips with her own. With a growl, he fists a hand in her hair and tilts her head back, ducking his—

Without warning, Mallux pulls away from her, body tensing up. She feels him loosen his hold on her and lean back slightly. She looks up at him in confusion, lust-fogged brain uncomprehending. Mallux has his head cocked to the side, eyes far away as if listening intently to something.

'What—' she starts, but Mallux hushes her.

Telium frowns, struggling to fight off the haze surrounding her. Concentrating, she can soon hear the pounding of hooves.

Mallux turns back and places his forehead on hers, cursing colourfully. He roughly grinds his hips against her in frustration. The sensation causes her to gasp again and a sly smile spreads across his face. 'This isn't over, *upa.*' His promise brushes against her lips.

The air is cool on her skin as Mallux steps back, running his hands through his hair. Pressing a hand to the rough bark behind her, Telium steadies herself, attempting to squash the desire to use one of her hidden blades to slash the shirt right off Mallux's chest and carry on, approaching riders be damned.

He must have been able to read the yearning and frustration in her eyes because Mallux gives a husky laugh before turning away to collect his discarded blade.

Clenching her jaw so tight her teeth grind, Telium takes a deep, steadying breath through her nose before stalking a few steps away from Mallux, taking up position opposite him on the road. Silently cursing their bad luck, she keeps her hands close to her blades. The seven bodies on the path are glaringly obvious and they do not have the time to hide either themselves or the evidence.

Peace, Telium thinks, *I just want some cursed peace.* She craves the quiet of her forest, the calming darkness of the night under the boughs of the ancient trees. But there is a deeper part of her, one she is not willing to face quite yet, that tells her perhaps it was not the isolation that caused her peace but being among those who did not baulk from her darkness. Telium shies away from that train of thought.

A pair of horses come thundering around the corner. The two approaching Fae pull their mounts up short when they see the massacre. The lead rider curses and draws a blade from his belt, while his companion, a beautiful female with ebony locks, quickly knocks an arrow onto her bow. The weapon is lovely: carved with patterns up and down the length of it, the arrows fletched with snowy white feathers. A far more graceful weapon than Telium's bow that she left behind in her forest.

After a tense moment, Mallux gives a shout and steps forward. His gigantic blade is still sheathed at his side and he holds his hands up in the air. Telium tenses, unsure what Mallux is doing, preparing herself for a fight.

When the Fae female sees Mallux, her face splits into a grin and she lowers her weapon. 'Mallux!' she cries, jumping down from her mount.

'Lotte.' He smiles and starts forward. When they embrace, Telium's jaw flexes with a flicker of annoyance.

'*Vel thruik,* Mallux,' the other Fae calls.

Well met. Telium translates the Fae greeting, having picked up a few phrases during their times in town.

The Fae sheathes his blade and swings down from his horse. He is handsome, as all Fae are – sun-kissed with warm hazel eyes and hair the colour of strong black tea. He regards Telium who returns his gaze without blinking.

'*Vel thruik,* Hermitch,' Mallux replies, letting go of Lotte to clasp forearms with the male. 'What are you doing here?' He looks between the two newcomers.

'We were on our way from Polr'mine to Fexio,' Hermitch replies, raising an eye at Mallux's use of the Common Tongue, before glancing to Telium. 'To spread the word, but Lotte had a vision, so we decided to take a detour.'

Telium doesn't know these places or people they speak of, but her ears prick up at the word *vision.* She tucks the information away, eyeing the female across from her. Telium quietly observes the Fae as they chat about how quickly and quietly the word is being spread. Becoming bored, she draws a small throwing dagger and begins cleaning her nails with it.

The whisper of steel catches the attention of Hermitch. He looks over at Telium with keen interest. 'Ah, I see you have found your secret weapon, Mallux.'

Mallux glances over his shoulder at her. 'Yes, this is Telium, the Siren Queen's greatest assassin. The one who they say is kin to the Alkorian Goddess of Death.'

Lotte brushes past Mallux and walks towards Telium, who eyes her approach. Lotte surprises her by sticking out a hand for Telium to shake. Her grin lights up her entire face, making her green eyes shine. Really, she is more beautiful than any being has a right to be. Still, Telium takes her hand with bemusement and shakes it.

'*Vel thruik*, Telium.' The female's lyrical Fae accent hugs the vowels. 'I am Lottemeka. But you may call me Lotte; everyone does.' The Fae switches seamlessly to the Common Tongue. 'You poor thing having to travel with my *sk'ril* of a cousin. Goodness, your eyes are strange! How beautiful.'

Something eases in Telium's chest at the female's words. Lotte leans forward to look closer at Telium's eyes and she cannot help but grin at the Fae's eccentric chatter and bold manner. There is something instantly likable about the female.

'Thank you, Lotte. It is nice to meet you too.'

'Siren Queen, you say?' Hermitch pipes up, looking from Telium to Mallux, 'Does—'

'*De ves tor mesisil?*' Mallux is quick to interrupt. 'We do not have time to satisfy your incessant curiosity now, Hermitch. Here, help me dig a hole so we can get these men off the road. Telium, search the bodies for anything useful. Lotte, come here a moment, would you?'

Lotte rolls her eyes at Telium and grins before trotting off toward the two males. The three Fae lower their heads and huddle together as Mallux speaks to the other two. Apart from a word or two, Telium cannot decipher the Old Fae.

The authority in Mallux's tone makes Telium's hackles rise, but she cannot deny that she was planning to search the bodies for anything useful anyway. With a long-suffering sigh, she goes and crouches by the closest body and removes the dead male's weapon belt which has a sheath for his sword and dagger.

She discovers a small velvet pouch tucked away in the waistband of the fallen Fae's trousers. The clink of coins brings a smile to Telium's lips. Peeking inside, a scrap of cloth catches her attention and she pulls it out. Once unrolled, it is about the size of her outstretched hand. There is a portrait of a female that has been roughly painted on the square of fabric. Flame-red hair cascades around the female's shoulders and her soft, brown eyes are warm and smiling. A slight gap in her front teeth gives her an endearing look. The paint is faded and peeling like it has been handled repeatedly.

With a pang of sadness, Telium realises the female must be this male's wife. With a silent prayer for the slain male and an apology to the female, she rolls up the painting and replaces it in the male's tunic.

The last of Mallux's hushed conversation floats by her. Though she doesn't understand his words, the way the Old Fae rolls off his tongue is pleasing to her ears.

Looking up, Telium sees the pair nod. As Hermitch walks off to find a spot to bury the guards, he throws a contemplative glance over his shoulder at Telium. She studies him, trying to read the meaning behind his look, but he disappears between the trees.

Lotte joins her in stripping the bodies of anything useful. Once they are done, they drag the bodies over to the hole the males have dug, before returning and removing any signs of their conflict. It is hot, morbid work as the sun makes its trip across the sky and Telium is covered in a light sheen of sweat by the time they are done.

They mount their horses and ride for a few hours in silence,

Lotte behind Hermitch and Telium behind Mallux. The latter both try to ignore the closeness of their bodies, the spots where they touch.

Before the sun sets, they make camp. Lotte chatters endlessly as they eat. Telium is surprised the female manages to eat anything with the amount she is talking. Her behaviour is a stark contrast to Mallux's normally quiet presence.

Telium volunteers to take the first watch. She stands, dusting of the back of her pants.

'*You* don't need to take first watch – that won't be necessary,' Hermitch says.

Though his voice is flat, Telium can see the distrust lighting his brown eyes. She turns to look at the Fae where he is lounging, forearms propped on his knees. Taking a steadying breath to calm her ire, Telium opens her mouth to reply.

'Telium and I have shared watch shifts since we arrived in Thresiel,' Mallux says in the Common Tongue. 'You can trust she won't be amiss.'

Telium's eyes travel between Mallux and Hermitch, trying to gauge their relationship. The brown-haired male doesn't even bat an eyelid. There is nothing but respect in his eyes as he looks at Mallux and dips his head in agreement.

Telium raises an eyebrow at the exchange but says nothing. *Interesting.*

She moves well out of the circle of the firelight and scrambles halfway up a tree. Leaning back, she nestles into the nook between the branch and the trunk, scanning the forest with her eyes and ears and mind.

When the fire has burned down to embers, Mallux rises from his bed-roll and wanders in her direction. Telium is delighted when he walks right beneath her. She drops to the forest floor; Mallux starts and spins with unnatural speed, hand already on his half-drawn blade. When he sees Telium, he rises from his defensive crouch.

She snorts in amusement. Some great warrior he is. 'You should look up. I could have killed you,' she says, smirking.

It is Mallux's turn to snort, the sound oozing Fae arrogance. 'It would take a lot more than your slight body to kill me,' he replies haughtily.

I bet you a blade to the back of the neck would do the job, she thinks. But she merely hums in reply.

'You should sleep,' Mallux says, nodding towards his bed-roll.

The thought of lying down, the fabric still warm with his body heat and smelling of him makes her heart beat a little faster. Mallux must sense it because a sly, sensual smile curves his lips and he steps closer.

'Unless,' he murmurs, 'you would like to continue where we left off?'

Heat pools in her core at the thought. 'What did Hermitch mean when he said Lotte had a vision?' she blurts.

Just like that, the spell is broken. Mallux shifts back slightly, allowing her to breathe normally again.

'Lotte is an *Ochic'a* – an Eye; she has powers of foresight. Some *Ochic'as* can see visions of future events, while others, like Lotte, can see future visions of a person they have come into contact with. The more contact they have with that person, the more likely they are to have a vision of them.'

The thought unsettles Telium who has no wish to know her future or tamper with fate. The memory of her handshake with Lotte flashes in her mind. 'Does Lotte have to physically touch a person to have these visions?'

'Yes,' Mallux replies. 'There are very few Eyes powerful enough to have visions of a person without skin-to-skin contact.'

Telium makes a mental note to keep her distance from the female, not wanting to know what things Lotte may see in her future. She hums in contemplation, tilting her head back to look at the stars peeking through the branches of the trees.

Her previous ire has evaporated in the heat of Mallux's passion. She can't find it in her to dredge it up again. She can feel Mallux's eyes on her, tracking over her neck and lips.

Fighting off her lustful thoughts, she looks over at him with a grin before taking a large, deliberate step backwards. Despite herself, her voice is unintentionally throaty.

'Goodnight, Mallux.'

CHAPTER
27

Trigg is beside her, russet skin shining in the sunlight. They sit by the outer edge of the training arena in the palace grounds, watching the off-duty guards go through drills and sparring. Telium shifts in frustration, wanting to join in.

'Who is your fiercest opponent there?' Trigg asks, pointing to a group of men taking turns wrestling.

Telium pauses a moment, giving the question the thought it deserves.

'Lieutenant Cole,' she says, pointing to the towering redhead.

Trigg nods, black braids swaying. 'And how would you best such a giant?'

'Stay out of range. Don't grapple with him. Sharp quick strikes to pain points and spots of weakness.' Telium lists the plan as if she were reciting lines from a book. 'Specifically, his right knee, which he favours.' She points as the Lieutenant spins. 'There.'

Trigg nods, the only sign of her approval. Pivoting on the stone bench, she turns her attention to a vicious bout of swordplay.

'Who is your fiercest opponent?' she asks again.

Wrestling. Swordplay. Archery. Poleaxes. Trigg quizzes her on it all. Sharpening Telium's mind into a blade of polished steel.

Telium opens her mouth to answer yet another question when Trigg suddenly scrambles away. Trigg's face warps and changes. Her deep-umber skin pales and her lush braids are replaced by dirty brown locks. Telium finds herself staring at the young woman from the passage, who looks at Telium in fear and falls backwards.

Telium starts forward, hands outstretched to help the woman. 'Let me help you. Run! Do not let them keep you a slave.' But the words do not come and Telium can do nothing but scream them uselessly in her head.

'No! P—please, no! Help!' Screeching, the woman continues to scramble away from Telium, screaming herself hoarse.

Telium stares at her hands as her nails blacken and lengthen, turning into talons. Her skin pales to a sickly grey colour as her mouth fills with needle-sharp teeth. Frantically, she tries to clamp down on her Gifts, forcing them into their cages and chains, but they evade her grasp. Telium's panic rises as they slip through her hold like smoke.

The woman at her feet screams and cries hysterically, begging for mercy. Telium backs away from her, desperately trying to push down her black powers, to smother the dark glee rising at their freedom.

Failing, she spins to flee, hoping to outrun the scene, only to collide with Lotte. The female smiles sweetly before catching Telium by the throat, her grip like a vice. Telium slashes at the Fae's face and arms with her talons, but while her skin is flayed apart, she does not bleed. Her wounds open to reveal clean white bone beneath; muscle, blood and tendons nowhere to be seen. Her efforts do not even earn a flinch from Lotte.

Realising her attack is ineffective, Telium stills, dropping her hands to her sides and snarling at Lotte. The female's grin does not waver. She looks at Telium with blank, empty eyes. So at odds with her innocent smile.

'Tenebris Kin,' she whispers.

The words echo all around, the sound of her Goddess' name on the Fae female's lips makes the hair at the back of Telium's neck stand on end.

'Killer of kings. Betrayed by your heart and drowned without water. The end destination for a soul and start of a journey for a heart. He drank her dry and you chase her still. Gifts corrupted and marked – bargains made. Killer of kings. Your darkness will save you and condemn you.'

Visions flash before Telium's eyes. She sees her body on a barren, snowy slope, lips blue and lifeless. Clad in red silk and armour, she stands at the head of an army. Then she is wandering through an endless, black abyss, a keening moan emerging from her throat and a necklace of burning coals around her neck. Sitting atop a throne of ebony and bones. Walking through a field of wildflowers, the sun warming her face. Standing in an endless ocean of sand, the harsh sun beating down on her head as she stares out at a sea of corpses. Draped in chains and spider's silk as a shadow hovers over her body.

Faster and faster the visions come in a whirlwind of colour. They move so fast that she cannot keep up, before disappearing between one moment and the next, the transition so violent that it leaves her head spinning.

Lotte's face warps, becoming sharper and more angular. Her eyes fade to grey and her nails lengthen, digging into Telium's neck. Suddenly she finds herself standing face to face with the Mad Fae King, his face shifts like vapour, never staying the same. One moment he looks like an old man, the next, the young lord from Lampart. Telium has never seen his real face, but she knows in her bones that it is him. He sneers at her, releasing her neck to stroke her hair. 'Pretty Half-Breed,' he slurs.

With a snarl, Telium grasps his wrist, twisting savagely, the resulting snap makes her laugh with glee. Her Gifts are running rampant. The King screams and she turns, bringing her sharp claws up under his ribcage. He collapses to the floor and she follows him, crouching on his chest and ripping at him. Bloods splatters her face and clothes but she pays them no mind until she reaches his heart. She digs her talons in, feeling the warm gush of his life-blood slipping through her fingers as she pulls the organ out. She brings it to her lips and places a smacking kiss on it, laughing at the King's demise.

From behind, she hears someone shout her name. She spins, only to find Tenebris, her Dark Goddess holding Mallux in her shadowy tentacles. They wrap around his legs and pin his arms to his body, leaving him helpless to her ministrations.

The Goddess circles around the Fae, her hips swaying hypnotically. With each rotation, Tenebris places a kiss on his mouth, and from her lips black smoke curls and pierces Mallux's face. The blackness threads itself through flesh, entering through his cheek and popping out through the bottom of his jaw before twisting itself up in a neat little knot. The darkness then hardens and shines like steel. By her fourth rotation, Tenebris has his mouth completely wired shut.

Mallux glares at the Goddess with hatred before turning his eyes on Telium. When she meets his stare, lust hits her like a blow to the gut. His seductive gaze fills her vision until that is all she can see. She is drowning in the blue of his eyes. She takes a step backward and her calves hit the edge of a bed. Suddenly, Mallux is there in front of her, shirtless, wet hair mussed; gone are the ties from his mouth, and instead, his lips curve in a sinful smile. His hands grip her arms and he slowly lowers her to the bed. When she is lying back, he smiles and clambers into the bed next to her, leans over and puts his mouth close to hers.

'Fae Thief,' *he whispers.*

CHAPTER
28

With a jolt, Telium wakes, blanket tangled about her body and skin sticky with sweat. Scrubbing her hands across her face, she fights the urge to groan in frustration. Her heart flutters in her chest and her hands are clammy.

Tenebris has never appeared to her in a dream before. Something had shifted; when the slave woman appeared before her, the dream had lost its fuzziness and came into razor-sharp focus. It was so lifelike that Telium could feel the phantom claws at her fingertips, hear the woman's screams still ringing in her ears. Telium feared if she had tried to wake from it, she would have found herself trapped.

Shaking off the ominous feeling the dream has left behind, Telium untangles herself from the blankets. With a sigh, she sits up and looks around the camp. Mallux must have woken Hermitch for the next watch and decided he liked the look of the other male's bed, because he is now lying on his friend's bed-roll, snoring softly. Lotte does not look like she has been disturbed all night.

The sun has barely poked above the horizon, but Telium gets up and moves about the camp, packing up the bed-roll and drawing on her Gifts to heat some water in her flask, like she has many times since their travels began. She pulls some herbs and a cup out of her pack and once the water is warm, she tips it into the cup along with the herbs. Steam curls up into the morning air.

A soft gasp alerts her; across the now-cold firepit, Lotte has propped herself up onto her elbow and is watching Telium with rapt attention.

'It is true,' she breathes. 'You do have Power.'

Telium's recent dream flashes in her mind again – Lotte's hands around her throat. She rolls her shoulders, banishing the thought. The female has been nothing but kind to her. She offers Lotte a crooked smile. 'In Alkoria, we call them Gifts.'

'Are you an *A'gnis?*' the female asks, sitting up and running her fingers through her black hair.

'A what?'

'*A'gnis.*' She repeats the word as if its meaning is obvious. When Telium does not reply she adds, 'You can create fire.'

'Oh.' Telium huffs. 'No, I cannot create fires. I could use my Gifts to encourage dry grass to light, but I cannot create fire from nothing.'

'Can you control the fire with your ... Gifts?'

Telium shakes her head, handing Lotte a steaming cup of tea. The female takes the proffered cup and takes a swig. Telium notes the way Lotte drinks without hesitation. She could have put anything in it. Maybe Fae are not susceptible to poisons the way humans are. 'No,' Telium replies, 'I could perhaps smother a small fire. But I cannot *control* the way it rages. Can your *A'gnis* do this?'

'Yes,' Lotte says and shrugs. 'To a varying degree, depending on their strength. They can create fire using the Power from their body. Some can only manage a small flame, perhaps a bit larger than an apple; others can engulf their entire body in flame and yet not suffer so much as a singed hair. They can manipulate a flame large enough to burn a house. I am told the skill takes years to master, and Fae with the Power tend to have a temper that burns as hot as the blazes they manipulate.'

Lotte snorts to herself at the last bit and Telium cannot help but huff out a dry laugh. Although she will endeavour to avoid physical contact with the female, she cannot help but like her lively and witty conversation.

'What are you two talking about?'

Mallux's voice causes Lotte to jump. He had been so still, they thought he was still asleep.

Lotte quirks an eyebrow at her cousin, crosses her legs neatly under herself and takes a dainty sip from her cup. 'This and that,' she replies, grinning at Mallux's obvious annoyance.

'Well, I would not want to interrupt your incessant need for chatter,' Mallux fires back, rolling onto his back and stretching his arms above his head. Telium's eyes slide over those black rings inked around his forearm.

Lotte fakes an indignant gasp. 'I do *not chatter!*'

'Oh really?' Mallux continues to taunt her, grinning with glee that Lotte has taken the bait. 'What about the time you ...'

Telium tunes out their friendly bantering. The two are more like siblings than cousins. As they bicker, she wonders about the Fae and their Gifts. Mallux had told her that while they are more powerful than those of the Alkorian Thieves, they are far fewer in number. She wonders just how many 'Gifted' Fae the King has at his disposal. *How will I recognise them?* she thinks.

Telium scrutinises Lotte from the corner of her eye. Nothing about the Fae seems different compared to her companions. No physical differences mark her out as being Gifted.

'How can you tell who are Gifted Fae and who are not? Could you spot one in a crowd?'

'You cannot.' Hermitch appears from between the trees, shooting a dark look at his friend who has made himself at home in his bed-roll. Mallux ignores him, pretending he hasn't noticed.

'Some Fae,' Hermitch continues, 'can be picked out by characteristics, like the way *Cirrus* tend to be wanderers, too restless to stay in one place for too long. Or how a *Ha'lau* is stubborn.'

'The way an *Ohic'a* is a know-it-all,' Mallux adds, tossing a pebble at Lotte.

Lotte opens her mouth to snap back a reply, but Telium beats her to it. 'So, how will I know who are Gifted and who are ordinary Fae when we fight the King if they all look the same?'

'Royals and their guards are marked with their station and their Power,' Mallux replies. 'Anyone with Power guarding the King will be marked with a coloured band stitched into the forearm of their uniform. White for *Cirrus* who command the wind, blue for the *Altums* who can bring water to heel, red for *A'gnis* and so on. Many civilians favour the trend, and you will see *Ka'hine* with decorative armbands to denote their affinity.'

As Mallux speaks, Lotte lifts her left arm, turning it this way and that. Tied around her forearm is a purple ribbon, braided through with silver thread. It catches the light and glimmers in the rising sun. Telium hums in contemplation as she tries to decide whether this newest bit of information will be an advantage or a pitfall.

'Come,' Hermitch says, his voice solemn as ever.

As they move about the camp, packing away their things, Lotte sidles over to Telium who flinches away as the Fae reaches a hand out to her. A flash of hurt crosses Lotte's face at Telium's reaction. 'Can you tell your Gifted apart from normal mortals?' Lotte asks.

'Yes,' Telium says, 'in a way.'

Lotte waits for her to elaborate.

Telium shrugs one shoulder and hefts her bed-roll. 'Power-Thieves are always draped with precious jewels. Blood-Thieves' are always guant and a bit dour, no matter how long they spend in the sun. A Mind-Thief looks …' she trails off, pursing her lips as she searches for the best word, 'shaggy.'

Lotte chortles with laughter at that.

They finish packing up camp, covering the remains of their camp fire lest anyone come across the clearing, before mounting up, two astride each horse, and heading towards the next town. Telium and Mallux awkwardly avoid each other's eyes. Telium tries to ignore the way they are pressed up against each other, her chest flush against his broad back and her thighs hugging his.

Lotte and Hermitch decide to travel with them to the next town before splitting off and travelling to Fexio. That is, *Lotte* decides; Hermitch seems to have no say in the matter. Lotte demands Hermitch keep his mount close to Mallux and Telium's so she can continue her endless chatter.

Telium listens politely as Lotte speaks about her childhood and her schooling, how she learnt to control her Powers, and her joy when she realised she was *Ka'hine*.

'When did you realise you had Power, Telium?' Lotte asks.

The question seems offhand, yet it puts Telium on edge. Mallux looks over his shoulder, awaiting her answer. Telium studiously ignores his gaze. 'My Gifts started to manifest not long before my twenty-first winter.' Out of the corner of her eye, she sees Hermitch and Mallux exchange a glance.

Lotte nods, either not noticing or caring about the two males' silent conversation. 'It is the same with all Fae.'

But Thieves come into their Gifts much younger than that, Telium thinks. *What makes me the exception?* If a child has not shown signs of a Thief-Gift by their sixteenth winter, parents can kiss goodbye to the dream of lavish living funded by their child's Gifts. She keeps her lips sealed, for some reason not wanting to share this information with these Fae. Instead of replying, she turns her eyes to the sky and stretches out her consciousness, letting her mind drift.

By the end of the evening, the shadowy outline of the next town comes into view. Within a few hours, they have reached the outer limits of the buildings. When they all dismount, Mallux clears his throat. 'Lotte, perhaps it would be best to assume Telium is your handmaiden. It will not look so suspicious if she is to have a bed that way.'

CHAPTER

29

The last of the sun's light bleeds from the sky as the four of them make their way into town. Lights shine in the windows of homes and the sound of a fiddle playing a vigorous tune tumbles down the main road toward them.

Telium pretends not to hear Mallux's words, pushing aside her anger as she takes the shawl to cover her hair. She notes the way Mallux's hands twitch as if he is about to help her.

'Excellent,' Lotte says at Mallux's suggestion. 'She will have a room with me, of course. You two old *lotos* can have your own.' She turns to Telium, barely taking air between sentences. 'Have you ever tried to dye it? Your hair, I mean. We have a paste we make – *rai'na* – that lets us put colour into our hair for special occasions. It lasts until it gets wet and then rinses out. I would imagine everyone will be buying it for the King's— ouch!' Lotte slaps Hermitch's hand away from her arm. 'For the celebration.'

'Will you stop chattering?' Hermitch murmurs, seeing Telium's eyes on him.

They move on through the town until they reach the inn, Telium trailing dutifully behind Lotte as they enter. They pay for their two private rooms and request supper to be sent up.

'Oh, and, girl?' Lotte calls after the retreating young Fae. 'We have had a hard day's ride. Make sure they are good portions.' She turns and winks at Telium before sweeping up the stairs. 'We will share a meal,' she whispers.

Telium bristles at the implication that she is not included in the meal purchase because she is a 'slave'. *No more,* she thinks, *after this, my people will be free.*

They settle into their rooms which are small but clean and have real beds with big soft pillows. Conveniently, there is an adjoining door between their room and the males', which is left unlocked.

Telium spreads her consciousness out, stretching it like a cat in the sun. She feels the stone walls of Mallux's mind alongside Hermitch's. The males' defences feel similar, but Lotte's mind is like trying to look in a mirror with the sun's reflection in it. Pushing her mind out further, she can feel the voids of Fae consciousnesses in the rooms around and below them.

Many are like Mallux and Hermitch – solid stone fortresses surround their minds with small points of difference to mark their personalities. A Fae below feels like they have a moat around their mind. There is one in the dining room that Telium swears she can *hear* the rustle of feathers atop his walls.

Her searching is interrupted by Lotte kicking off her boots and flopping onto one of the beds with a dramatic sigh. 'Gracious, I *despise* sleeping on bed-rolls,' she says as she snuggles into the softness of the mattress.

'Not one for the road, then,' Telium notes.

'I would like to say I do not have a taste for lovely things, but that would be an untruth. Mallux, on the other hand, cannot deny his taste for unique, beautiful things. It is entirely his father's fault, of course. Spoiled him to the core in the palace. But then, who could deny such sweet comforts? Surely you prefer this to a hard bed-roll, Telium? Ohhh! Tomorrow we shall go to the market and find some *rai'na* for your hair!'

Lotte squeals at the prospect but Telium's ears have pricked up on Lotte's mention of Mallux. 'Palace?' she questions, 'Mallux was raised in the palace?'

Lotte looks over at her with big eyes, opening her mouth to answer. 'He—'

The banging of the door between their rooms interrupts her. Mallux strides into the room, throwing a daggered glance his cousin's way. '… Was merely a distant cousin to the Ivory Crown,' he finishes for Lotte.

Telium quirks an eyebrow at him. Mallux shrugs as he moves aside for Hermitch, who leans against the doorframe, folding his arms across his muscular chest.

'My father was married to the Queen's younger sister.' Mallux clarifies. 'Hardly royal by any count, but the sisters had an unbreakable bond, and when the Queen's sister recognised my father as her *Wai'tan*, the pair were inseparable. So, I grew up on the palace grounds, getting underfoot as a child with my friends. Then as I grew older, getting into other … mischief.'

Telium can guess *exactly* what type of trouble he got into. With his gaze on her, the room suddenly becomes too small and hot with all these bodies in it. Her pulse races. She can feel it flutter at the base of her throat. Mallux's nostrils flare and his eyes track down her neck to the sensitive space of skin where her heart thumps.

A knock on the door breaks the silence. Mallux's eyes slide away from her to the door. A flush rushes to Telium's cheeks as she remembers Lotte and Hermitch are still in the room while they have been undressing each other with their gazes. She frowns as her mind clears, trying to map out the family tree in her head, and where Mallux sits in it. Having the Queen as your aunt, even by marriage, didn't seem like a trifling thing.

Telium jumps to her feet, attempting to hide the heat in her face. She crosses to the door quickly and opens it. The smell of meat and vegetables greets her. The young Fae girl from before hands her a tray loaded with plates piled high with food and mugs of ale. Taking the enormous tray from her, Telium turns, struggling to close the door with her hip, the crockery clinking softly as she moves.

Hermitch nudges Mallux forward. Telium deliberately avoids his eyes as he picks up a mug and a plate to hand to Hermitch. He then collects his own and retreats to the corner where he perches on a stool in front of a small mirror and basin.

The sight of his towering frame hunched onto the tiny seat makes her lips twitch. The small stool groans with his every move. Telium perches next to Lotte on her bed, balancing the tray of food on the soft surface between them. They pick at the generous plate of food together. Telium declines the ale.

They speak in quiet tones about their plans going ahead. Lotte and Hermitch have a few more towns to travel to where they will gather the last remnants of their rebellion before heading to the capital: Meannthe. Mallux and Telium will leave here after gathering more supplies and head to a small encampment of rebel soldiers hidden in a valley a few days' travel from here.

There, Mallux will coordinate with leaders before the army disperses to travel across the country, regrouping in secret in Meannthe.

Excitement and apprehension flutter in Telium's heart. The plan is beautiful in its simplicity but all the more deadly for it. There is no backup. No escape routes or reinforcements.

It does not take long for their conversation to peter out.

Lotte sits sprawled out with her head resting against the wall, her beautiful raven hair spread about her. Hermitch perches on the foot of Telium's bed and shifts restlessly, looking uncomfortable in the small space of the room.

Telium's eyes trail over to Mallux, finding his gaze already on her. The air between them zings with tension. Forcing her eyes away, she busies herself collecting the empty plates and cups and returns them to the tray.

Telium carries the dirty dishes to the door, intending to take it downstairs, but Hermitch comes up behind her. '*Niya*, Telium.' He takes the tray from her hands, careful to avoid touching her. 'It would be unwise for you to wander alone.'

Telium is about to protest, thinking if they are to make this whole human slave illusion convincing, then she should be the one to take it, but Lotte interrupts her. 'Oh, let them go, Telium. The old *lotos* can go downstairs to catch up.' She stands and flicks her hand dismissively at the two males. 'I, for one, would like to get some sleep, not listen to them drivel endlessly.'

Mallux glares at his cousin, but there was no real venom behind it. Then crosses to the threshold where Telium stands by the open door.

Mallux pauses a moment before saying, '*Vel,* Hermitch is right. It is not safe for you here; I think it is best you stay here with Lotte and not go … wandering after dark.'

His meaning is clear; he knows about her antics in Lampart. Not to mention when she snuck off to hunt down those bandits. She fights the blush trying to rise to her cheeks, tapping her fingers on her empty thigh where her dagger usually sits. She nods in agreement and watches as he disappears down the hall.

CHAPTER
30

The next morning, Lotte heads to the markets with Telium in tow under the guise of her handmaiden. They purchase some more food for the journey before Lotte stops at a stall full of interesting trinkets. Telium is standing quietly behind her, careful to keep her face expressionless, when her Gifts give a mighty surge, straining against their confines. Telium nearly chokes on the effort of keeping them under control. Something catches her eye in the corner of her vision. Her head snaps to the side, bicoloured gaze scanning the crowd with razor focus.

Nothing seems out of the ordinary. Fae are going about their business in the square as normal. She notes the bustle of colour and smells, a glint of silver in someone's dark hair, shouts echoing between the buildings.

Turning her attention back to Lotte, who has made a purchase and is moving on, Telium swears her Gifts give a contented sigh before settling back into the corner of her mind. She can't help glancing around one more time, trying to see what is the cause of her Gifts' reaction.

Baffled, Telium shadows Lotte's steps as they wind through the crowd.

'Is Thresiel really so vast that you could hide a large group of Fae?' Telium asks once the crush of people thins.

Lotte glances backwards at her, green eyes bright in the morning sun.

'I suppose you could, but Mallux would not take such a risk. He has recruited a trio of *Ra'sito* to help conceal the camp. How he found one, let alone three, is a feat in itself – they are rarer than *Tia'tums!*'

'Teyatum?' Telium asks, taking one of Lotte's paper-wrapped parcels from her.

Lotte shakes her head. *'Tee-ah tum,'* she says, drawing out the sounds. 'They, *hmm,* how do I say this? Reflect. No ...' she holds out her free arm across her body, fist clenched. 'You use it with a sword to protect yourself.'

'Oh.' Telium understands. 'A shield.'

'Vel, shield.'

'Mallux said he was to send a runner ahead of us, because they needed time to mobilise?' Telium asks, jumping at the chance to gather more information from someone other than Mallux.

Lotte stays silent a moment as a small group of Fae passes them. Once they are out of earshot she replies quietly.

'The camp has been sitting stagnant for more than two moons awaiting his return. Such a large amount of Fae will take time to prepare for the coming journey.'

They round a corner and head for the inn to meet up with Mallux and Hermitch, who have spent the morning going through their plans.

'So you and Hermitch are spreading the word of his return?' Telium clarifies.

'Amongst others.'

Telium stays silent, not wanting to push her luck. Too

many questions may make Lotte suspicious of her, even if Telium is only asking them to fill the gaps in her knowledge.

They pick up Mallux and Hermitch, who are waiting out the front of the immaculately carved door.

Not a single side glance or guarded look, Telium notes as they move through town.

'How?' Telium wonders out loud. When Hermitch casts her a look, she shrugs a shoulder. 'Such an undertaking must have taken moons, winters, even.'

Hermitch snorts. 'You are merely seeing the tail end of *many* winters of work, Assassin.' He boasts, 'Winters slowly infiltrating every town, city and farm. Sifting out those who are loyal, and those who are not.'

His Fae accent is thicker than that of Mallux or Lotte, his voice hugging every vowel and drawing it out slightly as if he were holding the words on the back of his tongue.

Telium looks across at Mallux. The whole ordeal must have taken great stealth and skill to pull off. She is just the cherry on top of this entire plan. Something tells her that if Mallux had returned without her, he would have still managed to rally his people to make a stand.

How he manages to direct and inspire is a mystery to Telium, who has neither the drive nor passion to lead. She peeks sideways at him as they walk, only half-listening to Lotte's endless chatter. A clever and brave mind, indeed. She just hopes they can pull the scheme off.

They walk the horses to the edge of town where they wait under the shade of a large tree. The day is already warming up. Though they are all used to such temperatures, sweat still beads Telium's forehead along the line of her headscarf. Lotte continues with her cheerful talk, requiring only a grunt or nod from her companions before continuing.

The clop of hooves announces a young Fae who vaults off his mount to stand in front of Mallux. Nervous excitement pulses off the Fae in waves. With bright blond hair and warm brown eyes, he is perhaps, Telium thinks, the youngest-looking Fae she has seen. If he were human, she would have guessed him to be in his late teens, drawing close to the cusp of manhood.

'*Rel sekta,*' the youth proclaims, grinning like a fiend.

'*Bonai,*' Mallux says, his voice all business. He throws his arm around the youth's shoulders, walking a distance away from the others as he continues to murmur to him in lyrical Old Fae, pointing towards the direction they are headed.

'Telium.' Lotte's voice draws her attention from the two Fae. When Telium turns, the female has her hands outstretched, a small, corked glass vial nestled between them. It glints in the sunlight and smells faintly of aniseed. 'I got this for you at the markets. It's *rai'na* – dye. For your hair. Black. I thought you would want something inconspicuous. Although I would have much rather bought a beautiful purple for you.'

'A gift? For me?' Telium is stunned beyond words. Besides Trigg and her Queen, nobody has ever given her a gift, certainly not someone who knows her so little. Emotion wells in her throat, surprising her.

Lotte nods her head enthusiastically, explaining how to apply the dye to her hair and warning her to wash her hands with crushed *beliark* leaves immediately after to stop the colour from staining them.

'Thank you, Lotte,' Telium whispers in a tight voice. She presses the vial to her chest, looking up at the Fae with a smile. She pulls off her headscarf and wraps it around the fragile bottle, before carefully placing it in her pack. 'I love it,' she adds sincerely.

Telium means it too. Her bone-white hair was often a burden when she was spying or doing other unsavoury tasks for the Siren Queen, and now, with this seemingly endless summer, her hooded cloak is impractical. But Lotte could have given her green *rai'na* for all she cares. She is touched and moved by the female's thoughtfulness. Telium rarely had any friends her age growing up.

A friend, Telium realises with a start. That is very much what Lotte had the potential to mean to her, despite only knowing her for a few days. The female's chatty, lively personality and sunshine smile is so at odds with herself, yet Telium cannot help but be drawn to the Fae's contagious light.

Lotte's smile is like the sun coming out from behind a cloud. It makes her already beautiful face breathtaking. She squeals with joy, jumping up and down like a young girl before wrapping Telium in a crushing hug.

Telium tenses at first, cautious of any contact with the Eye, but quickly realises no skin is bared to her Fae hands and she returns the hug, careful to turn her cheek away. They break apart and Telium gives Lotte a hesitant but genuine smile. Together, they turn at the sound of pounding hooves. The young Fae is urging his horse down the path to carry out his instructions.

Mallux joins them and they say their goodbyes. Hermitch is formal as ever with Telium but claps Mallux heartily on the back. Lotte throws her arms around her cousin, kissing him on the cheek before allowing him to boost her onto her mount. The two Fae wave as they spur their horses forward. Then it is just Telium and Mallux again.

'What did Lottemeka give you?' Mallux enquires as they begin to walk.

'Black *rai'na*. For my hair when we get to the city. She says amongst so many I need not pretend to be a slave. Hiding my ears and the colour of my hair will be enough to help me blend in.'

CHAPTER
31

Telium watches impassively as the man scrambles frantically away from her. His retreat leaves streaks through dust clinging to the floor of the quiet attic room. He is younger than she would have thought. At sixteen winters, she must be half his age.

When the man fetches up against the wall on the other side of the room, he sucks in an odd, gasping breath. His fingers curl into the worn floorboards.

'Y—you've got the wrong man.'

His voice shakes with fear as Telium watches him. She pulls the wine-red covering from the bottom half of her face. There is no point in hiding it. Not with her pale hair a blaring sign; like she has been raised from the Underrealm to do the Siren Queen's bidding.

Telium intentionally walks slowly towards her prey. She watches his nerves fray with every slow, stalking step. Coming apart under the pressure.

Clip.

Clip.

Her boots send up little puffs of dust, sending the motes dancing in the streaks of early morning light that slant through the boarded-up window.

Clip.

Clip.

The man begins to tremble, his body vibrating with fear. Telium stops so close to him her black boots nearly touch the edge of his pant leg. The garments were fine before the man fled upstairs from Telium and scrambled through the dust.

'You have been conspiring to kill the Queen for the past moon.' Telium's voice is dead. 'Don't tell me you did not foresee my coming.'

'We were not planning to kill her!'

The man gasps, slapping a hand over his mouth. His eyes are so wide, Telium can see all the whites in them as he looks up at her, pupils blown out. A muscle in her jaw ticks.

This is too easy.

Trigg had assigned this man as Telium's first solo mission for exactly that reason. The small coup is conspicuous and disorganised, this man heading them merely a spoilt lord playing a game he is ill equipped for. But Telium had not thought it would be this *easy. A simple twisting of words was all it took for him to confess.*

The man is begging now. Pressing himself so hard into the wall the faded, floral tapestry behind him tears away. Telium's face is a mask of blank indifference.

'Get up,' she barks.

The man's mouth snaps closed, cutting off his pleas. When he doesn't move, Telium reaches down and grabs him by the collar, heaving him up. It barely takes any effort. As soon as her fingers curl into the fabric, the man scrambles to his feet.

'There,' Telium says, smoothing down his shirt front. 'Now tidy yourself up, you can't go looking like that.'

In a daze, the man brushes dust from his pant legs. The movements are wooden. His eyes lock with Telium's, looking for something. Hope, perhaps.

'Go where?' he asks. That is definitely hope colouring his tone.

Telium watches as he pats his mussed hair, wondering how such a daft, unassuming man thought he would get away with going against her Queen. Traitorous cowards.

Telium moves closer to him. 'To Tenebris.'

Telium rams the dagger into the back of his neck. The blade scrapes against bone as it severs his spinal cord. When she jerks it free, blood gushes from the wound. It paints the wall in a grue-some streak as he sags back against it. Without a sound, the man slides to the floor like a child's forgotten doll.

Telium is already heading for the door.

∾

She paces across the carpeted floor of the great library. The soft whispers and gentle turning of pages in the distance puts her even more on edge. She attempts to harden her heart against the knowl-edge that a man has died by her own blade. She can still feel the blood between her fingers, viscous and sticky.

Trigg finds Telium in the stacks, eyes bright with unshed tears and an angry, restless energy that makes her movements jerky. As always, her mentor commands the space without effort, her keen eyes missing nothing. Today, Trigg's hair is out of her usual braids, her curls a halo around her head.

'I should just forget him,' Telium says by way of greeting.

'You should not.' Trigg speaks calmly, gently grasping Telium's wrists in her callused hands and guiding her to a seat. 'You should never forget those who have fallen to your skill. To do so would be a great insult to your training, and to yourself. To hurt or kill and forget is the way of a monster.'

'So, I am to let him haunt me endlessly?' Telium snaps, then grumbles an apology at Trigg's sharp look. They often do this, speak without words. But Trigg has known Telium her whole life, she knows that sometimes, words are what she needs.

'No, Telli. We have other ways; ways that show the sacrifice of
their life and the sacrifice of ourselves.'

Trigg stands and turns her back to Telium. She shucks up her
shirt, baring her spine. There, etched on her deep mahogany skin,
is a swirling white tattoo. The patterns whorl and twist like ink
in water, the white standing out starkly against her teacher's muscled back. It starts at the base of her neck, covering her spine and
ending just below her shoulder blades.

How has Telium gone her whole life and never seen this?

'This is my Ta Vir – my penance and my strength.' Trigg's
voice is uncharacteristically solemn.

She drops her shirt and turns back to sit beside Telium.

'It's beautiful,' Telium whispers. It is. She has never seen such
intricate artwork of whirls and lines – a patchwork of ink that
comes together in a violent, beautiful melody.

Trigg nods her agreement; the older assassin was never one for
bashfulness. 'The mark is made with a large needle; the wound
rubbed with salt and ink.' She turns her deep brown eyes on
Telium. 'The pain is ours to remember the cost of our skill. The
colour is for others to remember the cost of crossing us. With it, we
honour our dead and carry the memory of life on our skin.'

Trigg puts her fingers under Telium's chin, tipping her head up
so their gazes meet. Her teacher's touch is maternal and familiar.
It grounds Telium and soothes her ragged emotions. Swallowing,
Telium nods.

'I will not forget,' she promises.

'You will not,' Trigg says, standing. 'Come. We leave for the
Academy tonight. It is time for your Colour to be chosen.'

CHAPTER
32

The sun beats down on the open patch of camp. Despite a large section of the tents being set up in and around the sparse woodland, the heat is still uncomfortable. The camp itself is in an odd limbo of being partially packed. The bare minimum remains: shaggy lean-to tents, cooking pots and fires, carts loaded with supplies.

Telium watches with keen interest as Mallux dispatches his opponent. The young warrior lands flat on his back in the dust with a grunt, hands out in supplication as Mallux presses the tip of his blade to the male's sternum.

Around them, Fae cheer and yell. Mallux sheathes his broadsword, reaching down to help the male up. He grips his forearm and hefts him to his feet. The young male laughs ruefully and shakes his head, nodding at Mallux in acknowledgement of his loss, before retreating out of the circle.

They arrived at the camp in the late morning, three nights after leaving Lotte and Hermitch. Telium had been apprehensive about travelling alone with Mallux after what had transpired between them, but Mallux was distracted, and the

days passed without incident. Telium pretended it didn't dis-
appoint her.

Today, after introducing her to the Fae in charge, Mallux
spent the better part of the day convening with the others,
while she was secluded quietly in a corner of the tent, enjoying
the cool, shady depths as she listened. She understood very
little still. Not enough to completely follow the conversation.
Telium wished Lotte had come with them, she would have
liked to ask the female to teach her more of the language.
No-one asked her opinion on matters, so she did not offer it.
The Fae here are polite, if not hesitant to talk to her, answering
her questions in the Common Tongue and making small talk
when she approaches them.

Now she is watching Mallux spar with other Fae from the
camp. The contest has drawn a crowd, with spectators ringing
the packed dirt to watch.

A female steps forward. Her jet-black hair shines in the
light and her eyes are outlined in black, making them stand
out against her deeply bronzed skin. The onlookers jeer and
hiss. One male catcalls at her as she passes, yet the female keeps
her back straight as she draws her blade, not even favouring
the whistling male with a glance. The muscles of her arms and
shoulders, exposed by the cut of her vest, ripple under her
skin. She is enormous by Alkorian standards; a good foot taller
than Telium and nearly twice as wide.

Mallux's blade sings in response as he withdraws it from
its sheath. Hefting it in one hand as if to test its weight, he
rolls his neck to loosen the muscles. A distraction, Telium
knows, to try and intimidate an opponent with his strength.
A broadsword like that is heavy, yet Mallux holds it as if it
is a rapier.

His opponent knows this too. The female eyes his strong

arms with caution. Without preamble, she advances, and the fight begins.

She is a fearsome fighter, but Telium can tell from the start the female is not going to win the battle. Already, she is cowed by Mallux, either by his size or his reputation, and that is half the battle lost. Still, she fights bravely and the clang of steel rings out across the watching crowd. The female manages to land a slashing blow to Mallux's thigh; the impact will leave a bruise.

As they continue to fight back and forth, Telium watches the *Tia'tum* across the way, whose brow is wrinkled in concentration as she holds her thin shield around the blades of the fighters. Mallux explained earlier how they rely on *Tia'tums* to lay their Power over the sharp edges of the blades so the contestants do not cut each other to ribbons when sparring with real weapons.

That does not mean the fighters walk away unharmed, however. The blows from the blunted blades are still forceful enough to leave the receiver battered and bruised. A poorly timed blow could still break bones.

Telium watches as the female fights hard, with no small amount of skill. Yet Mallux still bests her. She lasts a good two minutes longer than the male before her; double the time of anyone else who has entered the ring. With a flashy move, Mallux disarms his opponent, knocking her to the ground with a sweeping blow of his massive sword. The crack of steel makes Telium cringe and the female cries out as she falls into a heap, clutching her ankle.

The crowd cheers at his victory and Mallux looks down at her a moment longer before reaching down to help the female to her feet. She dips her head in acknowledgement and retreats from the circle in defeat, followed by the jeers of the onlookers. None so loud as the male from before. Again, he catcalls to her retreating form, leering at her in a way that makes Telium clench her teeth. She eyes the offending male who has the handsome look all Fae carry, yet one too many fights has left his nose crooked and ears thickened. Telium decides he looks much like a pig.

'Any more challengers?' Mallux booms, holding his arms out wide and turning slowly.

The Fae around him cheer, but none step forward. Suddenly, Telium's scalp prickles and she glances over her shoulder, feeling a shadowy presence at her back. There is nobody behind her, apart from the rowdy Fae from before. She turns to face forward again, cocking her head to the side as she admires the way the sweat gleams on the strong column of his neck.

'No?' Mallux rumbles. 'Is no Fae willing to pit his sword against mine?'

At his words, Telium feels the sharp press of nails in her back, urging her forward. *Tenebris curse me,* she thinks, reluctant to bow to the Dark Goddess' tampering. When her soul reaches the Realm of Tenebris, she and the Goddess are going to have *words* about her meddling.

No Fae? The words whisper in her mind, taunting. Her Gifts stir in challenge, lusting for carnage, for a fight, for blood.

Mallux's back is turned to her when she steps into the circle of packed earth. The crowd's cheering peters out to curious murmurs. The Fae gathered eye her like wolves watching a sheep. Some nudge their companions; others who are passing by stop to watch.

Telium stands still, paying them no mind, as Mallux turns to face her. She watches his face as a flurry of emotions crosses it, too fast to catch, before settling into the blankness of a warrior. She nods at him, then strides to the edge of the circle where the *Tia'tum* is standing.

The *Tia'tum's* face is empty of all emotion, her consciousness feels like a seamless ball of steel – smooth, shiny and strong. She gazes at Telium with stormy grey eyes.

'How fast can you shield a blade?' Telium asks.

'I need a moment or two to see the weapon and conform my Power to its shape, no more,' the Fae replies, her voice low and even.

Mallux grins at Telium and looks from side to side in an exaggerated gesture. 'As the lady wishes,' he says loudly, before pacing a few steps backwards, drawing his broadsword.

The crowd looking on erupts into cheers and shouts of encouragement. Some even snicker, no doubt thinking her easy prey, like a stunned deer.

Telium cocks her head at him, looking him up and down in a slow sweeping motion as the corner of her mouth twitches up – one predator surveying another – before tilting her head back and looking down her nose at him. A muscle in Mallux's cheek jumps.

She takes a few large, deliberate steps backwards, before drawing her haladie from her hip, unfolding it with a snap and locking it into place. Holding the weapon out to the side, Telium ensures the *Tia'tum* gets a good look at the blade, allowing her time to survey its unusual curves.

Mallux barely spares the weapon a glance, trying to appear unperturbed. Telium sinks into a fighting stance.

As both she and Mallux step towards each other, the pig male from before whistles at her. Telium sees him nudge his companion and chuckle. With a snarl, she draws herself upright, whirling to face him while simultaneously pulling a throwing dagger from her bandolier.

Her throw finds its mark. The blade sticks quivering in the tree stump that the male is sitting on, right between his legs. Any higher, it would have stuck through his trousers. The crowd goes deathly silent. The male stares dumbly at the blade before looking up at her with his mouth hanging open. Telium's response is to glare at him before she turns her gaze to his companion who wisely avoids her eyes and looks to Mallux instead.

With all the arrogance of her younger self, Telium turns her back on the two males and advances on Mallux without looking back. Besides putting that pig of a Fae in his place, the throw also confirms her suspicions that the *Tia'tum* is unable to coat one of her daggers fast enough to avoid injury. A good piece of information to tuck away for later battles.

A cackle from the other side breaks the silence and the dark-haired female who had fought Mallux muscles her way to the front of the crowd. 'Ten *sens* on the Half-Breed!' she crows, staring directly at the male with the dagger between his legs.

Her declaration is met with a flurry of wagers, counter-bets and cursing as the crowd starts up its rowdy chatter again. This time, the cry of odds can be heard and several Fae move about the crowd collecting money.

Telium blows out a gentle exhale, calling on her Gifts to quicken her reflexes. She waits for him to make the first move, holding her haladie out in front of her. The moment spreads out indefinitely and Mallux shifts the grip on his sword.

The onlookers cheer, most urging Mallux on. A few, like the female with kohl-lined eyes and copper skin, shout for Telium, placing their coins on her victory.

As she waits, a flicker of movement in the crowd draws Telium's attention. Despite all her training and instincts, despite her brain screaming not to, her eyes flick away from Mallux of their own accord.

Behind the crowd, a male is chatting with one of the sentries next to a cold camp fire. His clothes are dusty and stained; another warrior come to join the ranks of the rebellion. But there is something familiar about this male. He throws back his head, laughing with his companion, the motion showing straight, white teeth, stark against his deep-copper skin. Without warning, all her Gifts rear in response, each Thief power fighting and scratching its way to the surface.

The reaction is so severe it forces the air from her lungs. At that exact moment, Mallux sees her distraction and launches into an attack. Telium's skill and handle of her Gifts are put to the test as she wrestles to put a dampener on them and fend off the wicked-fast blows of Mallux's broadsword. The effort nearly brings her to her knees. Keeping a grip on her Gifts takes all but the last shred of her concentration.

She fends and parries as best she can, retreating from Mallux around the circle. Desperately trying to put some space between them to give herself a moment to collect her scattered thoughts and wrest her Gifts under control. Every blow she deflects jars through her. Before long, she is breathing hard, the dry summer air carving a path down her throat.

With a grunt, she blocks a particularly forceful blow, shoving at Mallux. She dodges to the side a moment too late, feeling the tip of his blade nick her hip, the tender spot bruising instantly.

The hiss that escapes her lips is nothing human. Nothing Fae. It is something completely *Other;* dark and vicious and deadly. She can feel the sharp point of fangs against her lip as she is unable to stop some of her physical Gifts from taking form.

Her reaction shocks Mallux enough that he hesitates a second, long enough for her to flick her eyes back to the strange newcomer. The sentry now stands alone; his laughing companion gone.

There, see? He is gone. Her inner voice snarls at her Gifts, trying to wrest them into submission. Fear of losing control gives her strength but the effort leaves her panting through her clenched teeth – now fang free.

That is all the reprieve she gets. Mallux pushes his advantage, chasing Telium around the ring as she deflects his attacks.

When he aims a slicing blow at her head, Telium dives out of the way, rolling in the dirt. Dropping her haladie, she twists onto her back, propping herself up onto her forearms, panting with exertion. Mallux takes the bait and strides over to her, assured of his victory. Oozing Fae arrogance.

Telium allows him to approach until he stands between her legs, looking down at her. She kicks out, tangling up their legs and tripping him to the ground with a heave. Still half-feral, she leaps onto him with a snarl, teeth snapping. Planning to put him into a lock hold until he submits, but her mind is still distracted as she tries to stop her Gifts from blowing out of control. Mallux catches her before she can get a good grip and tosses her bodily across the circle.

She balls herself up and hits the sand at a roll, allowing the momentum to carry her back to her feet. She stinks of dust and sweat. Her haladie glints in the dirt a few feet away. She turns to face Mallux. Only to find him slowly standing from where he had fallen, dusting off his shirt with his free hand. He pauses a moment, watching her warily now. The reprieve allows her to take a few deep, steadying breaths and quell the darkness roiling under her skin like a storm.

Something in her look must have changed because Mallux

holds his sword up in front of his face and nods at her. She picks up her blade and mimics the gesture.

Now their battle begins in earnest. With her full concentration on the fight, Telium goes into offence. She is able to land a few bruising blows of her own. Mallux is an exceptional fighter, strong and fast, with a good eye for swordplay and the habits of his opponents. They battle back and forth, their feet kicking up dust in the late afternoon air. Soon they are both panting hard and covered in bruises.

Mallux is flashy with his swordsmanship and likes to use little flourishes that make his attacks look more difficult than they are. That, matched with his intimidating size, is more than enough to cow any opponent and cause them to doubt their chances of beating him.

It is a clever tactic. Telium finds herself enjoying the fight, allowing herself the simple joy of sparring with someone of great skill. Without her Blood-Thief Gifts, she would be hard-pressed to beat him. His superior speed and strength would mean she would be fighting for her life.

It is not long before they are both battered and dirty, winded from exertion. They clash and separate before coming back again and again. With a final burst of energy, Telium spins, ducking under his guard and swinging her haladie up. At the same time, Mallux chops his blade downwards.

They both come to a halt, panting, as the dust settles around their feet. The tip of her haladie rests just behind his ear, its shielded length kissing his neck. She grins up at him, gently tapping the steel against his flesh. Goosebumps chase across her skin at her sudden awareness of his closeness, setting her nerve endings on fire.

Mallux's responding smile is full of charming arrogance as he taps his blade against her hip in return, his meaning clear. While she may have struck the deathblow, with his giant broadsword embedded in her side, it is unlikely she would have lived out the night.

'Oh, *pay up,* Reynold!' The kohl-eyed female's voice breaks through Telium's hazy thoughts and she chuckles as she looks over her shoulder at the female, who is standing triumphantly with one hand on her hip and the other stuck out to the companion of the pig Fae. She wiggles her fingers and bats her dark eyelashes sweetly as the male hands over a small bag of coin while muttering under his breath.

The Fae around them watch her with a mixture of surprise, anger and wariness; wolves realising the sheep they have been circling turned out to be a dragon.

You don't belong here *either.* She pushes the thought away.

CHAPTER 33

As the watching Fae collect their winnings and disperse back to their tents and fires, the female makes her way over to her. Telium turns back to Mallux, only to see his retreating form heading towards camp. She studiously ignores the heat pooling in her core. Unlatching her haladie, she snaps it shut. There is *no way* she is going after him.

The female reaches her just as she begins to sheathe the weapon. 'May I?' she asks, holding out her hand.

Her voice has a slight accent like she is about to start laughing at any moment. With a shrug, Telium hands the weapon over to the Fae who turns it this way and that, rubbing a thumb over the carvings on the handle and holding the blade up to the light.

'What a fascinating weapon,' she says, passing the haladie back. 'I am Lillian.'

After a quick glance at Lillian's arms to check for coloured bands, Telium takes her outstretched hand and shakes it. 'Telium,' she says, sheathing her blade.

'Nobody here will tell you this, but I have never seen anybody best the General. You fought well … in the end.'

The statement is more a pointed question. Lillian is likely curious about how Telium went from barely holding her own to beating their *General*. Telium just shrugs in response, ignoring the uneasy feeling her Gifts' outburst has caused. Maybe she doesn't have as much control as she thought she did.

'You seem like you could be deadly with those blades, girl,' Lillian continues, unperturbed by her silence.

The endearment makes Telium bristle, but she lets it pass without comment. 'I have had some practise,' she replies evenly, looking over Lillian's shoulder in search of Mallux.

'No kidding. I am glad you shut Erin up with that blade between his legs. Pity you did not aim a bit higher; we could do without that cursed seed in the world.' Lillian winks at her.

Unable to spot Mallux in the crowd, Telium gives up and turns to wander toward the cook's tent that has been set up at the edge of the camp with Lillian dogging her heels.

The cook is a lean male who has a team of females working under him. Telium assumes they are wives or sisters, either too young or too heavy with child to fight. Too vulnerable to be left at home without protection.

The smell of cooking lures warriors from all over camp. Some are walking around with a bowl of stew and bread. Others seem to have skipped dinner completely in favour of starting on the ale. Both male and female Fae sit around fires, laughing and arguing, some playing cards.

'Tell me, Lillian, are your females trained to fight the same as males?'

The muscular Fae gives her a strange look as if the question is absurd. 'Yes, we are able to train the same, except, of course, those with Power, who are sent to train with the highest of their order.'

'Can they not learn to fight?'

'They can, if they choose to, become fearsome warriors, honing their skills in both Powers and combat. Others choose to just focus on their Powers and become *Kia'ra*. I do not know the translation in the Common Tongue … ones of great knowledge; those who learn from books and scripts.' Lillian says the last bit with distaste.

'Not a book person, then,' Telium notes, as she gets in line for food behind another Fae who eyes her curiously but says nothing.

Telium's mouth waters as she nears the cook's tent; the flaps are tied back and Fae rush about preparing meals, heat pulsing from the collection of cooking fires.

She has been keeping the net of her consciousness close to her so that only those who come within arm's reach register. While the Fae do not overwhelm her with emotions the way humans do, the constantly moving black spots of their minds give her a headache, the feeling akin to the dots that swim before your eyes after staring too long at the sun.

Telium quickly reaches the front of the queue and receives a steaming hot bowl and a dense fire-baked roll. Finding an empty spot by the fire, Telium sits down, stomach grumbling as the smell wafts up from her meal. The female next to Telium looks at her as she sits but quickly turns back to her food without uttering a word.

Telium is always hungrier after exercising her Gifts or having to subdue them. Lillian sits by her with a grunt but quickly scoots back from the heat of the fire. Telium takes a huge bite of her roll. It is dense and a little dry, but warm and filling. Her jaw aches as she chews but at least it will fill her stomach.

Lillian keeps glancing at her sidelong, chewing her food slowly. Her dark eyes flash with curiosity. Telium quirks an eyebrow at her.

'Will you start sparring with me?' Lillian blurts.

Telium pauses with her spoon halfway to her lips, before shoving the stew into her mouth. 'You already know how to fight; I saw you spar with Mallux,' she says around her mouthful of food.

'That was not just any spar. Mallux had challenged those who think themselves worthy to fight him in single combat. Those who pleased him will earn a place on his war council.'

Telium's ears perk up. 'War council?' she asks.

'*Vel,*' the Fae nods, 'but nobody was expected to actually *beat* him. Besides, you know what I mean; I want to learn to fight like you, like a demon.'

The word sends chills down her spine and she takes her time chewing. Swallowing, Telium points her spoon at the cook, avoiding Lillian's question. 'His food is good for what he has to work with and he's very fast.'

Lillian glances over at the cooking tent dismissively. 'Of course he is. He was the cook in the King's kitchens before that little—'

'*TO'A KEP!*' The cry echoes through the camp, silencing all conversation. '*VE TO'A KEP! Seuth!*'

Like they are one entity, the Fae rise to their feet and look south. All, that is, except Telium. *Scouts. South.* That is what the Fae had shouted. She looks down at the food longingly. Her few mouthfuls are enough to quieten her growling stomach, but not enough to fill her.

The rebel comes careening into camp, his hair windblown and mussed. He is instantly swamped by Fae asking questions and demanding answers. The cook bellows for someone to fetch Mallux and others who, Telium assumes, are part of the council. Quickly pulling on her Mind-Thief Gifts, Telium listens to the out-of-breath Fae from her spot by the fire. She is only able to pick out every third word or so of the pattering Old Fae.

Those surrounding him begin asking questions. Voices overlap as more crowd in.

Telium slams her bowl down and curses colourfully. The smell of the stew and bread taunts her as she rises to her feet and weaves through the crowd, away from the newcomer and to the east. She stalks away as the Fae continue speaking.

Telium recognises the word for a Flame – *A'gnis* – but nothing else.

Instead of going after the scouts on their way to warn the King about their rebellion, the Fae around him keep questioning the poor male. 'Idiot Fae,' she snarls to herself.

CHAPTER
34

Telium slips through the mass, picking up speed as the crowd thins. Soon the camp is empty, everyone heading towards the commotion at the southern edge of the tents. Calling on her Blood-Thief Gifts, Telium puts on a burst of speed, leaping over discarded armour and barrels. She zigzags between tents and flashes by the sentries standing watch at the outer edge of the encampment. Once free of obstacles, she pushes herself hard. Pumping her legs, she flies across the ground.

Planning to cut them off before they get too far, she throws out the net of her mind, hoping to pick up on the runaway scouts so she can pinpoint their location. Her Gifts rumble under her skin; the feeling a death toll to her prey.

Soon, Telium feels a flicker of emptiness at the edge of her perception. Altering her course slightly, she keeps up her pace, straining her mind to try and pick up the feeling of the scouts. One moment she can barely sense them, the next, there are two empty holes in the net of her consciousness. Drawing her Gifts close to the surface, she prepares for the fight ahead. She runs hard, keeping her feet as silent as possible on the forest floor. She dodges around a large tree, leaps over a fallen branch, and suddenly, there they are.

The male has flame-red hair, straight as an arrow; the female is honey-blonde with a braided green and brown ribbon tied around her arm.

Telium has not even come to a complete stop before she launches her Gifts at the female, throwing her sideways into the trunk of a tree. The male comes to a skidding halt, ripping his bow from his shoulders and knocking an arrow within a heartbeat. He has it trained on Telium's chest and lets the arrow fly with deadly accuracy. Only her Blood-Thief Gifts save her as she dodges to the side, the arrow ripping through the sleeve of her shirt instead of her chest.

Freedom-Thief Gifts are useless here; Fae are not susceptible to the Song, able to resist being bent to her will. Instead, she pulls on other Gifts – all but those of a Life-Thief; she keeps those chained. Her answering dagger embeds in the Fae's shoulder, causing him to drop the next arrow he pulls from his quiver.

Telium takes a step toward him but is abruptly knocked off balance as something hard and rough crashes into her. It knocks the breath from her and scrapes her skin as she goes flying sideways before slamming to the dirt. Instinctively, she instantly pushes to her feet, ignoring the searing pain, and whirls around to find one of the large trees righting itself. Its branches uncurl before settling back into their natural position. The female she tossed is staring at her and a faint green shimmer wreathes her outstretched hands.

Well, she knows what a green armband means now. A *Na'tai* – Seed – that is what the rebel Fae called her.

The *Na'tai* begins to stride toward her. Without warning, a mass of vines seethe from the earth and begin to tighten around Telium's legs. Slashing at them with her haladie in one hand, she looses a dagger at the *Na'tai*, who smoothly dodges out of the way. Her Fae reflexes save her, but the distraction is enough for Telium to hack and rip herself free of the creeping plants and bring up her blade to deflect the slicing blow the male swings at her head.

The clash that follows, while swift, is by no means easy; made harder by the constant need to keep moving to avoid the vines trying to ensnare her. Every so often, Telium hacks her haladie downwards to free her legs, each time missing her own skin by a hair's-breadth.

The male is inhumanly quick but obviously favours bow over sword, and with his wounded shoulder, Telium has the advantage. She runs her blade through him just as a vine entangles her ankle again, grounding her as it quickly works its way up her leg.

She rips her blade from the male's chest and twists as best she can, hurling another dagger at the *Na'tai*. The female is wise to the trick and has already flashed out of the way without losing her grip on Telium's leg. Lashing out with her Gifts, Telium catches the Fae around the throat with invisible hands and *squeezes*, lifting her off the ground. The attack is enough to halt the crushing vines from creeping any further up her thigh.

The male has slumped to his knees, heart failing him, but manages to slash out with a tiny dagger he pulls from his belt. The steel leaves a line of fire down Telium's arm. She cries out in pain and surprise. Her invisible grip loosens on the *Na'tai* as she spins back to the male with a snarl, white hair whipping about her. But he is already on the ground, dagger fallen from lifeless hands, eyes dimming.

Behind her, the *Na'tai's* feet kick at nothing as she sucks in a gasp. Telium's distraction has caused the vice around her neck to loosen just enough to let a trickle of air down her throat. The *Na'tai* throws out an arm, calling on her own Powers to form a vine with huge, wicked thorns; the largest growing right at the tip, sharp as any blade. The vine spears towards Telium who throws her arms up to protect her face and she catches the thorn on her forearm.

The pain rips a vicious growl from her as she slices at the plant and grips the *Na'tai* with her Gifts hard enough to make her ribs grind. Again, she lifts the Fae and tosses her savagely. Before the *Na'tai* even hits the bark, Telium is slashing at the vines coating her legs. They fall free and the blood rushes back to her feet, causing her toes to tingle.

Gritting her teeth, she rips the giant thorn from her arm. Her Gifts rapidly patch up the gushing wound. It is far from healed, but at least it will prevent her from bleeding out during the battle. She stalks toward the *Na'tai*, noting how the tree has bent out of shape. The Fae using her Powers to allow it to cushion her impact.

The *Na'tai* looks up at Telium striding toward her with blade drawn. She frantically raises her arms, hands glowing faintly green, and focuses over Telium's shoulder. The rustling of leaves closing in on her is all the warning she gets before she drops her haladie and hurls herself sideways. The main trunk of the tree crashes into the ground, missing her by mere inches, but branches batter her and knock her about. One of the larger ones pins her arm to the ground and Telium shrieks in pain, drowning out the resulting snap of bone.

Before she can draw a breath to curse, the tree shifts again, unfolding like a man from a bow, and returns to its natural position. Leaves and twigs shower Telium's head and shoulders. Shoving to her feet, pain barks up her arm, causing her vision to spin. She swivels her head back and forth as she looks for her opponent, only to see the honey blonde of the female's braid as it disappears through the trees. Retreating to the other scouts to regroup, no doubt. If they are given forewarning they could easily split up and take days to track.

Telium yanks sharply on her broken arm to set it, unable to stop a scream slipping past her lips. The pain quickly subsides, though, as the Gifts of a Mind-Thief mend the bone. She takes a moment more to knit the muscles back together from her other wounds. The spots are still tender, but she does not want to expend any more energy by healing them completely. At least they will not hinder her for now.

Picking up her fallen blades, Telium sheaths them before sprinting off in the direction of the fleeing Fae. A feline smile curves her lips as she races through the ever-darkening forest. Oh, how she *loves* a hunt.

As she flies over the ground, she throws the net of her mind out, using the ever-moving void to track the Fae fleeing before her. Her eyes become reflective and lupine as Gifts change her physical form to allow her to see in the dimming light. Along with short, sharp fangs as she cedes a little bit more to her Gifts that roil and howl under her skin as she hunts the *Na'tai*, thrilling in the chase.

Telium has only been in pursuit a short time before she feels the gap between them closing in her mind. The *Na'tai* must have slowed down to conserve energy, apparently thinking Telium would not have the strength to follow her. Trigg's words flash into her mind.

Unless you see the life-light leave their eyes right in front of you, you should never consider your enemy dead. I do not care how grievous a wound you inflict; if you don't see them die, you should always act as if they are alive and coming back to seek revenge upon you.

Obviously not a lesson this Fae learned.

As the distance between them lessens, Telium concentrates hard on the essence that is the *Na'tai*. The protection about her mind feels like the densest of bramble bushes – thick, sharp and convoluted.

She breaks away from the trees and onto a grassy knoll. Ahead of her, the *Na'tai* races up the hill. Barely skipping a stride, Telium pulls back her arm and whips it forward. An invisible Power-Thief javelin shoots from her hand and spears the *Na'tai* in the back.

The female cries out as she falls to the ground, of course bearing no physical evidence of a wound. Telium is unable to pierce flesh with her Power-Thief Gifts. Instead, she coils it back into herself and throws an invisible shield around her legs as she slows to a walk and stalks toward the Fae; the idea courtesy of the rebel *Tia'tums*. Her feet whisper above the ground as her boots fall upon the shield instead of earth.

The *Na'tai* pushes herself onto her back and throws out her green-hazed hands. This time, the vines cannot get a purchase and instead slide helplessly around the shield Telium has created before slipping harmlessly off as she walks by.

From atop the hillock, another Fae appears. Seeing the female on the ground and Telium advancing on her, he draws his sword and races down the hill.

Telium rolls her eyes. Honestly, why do males *run* with swords? It uses up valuable energy hefting the heavy things in your arm while you run, and you are more likely to cut yourself or a comrade before you reach your rival.

His cries must have drawn the attention of the rest of the King's scouts because one moment it is just the *Na'tai* and the Fae racing down toward her. The next, an assortment of Fae appear above the crest of the hill. Six in total, besides the *Na'tai*.

Telium smiles savagely. *A fair match.*

The breath whooshes out of her as she calls upon her most violent and deadly Gift: that of a Life-Thief. Unlike her other stolen Gifts, she has only come across two Life-Thieves in her time. If it were not for her reserves of other powers, she would have perished in the battle. As it was, one Thief was already wounded from fighting with its kin. Once she had ripped his Gifts from him, she turned them on the other.

The power she gained from those despicable beasts frightens her, not the least so because they marry so well with her own dark Gifts. So easy for her to shape them to her will, like a sixth sense she has just found. Her mind somehow already knew how to handle them, where she had to teach herself how to wield the power from other Thieves.

Now, however, she turns them on the King's scouts. She calls to life falkir-shaped shadows – dark beings with eyes red as blood. The two shadow-falkir howl and rush toward the charging Fae, some of whom stop and draw arrows and spears to fight the beasts from a distance.

One female has flame-red hair and looks startlingly similar to the fallen male from earlier. She calls to life a small ball of flame and flings it toward Telium. Telium easily dodges the missile, but the resulting flame that detonates in the grass moves against the wind, leaping at her with red tongues. The heat kisses her face, hissing like a pit of snakes as she throws a barrier of Power-Thief Gifts to deflect it.

The *Na'tai* screams as the falkir reach her. A few of the others vainly stop to help, but the rest charge on to engage Telium.

Like a wild thing, Telium throws herself into the fray, her blades flashing in the burning red light of the *A'gnis'* fire. She holds her Power-Thief Gifts close to her body, pulling them up over herself like a second skin to protect her from lethal strikes.

Fighting in close quarters with the other Fae stops the *A'gnis* from being able to use her Powers on Telium without fear of harming her companions. As the falkir rage about her, Telium cuts down any Fae in her path, seeing only the faces of the human slaves in the pass, hearing only the phantom weeping of her Queen as she begs the Mad Fae King for mercy.

Her Life-Thief Gifts draw on all the darkness and hate and rage in her soul, throwing them into battle. These Fae are helping protect that monster. If she has to become a monster herself to destroy him, then so be it. For the slaves suffering here, for the woman who fell to her Gifts. To repay the debt owed to her Queen. To save innocent Alkorian lives, she would.

One moment she is snarling into the face of a Fae as she pulls her haladie from his stomach; the next, she stands alone.

Glancing up the hill, Telium sees a regiment of the rebellion with Mallux at the lead. The two remaining scouts are on their knees, hands behind their heads in surrender in front of them. The red-haired *A'gnis* is with them. Even from this distance, Telium can see the hatred in her eyes as she glares at her.

Wiping her blade clean on the grass as best she can, Telium calls her shadow-falkir back to her side and ravels the dark wind back into herself. One of the falkir nuzzles her hand before melting away into nothingness at her command. A rush of energy that soothes the ragged edges of her mind and sore muscles seeps into her as the falkir dissipate.

Oh.

The sensation is startling but not wholly unwelcome. Never before have her shadows passed on a life-force to her, she only ever acquired it though pulling it from someone with her mind. She had always assumed by the time her shadows were done, there was nothing, neither life nor energy, left. It seems this new development is unique to the Fae. *Maybe it has something to do with their long lifespans.*

Aided by the stolen life-force, her rage slowly settles, her bloodlust eases and she cannot help but feel loathed at the carnage. For so long she had kept peace in her forest; not spilling blood or stealing life with her Gifts. But it seems Tenebris has a different plan for her – thrusting Mallux into her path and dangling the chance to avenge her Siren Queen, adding the promise of answers to ensure she would not turn away. She was made for killing; this she cannot deny. The perfect dark weapon to be wielded.

With a growl, she stomps up the hill toward the retreating rebels. A few cast glances at her over their shoulders. Looks she has seen time and time again in the eyes of courtiers and commoners alike. *Bloodless Maiden. Tenebris Kin. Other.*

By the time she reaches them, her rage has cooled entirely. All but Mallux and another male stand talking with each other. Seeing her approach, Mallux dismisses the other Fae who nods before casting Telium a look that is equal parts curiosity and caution. Of their own accord, her lips twitch up in a snarl at his gaze. She can feel the scrape of fangs against her bottom lip and banishes them with a thought, along with the black claws curling at her fingertips.

She stops in front of Mallux who is surveying the battle-field, noting the two corpses the falkir took, the bodies now thin and wasted, paper skin stretched over bones. The life has been sucked from them; the energy their bodies had produced now heals Telium's wounds and bolsters her strength.

When Mallux turns back to her, she sets her jaw and eyes him defiantly, refusing to allow her shame or fear of her Gifts to reach her eyes. He came to find *her* for help. Not the other way around. If he did not know what he was getting when he bargained with her, he certainly does now.

As if he can read her thoughts, Mallux nods slightly and quickly moves his gaze away.

'What will happen to the remaining two scouts?' Telium asks, voice harsh in the suddenly quiet evening.

'They will be questioned,' he replies evenly.

Oh yes, Telium knows exactly what type of questioning he has in mind. She could never find the stomach for torture, despite her dark Gifts. To kill or maim in the fury of battle is a different thing entirely. Telium much prefers skulking around the dark corners of taverns for her information.

'I see,' is all she says.

She hesitates a moment longer to see if Mallux will meet her eyes. To check her wounds like he did before. To *thank* her. Make her feel less apart from the world. When he does not, she ignores the hurt feeling in her chest and spins on her heels to head back to camp.

She needs a bath, and her hunger chooses this moment to flood back with full force, reminding her that she battled with Gift and blade on a near-empty stomach. As she walks away, she hears Mallux murmur to himself.

'Tenebris Kin, indeed.'

CHAPTER
35

The sun has finally released the land from its fiery grip, allowing a cool breeze to sweep through the camp. Telium sits on the floor wearing nothing but a long tunic and her undergarments in the glow of flickering candlelight, thinking of the time Trigg cleaned the blood from her hands after a mission, unfazed by young Telium's brutal efficiency.

Mallux enters the tent, pushing the burgundy flaps aside and interrupting her reminiscing. He blushes furiously and turns away, fumbling an apology when he notes the length of her exposed leg.

Telium chuckles and pauses her work on her tattooed leg to look over her shoulder at him. 'Honestly, Mallux,' she says. 'I am sure you have seen a woman's legs before.' She eyes him, noting how his shoulders bunch as he fights the urge to turn around. His reaction sparks something in her chest. She shrugs, faking nonchalance. 'You can watch if you like; I have not yet finished.'

As she expected, his masculine curiosity wins. She pastes a look of innocence on her face as he turns around. He valiantly tries to keep his eyes on her face and not her bare legs. Telium flicks her eyes up and down his form, before turning back to examine her work, pretending her skin does not feel hot and tight across her body.

She reaches to pick up her needle and the *Ta Vir* along her leg catches the candlelight. The fresh ink still shining red in the tent's dim interior, adding to the markings already curling up her thigh. Mallux snarls, moving to her side with Fae swiftness, and snatches the needle out of her hand. Clenching her teeth, Telium attempts to keep her anger in check, lest her tenuous hold on the darkness slip.

'What do you think you are doing?' he growls as he scrutinises the fresh swirls of ink snaking down Telium's thigh. 'A *female* should not ink herself.' His voice is low and deadly. 'Only the most sacred of our healers may mark skin.'

Telium's eyes flash in the soft light as she looks up at Mallux. 'How nice for your healers,' she says, voice heavy with sarcasm.

'You will not practice such things in my camp,'

Mallux's voice rings with authority as he tosses the needle back into the bowl of blood-red ink. Telium snaps at his tone. Snatching the needle in midair, she kicks out her legs, hooking them around his ankles. With a jerk, she topples him to the ground where he lands with a grunt of surprise.

Telium is on top of him in an instant, needle pressed to his neck and teeth gleaming as she snarls in his face. Mallux goes deathly still, holding his hands out in supplication.

'That's twice in one day,' she purrs, stroking the needle along his jawline. 'You seem to forget that I am not Fae, nor am I one of your warriors.'

She pauses, leaning forward so that her lips are a whisper away from his. The collar of her shirt gapes at the neck. Telium watches Mallux as his mind wars with outrage and lust. She cannot stop the smirk curling her lips and her own rising desire, especially when she feels his callused hands rest lightly on her hips. Using the needle, she tilts his chin up and puts her mouth to his ear.

'And considering I just saved your whole goddess-damned rebellion, you would do well to remember that it was *you* who came looking for *me* and *why* exactly you did.'

She pushes off him, standing in one fluid motion, ignoring the ache in her muscles and the heat pooling in her core. She turns her back to him, pretending to busy herself cleaning down the needle and setting it aside with the others, giving Mallux the time to clamber to his feet with as much dignity as he can muster.

'We will be departing for Meannthe at dawn. Be ready to leave,' is all he says before retreating out of the tent.

She sits back down and passes the needle through the candle's flame before continuing with her tattoo, each whirl and stroke telling a story of her battle today – if it can be called such a thing. The King's scouts had fallen before her blades and Gifts like wheat to a scythe. The survivors now somewhere in the camp, imprisoned and probably being tortured for information.

Telium dismisses the thought; the tiny pricks of pain soon pass and the salted ink will forever be a reminder of the encounter today and the lives forfeit to her skill. Her newest addition sits curled around a small whirl of lines that honour the slave woman from the pass, the details twisting like smoke.

She doesn't know why she continues with the tradition. The assassin's artist had preserved the stories along her spine – all her triumphs and failures marked in blood-red ink. Once her madness had cleared, she had picked up the custom, practising again and again with charcoal before taking a needle to her skin, doing her best to replicate the detailed work of art staining her back. At first, her hands had felt foreign and clumsy but as she progressed, she became more confident in her abilities.

Telium drags her mind back to the present, turning her leg this way and that to study her latest piece. She hums in satisfaction at her work, before smearing a poultice over the area and wrapping a bandage firmly around her thigh to keep it clean.

As she begins packing everything away, her mind turns back to her recent encounter with Mallux and she snorts. Wonders if he can see the lust in her eyes. Because that is all it is. She enjoys flirting with him, finds him undeniably handsome and would even admit that she craves his touch. But that is all.

Catching herself, Telium shakes her head to forcibly remove such foolish thoughts. It does not matter what Mallux thinks of her, or she him. Their pact is that she will help assassinate the Fae King, then they will part; Mallux to his ruling council and her to the Fae teachers. She pretends this knowledge does not sting.

Outside, she can hear some of the rebels laughing and drinking around the fire, toasting their triumph. She feels no urge to join them. Though they may rejoice in the victory she brought them, she knows she will not be welcome in their circles. It seems they are no different from Alkorians.

No matter how many years pass, she will never forget how the castle guards scorned her or how the soldiers barely tolerated her. If it were not for her prowess and skills, they would not have bothered to acknowledge her existence. After all, as the Queen's pet, she far outranked them, and the idea that she would grow to become the Siren Queen's closest confidante and adviser irked the men in power.

It would not do to have a *child*, an orphan at that, have the Queen's ear. They would have preferred some dithering old man who read books and had been on the council for *eons*. But Telium *did* have her ear, and those men learned to fear her, if not respect her. But they never accepted her.

With a sigh, Telium banishes such morose thoughts and dons loose-fitting trousers, carefully slipping them on over her tender leg. Pouring herself a mug of ale, she downs the entire cup in a few gulps, cringing at the taste. She much prefers the hot burn of rum.

Another bout of laughter sneaks through the flimsy walls of the tent, grating on her eardrums. With it comes a sudden rush of claustrophobia and the urge to lie under the stars.

She grabs her cloak and leaves her tent, heading for the edge of the camp as she weaves between bonfire and canvas, her feet unconsciously sticking to the shadows. Unless someone is looking hard for her, they would not notice her passing.

A Fae snags her attention as he hurls up the contents of his stomach behind a tent. Curling her nose in disgust at the sour smell, Telium begins to move on when the voice of his companion catches her interest.

The lyrical Old Fae reaches her ears, the tone teasing as he shouts to the male who heaves again. She picks up on one word. *Pito*. Rum.

The jeer is followed by a round of raucous laughter. On closer inspection, Telium spots a large flask hanging from the male's hip. When he leans over to retch again, she pads over to him, liberating him of the drink. She ghosts away, quiet as a shadow.

When she reaches the outskirts of the camp, she surveys over her shoulder making sure no-one has followed, before easily slipping by the poor soul stuck on night watch. She wanders out into the blackness, leaving the bright circle of camp fires behind her. Not ten paces past the guard, the camp disappears entirely. Telium pauses a moment, admiring the work of multiple *Ra'sitos* working together to hide their large camp from sight and sound.

The illusion was the reason so many had been shocked earlier in the day when the scouts found the camp. Already, rumours of spies are flying around. It will be an effort to remove the signs of their camp when they move on, but that is not a problem for her.

Telium walks without direction until she finds a soft patch of grass to lie on and flops down hard enough to slosh some of the ale from her mug. She takes another great swig of the brew, hacking in disgust at the taste. Using her free hand, she uncaps the lid from the intoxicated Fae's flask and sniffs its contents. Telium hums in satisfaction, before glaring down at the mug with its remaining ale. With a shrug, she upends the contents and takes a hearty gulp of the rum instead. The resulting burn near makes her purr.

Lying back, she gazes up at the stars, bright and brilliant against the inky blackness of the night and wonders, not for the first time, what the hell she is doing here. Is it really to kill a king who wronged her Queen and learn to control her Gifts? Or is it the urge to chase her past? She thought that desire had long since left her. That was a wish of a young Telium – a foolish Telium.

Once, when she was very young, she had asked Trigg about her real parents. Telium had spat blood from the resulting strike.

Never ask that again, Trigg had whispered harshly. *It matters not, and the knowledge would only endanger you.*

The fear and rage in her teacher's voice had shocked her into silence. Trigg was such an even-tempered woman; her patience knew no bounds. Telium had never heard her raise her voice in anger. Despite this, Trigg commanded the utmost respect from soldiers and guards, who were well aware that her skill with fist and sword far surpassed their own. A ghost of a smile curves Telium's lips as she thinks of her old teacher, even as her heart mourns.

Telium thought her wish to know her history had been buried under years of training and darkness and rage. Apparently not.

What monsters must her parents have been – what dark path had they walked – to bring a child of the night into this world, then abandon her to another? Did they know when she was born how apart she would stand from the rest?

She rarely thought about her birth mother; to her, Trigg was her mother, had cared for her and trained her. Even the Siren Queen had done more to raise her. Yet, during all those years in her forest as her powers had developed, Telium had begun to wonder more and more *what* her parents were.

This trip has forced her to face a truth that has long skulked in the back alleys of her mind – she is not wholly human. What is she then? Not Fae. She lacks the slightly tapered ears and elongated canines, the deadly fast reflexes. Not a Thief, for as Mallux said, they still had a mortal life span.

All these thoughts and more drift through her head as she lies under the stars, her mind straying between past and present, then somewhere in-between.

సా

After what may have been bells or minutes, she feels someone approaching. The black void in the net of her mind marks them out as Fae. This consciousness feels decidedly different; instead of being a stone for the river of her mind to part around, this one is a great black nothingness.

Telium pushes a little harder, trying to find the mark of the Fae's void, in the way Lotte's is the sun and Mallux's a stone wall. But this shield is like walking through a field on a foggy night with no moon; you're unsure where the fog starts and where it ends, and you wonder if you will find anything in-between as you search for a light, a mark – anything.

Something about this consciousness makes Telium's Gifts stretch and purr under her skin like a great, living beast.

Swallowing her mouthful of rum, she tightens her hold on her Gifts, pulling the power of a Mind-Thief to the surface. Her eyesight sharpens as the Gift takes hold, allowing her to see better in the night. The near blackness brightens suddenly, as if a full moon has come out from behind a cloud.

As the wind cartwheels across the grass toward her, she sniffs. *The first rain on a field of grass in the twilight, damp earth freshly planted and eucalyptus.* It is unusual and strangely pleasant. Telium pushes herself up to a sitting position and keeps her ears pricked.

Soon she picks up the sounds of someone moving through the grass, the noise so faint, if it were not for her consciousness spread about her, she would have mistaken the soft padding for a wild animal.

Moments later, a male appears from the trees, heading towards the shielded camp. Like it has been pushed by a *Cirrus*, the wind changes suddenly, turning on itself, pushing her scent directly towards the stranger.

He stills and jerks his head up to sniff the air. The motion reveals his face in the gentle light of the moon. With her enhanced sight, she recognises him as the laughing male from the sparring match with Mallux; the one who made her Gifts nearly rage out of control.

In a panic, Telium clamps down on her powers with an

iron will, just a moment before they try to surge to the surface. Her consciousness snaps back into itself like a trap. Her vision flickers between human and Mind-Thief as she wrestles her dark Gifts into submission.

You do not rule me, she snarls to the thunderclouds threatening to black out the desert in her mind. Ignoring the prickle of sweat on her palms, she struggles to maintain her hold. With visible effort, she wrests control of her black Gifts. It leaves a metallic taste in her mouth where she has bitten the inside of her cheek.

The stranger sniffs again. His eyes sweep the clearing before landing on Telium. He hesitates a moment. Unsure what else to do, Telium nods her head in greeting and takes a sip from her stolen flask. Her eyes never leave the male, even as the rum stings the wound inside her mouth and burns its way down her throat.

He begins making his way over, his casual, prowling gait setting all her instincts on edge. She recognises skill when she sees it – who holds a sword with confidence, who stands in a way that says they know how to hold their own in a fight. This male has that look about him. He carries himself with a lethal grace that screams one word: predator.

Telium looks him up and down as she prods the inside of her cheek with her tongue. Dark pants are tucked into practical leather boots. His midnight-blue shirt is crossed with leather straps that hold his weapons.

Twin blades peek over his shoulders, the hilts twined with red cord. Another dagger is strapped to his side, simple and well-worn with use. He has night-black hair that hangs in ropes tied back at the nape of his neck.

When he reaches Telium, he dips his head forward in what looks like a bow. Unable to return the gesture from a sitting position, she raises her flask awkwardly, silently wishing for Tenebris to come save her from these goddess-damned flawless Fae.

Like Lillian, this Fae's skin is the deepest bronze; not as rich as the mahogany of the Ereak Desert, yet not as fair as Mallux or Lotte either. His eyes are a deep, warm chocolate with flecks of hazel near the centre. Now that he is closer, Telium can see twisted string, beads and silver in some of his locks. He is not stunning in the flashy way that Mallux is, but he is still breathtakingly handsome. His rugged dark looks cause Telium's Gifts to roil.

The male studies her just as intently as she does him. Telium's Gifts continue to undulate under the surface. She refuses to let go of the white-knuckled grip she keeps on their leash. The air around them hums with Power and she tries to keep her face expressionless, not wanting her distrust to show.

'*Pae'ri,*' the male says suddenly, blinking. '*Paxium, sekta. Pax, gari de sethta.*'

His voice is a deep, rich timbre but with that same lilt as Lillian's – as if he knows a hidden joke you do not and is struggling to restrain his chuckle.

'I know very little Old Fae,' Telium replies, confused at the blush staining her cheeks. 'Uh, *pae'ri.*' *Forgive me.*

'I am Paxium, but you may call me Pax.' The Fae translates in perfect Common Tongue.

'Telium,' she replies, then adds after a moment's hesitation, 'you can call me Telli.'

Pax nods and smiles. He looks around. 'You are out here all alone?'

The question sounds more like a statement, yet she nods anyway, suddenly feeling foolish. Like a child running away to hide under her bed.

'It seemed like a lovely night to lie back and look up at the domain of Tenebris,' she says, waving her hand toward the stars.

Pax watches her for a moment longer, before tilting his head and rocking back on his heels. 'Indeed, it is,' he says after a moment's contemplation.

Telium offers him the flask and Pax takes it from her with a wry grin. Settling in the grass a comfortable distance from her, he takes a swig. With a start, he peers into the flask and swallows audibly. 'This is not ale.'

'No,' she replies, 'it's rum. I cannot stomach the taste of ale.'

He looks at her intently. When the wind picks up her bone-white locks and shifts them about, his gaze zeros in on the rounded tips of her ears. They sit in silence for a while, heads thrown back to bask in the cool light of the stars.

The only sound is the quiet chirp of crickets and the screech of an owl hunting in the distance. Pax's presence makes her Gifts churn under her skin, rising and retreating like the waves against the shore. Distracting herself from the unnerving feeling, she turns to the male. 'Are *you* all alone out here?' she asks, quirking her head to the side.

The moonlight bathes his deep complexion in its silvery light, making the metal in his hair glint. He holds himself with the unnatural stillness of the Fae. If it were not for the steady rise and fall of his chest, he could have been carved from stone. He studies her face intently, as if looking for something. She feels her brow crease into a frown.

'I am. I volunteered to scout the path ahead for tomorrow. I find the chaos of camp too much at times and like to find peace under the stars.' Paxium throws a sidelong glance at her. 'A sentiment I am sure you appreciate.'

She nods without replying and takes another sip from the flask before handing it back to Pax who shakes his head.

'You are a long way from home, Telli,' he says. 'Came all this way to aid a Fae rebellion?'

'Home,' she says slowly, savouring the taste of it on her tongue. She tips her head back, looking at the glittering blanket of diamonds. 'I don't think I know what that is anymore.'

She shrugs a shoulder, peering down into the contents of her flask. There is something about the male she cannot put her finger on, despite the unnerving effect he seems to have on her powers. But Telium sees no need to hide the truth; they are all working for the same end goal.

'As for the rebellion, do not think that I have not been offered something in return for my services,' she answers. She shares a conspirator's grin with him, which he returns willingly, exposing his elongated canines.

'I understand the sentiment … of home,' he adds. 'If you asked me where I am from, I would tell you Dal'Kreath – the great Fae kingdom to the east. But *home?*' He shakes his head. 'I have spent many a night wondering if I will ever find it again.'

Paxium cocks his head to the side and studies her. They lapse into silence. Though she isn't looking at him, Telium is hyper-aware of where Paxium sits. Her skin prickles as if she has her back turned to a falkir.

To distract herself, Telium asks, 'So is it clear?' When Paxium turns to her, she adds, 'The path you scouted, I mean.'

Something flashes in his eyes that puts her mentally on the defence. Her muscles tense, as if readying for a fight.

'Yes,' he replies, 'all clear.'

'*Bonai* – that's the word for good, isn't it?'

Paxium's face clears and he nods, his smile flashes. Teeth startlingly white against his deep bronze complexion. 'Yes, that's right. What other Old Fae do you know?'

Telium shifts, suddenly embarrassed. Though she isn't sure why, no-one in Alkoria knows Old Fae. There is little use for it in a kingdom full of humans.

'Very little,' she admits, sipping at her rum again.

She expects him to say more. She can sense he has other questions, but he only says, 'I must be going. We have an early start in the morning, readying for the journey ahead.' He stands and dusts the dry grass off his pants before he turns to her. 'Shall I walk you back to camp?'

He reaches down towards her, as if to help her to her feet. Her Gifts explode in her chest, forcing the breath from her lungs. Telium twitches away from him, too quickly to be anything other than an outright refusal. A slight frown creases Paxium's brow as he withdraws and runs a hand through his locks.

'Thank you, but *niya*,' Telium says before he can speak. 'I would like to spend a little longer away from the … chaos.'

She smiles, hoping to disarm him. His returning smile makes her Gifts surge against her skin yet again. His depthless brown eyes do not leave her face as he dips his head in farewell. Telium forces herself to still under the scrutiny, bracing for … she isn't sure. Only that his male sets her nerves on edge.

'*Nai vel'e*, Telli,' he says. '*Sek lith ses de mo'ra.*'

'I do not speak Old Fae,' she reminds him.

A growl creeps into her voice, surprising her. She is usually much better at monitoring her emotions. Paxium's deep chuckle jitters along her bones, making imaginary hackles rise.

'I know.'

With another nod of farewell, he pads off towards the camp, silent and graceful as a falkir.

Telium watches him go, touching the claw and greenstone hanging around her neck absentmindedly.

'Asshole,' she murmurs.

Her Gifts finally settle as Pax disappears into the dark. She wonders what sort of male would make her Gifts react so. It feels as if they are trying to burst through her skin when he is close.

She is tired from using her Gifts in battle and decides to take a rest from the vigorous training schedule she has undertaken every night since Mallux's arrival. Still, after Paxium leaves, Telium is unable to help throwing out the net of her mind again as a precaution.

CHAPTER
36

Some time passes before she feels another Fae approaching her from the direction of the camp. *Mallux.* Their travels together mean the feeling of his mind is familiar to her. The walls of his consciousness are strangely blurry, like she is viewing the stone from underwater. She turns and waits for his approach, still and silent.

Mallux appears out of the darkness, his usual stalking gait softened. His steps sway slightly as if he is walking on the deck of a rolling ship. His head swings back and forth as he looks for her, nose flaring as he sniffs the air.

'Mallux.' His name escapes her on an outward sigh before she can stop it.

His head whips in her direction. He sees her standing in the moonlight and Telium holds her breath as he comes toward her. She frowns at the bottle hanging loosely from his fingertips.

His eyes are unfocused as he rakes his gaze over her body. She starts to ask what he is doing there, only to gasp as he crashes into her. He drops the bottle as his hands encircle her waist. He leans down and their mouths collide. Every nerve ending in her body is set alight as his essence washes over her.

He kisses her savagely and she fists her hands in his shirt as she stands on tiptoe to answer the kiss. With a growl of pure masculine satisfaction, Mallux runs his hands up her back and plunges them into the white length of her hair. Twining it around his fingers, he tugs her head back and deepens the kiss.

A noise escapes her mouth that she is not proud of – something between a gasp and a moan. She delves her hands under his shirt, running her fingers over the hard planes of his muscles. Goddess, what is she doing? Has she so little control of herself? She flattens her hands on his stomach and pushes gently.

Mallux must feel her body tense because he tears his mouth from hers and looks down at her. His pupils have dilated, obliterating most of the blue in his eyes. His chest rises and falls in heaves. She stands silent, looking up at him, trying to control her lustful thoughts and calm her pounding heart. When he pulls her close again, her breathing hitches. Mallux holds her against his hard body. He dips his head, stopping just short of her lips. His citrus and fire scent washes over her, curling around her body in a warm embrace.

'Telium, my *upa*,' he whispers, his honeyed voice brushing over her skin.

The sound of her name in his mouth is like a plea and a demand. Her body goes hot and cold all at once as she breathes in the smell of him. Without conscious thought, she melts against him, breath sighing out of her.

With a growl that rumbles through her bones, he bends his head to claim her lips. Molten heat pools in her belly and she twines her arms about his neck. He removes the hand from her hair and slips it up under her shirt to cup her breast.

Telium gasps against his mouth at the sensation of his rough hands on her sensitive flesh.

With her remaining dregs of control, Telium pulls back from him, gripping his wrist to stop his exploration that threatens to overwhelm her senses. 'Mallux …' Her voice comes out breathy. Clearing her throat, she tries again. 'Mallux, are you drunk?'

Instead of answering, he pinches her. She moans as her head rolls back. With hot lips and tongue, he teases the skin at her throat, laying claim to it with soft nips. When she does not remove her hand from his wrist, Mallux leans back and frowns down at her. With less grace than usual, he flops to the ground, dragging Telium down to sit astride him.

'No,' he finally answers. 'I am not drunk – I am *drinking*.'

From his obvious state of intoxication, she is inclined to argue, but when his hands settle on her hips and his lust-hazed eyes meet hers, she cannot stop herself from meeting his kiss. One broad hand roughly strokes up her spine to her shoulder blades, pressing her into him.

She arches into him, wriggling into a more comfortable position on his lap. The movement wrenches a groan from Mallux that is like pouring oil on a fire. Telium threads her arms around his neck and their kiss deepens.

Mallux's hands and mouth are everywhere, leaving little trails of fire in their wake. He slips a hand under her shirt again as they break for air. His calluses scrape gently against her waist, sending shivers skittering across her skin. Their rasping gasps break the silence. Telium can feel every inch of where her body is pressed against his.

Mallux presses his forehead against her own and breathes deeply as if attempting to rein in his raging desire. The gesture causes a pang in Telium's heart and she closes her eyes, savouring his warm scent.

The sudden cool air against her skin causes Telium to gasp as the warmth of Mallux's body retreats. She snaps her eyes open to see he has flopped back against the grass, hands resting on her thighs. His position causes the bottom of his shirt to ruck up, exposing a thin line of stomach. Unconsciously, she smooths her hands over his skin, baring more of his chiselled muscles.

'Telium?' Mallux's voice is soft and husky.

She replies with a noncommittal sound and continues her exploration. When she gently scrapes her nails along his stomach, his muscles flex in response. Telium's pulse thuds in her ears.

'Telium.' This time her name is accompanied by a squeeze on her thigh.

She looks up to see Mallux watching her with those piercing blue eyes. The side of his mouth crooks up in a grin. Waving behind her, he murmurs, 'Will you pass me my ale?'

A husky laugh escapes her and she glances over her shoulder, spotting the discarded bottle. Unwilling to move from Mallux's lap, she lies back and stretches her hand all the way out to reach the ale. She drags the bottle toward her, sits up and turns back to Mallux, a coy smile on her lips ... only to find his eyes closed and his breathing deep and even.

'Mallux,' she scoffs.

When he does not reply, her mouth falls open. She grinds her hips against him and tries again. *'Mallux.'*

He merely murmurs sleepily and shifts his head. Telium could have shrieked in frustration. Throwing herself off him, she flops onto her back out of reach and inhales deeply through her nose. Trying to temper her raging desire. Tenebris curse him. *He is going to pay for that.*

CHAPTER
37

Telium hums to herself as she sits on the carriage, jostled by the bumps in the road. The midmorning sun warms her face as they trundle along. Two days ago, the camp split up, some heading across the country to Meannthe from a different direction, while others set off in small groups like the one she and Mallux now travel in.

The rickety wagon creaks as it makes its way across the grassy plain, pulled by a pair of sturdy horses. Thankfully, no Paxium. Something about him sets her on edge. She can't say she dislikes the male, but she would not have enjoyed spending the entire day keeping her Gifts on a tight leash.

She sneaks a glance at Mallux, only to find his eyes already on her. Her cheeks colour as she glances away from his strong jaw that she trailed kisses along mere nights ago.

She had awoken to him groaning and rubbing his hands across his face hours later. What followed was a series of stumbling apologies, Mallux barely able to look her in the face as a high blush warmed his cheeks. Telium worried he would regret his drunken passion and things would change between them.

Instead, in the following days, he found any excuse to touch her – a hand on her arm to draw her attention or on her back to walk her into yet another council meeting. Leaning in close to translate a conversation of Old Fae to her. Each brush of his callused hands a whispered promise, reminding her of what lay unresolved between them.

That is how Telium has ended up here, days later, leg jittering as she sits in the back of the wagon, chafing at their crawling pace. They can hardly go rushing into the city on galloping horses without raising suspicion, but that does nothing to help ease her nerves. From what Mallux has told her, it will take them at least another two days of travel until they reach the city.

Telium marvels at the sheer size of Thresiel. It must be double the size of Alkoria; its borders stretching from the impassable mountains to the east to the vast Sordu'era to the west. Alkoria hugs much of its southern border, but what lies to the north, she doesn't know. Perhaps she can find out, once all this is over.

Once she has driven her blade through the King's heart and wiped his blood from her soul.

She alternates between walking and riding in the wagon. The others speak to her rarely and so she occupies herself watching the passing landscape and the few Fae they see. By the time they stop for lunch, Telium is going out of her mind with boredom. She leans back on her hands in the grass, head tipped back to bask in the sun, hair kicking up in a light breeze.

Up ahead, one of the smaller roads converges onto the main thoroughfare where small groups or the odd lone traveller head towards the great city of Meannthe. A travelling couple passes by and she nods to them in greeting along with some of her other companions. The male's face is set into stern, hard lines as he mumbles something under his breath. The concerned crease of the female's brow makes Telium sharpen her hearing.

The male's voice is harsh and grating as he berates the female soundly, before falling silent. When she begs him to let them stop – even Telium knows the Fae word for stop – he ignores her with a contempt that makes Telium's lip curl.

With an inconspicuous flick of her wrist, Telium shoots out a line of her Gifts, shaping the malleable power into an invisible rope that wraps around the male's ankle and holds firm. The Fae does not even have a chance to be surprised as he topples to the ground, hitting the packed earth with a grunt. One of the rebels barks out a harsh laugh, raising his waterskin in mock salute.

The female rushes to his side but he waves her off angrily, face blazing red. Telium allows her Gifts to unravel and slither back to her. The Fae rises, dusting himself off to the brash laughter of more of the rebels and other Fae who are watching nearby.

Even Telium manages a dry chuckle at his beet-red face as he storms off, his poor companion trailing behind him.

Warm ember and citrus washes over her as Mallux settles next to her. She can feel his eyes burning a path across her cheek as she watches the humiliated male retreating with a smirk on her face.

'You know he will likely take his anger out on his *Wai'tine*,' Mallux says with reproach.

Telium turns to look at him, eyes wide with false innocence.

Laughter shines in his sea-blue eyes. He had donned a sleeveless cloak when they left that morning, keeping the hood up when strangers pass by. The closer they get to the capital, the more careful Mallux will have to be, along with some of the other Fae leading the rebellion, whose faces may be recognised. While they are confident that the rebellion is not common knowledge, their presence will raise too many questions. Telium thinks it makes him look brooding and handsome.

'*Whyy tin-eh.*' Telium says, sounding out the word. 'Have you told me that one?'

Mallux shakes his head. He studies her so intently she cocks an eyebrow at him. With a huff, he runs a hand across his jaw and looks up at the clouds.

'*Wai'tinate,*' he says after a moment. 'The Bond. A tether between two souls. Created by the All-Mother.' He looks after the disappearing couple. 'Not all Fae are blessed with finding the other half of their soul in this lifetime. It is the greatest honour.'

Leaning back on one hand, he points at the retreating male's back. '*Wai'tan,*' he says. Before indicating the female, '*Wai'tine.*'

Telium repeats the words, drawing out and curling her tongue around the vowels in the way of Old Fae. Mallux nods in approval.

'There is no direct translation in the Common Tongue for either … like beloved. Keeper of my soul.' He shrugs. 'The closest Alkorian equivalent would be becoming man and wife. But it is more than that. Deeper. Fiercer.'

There is a beat of silence. When Mallux turns those stunning eyes on her again, she realises she is staring.

'Why, Mal,' she quips, blushing and turning away, 'who knew you were such a hopeless romantic?'

'*Mal?*'

Telium snickers at the look on his face, 'Don't like that one?'

Mallux's look turns heated. All Telium's senses jump to prickling awareness as he leans closer.

'I can think of many other things I could get you to call me.'

His words wrap around her, making her toes curl in her boots. She blinks, the only outward sign she heard the underlying promise in them. Behind them, a horse snorts into its nosebag. Clearing her throat, Telium leans back as she remembers how close the other Fae sit to them.

'How do you know she is his *Wai'tine?'* she asks, genuinely curious.

He shrugs one muscular shoulder as he hands her the end of a loaf of bread and some cheese. 'You can sense it, the Bond, like a living tether between them.'

'Huh,' is all she says, munching on her food thoughtfully.

They sit that way in silence, chewing on their bare lunch. As always when Mallux is near, she can feel the tug of him, like he is the sea and she is drowning. His enticing scent seems to envelop her in its embrace – warm and rich and sexy.

A familiar consciousness blazes to life at the edges of her net. She sits up and looks towards the source, calling upon her Gifts to sharpen her eyesight as she stares towards the crossroads further down.

Mallux notices the change in her. He grips the broadsword at his side and leans forward, eyes darting between her face and the road. 'What is it?'

A pair of horses and a head of black hair catch her eye, confirming the consciousness she could feel. 'I think Lotte may be up there.'

Mallux frowns at her and narrows his eyes. She expects him to ask her more questions but it seems he has travelled with her long enough now to understand that she senses such things. He rises to his feet, moving over to one of the other males in the group. He speaks to him in an undertone. The Fae nods at Mallux and jumps up, heading down the road at a brisk pace.

The rest of them quickly pack up and follow behind at a more leisurely pace, blending in with other travellers on the road.

A short distance away, Lotte and Hermitch have dismounted and are waiting on the side of the road with the Fae Mallux sent to catch them. When the group of rebels pass, Hermitch and Lotte fall into step with them. Hermitch barely spares Telium a guarded glance before he mounts up and moves away to ride by one of the other rebels. Lotte gives Mallux a brief hug, before handing him the reins of her horse and making a beeline for Telium.

Lotte greets Telium with her sunshine smile before gripping Telium's wrist and towing her toward the cart. Telium is careful to angle her wrist so that the Fae's hand clasps around the loose cotton fabric of her shirt.

'You,' Lotte says, flicking her hand at one of the three males riding in the cart, 'shove over, my ass is sore from riding all day and night.'

Telium glances at her with raised eyebrows. Lotte, it seems, has some bite.

The male she ordered to move gives her a grin that is all teeth. *'Li'ne,* Lottemeka,' he purrs, warm brown eyes sparkling with mischief. When Lotte tuts and slides her eyes to Telium, the male seamlessly switches to the Common Tongue. 'If your ass needs attention, I would be happy to volunteer my services.'

Lotte barks a laugh and Telium realises the pair must know each other.

'Last time I checked, Red, you were so besotted with me,

that when I invited you to my bed, you could barely form a sentence between the ale and lust addling your brain.'

The other two males on the cart crow with laughter. One slaps Red heartily on the back and receives a snarling shove in reply.

'That was fifty years ago,' Red replies, his voice smooth as silk. 'I think you will find I have grown a lot since then.'

Lotte's returning smile is full of sinful promise and she bats her pretty green eyes at him.

'Well, if you move out of my seat, I may just take you up on that offer ... Unless you would rather sit and listen to us females talk. Though, I cannot say I would be surprised. Last time you got drunk, I found you—'

Red explodes out of his seat.

'Fe'ta! Alright, alright!' he cries, hands held up in surrender.

He glances towards the other two males who are watching with such rapt attention, Telium has to bite her lip to hide the grin fighting its way to the surface.

Red shuffles to the end of the cart and jumps down, grumbling at Lotte as he goes. 'I thought we were past all that.'

The smile Lotte turns on him is as sweet as honey and as innocent as a newborn babe. 'It is our little secret, Red, you just needed reminding of my benevolent nature.'

Red snorts, but still eyes her backside as Lotte turns to be helped up into the cart. 'Always a pleasure, Lottemeka.'

Lotte sits primly on the hard wooden bench, a queen on her throne, and looks down at Red.

'You know how much I love to stroke your little ...' her green eyes flash down suggestively, 'ego.'

One of the males, who is halfway out of the cart, having wisely decided he would rather walk than sit with a silver-tongued vixen and her mad friend, chokes at that.

'You may have my seat, Assassin,' he says as his boots hit the dirt.

'Her name is Telium. You will use it.' Lotte's voice is a whip crack.

Telium feels her heart squeeze at the way Lotte defends her, even though she has no reason to do so. As she takes a seat, Telium sees the male bow his head at Lotte before moving away from the cart.

The remaining male takes one look at Lotte and Telium sitting across from each other, and vaults into the front seat.

CHAPTER
38

'Lotte ...' Telium starts. Then trails off, suddenly unsure of herself. She is not used to being in a position of being grateful to others. She clears her throat. *'Thril'ra.'*

Thank you.

Lotte just smiles and dips her head in a nod. As if she understands how uncomfortable she is. Understands the depths of her gratitude, not only for upbraiding the male, but for speaking with them in the Common Tongue. For making her feel less ... apart.

'No black hair today?' Lotte asks innocently.

'I am holding off until we reach Meannthe in case it rains.'

'A good idea. If it rains heavily enough, the dye will run. When we arrive, I will—' Lotte trails off abruptly, her gaze going blank and distant.

Telium remembers her dream and goosebumps chase across her skin.

'Lotte?' No reply. The Fae's eyes flicker back and forth as if she is watching a sparring match. 'Lotte?' Telium tries again, concern rising in her.

When the female still does not respond, Telium looks

around for Mallux. She is about to call out when she hears Lotte's voice.

'*Oh.*'

Telium whips her head back around to see the Fae blink a few times and her eyes come back into focus.

'Lotte, are you well?' Telium is startled to discover that she is genuinely concerned for the Fae.

A bright smile breaks out across the female's face. '*Threal;* peace. Yes, I am well. It was just a vision.'

Trepidation tickles at the edges of her mind, but Telium cannot stop herself asking, '… Who did you see?'

Unexpectedly, a blush rises to Lotte's cheeks.

'A, uh, male I met the other night in Pexio, while we were spreading the message.'

'Don't you have to have contact with someone to have a visio— Ah.'

Suddenly Lotte's blush makes sense.

'I see.' Telium smiles wickedly, a knowing gleam in her eyes. 'And where *exactly* did you touch this male to get this vision?'

Lotte bursts out laughing, covering her cheeks with her hands. A grin splits Telium's face.

'Oh no, no it's not like that!' Lotte's voice is shaking with suppressed laughter. 'I mean, it was heading that way but …' Lotte stops and scoffs with laughter.

'We were, you know, *getting there.* But he went to kiss me and …' Lotte bites her lip and shakily exhales through pursed lips, obviously trying to contain herself. Telium rolls her hands in a 'go on' gesture. 'He missed my mouth and he … *licked* me.'

Telium blinks, sure she heard wrong. Lotte is practically buzzing with suppressed laughter.

'He ... licked you? On purpose?'

Lotte puts her face in her hands, slim shoulders shaking with giggles. 'No, he went to kiss me, but he was so drunk, he *missed* and got my cheek instead.'

Telium pushes her knuckles to her lips, not wanting to offend the Fae by laughing at her. But one look at Telium's face and Lotte bursts out laughing, eyes closed and face tilted up. The female is laughing so hard she has to gasp out her next words. Telium is unable to help her own huff of amusement.

Lotte looks at her with mock seriousness, making a valiant effort to sound disgusted, despite the humour tickling her voice. 'Telium, I had *drool* all across my *cheek!*'

Lotte attempts to gather herself. Telium waggles her eyebrows suggestively, touching the tip of her tongue to her front teeth. That is all it takes for Lotte to burst out laughing again, this time so violently that she lets out a little snort. Her emerald eyes widen and she gasps, slapping a hand over her mouth.

Telium throws back her head, laughing in earnest this time. The sound rumbles up from deep in her chest. After a moment's hesitation, Lotte joins her and the pair hunch over, laughing hard.

Ridiculous, Telium thinks, as tears leak out of the corner of her eyes, *we are days away from confronting the greatest threat to Alkoria in half a century and here I am giggling over boys.*

Eventually, with great effort, they get themselves under control. Lotte sits back with a sigh and wipes tears from her face. Her other hand splays across her chest. 'All-Mother, I have not laughed like that in many a moon.'

Telium nods her head in agreement. She cannot recall the last time she had laughed like this: until her belly is sore and her cheeks ache.

They sit in companionable silence for a while, before Telium turns to Lotte, clearing her throat. She shifts in her seat and taps her nail on the leather sheath at her hip.

'Would you … like to play Bones?'

Lotte cocks her head to the side. 'I am not familiar with the game,' she says. 'How does it work?'

Telium looks at her in surprise. In Alkoria, Bones is a beloved children's game, even adults continue to play it in their later years. The game consists of five painted animal bones that players catch on the back of their hand and do various tricks with.

She pulls a small drawstring bag from her pack and upends the contents into her hand. Five black bones lay gleaming in her palm. The male Fae sitting in the front regards them over his shoulder, one eyebrow cocked.

'How many can play?' Lotte asks, noting his interest.

'As many as you like. But usually two to five.'

Lotte beams, turning to the male. 'Come join us. Telium is teaching a new game.'

Telium explains the rules to them. Then the game begins.

Lotte excels at it, teasing the male endlessly every time he drops a bone. The game comes to a halt momentarily while they set up camp for dinner but is quickly picked up again on a bed-roll by the fire. In the fading light, it is hard to see the dark bones, adding another level of difficulty.

By this time, Lotte's yells of triumph and the moans of defeat from the male have drawn some of the other rebels. They crouch behind the players, making bets and cheering wins. Mallux settles himself behind Lotte and Telium, slyly brushing a hand across the back of Telium's neck in the process. Friendly banter surrounds them.

Looking over her shoulder, Telium glances at Mallux, his

clear blue eyes already on her. A burst of warmth floods her. It takes a moment for her to identify the emotion.

Happiness.

As startling and beautiful as the first blooms of spring after a grey winter. She beams at Mallux before turning back to the game.

Afterwards, Telium sits leaning against the stationary cart with Lotte who has produced a small slice of sugared bread. She offers some to Telium who takes small bites of the sweet and chews slowly, savouring the sugary flavour. The warm glow of happiness settles in her chest as she watches the stars glint in the sky above the empty road. The moon is a night away from being full, casting her silvery light across the landscape.

The tread of many feet reaches them, echoing through the night. Down the road, a small battalion of soldiers appears. Telium does not move from her relaxed position but draws up her Gifts so they sit close to the surface. Beside her, Lotte shifts so that the quiver of arrows she has discarded is hidden from view.

'The King must have pulled all the *Ka'hine Lei'kah* back to Meannthe already,' Lotte murmurs, knocking her shoulder against Telium.

Indeed, as they pass, Telium can see that there are only two females in the battalion and neither has coloured bands around her forearm.

Once Telium is convinced the soldiers will move on without stopping, she turns back to Lotte, only to find her friend with an odd look plastered across her face as she watches the soldiers go.

'Lotte?' Telium ventures. 'What is it?'

The Fae shakes her head.

'I ...' Lotte frowns, looking after the battalion again. 'Nothing.'

Telium does not push further. Instead, she pops the last piece of sweet bread into her mouth, brushing the crumbs from her hands. Unconsciously, she reaches up to brush her fingers across the greenstone around her neck, then the falkir claw that hangs next to it – the last remnants of her gruesome crown she made in her lone madness all those long winters ago.

CHAPTER
39

Telium frowns down at her sleeping form. I am dreaming, *she tells herself as a wave of vertigo hits her. She blinks rapidly, looking around. The world is oddly silent, as if a thick blanket lays over everything, muffling all sound. Overhead, thick clouds blot out the stars.*

It feels as if her body is rooted to the spot, she is able to move her head, but nothing else. Telium has the bizarre feeling of having her consciousness deposited in another body, one she has no control over.

To her right, embers glow orange in the night as the camp fire dies down. The small coals the only source of light. On the other side, Mallux lies on his bed-roll. He is on his back with his hands threaded over his chest. Telium watches him a moment, the steady rise and fall of his breath.

Looking around, she tries to get her bearings. Work out where, and when, *she is. The rest of the scene is odd and hazy, as if the world ends just outside the light of the dying fire. She cannot pinpoint their location.*

From the bed-rolls and dying fire, she assumes it is from when she and Mallux were travelling along. But exactly what night she is seeing, she cannot tell. In the corner of her eye, sleeping Telium's white hair shines like a beacon.

When she tries to look at her slumbering form again, a wave of dizziness hits her. Telium screws her eyes shut a moment as her head spins. Her body begins to feel warm. Ember and citrus fills her nose. Mallux.

Opening her eyes, she watches as he meanders his way towards Telium's sleeping form. Or rather, his essence does. She watches it seep from his physical form like orange and red oil, making its way toward her bed-roll.

It winds sensually across the grass, skirting the fire like a serpent. All she can smell is him. The temperature ratchets up steadily. Hovering above herself, Telium watches that flame-coloured substance slither its way up her sleeping body.

She shifts in her sleep as it reaches her. The essence forms hands, stroking up her calves, binding her legs. Fingers of red and gold trail across her chest and abdomen. A breathless moan escapes Telium's sleeping form. Standing there watching, her breath comes faster.

Mallux's essence curls around the shell of her ear. Slithers down her neck. Telium swears she can feel the phantom press of lips on her as she stands there. Her body feels too warm; a bead of sweat slips down her spine. If she had control of her body, she would have shivered.

Inside her chest, her Gifts growl. But the feeling is distant. As muffled as the sounds of the world around her.

For a moment, Telium swears she can feel someone approaching. Moving towards the edge of the light with dark purpose. But she is distracted when Mallux's essence wraps itself around her sleeping form completely. A part breaks off, stretching up to encircle her throat. A tendril creeps over her chin, reaching up to caress her lips and—

CHAPTER
40

The next day the afternoon sun warms their backs as they trudge up the hill, stretching their shadows out in front of them as they walk. Up ahead, on the crest of a small rise, is a clearing. A little too large to be natural, Telium wonders at its purpose. Until she breaches the top of the hill where she has an unobstructed view of Meannthe, the crown city. Or more importantly, the palace it surrounds.

Creamy stone walls rise from the centre of the city, the multitude of glass windows reflect the sun and glint like diamonds. The building is perfect in its symmetry; its formidable main building flanked by wings that spread out to either side like open arms. A domed part of the palace roof seems to be capped entirely in glass. It catches the light in a dazzling display, looking like liquid fire. Everything, down to the emerald banners snapping in the breeze, is perfect. Even from here, Telium can see the royal crest stitched in gold – a pair of crossed swords behind a crown.

But it is not the palace that catches Telium's eye. Behind it are enormous grey slabs of stone jutting from the earth after centuries of quakes have raised them from the dirt.

They look like a handful of enormous daggers, the slate-grey tips ending in points. The palace huddles up against them like a child against its mother's skirts. From her perspective, Telium can see the long shadows the rocks cast that reach behind the palace like the fingers of a great beast. She feels a sense of foreboding as goosebumps chase across her skin.

The city surrounding the palace does not extend beyond the colossal stones. Instead, it sits in a semicircle around the palace. Two gates stand at the outskirts, the smaller facing the western road. The southern gate is larger and far more ornate. It sits supported between two pillars of stone, the same sort of pillars they came across after escaping the Infri Pass.

A stab of guilt punches her in the chest as the face of the elder slave from the pass swims before her eyes.

Your sacrifice will not be in vain, she silently promises the spectre. *I will dance with the Fae King and drag his soul down to the Underrealm.*

The columns supporting the gate are smaller than the colossal pillars she has noted in her travels, but they are carved with the same whirls and patterns. The art is so intricate, it could only have been created by a Fae. A single column would have taken many winters to complete. The swirling lines remind Telium of smoke and vaguely resemble the lines of the tattoo inked across her skin. Her hand grazes the fabric covering her leg where her ink lies hidden. *Strange.*

Telium draws on her Gifts to sharpen her eyesight. The gate itself is a work of art, fashioned to look like creeping vines. The brass twists around and back on itself and parts have been gilded. Stone as green as the leafy canopy of her forest has been inlaid at intervals. The deep-green stone has been carved with loving care, fashioned into leaves or flowers, and set into the metal of the gate.

She frowns as she toys with her necklace through the material of her shirt where her own green stone sits resting against her skin. She wonders if there is a connection. Trigg told her she was found with hers, yet the similarity between the two makes her uneasy.

Apart from the gate, there are no other defences around the city. In fact, the gate itself is supported only by the two pillars. No walls or fences surround the city, but there is a clear line between where the plains end and the city begins, marked out by more of the beautifully carved stone pillars.

As they descend the hill, the crowd thickens as more and more travellers join them on the main road running straight down through the centre of Meannthe. The enormous gate is guarded by soldiers, all done up in their military finest – emerald-green shirts trimmed with gold, covered by hard, black leather breastplates and vambraces; legs clad in black pants with boots laced up tightly, in place of greaves, polished so that they gleam in the sun. Leather belts crisscross the guards' arms and chests, holding everything from knives to darts to horns.

It is a far cry from the heavy metal armour the soldiers of Alkoria wear, but they are mortal and do not have the deadly fast reflexes or enhanced healing of the Fae. The effect of all the leather, fabric and gold is surprisingly intimidating. The lightweight material means the wearer has full range of movement with no heavy armour to slow them.

Telium releases her hold on her Gifts and her enhanced eyesight drains away. The soldiers return to blurry spots of black and green beneath the gate.

Her hair is now bare. She has braided it back from her face in intricate swirls that hide the rounded tips of her ears. The rest hangs down her back in pale sheets. While she is certain no-one will recognise her, Telium is mindful not to make eye contact with anyone. Still, she cannot help looking about, fascinated by the sheer number of Fae gathered.

The trees begin to thin as the hill slopes gently down to the expansive plain. A whole city of tents has been set up a short distance from the gate – Meannthe unable to hold all the Fae who have travelled for Rameris. Some of the tents are simple affairs, just a place to lie your head in privacy; others are enormous colourful structures capable of sleeping an entire family with room to spare.

Dotted outside tents are pots and meat strung over camp fires. The Fae gather in groups, laughing and talking. Faelings run around between the tents, nimbly avoiding the guy-lines that hold the shelters in place. A female chases a Faeling, no more than two winters, whose hair is so blonde it borders on white in the bright sun. Telium frowns at the pang in her chest as she watches the Faeling squeal with laughter when her mother throws her up in the air.

Telium is especially fascinated by the young Fae. She has not seen nor read about them before. For all the world, they seem like normal laughing, grubby children. But what marks them apart from mortal children is not just their pointed ears, but the slight luminescence of their skin.

They do not shine or sparkle; nothing so obvious as that, but there is something about them. Telium is reminded of a bride when she walks down the aisle or the look of a woman when she discovers she is with child. *Radiant.* That is the word she would use to describe the young Fae.

Mallux must have seen her tracking the Faelings with fascinated attention because he steps closer to her, his shoulder brushing hers and says, 'It is their magik. All Fae are born with the magik of the land but as they get older, it slowly fades. For females, sometimes it will morph into their Power and stay with them into adulthood.'

Telium watches a group of Faeling males no older than ten winters hurtle between tents, cracking their makeshift swords.

'And the Faeling males?' she asks. 'What happens to their magik?'

Mallux shrugs in reply. 'Males are not made to carry Power; it dissipates back into the land.'

Though he tries his best to sound nonchalant, there is something bitter in his voice. Anger too, simmering deep under the surface.

Telium glances sideways at him. A muscle feathers in his jaw and his lips are pursed. She reaches out, brushing her fingers along the back of his hand. When he looks over at her, she offers him a small smile and nods toward the giant gate.

'Why the gate, when there are no walls surrounding the city?' she asks, hoping to distract him from his thoughts.

He smiles, sending her heart fluttering in her chest. He points to the stone pillars that dot the circumference of the city's outskirts. 'The columns are imbued with Power. They form a sort of net, similar to what a *Tia'tum* can produce. Except one can pass through it if the net allows you.'

'*Allows* you?' she repeats, not sure if she heard him right. She eyes the stone again.

'It is an old Power,' Mallux explains. 'From Fae who are no longer found amongst our gifted. The stones have been standing since long before my time and even before that of my father. It is said that the Fae who created them used the carvings to transfer parts of their consciousness and Power into inanimate objects.

'So, when discussions were made about how to protect

Meannthe against an attack, those females with the Power gave their lives to guard the city and created the pillars. We call them *Lei'sidio*. The guard.'

'So, the pillars … are Fae?' Telium struggles to wrap her mind around the implications.

'Niya.' He shakes his head. 'Not anymore. They are simply something else – Other.'

Telium falls into silence as she contemplates what Mallux told her.

They walk side by side in companionable silence, leaving Lotte to ride in the wagon with Red and another male. Even from here, she can hear Lotte and Red taunting each other, although Lotte is missing her usual bite. The female seems distracted today, but if any of the others notice, they say nothing. Hermitch had ridden on ahead of the group in the early hours to scout. Good. Telium was quickly growing irritated by his guarded looks and sideways glances.

The smell of camp fires and cooking food wafts up toward them. A distance away, one of the Faelings has a makeshift kite and is flying it with the help of a *Cirrus* who uses her Power to help keep the ragtag kite aloft on a gentle gust of wind. The young male runs back and forth, squealing with laughter.

All around her are signs of contentment and happiness, Fae talking and laughing with one another. She spots a group of Fae making bunting in the emerald and gold royal colours. Some males have cleared a space between the tents and removed their shirts, muscled bodies gleaming with sweat under the summer sun as they wrestle each other to the cheering of their companions.

This is not how she pictured the Fae. Despite knowing better, she pictured them all like the Mad Fae King – corrupt, dark, twisted creatures with no room in their hearts for light or love. She thought perhaps Mallux was an exception. But these Fae, they seem ... normal. Telium is forced to admit her childish view of the Fae has been greatly challenged.

As she observes the goings-on from under lowered lashes, she feels her skin prickle as if someone is watching her. She glances around, spotting a familiar form moving with the crowd a short way behind them. Paxium.

Reflexively, she tightens her hold on her Gifts. They stretch and sigh under her skin, the motion soft and languorous. She swears she can feel an internal vibration from them, the hum feeling peculiarly like ... *purring?* Telium's eyes widen in surprise and she glances back again at the Fae with his prowling gait.

Their gazes meet. For a moment, Paxium's brow creases in confusion but then he blinks and the look clears. He smiles brightly and throws her a little wave. Telium merely nods at him and turns away, ignoring the itch of unease he causes. She fidgets with her necklace, running the pendant back and forth along the thin strip of leather.

When the slope levels out onto the plains, they move away from the main thoroughfare, planning to set up camp and watch the gate from afar. At the entrance, the soldiers are hard eyed and alert. They scan the crowd as they pass through, checking the backs of wagons and ordering Fae to remove their hoods so they can see their faces.

While most of the rebellion will be able to pass by the gate unnoticed, there are those, like Mallux and Lotte, whose faces are too noticeable. They will have to find another way in. With the consciousnesses of more than a dozen Fae locked into the pillars surrounding the city, it will be no easy feat.

They find a clearing at the western edge of the tent city, closer to the smaller gate, hoping they will be able to sneak through later in the evening. Mallux passes her his waterskin. A few other rebels join them, including Lotte and Hermitch. Telium has watched him from the times she has sat in on the meetings, listening to them discuss logistics. From what she gathers, he grew up with Mallux, and as such has turned into something of a loyal hound.

Telium eyes the male closely, sizing him up. He could be another vote for the release of human slaves here. While she does not doubt Mallux's commitment, it will not hurt for her to try and win over another Fae to her cause.

She waltzes over to Hermitch, determined to play politics – a game she had been forced to master in her time as an assassin, despite her loathing for it. Sitting down beside the Fae, Telium offers up the waterskin. He looks at her with a guarded expression, as if she would try to poison him, before shaking his head.

Hermitch watches her with bright hazel eyes. He has cut his hair shorter since she last saw him and now it sticks out in rebellious waves. Coupled with his smattering of freckles, it gives him a look of innocence that is at odds with his stormy demeanour.

She strikes up a conversation with him, talking about things of little consequence, like the heat and the hard march and what they will have for dinner. Determined to make an ally out of Mallux's friend.

He seems hesitant to talk to her, but she turns her brightest smile on him and continues to chatter about boring things. He begins to relax, probably thinking he has overestimated her and her prowess.

She passes him the platter of dried fruits that is being handed around. She notes Mallux watching them from across the fire, staring at the hand she has now returned to her lap.

There is suspicion and a hint of jealousy in his eyes. The look squeezes her heart.

She gestures him over to sit next to her and they begin to talk about more important things, like how to get into the city unnoticed. Mallux has discreetly sent runners with messages to those rebels already stationed inside the city, to see if they can find a way in.

Lotte is sitting across the other side of the fire, playing Bones with two other Fae. Telium decides to find a butcher in the city once all this is over so she can make Lotte a set for herself. It would be the least she could do to repay the Fae's kindness.

There is a flurry of movement across from them as Lotte stands up abruptly. When everyone turns to look at her, she flushes and focuses on wrapping her cloak around her body. 'I am going to stretch my legs before dinner,' she says before levelling a threatening finger at the two remaining males. 'You will give those straight back to Telium when you are done, *vel?*'

'Lotte,' Telium says, surprised by the venom in her friend's voice. 'It's fine.'

The raven-haired female stalks out of camp. Telium only half listens to Mallux and Hermitch's murmured conversation. Worry nags her, twisting in her gut. Since seeing the King's soldiers the other night, Lotte has been out of sorts. Though hesitant to overstep the bounds of her new-found relationship with Lotte, Telium is unable to brush aside her concern. Such intuition has proven well-founded in the past. So, after eating her handful of dried fruits, she dons her cloak and rises, planning to follow Lotte.

Hermitch gives her a sharp look and opens his mouth as if he is about to argue, but Mallux stops him with a hand on his shoulder. 'Let her go,' he murmurs.

Mallux walks with her a few steps, giving them the illusion of privacy, though she does not doubt the other Fae can still hear them with their sharp ears. He grips her arm, spinning her around to face him. 'What are you doing?' His warm words skim across her skin.

His suspicion rankles her, but she reminds herself that she is foreign to these lands, and is Mallux's secret weapon. He is just worried for her. She smiles up at him with a mischievous curve to her mouth and trails her fingers along his chest. 'Nothing reckless,' she whispers. 'I just want to walk, to watch and listen, see if I can find out anything useful. Check on Lotte.'

Mallux searches her face intently. He leans down so that their lips are a hair's-breadth apart. Citrus and embers. Telium cannot help tilting her chin up in anticipation of the kiss. Her eyelids flutter down as his breath warms her cheeks. Her stomach clenches and butterflies dance as he parts his lips.

'Be back before the next bell, *upa*,' he purrs, squeezing her arm and stepping back. He turns on his heel and walks back to their little camp, sitting down next to Hermitch without a backwards glance.

Well. With that unspoken promise simmering under the surface, she will be back long before then. Telium rolls her neck, shaking off her lingering lust and strides away, her hidden daggers and knives constant companions.

CHAPTER
41

The sun is close to touching the horizon and the sky lights up in fantastic splashes of pink and gold. Telium wanders through the tent city, trying to find Lotte by stretching out the net of her mind, but the area is so crowded, it is difficult to distinguish any one consciousness. She feels like she is standing above a bustling street, its colours and shapes bombarding her senses.

The sounds and smells of hundreds of Fae together briefly overwhelm Telium, who has spent the better part of her life in solitude. But there is a part of her that thrives in the colourful, organised chaos. That long-buried part of her that wants to kick up her heels and dance alongside the pretty Fae maidens. She drinks in her surroundings – the songs and food and people. Eventually, she pulls her consciousness in close, leaving a small bubble around her immediate surroundings instead. *I'll just look for her the old-fashioned way.*

Telium is not far from the edge of the tents when she spots Lotte from the corner of her eye. She starts towards her, noting an odd look on her face. It is not quite sadness but something else – softer.

Lotte looks up in surprise when Telium reaches her. 'I have the oddest feeling that I have forgotten something,' she says.

Telium cocks her head at the female. 'Like what?'

'I do not know.' Lotte sounds disappointed. 'I feel like I need to go somewhere, then the feeling vanishes and I feel silly for entertaining the idea.' She shakes her head, throwing her sunshine smile at Telium. But it does not quite reach her eyes.

Telium frowns.

Lotte checks over her shoulder, eyes scouring the crowd. Catching herself in the act, she turns back around, straightening her spine resolutely.

Telium can tell Lotte does not want to be questioned so she walks quietly beside her friend, offering whatever silent comfort her presence can provide. As they make their way back to the others, Telium thinks of all the times she has felt the ebony brush of Tenebris and wonders whether some deity hounds Lotte too. She is about to ask when Lotte stops dead in her tracks. Her green eyes go wide, full lips parting in shock.

Telium frowns again and gazes over the crowd to see what has caught the female's attention. *Or who*, she thinks as she sees a handsome Fae with short-cropped brown curls and stormy blue eyes. He is frozen in an awkward half-crouch after rising from his seat. His eyes are riveted on Lotte.

Turning back to her friend, Telium watches in confusion as Lotte raises a hand to her heart on a sharp intake of breath. Some of the male's companions have noticed his odd behaviour too and turn to him in question.

As if he is afraid of startling her, the male straightens slowly, never taking his eyes off Lotte. When she does not move or flee, he steps towards her.

Telium's eyes dart between the two and she slides a hand surreptitiously to a blade beneath her cloak. Who is this male?

Does Lotte know him? Has she had a vision of him? A thought chills Telium to the core and she turns a hard, calculating eye on the male, noting the leathers covering a fine emerald shirt. *Is he with the King?*

But the look on Lotte's face stills the questions on Telium's lips. Her friend is wearing a look of such unabashed joy that it makes Telium blink in confusion. *What in Tenebris' name is going on?* Her head whips around to level a threatening glare at the male as he moves closer to Lotte. Telium swears she can feel Power buzzing in the air. The tension between the two so thick she could choke on it.

The movement he makes seems to break whatever leash held them and Lotte takes a shaky step forward. Tears glitter in her eyes and she begins to sway. Telium realises with a jolt that Lotte is about to collapse. Before she has even finished the thought, the male sweeps Lotte into his arms and crushes her against his chest. When they part, his blue-grey eyes devour her. Lotte's gaze is just as heated as it tracks over him. The embrace is so passionate, despite its innocence, that Telium glances away, the tips of her ears going red.

The nearby Fae watch the scene with rapt attention. Their wistful looks only add to Telium's confusion and she turns back to the couple with a spark of irritation, preparing to demand the male get his goddess-damned hands off her friend and start explaining. She is stalled by the fervent words that fall breathlessly from Lotte's lips.

'*Keth rel amrath thro'sul, Wai'tan.*'

The male's eyes brighten and he swoops down to claim Lotte's mouth in a passionate kiss that has some of the watching females sighing. Telium's mouth is still hanging open, ready to spew out profanities. She snaps it shut. She knows *Wai'tan* is the equivalent of husband. But deeper. Stronger.

A soul-bonded partner. And *thro'sul* means *soul* ... but she doesn't know what the rest means.

Lotte pulls back and gazes into the face of the male who holds her, her cheeks flushed red.

'*Tanu de rel'ak,*' he breathes, his voice a deep rumble.

'*Vel,*' Lotte replies.

The tension in the air shatters and Telium swears she can *feel* the tether form between their two souls.

A cheer goes up from one of the male's companions, which is quickly taken up by the rest. Even passers-by clap and cheer. The noise seems to break the haze that surrounds Lotte and her flush spreads even further as she steps back from the male. She keeps a hand outstretched, fingers resting lightly on his chest as if she cannot bear to let him go.

'Lotte,' Telium whispers as she stares at the green shirt and leather armour of her *Wai'tan's* uniform.

He has turned to beam at another Fae who is thumping him on the back in congratulations.

A slight frown creases Lotte's brow as she follows Telium's gaze. Lotte's face goes pale and she takes her *Wai'tan's* shirt front in a bloodless grip. Panic flares in her eyes.

As if he can sense it through their newly forged bond, the male turns back to Lotte with a concerned frown. Lotte spins to face Telium, still holding that damning shirt in her white-knuckled fist.

'Telium,' Lotte gasps and reaches out with her other hand to take Telium by the sleeve and pull her close.

Telium is startled by Lotte's strength, then berates herself immediately. While she may look like a delicate maiden, Lotte is still Fae and therefore stronger than any human by a good stretch.

'Telium.' Her voice is breathless. 'You must not tell him. You cannot, he will not understand.'

Mallux. Lotte is talking about Mallux.

A low growl rumbles from the male's chest. Telium does not care how this conversation sounds to him.

Lotte must see the indecision on her face because she tightens her hold on Telium's sleeve, tugging her a little closer. *'Please.'*

That single word, so full of terror and heartache and desperation. So much like the time Telium had lain at the foot of the Siren Queen's stairs and begged. The memory lashes through her like lightning. Telium looks at Lotte; the friend she is only just beginning to make, the female who barely knows her but bought her dye to hide her white hair, the Fae who recklessly leaned close to her knives to examine her strange eyes.

She knows right then that she will not betray Lotte; she will take this secret to her grave. Knowing Lotte and her *Wai'tan* won't be able to live peacefully until the Fae King is dead adds another flame to Telium's burning desire to bring the bastard to his knees.

Telium places a hand over Lotte's in a blaring display of trust, her bare skin against the *Ohic'a's* own, and nods.

Lotte sags in relief, turning to murmur soothing words to her *Wai'tan*, who is growing agitated at the conversation, no doubt thinking something completely different. Certainly not that his new *Wai'tine* is part of a rebel alliance a day away from bringing down his King.

The male's next words leave him in a reverent whisper of melodic Old Fae, tilting Lotte's chin up with such tenderness that any reservations Telium has are immediately erased.

This male will do anything Lotte asks of him. Once she recovers from the shock of the *Wai'tinate* Bond locking into place, that will likely be a great many things. Telium ducks her head to hide a smile as Lotte releases her. The poor male has no idea what he is in for.

'Lottemeka,' the female replies.

'Lottemeka,' the male murmurs. 'With eyes like spring and hair like night.' He picks up a strand of Lotte's ink-black hair and runs it between his fingers before dropping his gaze to her lips, his eyes blazing with masculine hunger. 'I am Orion.'

'Orion,' Lotte says, her voice husky. 'I would take a moment, to gather my thoughts ...' She gazes around at the gathered Fae. Some are drinking on behalf of the Bonded couple, while others stare at them unabashedly. '... In private,' she finishes, but her fingers stay fisted in his shirt as if of their own volition.

Orion nods, his fingers curling around her wrist as he gently pries her hand from his shirt before bringing it to his lips to kiss her knuckles. 'If it pleases you, I will accompany you.'

The male sounds as if he is worried Lotte will reject his offer. The dark-haired beauty beams at him, nodding her consent. They manage to let go of each other long enough for Orion to farewell his companions.

With sudden intensity, Lotte turns to Telium and grasps her wrist in a bruising grip. 'You will not tell him, will you?' she whispers.

'Of course not.' Hurt flares in Telium's chest that Lotte would trust her so little. The Fae's face softens as if she has sensed Telium's hurt. 'But Lotte,' Telium adds, 'he's the *King's* soldier.'

'I know, I know. I will sort something out.' She pauses a moment before pulling Telium into a bone-crushing hug. 'Thank you, sister,' she whispers in Telium's ear, 'and tell Mallux ...' Lotte glances over her shoulder at her *Wai'tan* who is waiting for her. 'Tell him I had a vision and left in a rush. Tell him I said I did not know when I would be back. He will be too preoccupied with tomorrow anyway. I just need a little while to figure this out. But I *will* figure this out. It will all be fine. Fine.'

Telium senses she says this last part more to herself. Everything is happening so fast, Telium just hugs her friend one last time and whispers, 'Be careful. Tell him if he hurts you, I'll hunt him down and add him to my necklace.'

Lotte laughs. Then she is gone, folded in her *Wai'tan's* embrace as they head for the empty plain.

Telium watches them go, suddenly feeling very alone in a crowd of Fae, one of whom appears right beside her, offering her a mug of ale to drink to the new *Wai'tinate* Bond forged between two Fae. She politely declines, slipping off between the tents in the direction of Mallux and her bed.

Though she has never seen the ocean, she imagines this is how men on a boat must feel, lost on an endless, stormy sea. Like they are utterly alone in the vast expanse of cold waves. In a way, Mallux makes her feel a little less alone. She finds herself looking forward to the comfort of just being in his presence.

Her feet change direction of their own accord as she is drawn to the furthest edge of the tents to the quiet space between civilisation and wilderness, fascinated by the way the light bleeds into darkness. Telium tilts her face up to the sky, watching as the last light fades to blackness and the stars begin to come out one by one. Everything seems quiet and still. Even the wind is the softest whisper across the plains. The stars are dimmed by the multitude of camp fires at her back. Telium glances at them once more before turning on her heel and heading back towards their little tent.

CHAPTER
42

Telium moves through the city of tents with a smooth gait, passing groups of Fae who gather around camp fires together to share a meal. The smell of cooking meats and spices makes her stomach growl, but she ignores it. She wanders about for a little longer, hoping to catch a snippet of conversation, a whisper, *something* that can help them get inside those walls by tomorrow.

Nothing. None of the Fae gathered seem concerned about passing through the gate in the morning. All they speak about is trivial subjects: their journey, the weather, family, the food.

With a twinge of disappointment, Telium turns and makes her way back to Mallux and the others. Consciousnesses touch the edges of her net as she walks, each one unique to its owner. The walls protecting their minds range from the more common towering stone fortresses to tangled briar bushes. One Fae's mind even feels like the snarling jaws of a wolf. Telium glances sideways under lowered lashes and spots a young female with ebony hair cropped short around her ears and lovely blue eyes. A band of green, black and yellow is tied about her arm. Telium does not know what the colours represent, but judging by the female's consciousness, it must be something fierce indeed.

Something beyond the Powered Fae catches her eye – a glint of metal in dark locks and a flash of white teeth. Paxium stands talking to another male, laughing as they clink wooden mugs together. He downs the ale in a few quick gulps, then claps the male on the shoulder and hands him the empty cup, before moving away.

After many years as an assassin, Telium has developed a sixth sense for certain things, so when her feet move instinctively to follow, she does not question it. She ghosts after Pax as he moves through the camp, generous with his smiles and greetings, waving at those he passes.

At one point, a young female, no more than five winters old, points a toy bow at Paxium and fires an imaginary arrow, making the *shhk* sound of a bowstring as she does. He gasps dramatically, throwing his head back and clutching his chest, before looking down and grinning at the little Fae. The young female smiles at him, eyes bright, before being ushered away by her mother.

The interaction makes Telium frown, even as a smile curves her lips. For one with such a dark soul, Paxium is charming. That alone makes him even more deadly. Telium knows all too well how to act the part of appealing innocence. Always considered herself rather good at it. But if she is good, then Paxium is a master; his mask does not falter once. Not a hint of what lies beneath reaches his eyes. Chills skitter across Telium's skin. *Dangerous,* her Gifts whisper to her, *this one is dangerous.*

Paxium reaches the edge of camp and moves off to the plain beyond in the direction of Meannthe. He moves in lazy lines as if going for a late stroll because he was unable to sleep.

With a flare of suspicion, Telium follows behind him, careful to keep her feet quiet on the ground. She moves slowly with stealth that comes from years of training, eyes flashing in the dark with an animalistic shine. She slinks from straggly trees to weeds, keeping her body hidden by the sparse cover where she can.

Where is he off to?

Paxium heads away from the tents to the eastern side of the city. He seems to be counting the pillars. The huge daggers of stone tower over everything, their presence ominous as they loom over the city and its inhabitants. Why anyone would want to build a city here is beyond her. The massive grey slabs of granite make her Gifts itch. She cannot imagine what it is like for the townsfolk who spend their days under their presence.

Pax stops before one of the columns, his shoulders rising as he takes a deep gulp of air before stepping forward and placing his hand on one of the pillars. Alarm spikes in her chest. Surely the *Lei'sidio* will punish him. If he is the kind of male Telium suspects, certainly the pillars will not let him pass?

Paxium's head bows under an invisible force, the motion causing his long locks to slip to the side. Pale moonlight glows against the warm-copper skin of his neck, highlighting the cords standing out as his muscles strain.

Telium does not move, barely breathes, as she watches him for long moments, convinced the *Lei'sidio* will see the darkness in his soul and turn him into a pillar of fire. Finally, the tension ebbs from his shoulders and Telium feels her unease melt away. With a shuddering inhale, Pax removes his hand from the column of stone and walks into the dark city streets beyond.

'*Tenebris* curse him,' Telium swears under her breath as she moves forward, eyeing the stone with caution.

Her instincts tell her she needs to see where the Fae is going.

She eases out her consciousness, spreading it out like a net around her. She creeps forward. At the first brush of her mind against the shield of pillars, she stops. The invisible wall feels like a great sleeping beast: slow and slumberous, but powerful. Telium is reminded of the ancient trees of her forest: alive but not. A force pulses there; it is lacking the sharpness of a human mind. If she could encompass all her trees in her mind-net, it would still pale in comparison to what she feels radiating from the wall.

Telium stands still for a handful of heartbeats. The wall shows no signs of noticing her presence. Brazened, she moves forward another step. Still nothing. Her heart pounds in her ears and sweat slicks her hands. She is hyper-aware of every second as it ticks by; each moment allowing Paxium to slip further from her. Gritting her teeth, Telium takes another step. She is close enough that she could reach out and brush her hand across the cool, carved stone. She does not dare.

Her eyes track the whirls etched on the pillar's surface. She looks up and to each side of her, waiting for something to happen. When it does not, she releases a shuddering breath and moves on. She has barely taken two steps before the combined consciousness of the *Lei'sidio* is turned upon her. Telium gasps, yanking her Gifts to the surface, pushing Blood-Thief power into her limbs to grant her the speed to flee. But her body will not obey her. Her mind is held tightly in the *Lei'sidio's* grip.

Without effort, the not-Fae of the wall brushes aside her defence and strips her mind bare. Telium cries out in her mind, fear and pain warring inside her. The power that fills her is so vast she cannot comprehend it. Her mind feels like a great weight is pressed upon it, smothering her senses – her very soul. Telium throws her head back in wordless agony, jaw clenched so hard the tendons stand up in steel ropes. Her muscles tighten and tremble under the onslaught.

Every dark crevice of her soul is pulled out and scrutinised. Every happy memory, taken out and turned over. Examined like some interesting trinket. There is nothing she could have hidden from the invasion if she wanted to. Her Gifts hiss. Those too are taken out and inspected, like an unruly kitten, before being shoved back into the restraints Telium keeps them in. Surprise emanates from the combined consciousnesses.

A patter of ancient lyrical Fae words whisper into her mind. The headache it causes is instant and throbbing, making her squeeze her eyes shut against the pounding in her skull. The voices seem to come from everywhere and nowhere at once; the sound of a dozen voices speaking in perfect union. Though they speak in Old Fae, Telium somehow understands every word.

What a curiosity. What are you?

The wall hums in response to the image of the Power-Thief who asked Telium the same question a lifetime ago.

You are not mortal.

It is not a question, but the answer bursts forth in Telium's mind regardless, her mental voice breathy and tight. *No.*

But completely Fae, you are not.

Again, Telium can do nothing but gasp out her agreement. *I am not Fae, no. I am not mortal.*

Then what being are you?

The voices sound displeased this time, their irritation raking across her senses. She can feel a storm building, knows her life likely hangs on the answer. Her heart beats erratically in her chest, fluttering like a trapped bird. Her muscles tremble. *I do not know,* she answers truthfully, teeth grinding under the strain, *I am neither human nor Fae. Like you, but not. I am simply* Other.

The building power hesitates at that. Turns away for a

moment. Telium has the impression of the consciousnesses whispering to themselves.

She could bring about the new age! She is—
Hush.
Her soul is dark.
Her intent is pure …
She bears the mark of …
It is unprecedented.
But she could be the—
Hush!
It is the will of …

The barrage of voices rise and fall about her. Telium feels like she is caught up in the middle of a storm, certain her brain is going to explode out of her ears. She feels a trickle of liquid run over her lip and knows without raising her hand that her nose has begun to bleed. Her skin feels tight and hot, stretched thin across muscle and flesh. She is going to die. She should be panicking, but with her mind held in the vice-like grip of the *Lei'sidio,* she cannot summon the emotion.

As abruptly as it began, the assault ends. The sudden lack of noise and movement causes Telium's ears to ring with a high-pitched whine. She flexes her jaw, trying to release the built-up pressure. She still cannot move other than to draw in great shuddering gasps. Tears spring to her eyes and she bows her head reverently. Her haughty arrogance chastised by the consciousnesses that saw through her very being; her stubborn pride, humbled by the immense Power.

The consciousnesses seem to watch her for a moment longer, then with what feels disconcertingly like a sigh, release her from their grip.

Do not make us regret this decision, little half-Fae.

✑

Telium stumbles forward at the sudden freedom, knees cracking on the cobblestone road lining the city streets as she collapses. Her body, her entire soul, feels like it has been twisted and wrung dry. Muscles tremble while she kneels, taking deep, steadying breaths as she slowly pieces her entire being back together.

Remarkably, she is unharmed. Even her sudden vicious headache has disappeared. All that's left is an odd sensation, like a second skin sticking to her. With the back of her hand, she wipes the blood from her mouth and chin. Taking a moment to centre herself, Telium draws up her Gifts once more, climbing gingerly to her feet. Every hair on her body stands on end at the *Lei'sidio's* presence at her back, but she is too cowardly to speak.

She does not need her Gifted eyesight with the lamps casting soft buttery light at every corner. Still, she closes her eyes and inhales deeply, Mind-Thief-enhanced nose picking up the trace of rain and eucalyptus that is Paxium.

With a tentative peek over her shoulder at the carved stone pillar, she moves off after the male. She is determined to find out why he is sneaking about, driven by the sense of unrest her Gifts cause around him. She tracks his scent like a hound, moving swiftly through the night, hugging the walls and shadows. Telium has not gone far when the sound of soft knocking reaches her. She slows to a slink, crouching down to peer around the corner.

Paxium stands on the doorstep of a home, hands in his pockets. He shifts his weight from foot to foot, glancing up and down the street. Telium ducks her head in the shadowed cowl of her hood and holds deathly still, willing her heartbeat to quieten. She need not worry. The male merely turns back to the faded-green door and knocks again.

'Alinte,' he murmurs.

After a moment, a female opens the door. Her upturned face catches the moonlight, highlighting a sweet round face framed by thick chestnut waves and wide eyes of verdant green. The Fae's face lights up in surprise and she glances over his shoulder. 'Paxium,' she whispers, her voice melodic. 'You should not be here.'

'I had to come,' he replies, leaning in close.

Oh.

A flush creeps across Telium's face. It is suddenly quite obvious what Paxium is doing here, with this beautiful female with a face like springtime. Feeling like a foolish peeping Tom, Telium turns quickly to go, cursing herself. But Paxium's next words stop her dead in her tracks.

'An opportunity has arisen and the news could not wait. Can we speak inside?'

'Yes, yes. Of course.'

Telium's curiosity flares. Those are not the words of secret lovers. She watches as Paxium follows the female inside before she creeps across to the house. She dares not touch the building or even lean against the cool brick, for fear of triggering some sort of trap. She still wasn't familiar with the full extent of the Fae's capabilities.

Even with her enhanced hearing, Telium has to strain her ears to hear. The thick walls muffle the Fae's quiet voices. Every muscle in her body is taut as she creeps up to the front door, hugging shadows as she goes. She has to shuffle so close that her ear is nearly pressed up against the green wood of the door.

Risky, a voice echoes in her mind, *very risky*. Trigg is oft the voice of wisdom that creeps up through time, cautioning her when she behaves too rashly. Emotions and control still scattered after her trial by the *Lei'sidio*, Telium recalls the rich, warm voice of her teacher with a flare of heartache. She twitches her shoulder, pushing away the voice as she would an annoying fly. Buries her pain and sorrow deep down. She needs to concentrate now. She can grieve later.

Leaning forward, she listens intently. The smell of dirt and paint mix with the damp earth smell of Paxium that lingers in the doorway. Another smell, one she assumes belongs to the female, dominates. Wildflowers and sunshine tickle Telium's nose. She hears the pair moving about inside and the sound of liquid being poured.

'Alinte, there is no time for tea.' That is Paxium, his voice slightly exasperated.

'There is always time for tea,' Alinte replies matter-of-factly.

'Hermitch and some of the others are here … Mallux too,' the male states bluntly. 'The others must not be far behind if they are not here already.'

A cup rattles in its saucer. Telium cannot feel the surface emotions of Fae the way she can mortals, but she imagines the female is shocked. Their consciousnesses sit like stones in her mind; the dark mist-shrouded strength of Paxium in sharp contrast to the ivy-wrapped stone walls of Alinte.

'I fear the palace may be compromised; that they may have managed to sneak in spies of their own. All-Mother knows how many are already in the city.'

A snort. 'Paxium, none but the most trustworthy are allowed to serve. Many of the staff are hired by the King's guard. Do you think we could not smell out a rebel spy?' The female's tone is haughty.

Telium growls internally. *Tenebris curse him! The traitor is a goddess-damned spy!* Anger and disappointment war in her chest. She had hoped, for some reason beyond her ken, that she was wrong about him. That despite the way he affected her Gifts, he was not the dark, dangerous thing she suspected him to be.

He has sided with the Mad Fae King, with everything Telium stands against and is actively working to undermine everything Mallux has worked for. Her jaw clenches and she grinds her palms hard into the ground. She snarls silently. Under her skin, her Gifts sit eerily quiet.

'If those of the council are here, I will alert the King immediately,' Alinte says. 'We will have guards out within the hour to apprehend them.'

Icy fear sloshes through her. *Shit, shit, shit! I have to warn Mallux—*

'No.' Paxium's voice is no less commanding for its quietness. 'Too messy. And they have not all arrived. We cannot afford to leave but one rebel behind. They are a weed and should be treated as such. We need to pull out the entire plant, roots and all.'

'We cannot afford to waste time,' the female argues. 'Every moment we delay puts my King at risk.'

'The King's feast,' Paxium replies evenly.

'What?' Alinte snaps.

'That's when they plan to attack. All the council members and courtiers will be there. They will be dominated in one fell swoop, held hostage until they swear fealty.'

Telium frowns. Now where had he got that information from? *Twisted, cunning little spy.* Despite the disgust warring in her chest, she is grudgingly impressed with his skill. The plan had been devised with the highest order of secrecy; it was near impossible for someone working against them to get hold of that news. Her mind races. She can't risk taking them out on her own. If Alinte is part of the *Lei'kah*, surely someone would notice her missing.

Even if they didn't, Telium can't risk alerting others in the ensuing scuffle. She has to get back to Mallux and tell him. Together, they could work something out. Adrenaline spikes through her limbs; she has to hurry.

I did not come this far to fall at the last hurdle. Telium's skin itches as the residual sensation from the *Lei'sidio* feels like it begins to drip from her. She rises from her crouch, meaning to leave when the lilting female voice catches her attention again.

'Paxium, this news is crucial, but you risked much coming here. I expected you to know better than to come skulking through the front gate at night.' Her tone is accusatory.

'I came through the wall,' Paxium replies tightly as if she has offended him. 'Fae nor mortal would have been able to follow me with ill intent. The *Lei'sidio* may not care who leaves the city but they certainly care who enters.'

'Through the wall?' Alinte hisses. 'Paxium, are you mad? You—'

'Did not have the time to lose a tail, on the off-chance I was followed after coming through the gate.'

Telium has heard enough. Cursing Paxium colourfully in her head, she creeps away from the door, careful not to crunch any dry leaves underfoot. Then she is off, running through the streets, urgency dogging her heels as she skids around corners and hurtles toward the edge of the city.

She has not come this far to fail now. Has not fought bandits, outrun fires, bloodied her hands, been looked down on and outcast by these Fae, to sleep in the same city as the Mad King and not run her blade through his black fucking heart.

She grits her teeth so hard they grind together as she pushes on. The last of the odd sensation falls away. With it, Telium picks up the murmured conversation of Old Fae as families sit down to their dinners. With an iron will, she clamps down on her panic, mind racing as she tries to come up with a solution to get them out from under Paxium's spying eyes. Telium and Mallux, along with the rebellion, are all that stand between the Mad Fae King and Alkoria. The Thief children there. They cannot falter.

Without warning, the thought of Mallux's body, bloody and broken, flashes in her mind. The screams of her Queen echo in her ears. *Treason.* But this time, it is true. What she is conspiring with Mallux and the others to do is treason of the highest order. They would be imprisoned and killed. Or worse.

Alkoria's army cannot stand against the might of the Fae, Telium thinks as she runs, *they will be slaughtered.* The invisible presence of the slave woman haunts her steps accusingly. If they are caught, Telium's promise will go unfulfilled. Not only will the slaves here be owned until the day they die if the King succeeds, but the rest of Alkoria would likely suffer a similar fate.

Once Alkoria falls, he will have unlimited access to Thieves for his experiments. There would be no stopping him. His power would be absolute.

The invisible border between the city's edge and the field comes into view. Her chest tightens with apprehension, but Telium is banking on what Paxium said about the pillars not caring who leaves the city. The Power hits her like a slap, and Telium gasps despite herself. She can feel the combined consciousnesses of the not-Fae are aware of her, but this time it seems they will let her pass without contest. Her body feels like it is running through syrup.

Hello. A sweet tinkling voice makes Telium skid to a stop.

The hairs on the back of her neck stand on end, pre-empting the pain that is about to envelop her again.

You are Telium. The voice speaks again. As before, it is everywhere and nowhere all at once. It echoes in her mind. But unlike before, this is distinctly one voice, high and clear as a bell.

Telium can still feel the immense Power behind it so thinks it wise to answer the question. 'Yes,' she whispers aloud.

I am Elanora. The voice pauses as if waiting for something.

'Hello, Elanora,' Telium replies politely, unsure who exactly she is having a conversation with.

Suddenly, an image flares to life in her mind's eye: a young Fae, no older than ten, stands before her. She has silky deep-brown hair that falls in straight sheets about her waist. Round, bottomless brown eyes stare out from an innocent face with fat rosy cheeks and full lips. She is suffused with a soft, warm glow, stronger than that of the Faelings.

We are alike, you and I. Other – Fae, but not quite.

'Are you one of the *Lei'sidio?'* Telium asks softly.

The girl nods.

Unexpected tears prickle Telium's eyes. *So young,* she thinks, *to give up her life in defence of her people.* She watches the girl check over her shoulder furtively. 'Are you allowed to talk to me?' Telium asks suspiciously.

Elanora ducks her head, shaking it as she toes the dirt with her bare foot. *I like to talk to people sometimes; those brave enough to touch our Power. The others say I should not speak to Fae who walk through the wall. But you are not Fae; you are like me.*

Telium smiles at the childlike reasoning and waits for her to continue.

I just want a friend, the girl says quietly after a moment, scuffing her foot again.

Telium feels her heart crack open in her chest. This girl never had the opportunity to make friends or learn her path in life. Never to fall in love or have her heart broken. In her mind, she crouches in front of Elanora, taking one small glowing hand in hers. Telium can do naught for this child who lost her life before it had really begun, but she *could* do this.

'Tell you what, I will be your friend, but you must promise me you will do as the others ask and not speak to any more *beings* that walk through the wall, okay?'

Pure joy lights up the child's face and a smile spreads unchecked across Telium's own.

Elanora nods vigorously.

'Good, it is settled then. Friends?'

Friends! The girl shrieks and throws her arms around Telium, who gasps as the child's vast unfettered Power brushes against her.

Did you like my gift?

Telium pulls back from the girl, looking down at her happy, round face. 'I'm sorry?'

When you went to see your friends, you understood them. Did you not? Elanora frowns, touching Telium's cheek, *Though it seems to have worn off already.*

Telium's brow bunches in confusion as she lets go of the child and looks down at her. While she is intrigued by the girl, Telium does not have the luxury of time to discuss what she means.

'Elanora …' she begins, unwilling to upset the powerhouse.

You have to go. The child nods. *I know.*

'Yes, I must—'

Help your friends, Elanora interrupts. *I know.*

'Ah.' Telium stalls, taken aback. 'Yes, that's right. But I will—'

Be back, the girl finishes for her, grinning deviously. *I know.*

Telium laughs, recognising the girl's forced innocent smile and the cunning that shines in her eyes. Of course, she knows. This girl, along with the others, has just waltzed through her mind and soul as easily as taking a leisurely stroll through a rose garden. Throwing her own wicked smile at the child, she waves as Elanora vanishes from her mind.

Telium blinks, refocusing on the world around her, then takes off toward the tent city, legs eating up the distance.

CHAPTER
43

Telium arrives at their tents to find most of the group have gone to bed. But Mallux is still up talking to Hermitch, who scowls at her approach.

Her legs itch from forcing herself to walk at a slow, measured pace through the tents when all she wants to do is run to Mallux with her news. When she spots him, pride flutters in her chest; she is eager to tell him what she has learned.

Mostly, she feels rather useless, sitting aside while Mallux and the others speak about plans and places she knows next to nothing about, in a language she is only just beginning to learn. It irks her to know so little, but as it was unlikely they would take her advice anyway, she has held her counsel. Subtly making her own arrangements to improve the plans. But this news is not only helpful, it's crucial. They cannot deny her usefulness now. It will prove her worth as a warrior – or at least, her reputation as an assassin.

Mallux frowns at her as she approaches. Her 'short walk' has turned into bells and she is sure he is furious. Telium sticks out her chin and ignores his expression. She speaks before he can get a word in.

'Paxium's a spy.'

'Who?'

'Paxium,' she repeats, exasperated.

'I know him,' Hermitch pipes up. 'He is a scout. He and the female, Lillian, came to join the rebellion many moons ago.' He curses at the news but Mallux waves a hand to silence him.

'How do you know this, Telium?' Mallux enquires, his voice hard.

She feels a small stab of disappointment at his callousness but pushes it aside. Quickly, she relays the events of the last hour, skipping the part about Elanora and her experience passing through the wall. 'We should go now. Sneak past the gate while we still have the element of surprise.'

Before Mallux can answer, Hermitch growls sarcastically. 'Oh yes! Shall we just … what? *Walk* on past the guards when they already know who to look out for? You think Fae so blind?'

Fast as a sand viper, Telium snaps shadows out from her fingers, cracking them at the male's face like a whip. He flinches back and half-draws his blade. When he recovers, Hermitch looks around, but Telium is nowhere in sight. He glances at his General who is staring at the shadows cast by the tent in the firelight, a slight frown on his face.

'Fae you may be,' Telium's voice sounds from the shadows. Hermitch snarls, narrowing his eyes as the outline of her body comes into focus. 'But assassin, you are not,' she continues, stepping forward into the light. 'The darkness is *my* domain.' As she speaks, the shadows cease curling from her fingertips and slide down her body, like ink dropped in water, to pool at her feet.

The male snarls again, but Mallux cuts him off before he can throw a retort back in Telium's face and start something he cannot finish. 'Go wake the others,' he demands, eyes not moving from Telium's face.

She stares back at him, defiance burning in her bicoloured eyes. Mallux is the first to look away, sighing as he runs his hands through his blond locks, his posture softening. She steps towards him, offering her thoughts on how to get past the gate in a hushed voice. He hums a noncommittal response, rubbing a hand across the stubble scattering his chin.

Abruptly, Mallux steps closer and reaches out to grasp her arm. His eyes bore into hers. He opens his mouth to say something …

The moment is shattered by the other Fae clambering out of their tents. Hermitch stalks out from behind them, glaring daggers at Telium, who merely looks at him coolly for a moment before turning away and presenting him with her back. She just hears his low growl over the crackling of the fire.

'Telium, repeat what you just told me,' Mallux says, his voice low and serious.

Again, she relays what she has found. Curses rumble in the chests of some of the Fae, others are more restrained and simply frown with displeasure.

What follows is a predictable argument that makes Telium sigh with frustration. So much talking and so little acting with these Fae. *No wonder it has taken them so long to form the rebellion.* She instantly feels shamed by the thought. Mallux and the others have worked for years, carefully infiltrating every city and town with a stealth that would make any assassin proud.

Huffing another sigh, she sits down at the fire, helping herself to the stew that is being kept warm by the coals. The smell of vegetables and meat mixes with woodsmoke, making her empty stomach rumble.

The lyrical Old Fae washes over her, Telium only picking up bits and pieces of the argument. *You understood them. Did you not?* She sits upright, turning to the Fae talking. Focusing on the conversation. Paxium and Alinte had been speaking in Old Fae, and yet she had understood them. *Did you like my gift?*

Telium recalled that odd feeling, like a second skin had been lain over hers once she passed through the *Lei'sidio*. The sensation had vanished as she raced back through the city. Suddenly, Elanora's words make sense. Telium shakes her head in astonished awe, making a mental note to speak to the not-Fae child again, see if she could make the gift permanent. Being able to understand Old Fae fluently would be a blessing indeed.

Turning her mind back to the issues at hand, she tries not to grind her teeth in frustration and scream at the gathered Fae. At least Mallux believes her. She has to trust him to push these Fae in the right direction. There is no-one who wants to see the Mad Fae King defeated more than she. But Mallux would come in at a close second. He will not falter.

'Go get Ariel,' a Fae commands one of the soldiers, sparking another round of debate between the Fae.

'Enough!' Mallux barks, sharp enough that Telium looks over at him. He must want her to hear this if he is speaking in the Common Tongue. 'Either you trust in what Telium has told us or you do not. Make your choice. I have made mine. I will not be staying here until the King's men rally. The plan is sound. Come or not; it is your decision.'

For the most part, Hermitch remained silent during the discussion, but now he speaks up. 'You are asking us to trust her, yet we know naught about her.'

Telium looks over at him from her place by the fire,

one side of her face bathed in flickering firelight, the other cast in shadow. Some of the Fae shift uncomfortably as she addresses him.

'There are many times in life you must put your trust in a stranger, not knowing whether the decision is the axis on which your life sits.'

'And if we choose wrong? What if we fail?' the male shoots back.

Telium's smile is wicked, full of dark promise. 'Ah, but what if you fly?'

Hermitch has nothing to say to that.

'*Sak*, enough,' Mallux says. 'You need not all make the choice; only those of us who are recognisable to the King or his guards. How many of the others are here already?'

One of the council members rattles off a short list of names.

Mallux turns to another Fae who has been travelling with them. 'Go find the others. Present them with our plan to get through the gate. Ariel will come with us too. Either they come with us now or they find their own way in later. Those who have not yet arrived will have to take their chances. Hermitch, you will stay behind to update them.' His voice rings with authority. None of the Fae dare oppose him. Those who will not be going with them retire to their beds once more.

Telium turns back to the fire, stifling a yawn.

Once most of the Fae have dispersed, Mallux sits down beside her. As always, when he is near, his citrus and fire scent envelops her. She breathes it in deeply as she turns Mallux's plan over in her mind. He says nothing as the warmth of his calming presence wraps around her. She sighs and leans into his shoulder. After a moment, his broad arm comes up to embrace her.

'Mallux?' she murmurs, the warmth of the fire and his arms making her drowsy. 'Who is Ariel? Why do we need her?'

'She is *Ra'sito* – a Fae who can change her appearance and that of others.'

Telium pulls back to gape up at him. 'She can *shapeshift?* I thought they could only lay mirages over objects.'

'She does not shift her form. Instead, she can drape illusions over herself or others. From what I understand, it is a difficult Power to master and cannot be used in battle.'

Telium smiles and shakes her head gently. Of course, Mallux, being a warrior, would see it as a rather useless Power. If it has no use in a fight, then it is no more than an interesting party trick. But to the Siren Queen's assassin, it is a great and intriguing Power indeed.

She returns her head to its place on his shoulder and draws his scent into her lungs, letting it soothe the ragged edges of her emotions.

They sit like that, bathing in each other's presence until the others return. The first Fae, his skin the colour of mahogany, arrives, and Mallux sits up. He runs his hand down the back of Telium's neck and shoulder with a proprietary touch. Telium shivers at the caress.

As Mallux rises to greet the newcomer, Telium rolls her head, trying to settle her Gifts pacing under her skin in anticipation of the coming trial. There was a time when she disliked her dark forest, resented its quiet stillness and how the days could pass by without one noticing.

My sanctuary and my prison, Telium thinks, *now I can think of nothing I would like more than to rest under the leafy canopy and watch the shadows play.*

She eyes Mallux out of the corner of her eye. Well, almost nothing.

And what will become of me after all this? Where do you think you and he fit?

She forces away the questions. Instead, she clutches her rage close to her breast, letting it fuel her.

CHAPTER
44

Over the course of the next half a bell, a handful of Fae arrive. When Mallux returns to her side, there are six others in total who will try to sneak by the gate with them.

'All but one have decided to take a leap of faith.' Mallux says at the question in her eyes.

The female, Ariel, had arrived shortly after the second runner returned. She bears no coloured band to indicate her Power and her dusty brown hair is tied back to reveal a stern, pale face, full of angles and set with strange icy-blue eyes. Telium watches her curiously but makes no move to approach her.

Ariel says little, merely standing beside the gathered Fae, observing them intently. A brief discussion ensues, and the others question Ariel harshly about the extent of her abilities. Their remarks would have rankled Telium, but Ariel simply replies in a soft, even-toned voice.

'I can veil you all.'

'That's it, *li'ne?*' Hermitch asks.

Telium notes the slight grimace as Ariel nods. 'Just stay in my line of sight, and no sudden movements, else the veil will slip. Wreathing all of you will push me to my limits.' Her voice wavers slightly as if she is unused to giving orders.

Her request sounds more like a plea to Telium. When Ariel's eyes rest on her, Telium smiles and waves her hand nonchalantly. 'You need not veil me,' she says. 'I am not recognisable, just too untrustworthy to be left behind.'

Mallux frowns at her sarcasm. Some of the others snarl, but none so loud as Hermitch. Telium cannot resist baring her teeth at him in a poor excuse for a grin. Ariel's lips twitch, fighting a smile.

A muscle ticks in Hermitch's jaw and he opens his mouth but is cut off by one of the other males before he can speak. '*Threal.* You should not let her goad you so.' His words are directed at Hermitch but his eyes are on Telium as he frowns at her.

Telium shrugs and turns away. She cannot help it if these Fae males with their delicate egos are so easy to rile.

They gather up what they need, leaving anything that is not necessary. Telium looks sadly at her bed-roll, knowing she cannot bring it and that likely means a night spent sleeping on the floor. With a resigned sigh, she wraps her cloak tightly, hiding the glint of weapons, and pulls up the hood.

They set off through the sleeping city of tents, leaning on each other in pairs or threes. Ariel has her arms around the waist of a male. A stunningly beautiful Fae, with long limbs and mahogany skin. Mallux drapes one strong arm about Telium's shoulders, while his other hand clutches a full tankard of ale.

The others are similarly burdened. One even has a small barrel perched on his shoulder to keep up the illusion. They pass the final tents and make their way to the main gate, swaying and stumbling the entire way. The beautiful male stops to plant a sloppy kiss on Ariel and the other males cheer raucously.

Telium swallows her distaste as the smell of ale wafts up from her clothes. Mallux had apologised before dumping half a tankard on her, hoping the smell will help cover her not-quite-Fae scent.

The three guards at the gate watch them approach. As they draw close to the gate, they hush each other, trying to stand up straight and walk without a drunken wobble, some of them failing miserably.

The ornate gates tower above them, glinting softly in the waning moonlight. Telium lolls her head to the side and studies them, careful to keep her gaze soft and languid. Just one of the gilded leaves would be worth enough to feed an Alkorian family for a year.

As expected, the guards stop them, questioning what they are doing entering the city at such a late hour. They reply with drunken, half-mumbled answers, along with a breathless giggle from Ariel as her companion nuzzles her neck. The guards frown in annoyance. Apparently, they are not the first drunks the trio has had to deal with tonight.

Telium edges up close to a pillar, pretending to lean against it in her inebriated state. Mallux grips her arm and draws her away carefully, pulling her against his chest where he rests a hand brazenly against her backside, giving it a squeeze. Her flare of lust is so sudden and all-consuming, her lips part and she gasps.

The guards demand they all remove their hoods. Even though she is expecting it, Telium is shocked to watch Ariel's male pull back his hood with milky-white hands to reveal a face completely different from his own. Complying, the rest follow suit, all exposing faces that are not their own, bar Telium and Ariel herself.

Telium turns her face to the guards, careful to keep her eyes lowered. She feels a tug on her hair as Mallux rubs a silky white strand between his fingers.

'I wish you had chosen a different colour for the celebration,' he murmurs to her, his voice somehow rough and silken at the same time.

'It was meant to be purple!' she protests a shade too loudly.

The guards frown slightly at her drunken outburst. One of them sighs in annoyance. The leader's eyes sharpen, mouth thinning as he looks over them.

Not trusting the plan to go off without a hitch, Telium sways backwards slightly and puts her hand out to the carved pillar to steady herself. Praying her gamble will pay off. The three guards zero in on her bare hand, resting on the cool surface of the *Lei'sidio.* Mallux, too, notices. He seems hesitant to touch her while she is tethered to the pillar.

A vision fills Telium's mind of a beautiful beaming face. *Hello, Elanora,* she says silently.

Telium. The Faeling greets her happily.

Elanora glances over at Ariel still standing beside her companion. *Your friend does not like the way the others address them. But they are too gentle to correct you.*

Telium will have to ponder the child's words later. Distantly, she notices a guard grilling one of the Fae on where they have travelled from and where they are staying in town, getting increasingly frustrated at the male's longwinded and slurred answers. Meanwhile, the other two guards and Mallux watch Telium with rapt fascination. Torn between wanting to tear her away from the deadly *Lei'sidio* and fearing to touch her.

Will you help me? Telium asks.

Of course, friend. Elanora replies without hesitation and disappears from Telium's mind.

Telium straightens and drapes herself over Mallux, nuzzling his chest. Mallux responds by gripping a handful of hair and inhaling deeply, before rubbing his lips across her cheekbone. Telium sighs and goes boneless in his arms, the lust raging through her – not entirely for show.

To the plains on their left, there is an explosion of light from the *Lei'sidio*. It brightens the plain for an instant, then disappears completely. Leaving an imprint on the backs of everyone's eyelids, like a flash of lightning.

All the Fae straighten and look toward the source. The guards' eyes flit between the wall and the handful of drunkards on their doorstep, unsure which warrants their attention more. The first guard waves a hand at them dismissively and growls, 'Be off with you. Go straight to your residence. If I hear that you have been causing trouble in town, I will *personally* send you to the stocks.'

He turns to his comrades, dismissing the group completely, and begins to talk in low, urgent tones. One of them runs off while the other two snap back to attention, eyes hard as they watch the group stagger through the gate and off into town.

'Was that your doing, *upa?*' Mallux murmurs in her ear.

Telium merely flashes him a conspirator's grin.

The small group continues their charade of loud, staggering drunkenness until a handful of turns stand between them and the guards. Telium sighs in relief.

'*Thril'ra,* Ariel,' Telium congratulates. 'That was quite a show of skill.'

The female seems surprised by the praise and smiles hesitantly before turning her concentration back to the males, unwilling to let her illusion go until they are hidden.

Tapping her free hand on her dagger, Telium thinks a

moment on Elanora's words. Stepping closer to the female, she lowers her voice.

'Your name ... do you dislike it?'

When Ariel shoots her a surprised look Telium adds, 'You sometimes seem ...' she pauses as she searches for the right word. 'Uncomfortable. With the way the others address you.'

Ariel sucks her bottom lip between her teeth and shifts her attention back to the others. She is quiet for so long, Telium thinks she will not answer and goes to move away.

'I am not she or her or female.' Ariel says in a quiet voice.

'How shall I address you then?' Telium asks gently, leaning in.

'They, them or just Fae,' the Fae clarifies.

Telium searches the Fae's face a moment, then dips her head in acknowledgement. Ariel moves away from Telium without another word and back towards their companion.

Mallux gently pulls Telium closer to his side and she squeezes his hand. His brazen idea has paid off. Luckily for them, *Ra'sito* like Ariel are few and far between. The chance of the rebellion having any is so slight that the guards will not suspect the trick.

Their place of residence, as the guard at the gate called it, turns out to be a store of some sort. One claims he knows the owner and that the shop will be closed tomorrow due to the celebration. When he raises a fist to a window, Telium hisses at him to stop. Rolling her eyes, she steps up to the back door and makes quick work of picking the lock, muttering under her breath. The door swings open with a gentle creak. Mallux watches her, blue eyes shining and a smile tugging the corner of his mouth.

The others say nothing, just follow her inside, Mallux bringing up the rear and locking the door behind them with a soft *snick*.

Glancing about the room, Telium guesses the shop belongs to a tailor of some kind. Bolts of different fabrics cover the walls in every colour imaginable. Drawers sit at random intervals, holding everything from buttons to trim to fine golden thread. She assumes this part of the shop is a storeroom.

Telium peeks through the other two doors leading off the room. The first opens up to the storefront where two mannequins sit in front of large glass windows. One displays a soft pink gown made of the finest silk and draped with lace; the other, a masculine outfit of forest-green suit tails, complete with shiny black boots.

The other door opens to a workroom with an enormous heavy wooden table taking up the majority of the space. Half-completed projects lie strewn about, along with a startling assortment of pins, needles and threads in a variety of colours. A small pile of brown leather catches Telium's eye. She picks it up, turning it this way and that as she examines it. Smiling to herself, she tucks the item under her arm.

She returns to find the others have made use of the softer fabrics, pulling them down and fashioning beds from the piles. The room smells of cotton and fur.

Telium pulls a fabric from the wall. The hideous olive colour is soft under her fingers. She looks around for somewhere to lie. Most of the floor space has been taken up by the six muscular males and Ariel, who has stayed close to their companion.

Telium has no desire to lay so close to any of them, bar Mallux, so she returns to the workroom. Once she pushes aside the piles of fabric offcuts and moves a chair to the other side of the workbench, there is ample room to lie down between the wall and the table, with only her feet visible from the room beyond.

She throws down the ugly coloured material, then, struck by inspiration, grabs an armful of the scrap cloth she had found earlier and stuffs it under her bedding. She now has a makeshift pillow. Pleased with her effort, Telium lies down, shifting to get comfortable.

In the sudden silence, she tries to push her mind away from what lies ahead. For the better part of her life, she has been haunted by the promise she made her Queen when she was barely seven winters old. She had been training for a few moons at that point and young Telium thought herself quite clever and brave.

Now, here she is, so many winters later, ready to fulfil her promise, her Queen gone.

Telium shifts, uncomfortable, before sitting up and shedding her bandolier of knives and resting them next to the haladie she smuggled in. Reaching into her pocket, she pulls out a small cloth-wrapped package that contains the black dye Lotte had purchased for her.

When walking through the tent city, a Fae had asked where she got such unique *rai'na,* thinking her natural white locks were dyed. White *rai'na* is not something the Fae commonly produce, so she will still use the black colour tomorrow. She holds the vial to her chest a moment, wondering where her friend is now. From the way she had fallen into her *Wai'tan's* arms, it does not take much imagining.

Telium smiles to herself and tucks the dye alongside her knives, planning to rise early to put it to use. She tosses and turns before finally settling in. A purring snore drifts through the open door, causing a pang of loneliness. Despising the emotion, she tries to shove it away but it digs in its claws and resolutely stays put. Even here, among the Fae whose strength and power are spun into hearth-tales, she is apart. Lotte seems to have accepted her good-naturedly, but she imagines the beautiful female befriends everyone.

It seems many of the Fae despise her for her part-mortal, part-Thief heritage. She snorts at the irony. The reason her mortal life was destroyed was because her Queen despised her part-Fae heritage. And no matter who it is, both sides fear and detest her Gifts.

Telium can feel herself being pulled down into a pit of self-loathing and fights hard against it. Tenebris knows how she sometimes hates her Gifts. She does not need the reminder from others as well. Her dark forest provided her with the closest semblance to peace she will possibly ever find. She sighs sharply, unwilling to be swamped by her self-pity again.

ళ

The gentle scuff of feet on the wooden floorboards pulls her from her morose thoughts and she reaches for one of her daggers. Ruffled blond hair and eyes a blue so deep she could drown in them poke around the doorframe.

Telium smiles up at Mallux and shuffles to the side to make room.

He takes the space without protest. 'Come here, *rel upa,*' he murmurs, opening his arms to her.

She goes without question. The warmth of his arms and familiar scent banishes her gloomy musings. From any other, the endearment would have rankled. From Mallux, it is a caress and a promise. She is his to care for, his to protect. She makes a happy sound in the back of her throat as she snuggles into his broad chest.

'You seem remarkably calm about this whole situation,' she whispers, conscious of the others in the room beyond.

Mallux's smile sends a thrill through her. 'I may not have the book smarts of Hermitch and the others,' he murmurs back to her, 'but I am well-versed in the game of warfare and secrets.'

She tilts her head to look up at him, raising an eyebrow. Mallux chuckles at her and presses a kiss to her brow. Telium all but purrs under the attention.

'I never actually planned on attacking during the feast,' he continues. 'I knew there would be those loyal to the King among us, so I planned as if I were unaware of that. Come the morrow I will pass on the *real* plan to those in the council who will carry out my orders. By then it will be too late for the King's spies to report to him and prepare a defence.'

Telium is impressed. The plan is beautifully simple. The risk he ran by keeping everyone in the dark, including his council, was great. Telium has done him a huge favour by uncovering a spy. The others will be that much easier to convince with this knowledge.

'Well,' she demands, 'when *is* it taking place?'

He smiles at her impatience, leaning down to kiss her passionately until she is limp and gasping in his arms. She has never been able to resist him. Even when he first came storming into her life, there was something about his silken smile and honeyed voice.

Mallux pulls back ever so slightly. When he speaks, his lips brush against hers, sending little sparks of heat dancing across her skin. 'Tomorrow afternoon, before the King makes his speech.' His words are so faint Telium has to strain to hear them. The words of his plan – his foolish, ingenious plan – dance across her cheek. Her heartbeat echoes in her throat as she drinks in every whispered word.

'Together, we will bring him to his knees,' Mallux finishes.

There it is. The moment her entire existence is centred around. Laid out so simply.

Mallux's hand skims up and down her sides, while the arm she rests on reaches down her back to play with the waistband of her pants. Heat pools low in her gut and she shifts so her body is flush against his. She will trust this male; he alone who can brush aside the darkness of her soul and pull her from her brooding thoughts.

They lay together for a time, murmuring in low voices about tomorrow and what it will hold for them until Mallux rolls her onto her back and covers her body with his.

As it had the very first time, his kiss threatens to undo her. But she cannot brush aside the niggling feeling of shame. This whole time, Mallux has put his faith in her, offered to help her … in exchange for her services, yes, but somewhere along the way, the lines between personal and business have blurred. With his hands on her in the relative privacy of the room, Telium can no longer pretend she does not care what he thinks of her. He deserves the truth; he would do the same for her. She gently pushes on his chest, breaking the kiss before she can lose her nerve.

'I have to tell you something.' Her whisper is tight, her palms sweaty.

When Mallux pulls back to look at her, Telium licks her lips and swallows. He leans forward and nuzzles her neck.

'Tell me.' His words are warm against her skin.

Having his piercing gaze hidden steadies her, though that likely makes her a coward. She takes a steadying breath.

'When I was very young, the Fae King came to Coronal. I was not allowed to see him, but I know at the dinner he was charmed by the Queen. They made a treaty to unite the two kingdoms. He was to send a suitor for her to marry. But later that night, hounded by lust, he visited her rooms.'

Telium has to drag another breath into her lungs. Mallux

pulls back, frowning. He searches her face intently. 'This tale is known here in Thresiel.'

'He raped her.' Telium's voice sounds small as her throat tightens. She clenches her jaw tight. The ugly word hangs in the silence, broken only by Telium's ragged breathing. Fearing what he will say, how he will react, she forces the next words from her throat. 'I did not come to help you for a noble reason, did not come just to save Alkorian lives ... I came to kill him for Selenia. For revenge. For me.'

Telium's gut churns as she waits for the disgust or anger that's sure to follow. But Mallux merely watches her quietly, an odd expression on his face. His eyes roam over her face and when his gaze returns to hers, a small smile tugs at his mouth. He moves to settle back on her and says two words that make her heart ache with forgiveness and acceptance.

'I know.'

The warmth of his body is a delicious weight against her, his smell dominating her senses. She hooks one leg around his, determined to make him finish what he started this time. Now his rough hands scrape gently as he grips her hip with one hand, keeping himself propped above her with the other.

With his hands and mouth on her, she forgets all about tomorrow and everyone in the room next door. Mallux has to clamp a hand over her mouth to muffle the noises she makes. But when he moves to fill her, it is his mouth that moans out her name. Telium smiles and nips at the hand covering her lips. Mallux's jaw clenches, the muscles standing out on his neck in an attempt to stay silent as he rises and falls above her, their bodies moving in harmony.

Telium rakes her nails down his back. The action must be his undoing because he buries his face in her neck and moans as he finds his release. At the same time, Telium arches up, head falling back restlessly against the makeshift pillow as her own climax tears through her. She goes limp, her muscles deliciously sore as Mallux settles next to her, throwing a possessive arm around her waist and tucking her in close.

Sated as a falkir after a hunt, Telium turns her face to his neck and sighs deeply, before falling into a dreamless sleep.

CHAPTER
45

Telium's dyed hair keeps fluttering in the wind and catching the corner of her eye. She touches a strand, twisting the inky blackness around her finger.

She had woken early and disappeared into the small chamber at the back of the shop, closing the door firmly behind. She unwrapped the package containing the vial of *rai'na* and some dried *beliark* leaves and set it beside the small basin in the corner of the room.

Telium had uncorked the bottle and dumped the contents on her head. Once she massaged the dye through, surprised to find it lathered, she patted her hair dry before pulling it away from her face with multiple little braids curling along her temples.

The style would conceal her rounded ears while leaving enough loose for her to hide behind a curtain of hair should she need. She had donned her loose cotton shirt again and picked up the item she had taken from the workroom the night before.

It was a female's tunic fashioned from hard leather to create a type of breastplate. Telium slipped it over her head and tightened the laces running down the sides. She strapped matching leather braces to her forearms over her soft white sleeves and slipped a tiny dagger into each one.

When she looked in the mirror, she had not recognised herself. With her obsidian hair and breastplate, and shadows playing behind her mismatched eyes. Her mouth set into a hard, determined line. Telium had to admit, the entire look was rather pleasing. She had smiled at herself in the mirror. Beautiful and feral. Tenebris reincarnate. When she sauntered out and Mallux did a double take, the tiny smile grew into a full-blown grin.

જ

Bells later, they move through the back alleys that pepper the city, trying to keep out of sight. Yet even they are busier than usual, with parties spilling over from the main streets.

All around them the Fae are celebrating, dressed in a colourful array of silk and cotton and tulle. They are all in different stages of celebration: dancing, singing, drinking. As she wades through the crowd, Telium notes more than one couple sharing a secret embrace in the quiet of the shadows. The Fae are, she decides, much more open with their passions than Alkorians, probably something to do with *Wai'tinate* bonds and other such Fae curiosities.

Exotic spices tickle Telium's nose as they mingle with the scents of a thousand different bodies. Banners and flags flutter in the breeze. Fae dance in the streets, their movements lithe and sensuous, belying their deadly strength. A handful of females twirl in a circle, colourful skirts swirling as they pick up their feet and spin around and around. Somewhere, a lute and a set of reed pipes pick up a jaunty tune. The females laugh, their faces bright and cheeks flushed as they dance beneath the midmorning sun.

One of the females begins to sing. Her voice is the purest thing Telium has ever heard – crystal clear and high. The melody is haunting. It seems to weave through the air like honey, reaching towards Telium and wrapping her in its warm embrace. She bobs her head to the sound, the sweet voice of the female twining itself around her very being. Her fingers tap along to the rhythm.

Come, it seems to say, *come join, little Thief. Come dance barefoot in the meadow, Assassin.*

Telium finds herself swaying to the music, breath leaving her in a contented sigh. The females spin and twirl, eyes as bright as their skirts that kick out as they go.

Come let the wind comb your locks and the sun crown your hair, little Fae.

In a semi-daze, Telium wanders closer to the dancing females. One wearing a bright-red dress, lips painted scarlet to match, reaches out to Telium as she spins by. Suddenly, Telium finds herself in the circle of dancing Fae.

The red female twirls Telium under her arm with lean strength. Telium's black hair whips about her as she pivots perfectly and comes back to face the female. Another of the Fae claps in joy at the display, draping an emerald-green wrap over Telium's shoulders. The green material is slippery and slightly transparent.

The red female grins and spins Telium again, this time letting her go so she can fall into step with the other females. In a rush, it comes back to her. The years of dancing in ballrooms. Sneaking into taverns for the more unstructured, but vastly more enjoyable, dances. She has forgotten the wild, unfiltered joy it brings her.

Telium throws out her arms and rolls her shoulders. Her booted feet pound the earth and she dances around the circle.

She flicks her wrists, using the silk wrap to imitate the twirling of a skirt. Her arms arch and flex in time with the melody as her spine rolls. Supple. Fluid. The music echoes through her.

Tilting her head back, Telium smiles so hard it crinkles her eyes. A genuine laugh bubbles up from deep in her stomach. The sound is light and breathlessly joyful. Her eyes catch a string of emerald and gold bunting just as the tune changes. The female stops singing and a male close by takes up the tune.

His voice is a deep baritone. Telium spins again, twirling the emerald silk around her body. The crowd begins clapping. The bunting flaps in the wind, the swords and crown of the royal crest glinting in stitched gold.

Her Gifts roil to the surface with an internal snarl, snapping her out of her trance. Telium gasps like she has just come up for air. Steadying herself, she loops the wrap around the female who gifted it to her and smoothly bows out of the circle.

She struggles against the melody still twining around her heart. The human in her lured by the Fae's underlying magik. Her Gifts recognise the Fae for what they are: predators, despite their shining faces and beautiful voices.

A chill skitters down her arms as she moves away. Here are the Powers of old – these Fae gathered in such numbers are unintentionally tapping into the magik of the land. She looks around. Where is Mallux?

Telium blinks, frowning. How long had she been dancing with those females? Surely it was only minutes? But it had felt much longer than that.

'Shit,' Telium swears under her breath.

Another Fae tune tugs at her, curling into her ears. She turns towards the sound.

A warm hand clamps around her own, fitting snugly as if

it were made for hers. Her eyes are still glued to the females as she is tugged into a shop. *Mallux.* Her fingers curl around his as the shop door cuts off the sight of the dancing Fae.

Her eyes drag across an array of delicate, beautifully painted crockery, before turning to—

'Paxium.'

Telium snatches her hand out of his, coming to an abrupt halt. Every sense snaps to sharp alertness. She tightens the coils of her consciousness even as her mind races. A reverent sort of silence hushes the shop.

Peace, she tells herself, *he doesn't know you saw him the other night.*

'Hello, Telli.' Paxium practically purrs out her nickname. 'I did not think you would have time for dancing, with the rebellion readying to fall upon the King this evening.'

Telium's eyes jump around the shop at Paxium's casual mention of the rebellion. Strangely, it is just the two of them, and stacks of lovingly crafted tableware. She can feel the heat suffusing her cheeks as she realises Paxium was watching her dance.

She focuses on that. Instead of the unspoken question left hovering between them.

He doesn't know.

Savage pride swells in her chest. He has not figured out Mallux's last-minute change of plan. Instead of answering, Telium flicks her hair over her shoulder. She picks up a blue and white teacup, turning it this way and that as she admires the tiny flowers painted on it.

'Thank you for pulling me away from that circle,' she says. 'Though I am surprised you recognised me from a distance.'

Paxium murmurs something under his breath. Telium turns to him with a raised brow.

'What was that?'

'Nothing.' He smiles at her with his perfect, straight teeth. Daring her.

Telium hums in response, putting the cup down and picking up a plate from the top of the stack. Her mind races. She has to get away from him. Her eyes drift lazily around the shop. At the back against the wall, partially hidden by shelves of bowls and vases, stands a miniature clock tower. In place of stone walls is exquisitely carved wood that stands a little higher than her.

She barely spares it a glance, but what she sees is enough to make her pulse kick up. Less than a bell before they need to be in position.

Tenebris curse me. She has wasted so much time dancing with those females. Lost Mallux and now managed to get tangled with Paxium to top it all off. The traitorous *sk'ril.* She forces her heartbeat to remain steady, sure this dangerous male can hear it.

The clink of Telium returning the plate echoes through the hollow silence of the shop.

'Is there a back door?' Telium asks.

Paxium nods. He has not taken his eyes off her since they entered.

She clears her throat. 'Good.'

Telium makes to move past him. Though shorter than Mallux, Paxium still towers over her. In the skinny walkway, there is barely enough space for the two of them. She has to put a hand on his chest as she squeezes past. Plates clink as Paxium leans back slightly.

She feels his muscles flex under her fingers. Without warning, he grips her wrist. Her Gifts come surging to the surface. She grits her teeth as they push at their restrains.

Battling with them as she tries to decide how much force she will need to—

'Telium.'

Her Gifts pause.

She turns to look at Paxium, eyebrow lifted in question. He swallows a moment, indecision written clearly on his face. The open look makes her cautious, like she is being backed into a corner. *Dangerous.*

'I have to go to Mallux,' she says, shaking her wrist clamped in his grip.

The plates behind Paxium protest the movement.

'Do not go to him,' he says, keeping her hand trapped on his chest, 'I know what you are planning.'

Telium yanks her hand from his grip. Her movement knocks a cup from its perch. It crashes to the floor, shattering in an explosion of white and blue. The sudden movement makes them both jump. Feral animals circling each other startled by a sudden noise.

'I have to.'

Spinning on her heels, she stalks away from him. *He doesn't know,* she tells herself, *he is talking about the feast tonight. He doesn't know where you are heading.*

She makes it to the little wooden counter at the back before Paxium stops her. Reaching around her, he plants his hand on the door that leads to the back of the shop and her freedom.

Telium comes to an abrupt stop. She makes to turn around, but her spine locks up when she feels Paxium's breath brush her ear. All the hairs on the back of her neck stand up. Her instincts scream at her not to turn her back to this male. She ignores the whispered words, *Treacherous.*

'I cannot let you,' he says in a low voice. 'I cannot let you kill the King.'

Her heart stumbles before leaping into a gallop. *Bastard.* She hauls on her Gifts. Spinning, she drives an elbow into his gut. Paxium grunts, his breath leaving him in a rush as he staggers backwards.

'You showed your hand too soon,' Telium growls, stalking towards him. 'I thought a spy of your calibre would know better.'

She reaches for her haladie but hesitates. Her eyes flick to the crowd, separated from them only by a thin pane of glass. It would only take one glance from a passer-by to notice them. The hesitation costs her.

Paxium leaps, tackling her to the ground. The move would have knocked the wind from her, but his foot catches on the edge of a shelf and they twist, landing on their sides instead.

Above them, the shelf rocks wildly in protest, the crockery ringing like a thousand angry bells.

'You hesitated,' Paxium mocks, 'I thought an assassin of *your* calibre would know better.'

Growling, Telium writhes out of his grip, headbutting him in the mouth. With a curse, his hands spring off her. Twisting, Telium pushes to her feet. Making for the door.

Paxium grips her around the ankle and sends her sprawling to the ground again. Reaching out for anything to break her fall, her hand catches a stack of plates. The delicate pile tumbles down.

It crashes on Telium's back and over Paxium's head. The male curses colourfully as he drags her back towards him. Bits of broken plate crunch under them as they scuffle. There is nothing skilful about their fight. It is a messy, graceless wrestle as she throws fists and elbows at him while he tries to subdue her.

Her Gifts seethe and hiss. Fangs glint as she snarls in

Paxium's face. The male snarls right back at her. The sound is low and threatening, sending chills along her skin.

Telium wrenches out of the hold Paxium has on her. His leg thumps into the table, sending a trio of teacups and an ornate pot smashing to the ground. The ruckus they are causing is sure to attract attention if it continues for much longer.

Telium growls, getting her feet in-between them. She did *not* get this close to fail now. With a grunt, Telium kicks Paxium off her. With her Gifted strength, he goes crashing into another shelf.

Cups and plates rain down on him, shattering on his head and shoulders. Taking advantage of his momentary distraction, Telium binds him with invisible weaves. Panting hard, she reaches for her haladie.

The grandfather clock chimes in the corner, signalling Telium has less than three-quarters of a bell to get into position.

Paxium is struggling against his bonds with such ferocity, Telium grits her teeth as she holds her Gifts in place. Stepping forward, she strikes him hard in the temple with the hilt of her haladie.

Paxium's head lolls and his eyelids flutter as he struggles to hold on to consciousness. *Hard-headed male,* Telium curses. That blow should have knocked him out cold.

Gripping his collar, she grunts as she hauls him towards the back door. Her boots crunch over broken plates. Panting hard, she shoulders open the door and drags him into the small back room of the shop. Dropping him unceremoniously, Telium looks around.

Stacks of crockery carefully nestled in crates of straw take up the majority of the space. There is a small cot in one corner with a rickety bedside table. An empty iron pot-belly stove to keep the space warm in the winter sits against the wall to her right.

Urgency rising in her, Telium pulls a length of rope from one of the crates. Glancing back at the deadly male swimming in and out of consciousness, she grabs a second rope.

Paxium murmurs incoherently when she drags him over to the stove. His locks slide over his face as he looks up at her. Her Gifts are howling under her skin, thrumming along her bones and keening in her chest.

'Sorry,' she breathes.

Paxium looks up at her, uncomprehending.

This time, when the hilt of haladie strikes home, consciousness flees him. Telium uses the rope to fasten his hands and feet together, then binds him to the stove. *Because he could be useful later,* Telium tells herself. That's why she hadn't been willing to kill him. He can give them information on other spies.

She doesn't allow herself to look back as she sheaths her haladie and barrels out the back door of the shop. Straight into Hermitch.

The male curses as he steadies himself. When he recognises Telium, his eyes narrow into slits.

'What are you doing, Assassin?' he rumbles. His eyes flick over her shoulder. 'Where is Mallux?'

'We got separated,' Telium pants, 'I don't have time to explain. Do you know where he is?'

Hermitch's hand grips her forearm, his mouth thins into a hard line as he looks her over and glances back to the shop. Her Gifts hiss threateningly.

'What were you *doing* in here?'

Telium groans in frustration. 'I got separated from Mallux in the crowd. Paxium caught me and dragged me into that shop. Now hurry.' She tugs her arm out of the male's grasp. 'We have less than a bell until we need to be in position.'

Hermitch lets her arm fall out of his grip but doesn't make a move to leave. He watches the back door for a moment more. Telium feels like she is practically buzzing with urgency. She has to fight the urge to bounce on her toes.

'Did you kill him?' he asks after a moment, eyeing the blood on her clothes from the broken crockery.

'Yes.' The lie rolls so easily off her tongue.

After a moment, Hermitch nods sharply and turns away. 'Hurry. This way, Assassin.'

CHAPTER
46

Telium and Hermitch move through the streets at a fast walk. The male all but ignores her, only glancing back sporadically to check she is still following. The hard look never leaves his face.

They weave through the crowd, keeping their heads low. Telium feels as though time is slipping through her fingers like sand. She discreetly runs her fingers through her hair, working out the knots after her tussle with Paxium.

They are only a block away from the palace grounds when they round a corner and there he is. Mallux. She has to fight the urge to run to him. Relief hits her in a dizzying wave, making her knees wobble.

Hermitch grabs Mallux's shoulder, pulling him to a stop. When he turns to her, Telium cannot stop herself from reaching out and gripping Mallux's forearm, her fingers digging into the tattoos inked there. As if she needs to anchor herself to him. Feel him under her fingers to know they still have a chance, not all is lost.

Hermitch speaks to Mallux rapidly in Old Fae, before clapping his friend on the shoulder and disappearing into the crowd. He doesn't even spare Telium a backwards glance.

The crowd parts around them like water. Telium still hasn't let go of Mallux's arm; his skin is warm and smooth under her fingers. She opens her mouth to explain or apologise, she isn't sure.

Up ahead, something metallic glints in the sun. Telium peers at it through her lowered lashes. A jolt runs through her as she realises who is approaching them at the same time Mallux must – *Kah*. His warm hand encircles her forearm and he spins her around, backing her into a tiny alcove beneath a doorway. His huge frame presses up against her, and despite the King's guards closing in on them with every step, the heat of him sets her body aflame.

She cannot tell if her heart is racing because the guards have just appeared in her line of sight, or because Mallux dips his head towards her, his sinful mouth hovering just inches from her own.

When her eyes flicker over his shoulder to the guards marching past, he drops his lips to her neck. She tilts her chin to give him better access, even as she assesses the guards. His hands tighten on her in response.

They pass by, unconcerned by the couple sharing a private moment in the shadow of the doorway. As Telium surreptitiously watches them walk past, she notes they are all males – no *Ka'hine*.

The heavy stomp of their boots fades away, yet Mallux does not move. Instead, he grazes his nose on the sensitive spot by her ear. He pulls back to look at her, eyes roaming over her face and landing on her mouth. 'Telium,' he murmurs.

'Yes?' she answers, breathless, already being pulled under.

'After all this is over – after we defeat the King – I want you to stay with me, help me … you could be an emissary of sorts. Help us reopen communication with Alkoria. Train here, yes, but then stay. Stay by me. You need not go back.'

A stupid grin breaks across her face at his words and her chest flutters with joy. *A place to stay, to live, to be wanted.*

'Of course,' she says … as if she can give any other reply.

In such a short time, he has become so important to her. Such a constant in her life. She cannot imagine now, not seeing his piercing blue eyes or hearing his silky voice call her name. The thought rocks her – at how quickly he has gotten under her skin and nestled there. He may not understand her darkness, but with his help, she can learn to control it and harness it better.

His only reply is to duck his head and kiss her roughly. In the back of her mind, something nags at her, but the thought slips through her grasp like water as her entire being becomes consumed by Mallux. He releases his hold on her and rests his hands on her arms, breaking the kiss.

Telium reaches a hand behind her to steady herself on the wall. The rough brick on her fingertips anchors her, and the reality of their situation comes rushing back in. How easily she succumbs to the touch and words of this Fae. He is like nothing she has ever experienced before.

Before she can be caught up in his current again, she straightens. 'We should go.' Her voice is unintentionally throaty.

Mallux frowns slightly and Telium fights the wave of sinful thoughts that come with it. But he nods and steps back out onto the street. In the distance, rainclouds stain the horizon.

They hurry for the palace at the edge of the city. The structure is even more impressive up close. It is set in front of those huge slabs of stone that jut out of the earth like a giants' blades. It looks as if the stones are cradling the palace, the soft creams of the walls contrasting starkly against the slate grey.

It is the only defence the King seems to have. The gardens that sprawl in front of the palace steps blend into the surrounding city seamlessly; commoners and royals alike celebrating on the wide expanse of grass. Small groves of fruit trees cluster together in bright bunches and Faelings climb their branches, tossing fruit down to those below. Older Fae wander through the maze of flowers or sit and admire the colours. Telium can just see the blooms as they curve around the corner of the palace walls.

How the land is so lush and fertile, she cannot understand. The grass and flowers should have been baked to a crisp by the unrelenting sun. The Fae King must be truly mad indeed if he is using precious water on *fruit trees* in a drought. She eyes the gardens with equal parts awe and disgust.

Mallux reads her look. 'The gardeners have one or two *Na'tai* among them. They keep the grounds flourishing even in the drought or depths of winter.'

Ah, of course, Telium thinks. *What a waste of Power.*

Instead of continuing up the main street to the palace, they take a circular route. Mallux has spies and other Fae loyal to him working in the palace. One of them is to leave a side door open so they can enter through the servants' quarters. From there they will make their way through the palace and hide in the large receiving chamber that leads out to the balcony, where the King will appear to make his speech for the celebration. Some of Mallux's best fighters will also be close by, disguised as handmaidens, cooks, cleaners – any position they can get their hands on. The palace is not as impregnable as the *Lei'kah* think. That arrogance will be their downfall.

When they strike, Telium will unleash her Gifts on those who remain behind, drawing the attention of the *Lei'kah* long enough to allow Mallux or one of the others to slip through their defences and get to the King. Never mind that Telium intends to be the one to deliver the killing blow.

So many holes, so many ways this could go horribly wrong.

She is not unfamiliar with poorly thought-out plans, she herself had many in her younger years as an assassin. Only her quick thinking and deadly skill allowed her to escape with her life.

But *this* ... this is a whole new level. Failure here will not just mean her death; it will mean Mallux's death, the death of thousands of people in Alkoria. Not to mention those who will be enslaved to the Fae or young Thieves who will be used in experiments by the Mad Fae King. People like that elder woman in the valley, who had never known freedom.

The thought hardens Telium. Despite the numerous pit-falls of the plan, she will ensure it ends with a blade buried in the Mad King's heart.

They make their way to the small wooden fence running at an angle off one of the palace's wings. Telium hums to herself every time they pass a group of singing Fae. Mallux's blue eyes dart about under his hood.

Eventually, they leave the city behind and make their way through the expansive garden encircling the palace. Mallux pulls her to his side and drapes her arm over his. To a passer-by, they look like any other couple enjoying a walk through the beautiful gardens, unremarkable in the sea of Fae who have turned out for the celebration.

They pass through the small gate set in the wooden fence and walk up the dirt path that curves around the side of the palace. The garden in-between the palace and the low fence contains more useful plants; vegetables and herbs line the garden beds in neat rows. Further down they see an orderly orchard.

Nobody is about, this part of the gardens off-limits to the public. The door they are searching for sits nestled at the end of the east wing of the palace, facing the towering stone wall.

It is partially obscured by a climbing vine with golden-yellow fruit. Telium reaches out to grasp the worn handle.

'*Sak!*'

A guard stalks between rows of carrots towards them. Telium's heartbeat spikes. The gold thread in his uniform glints in the sun. Telium shares a look with Mallux as the guard barks out another order.

Spinning, Telium draws a blade from her bandolier. In one swift movement, she uses the momentum to put strength behind her throw. The dagger hits home with a wet thunk. The guard stumbles a step backwards. Her Gifts are there to catch him, tripping his feet and sending him sprawling. She is there in an instant. Hand clamping over his mouth and slashing her blade savagely across his throat. Her jaw set in determination, Gifts howling and raging under her skin.

She doesn't remove her hand until the guard's gurgling breaths quieten and he stills. She looks over her shoulder at Mallux, whose face is studiously blank.

'We need somewhere to hide the body,' Telium says.

Mallux watches her intently for a moment. 'I know a place.'

Together, they heft the body. Hugging the wall, they move deeper into the palace gardens. Telium's eyes dart from tree to grass and back again. They have to get out of the open and rid themselves of the guard's corpse. Telium pushes the net of her mind out, straining her senses for signs of anyone approaching.

They reach part of the garden that backs right up to the enormous slabs of stone. The rows of edible plants stop a good ten feet from the wall. The area between is unkept, grass fighting for space amongst the weeds and brambles.

Mallux's eyes scour the ground as they tramp through the no-man's-land. *What in Tenebris' name is he looking for?* Telium is acutely aware of every moment as it ticks by. They are running out of time. They have barely half a bell to get into position and it is not as if they can just hide the body in the short grass.

'Mallux, we have to— *shit!*' Telium swears as the toe of her boot catches the sharp edge of a stone and she stumbles.

Mallux drops the guard's body so abruptly she is nearly dragged down with it.

'I knew it was here somewhere,' he grunts.

Dropping to his knees, he begins pulling away the weeds and grass. Telium watches with a frown for a moment, until she sees wood being revealed from under the vegetation. *A cellar?* Crouching beside him, she tears at the clumps of undergrowth.

Grasping the iron ring their efforts reveal, Mallux heaves the door open. Musty, stale air whooshes out at them, tainted with the smell of rot. Her Gifts hiss threateningly, making the hair on the back of her neck stand on end.

'What the hell is this?' Telium whispers.

Mallux is already dragging the body towards the edge of the pit. 'Hurry, hurry!'

Together, they shove and roll the body to the edge. Readjusting her position, Telium pushes alongside Mallux. After a moment, gravity takes over and the corpse tumbles down into the darkness.

The guard's body hits the wall, knocking loose dirt and a large stone. As Telium watches, the dead Fae disappears into the black. Tumbling beside him, the stone rotates as if in slow motion. The empty sockets of a skull gaze up at her. By the time she blinks it is gone.

Telium stares down into the pit a moment longer, eyes straining as she tries to catch another glimpse. Beside her, Mallux has already stood up and is brushing dirt off his knees.

'Mallux. What in the Dark Goddess' name is in this pit?'

When he does not reply, Telium looks up at him from her knees. Flexing his jaw, he holds a hand out to help her to her feet, refusing to meet her gaze. Once she is standing, Mallux leans over and grabs the rotting wood.

'This is where the King disposed of his experiments when they were no longer of use to him.' The wood bangs shut with a hollow thump.

It takes her a moment to register the words. By the time she does, Mallux is already moving back off towards the palace.

'Hurry, *upa*. We are running out of time.'

The empty black eyes of the too-small skull burn the back of Telium's lids as she sends up a prayer for the countless young bodies that must lay at the bottom of that pit. The King's *experiments*.

Tenebris curse me.

Gritting her teeth, Telium trains her eyes on the stone walls of the palace and the Mad Fae King beyond.

CHAPTER
47

The palace is enormous. If not for Mallux she would be hope-lessly lost as they skulk through the palace. It had been an easy task to slip in the door left ajar by one of the rebels. They walk through grey stone corridors with arching ceilings.

Many of the main hallways are decorated in the royal colours. Runners of emerald green are plush under their feet. Multitudes of windows are thrown open, letting the bright afternoon sun in. It makes the halls look warm and airy, the buttery yellow light combating the chill of the granite walls.

They turn a corner, coming to a corridor lined with ancient suits of armour. They are beautiful, violent things. Breastplates of snarling wolves, greaves etched with snakes and helmets shaped like the snarling jaws of a dragon. It makes the hair on the back of Telium's neck stand on end to walk through them; convinced one will jump out and attack her as she and Mallux walk brazenly through the enemy's palace.

Up ahead, the sound of shouting voices and clanging pans indicate they have reached the palace kitchens. Opening what appears to be a linen closet, Mallux steps inside. Telium fol-lows him curiously, closing the door behind her just as she hears footsteps in the hallway. She blinks, eyes taking on a reflective gleam.

Mallux crouches down and opens a large metal grate set into the corner wall of the room, muscles bulging with the effort. Straining her ears, she tracks the footsteps of the approaching Fae, drumming her fingers restlessly against her dagger as she mentally hurries Mallux.

He nods to her as he holds the grate up. Getting down on her hands and knees, Telium crawls through the opening. She has only gone a few feet when she feels Mallux following behind her. Glancing over her shoulder, she watches him gently lower the grate shut behind him so it will not clang.

The door of the linen closet opens. They freeze; Mallux holds a finger to his lips. Her heart beats in her ears as she listens to the Fae gathering supplies mere feet from them. With a thump, the Fae closes the door and leaves.

Mallux turns back to her, grinning like a fiend. Her returning smile is nothing short of savage. Her Gifts rumble, having not settled since they left the pit in the gardens behind.

The stone is chilly against her bare hands as she moves on. Less than a minute later, she comes to the end of the strange passage which opens to an internal hallway. From its odd, jagged shape, Telium guesses it must be disguised in-between the palace rooms. Behind her, Mallux stands up from a crouch and rolls his neck. Telium continues gazing down the corridor, listening to her heartbeat.

'A secret passage?' she whispers, conscious of how the sound will bounce off the bare walls. 'How cliché.'

His chuckle is near silent, sending a puff of warm air across the back of her neck.

'Technically they are servants' passages. They date back to the first King of Thresiel. He built them as a means of escape if he were ever attacked by the *Ka'hine*. He was … paranoid about how vulnerable he was against those with Power. He despised and feared them for their abilities.

'The tunnels took years to complete. They remained a secret to all, including the King's closest confidants. Not even his wife knew of them.'

Telium raises an eyebrow at him and he shrugs. They begin to walk, their footsteps falkir-quiet in the cool, stale air.

'And you are telling me no-one else knows about them?'

Again, Mallux bunches his massive shoulders in a shrug as he replies just as quietly. 'I am sure there are others who know of their existence, servants certainly use them as short-cuts often enough, but I had years as a young child to explore every inch of these tunnels. I do not think there is one who knows them better than me. The ones like this, that are harder to get to, have been forgotten.'

They lapse into silence once more as they move through the bizarre corridors. The walls are not smooth and winding like most hallways, but have sharp bends, like the outside corner of a house. At intervals along the way, they dogleg at bizarre angles to accommodate the rooms beyond.

Clever, Telium thinks. Nobody would notice the few feet missing between rooms in such a sprawling palace.

There is no sound to distract her from her turbulent thoughts as they pad softly along the rough floor. She forces her mind to stay in that still, empty place. Distance herself from the rage and disgust she felt standing above that grave. Her Gifts rise and fall like waves in a stormy sea. The whole way, a voice whispers through her mind, beating in time with her pulse.

Drive a blade through his heart.

In the distance, thunder rumbles.

CHAPTER
48

Telium dusts her hand on her pants as she gapes at the expansive room they enter. It had taken them a quarter of a bell, and one close call of being discovered by a maid, to make it through the passageways to this room.

Tenebris curse me, Telium's inner voice is breathless, awed by the grandeur of the space. It is circular like the inside of a tower, and more rooms and hallways branch off it at intervals. But it is the ring of arches that is the most eye-catching, making the space look like a room within a room.

The circular room seems to serve as the grand hall of the palace. Made from creamy limestone, the wall of arches reaches to the roof. The arches carved at the bottom are large enough for a carriage to pass through, each row above is staggered off-centre to the one below it. The rows of hollowed-out arches gets smaller and smaller as they reach towards the ceiling. The arches at the highest point are no wider than the length of Telium's forearm. The effect is a sort of optical illusion, making the room seem even higher than it is.

Which, Telium thinks, *is already ridiculously high.*

Huge banners, at least four-horse-lengths long, drape

down the walls at each point of the compass. Each bearing the golden crossed swords and crown of the royal crest. The emerald-green and gold material is the only decoration in the otherwise-bare room. The vast vaulted ceiling is made up of a mosaic of glass: thousands of geometric shapes held together with thick veins of gold.

The effect makes the roof look like it has been topped by a diamond, the sun throws rainbows onto the floor and walls as its rays pass through. The entire effect is startlingly beautiful – a grand display of wealth. It feels more like an enormous outdoor pavilion than a walled-in room in the middle of a palace.

Moving towards one of the arches, Telium hears the clomp of boots in the distance. The *Lei'kah*. One of Mallux's men, posing as a servant, is scrubbing the already spotless marble floor. He hurries across to the two of them, and lacing his fingers into a stirrup, he boosts Telium up to the top of the closest arch. Even standing on the male's shoulders, she has to reach high above her to hook her fingers over the lip. Her shoulders strain as she scrambles into place, turning to help haul Mallux up. The disguised rebel quickly returns to his position and continues cleaning.

When Mallux's warm hand settles on her neck, she closes her eyes, taking a moment to enjoy the weight of his touch. Turning to him, she gazes at his face, tracing her eyes over the strong line of his jaw. When she raises her eyes to meet his, she sees determination and steely resolution. Along with a touch of apprehension that he tries valiantly to hide. She feels partly the same. But instead of apprehension, there is only steadily rising bloodlust as she imagines how each step the Mad Fae King now takes brings him closer to her blade.

When she smiles at Mallux there is nothing of the woman he had spent the night with there. Her smile is predatory and feral. She lets the cold glittering rage she has held onto for so long spread through her limbs.

Mallux stabilises himself on the narrow wall of stone and turns so she can stand on his shoulders to reach the next arch. This one is easier. Quiet as a shadow, Telium moves up and away from Mallux. Once she has climbed another level, she begins to move around the wall, wanting to make it to the opposite side of the room before the King's guards arrive. They will enter from the large wooden doors set into the end of the room. Directly opposite is the only archway set into an external wall. It leads to a small antechamber and beyond that is the massive balcony where the King will look down on his subjects and deliver his speech.

Once she is in position, Telium settles in to wait. Her Gifts snarl and pace restlessly under her iron grip. She relaxes her hold ever so slightly, letting them swell under her skin and pool into every crevice of her dark soul as she watches the door intently.

She does not have to wait long. Her heart thunders into her throat as the doors bang open and the *Lei'kah* march in. From her perch hidden by the banner, she watches about twenty guards file in through the large double doors. All female. All with a coloured band denoting their Power stitched into the forearm of their uniforms.

The rebel disguised as a servant scurries off as the females arrive. They line themselves up facing each other and stand to attention, forming two rows for the King to walk between as he passes through the room and to the awaiting balcony beyond. Too bad he will never reach it.

Drive a blade through his heart.

As if the words summon him, the doors open again and Telium gets her first look at the Mad Fae King. He appears young, and despite her knowing how slowly the Fae age, the realisation still shocks her. This is not the twisted old man with a sneering face and evil eyes she had pictured. His face is smooth and unlined. Long golden hair tied back at the nape shows off the strong column of his neck; nestled on top of his locks is the Ivory Crown.

White as bone, it seems to absorb the light. The simple, almost crude, crown is both harsh and beautiful. His brown eyes lack the madness Telium had expected. There is something vaguely familiar about him. Telium cannot put her finger on it.

Tenebris claim you, murderer. Your pretty face cannot hide that. Vile, evil, cunning bastard. Torturing, raping, filthy—

Her snarling thoughts are cut short by a concussive bang and her heart leaps in her chest. Immediately, the lead female reaches out a hand and the King is wrapped in a near-transparent shield. *Jiah,* Telium recalls from previous rebel meetings, *Captain of the Lei'kah.*

Damn. She will have to be one of the first to go.

Telium stands up and drops the distance to the floor. Without a moment's hesitation, she loosens her grip on her Gifts. Fingers morphing into claws, teeth elongating into fangs before her feet have even hit the polished marble. She hits the ground at a roll to save her ankles and rises to her feet in one fluid motion, bringing her next to one of the guards. Before the Fae can react, Telium slashes a dagger across her throat with a snarl. This is the first and last easy kill she gets. If a twenty-foot drop into a hostile, powerful group of Fae guards could be called easy.

Telium lets the relentless grip she keeps on her Gifts slip a little more. Twin falkir of smoke burst from her, their eyes burning with fury. This is not the time for half-measures, yet the fear of her power-drunk madness causes her to hold back on releasing her Gifts completely.

A second explosion booms, closer this time. One of the doors leading to a corridor bows inwards as a crash sounds. Mallux drops from his perch and engages with the closest *Lei'kah;* the female's skin begins to thicken and turn grey like … *stone.* The female has turned her skin to stone.

Telium's attention is pulled away from Mallux as she begins the fight of her life. The door bows again under the weight of someone trying to barge through. Telium prays it is rebels coming to aid them, not reinforcements for the King.

She loses herself to the battle, raging like a wild thing. Any Fae fool enough to come within reach falls back, sporting wounds from knives and claws. Her mind strains as it tries to keep track of the voids sitting in her net like a sixth sense keeping her aware of her surroundings. At the same time, she wields her Gifts to devastating effect. With enormous effort, she snaps the spine of a *Na'tai* charging towards her. A trick she only has the strength to use once. The Fae tumbles to the ground without a sound, not dead, but unable to move.

With a start, Telium recognises Alinte, the Fae Paxium had gone to see the night before. She turns away from the look of horror in the female's eyes just in time to throw up a wall of invisible Power-Thief Gifts to block a fireball hurled her way. The ball bursts against her shield, a stray flame catching the tail end of a banner and setting it alight. The acrid smell of burning fabric makes her eyes smart.

Her falkir throw themselves at the guards, again and again, howling in frustration as they are thwarted in their attempts to draw the life-force from the Fae. A glance at the *Tia'tum* confirms Telium's suspicions; a light sheen of sweat covers Jiah's brow as she throws her shields around any Fae that the falkir stray too close to.

Goddess, she must be powerful.

A third bang. Screams from outside. The lead *Lei'kah* raps out an order in Old Fae. Two females who look like twins turn and rush forward to the archway leading towards the balcony at the other end of the great hall.

The pair move as if in question and answer to each other, their hair shimmering waterfalls of adamant down their backs. Their white and silver armbands mark them out as *Cirrus*. They clear the room in a buoyant leap that seems to defy gravity. A wave of wind ripples out from them as they reach the open doors of the balcony and leap through and over the railing beyond without hesitation.

Well, that's two less to worry about.

Telium's lips draw back in a snarl of challenge as a female with a halo of blonde curls stalks towards her. A band of yellow, green and black decorates her sleeve. The Fae's mind feels like a tangle of vines, thorns and snakes: wild and untamed. It brings to mind distant jungles, exotic and deadly. Between one step and the next, the Fae begins morphing. Her teeth elongate, her limbs lengthen and become more muscular. Her golden hair turns into fur that runs the length of her body. Her nails darken and curve into claws.

Before Telium can fully process the transformation, an enormous lioness leaps for her, canines bared, aiming for her throat. Telium throws herself out of the way, drawing a dagger and tossing it at the Fae-lioness, giving herself time to put some distance between them. Her Gift-enhanced ears catch the whizzing of an arrow through the air and she manages to get out of the way just in time to save her heart from being pierced by the deadly projectile. But she is not fast enough to avoid the line of fire that rakes across her bicep. The razor-sharp tip of the arrow has ripped through skin and muscle, soaking her shirt instantly with blood.

She shrieks in pain and clamps her hand over the wound to stop the flow of blood. She swivels her head around with a growl to find the shooter. The female already has another arrow knocked and trained at her heart. She snaps the bow with a twitch of her Gifts and snarls at the archer. The crack of splintering wood echoes throughout the room and a fragment of the bow rebounds and strikes the female across the face.

Then, she is dodging out of the way again, desperately trying to stay out of reach of the lioness' jaws, while trying not to be burnt to a crisp by fireballs.

The remaining Fae close rank around their King, facing the onslaught from the door that is bowing in further with each blow.

With a thought, Telium dissipates her falkir who are unable to do any lasting damage while the *Tia'tum* is still breathing. She focuses on the still-burning banner hanging far above them, and wraps her Gifts around the fabric, bringing it down on the guards with an almighty tug.

The distraction allows her a moment's respite so she can concentrate on one opponent instead of half the guards at once. In the same instant, the wooden door blows inwards, shattering off its hinges. Hermitch charges in with three haggard-looking Fae. It does not even the playing field by any stretch, but it means they are no longer fighting for their lives in a losing battle.

The King fights out from under the banner, along with those of his *Lei'kah* who are also caught up under the heavy burning fabric. When the King sees Hermitch, an angry flush creeps up his neck and across his cheeks. He draws his blade with a roar and throws himself into the fray, fighting alongside his guards, despite Jiah's protests to stay behind them.

Hermitch merely smiles and shouts a war cry that his

companions echo, before clashing with the *Lei'kah*. The odds are stacked against them. They are good warriors but not in the same league as Mallux or Telium, and they are fighting *Ka'hine*.

Telium throws her power into shoddily patching up her arrow wound. As soon as it has closed over, she stops retreating from the Fae-lioness and meets her head-on.

The female stops, all the hair along her back standing on end. Her growl rumbles through Telium's chest. She snarls right back at the lioness, her own fangs scratching her lower lip. The lioness pounces.

Fireballs continue to miss Telium by a mere hair's-breadth. By pure chance, one nearly singes the lioness' tail, her snarl of annoyance reverberating through the room and stopping the *A'gnis* from throwing any more.

Tenebris claim these Fae and their inhuman reflexes!

She does not have time to avoid the lioness' claws as they reach out to her. They rake a set of burning lines across her hip, but unable to find purchase, they fall away. Telium screams in pain and rage.

She has never fought so hard in her life. Her pants rasp up and down her throat as her lungs work hard to deliver enough oxygen to the rest of her body. Her mind strains. She is tiring from fighting and desperately trying to put a damper on her Life-Thief Gifts. There are still more Fae to come. Hermitch and his companions are the only ones keeping the King from retreating through the large wooden doors.

Snarling, she spins to face the lioness. This time, when the beast leaps at her, she does not dodge away. Instead, she steps up into the lunge and buries one of her daggers in the lioness' eye. The pain causes the animal to screech, setting Telium's teeth on edge. Unable to stop her momentum, the Fae knocks Telium to the floor hard enough that she sees stars.

The impact forces the breath from her lungs. Her body screams for air. She moves before the lioness does. Drawing her haladie from her hip, she does not even bother unlatching it as she stabs the double blades between the beast's ribs. Warm life-blood speckles Telium's face and chest, coating her hand in a scarlet glove.

As she dies, the Fae loses her grip on her Power and her body morphs back into her humanoid form. Her beautiful face marred by the mangled wound to her eye. Blood leaks down her cheek, staining her golden hair.

Telium has never really feared for her life, even when she was locked in the Siren Queen's prison. But here, among these Fae with powers akin to gods, the slightest tickle of fear squeezes her heart.

Her strength is failing rapidly and her mind feels like it is about to combust under the strain of wielding her power to such a degree for so long, while still holding back her Life-Thief powers. Yet every time she thinks she is done for, she catches sight of the Fae King from the corner of her eye and gets a burst of strength. She *will* kill him. He will not escape her judgement.

For her Queen. For her people. For the slaves trapped here, like that woman in the pass.

Across the room, Hermitch is struck down. He falls with a cry, holding his hand across his bleeding stomach. Telium reaches for her dwindling supply of daggers as the guard raises her sword over Hermitch's head. An executioner ready to deal the killing blow. Telium grunts with the force of her throw. Even for her, it is an impressive shot. The Fae is on the other side of the room and her back is covered by a thick leather breastplate, meaning that only the back of the female's neck is exposed to Telium's blade.

She does not see if the throw hits home as someone throws a bucket of water in her face. The water surges up her nose and down her throat. Telium jerks back, trying to gasp for air but the water *follows* her. Her vision blurs as the water covers her entire head. Panicking, she reaches up and tries to pull away whatever is covering her face, but her hands pass straight through. A bubble of water sticks to her. She can touch her cheeks and lips, but she cannot get rid of the water. Swiping at her face, Telium tries to slosh the liquid off. The bubble just parts around her hands and stays put.

Don't breathe in, don't breathe in, don't breathe in. She chants the words like a mantra, desperately trying to calm her frantic mind. Her haladie clatters to the ground and her fingers claw at her chest. She falls to her knees, her lungs burning with the need for oxygen. Her eyes smart and her sinuses sting as the water slowly forces its way into her body. *Tenebris curse me,* she thinks. *I am going to die here, drowned on dry land.*

A Fae appears before her, face serene, her hands raised in front of her like she is offering up a gift. A blue and silver armband glints on her uniform. An *Altum.* Water droplets condense out of nothing and whizz through the air to join the bubble stuck to Telium's face.

Her mind bleats in panic and her heart kicks into a gallop. She cannot even *think* around the driving, incessant need to *breathe.*

Don't breathe in, don't breathe in.

Telium reaches out to the corpse of the lioness Fae. She sways drunkenly, yanking the dagger out of the fallen female's eye. The steel makes a soft, squelching sound as it is freed from flesh. She flips the dagger, gripping it by the tip and flings it towards the *Altum*, aiming for her heart … and misses.

The effort drains the last of Telium's energy. Black spots

swim before her eyes. It feels like a vice is crushing her chest. Water rushes down her throat. The pain it causes is accompanied by the certainty that she is going to die. Right here. On the floor of the Mad King's palace, with the evil bastard himself still breathing mere feet away. She is not going to be able to go back and burn the body of the slave woman in the pass. Never see Mallux again. Her body will never reach the Underrealm.

Her usually unflinching grip on her Gifts weakens until it is nearly gone completely. Telium collapses to the floor, vision blackening as her Gifts throw off their restraints and howl with wicked delight. They stretch and snarl and writhe under her skin, through her soul.

And with that, one of her most rarely used Gifts swims to the surface. One she disregards most of the time, the powers it gives her coming from the weakest of Thieves. So they sit, quiet and near-forgotten, in the back of her mind. The Gifts of a Freedom-Thief. The Gifts of a siren.

Distantly, Telium feels her head knock against the marble floor. She feels leaden and detached from herself.

With a snarl, her Freedom-Thief Gifts burst to the surface, the feeling like cool sweet mountain water as it rushes through her veins and fills her chest. With it comes the Gift of compulsion, and while that power is useless here amongst the Fae, the other attribute it brings has just saved her life. The physical change rips through her with such force it is agonising, and she cries out, hands flying to her neck. Her fingers brush across strange, raised lines that run from the backs of her ears down to the hollow of her throat. The physical Gift of a Freedom-Thief that can only be accessed in water.

Gills.

CHAPTER
49

Telium sucks in a great heaving gasp, the force of it so strong it causes the water bubble around her face to warp. Tears of relief prickle her eyes, merging with the water still around her face. She wraps her hand around her throat reflexively and coughs, gills flaring. The motion causes bubbles to gurgle up from her mouth and tickle her nose. The feeling is bizarre.

Coupled with the light-headedness brought on from her brush with death, Telium cannot help the laugh that bursts forth from her lips. She puts a hand to her forehead, body shaking with incredulity. But her joy is cut off by a fearful curse and the sound of a sword being drawn.

She turns to see the *Altum* looking at her with a mixture of fear and disbelief, sword held out in front of her as if she can ward off Telium with the mere sight of it.

Her Gifts sing in glee, lusting for carnage. Her smile is feral. 'Oh, you're fucked,' she growls.

Telium lunges at the Fae, armed with nothing but her claws and quick reflexes. She dodges the *Altum's* blade and steps in close. The threads of her mind whip about her like the tentacles of a great beast. Reaching, grasping for anything they can. Bumping up against the shield covering the *Altum's* mind, they curl around the great waves protecting her consciousness, constricting slowly.

The Fae winces, her eyes bright with fear as she looks at Telium, who throws up a hand and cracks them in the nose with the heel of her palm. The satisfying crunch and resulting gush of blood makes Telium grin with fierce delight.

She reaches out and grips the *Altum* as they stumble from her blow. Her claws curl around their bicep, blood pooling in little spots where she pierces skin. Her Gifts screech and thunder rumbles as she drives the talons of her other hand into the Fae's stomach.

The *Altum* gasps. The water still stuck to Telium's face falls away, splashing to the floor and soaking their boots. The female sways, gripping Telium's shoulder as if for support. In response, Telium curls her fingers inwards, claws shredding through flesh, and jerks her hand back with a savage snarl.

The Fae cries out and hunches over. Slumping to the floor as blood patters to the ground like raindrops, mixing with the pool of water that had nearly drowned Telium.

She lets go with a contemptuous flick of her hand. The gills on her neck fade away as she takes another lungful of air. Some of the water dripping from her face turns grey as it makes the black dye in the whisps of hair framing her face run. However, her respite is short-lived.

The room is carnage. Bodies lay strewn among burning scraps of fabric.

Six guards are still left standing, defending their King.

This time, two *Lei'kah* engage her at once. The archer from before and another with such tiny stature and honey-blonde hair, she looks wholly non-threatening. Telium knows better than to underestimate her.

Her Gifts are running rampant. Of their own accord, the threads of her mind crack out and slither towards the pair, wrapping around the essence of theirs. They slide over shields of stone and marble, feeling along the boundaries for cracks in the seemingly faultless armour. Blades clash as Telium deflects a blow to her neck and shoves the archer back. Her purple band braided with silver catches the light. An *Ohic'a*, just like Lotte.

The two Fae facing Telium pause a moment, thrown onto unsure footing by her wild nature and unprecedented Gifts. She snarls at them like a wild beast.

'Get on with it, then.' Her voice is so warped she barely recognises it as her own. Without warning, she launches herself at them. Haladie glinting in the light.

Far above, the glass ceiling darkens as huge grey thunderclouds roll in, threatening rain. Lightning zings overhead and when thunder rumbles; Telium feels it in her bones.

Another great boom sounds, this time from inside the palace. It echoes down the hallways and bounces around the circular room. *That is not part of the plan.* Telium does not have time to ponder its origins as she re-engages with the two Fae.

Her Gifts roil about her. Without the mind to direct them, they manifest in different ways; a wind kicks up ashes from the burning banner, throwing them about the room, seeming to dance in time to the cracks of thunder far above. Obsidian smoke, viscous and dense, tries and fails to take form.

Telium attempts to clamp a tight hold on her Life-Thief Gifts with the last scrap of her will. But she is unable to subdue them completely and shapes rise and fall about the room. Nightmarish shadows flicker in and out of existence; falkir stalk through the columns, only to disappear a moment later; tall humanoid shapes with long spindly limbs and eyes of molten gold launch themselves at the Fae, only to evaporate into black mist the moment a blade is turned their way.

The scene is straight from the realm of Tenebris. While the creatures do not harm them, the Fae are spooked enough that they hold off attacking Hermitch and the other rebel. Unsure how deadly the shadows could be. The leader of the *Lei'kah* seems to be pushing herself to the limit, lips a thin bloodless line on her face twisted in pain. Sweat soaks her brow and the collar of her shirt. The amount of energy she is expending to keep a constant shield over the King, herself and the Fae standing with her plus every door coming in and out of the circular main hall, must be immense.

Telium throws herself at the smaller Fae who stands still, letting her get in close. The female surprises Telium by dropping her own swords and wrapping both hands around the blade. Blood blooms from between the female's hands and drips between her fingers. She does not seem to notice as she jerks the haladie towards herself. The unexpected move catches Telium by surprise and she stumbles forward a step before she recovers.

With a jerk, Telium recoils from the tiny Fae, who holds firm to the haladie. Without warning, the female lunges forward and grabs Telium's wrist. Pain explodes in her chest and stars dance behind her eyes. A scream rips from her throat. It feels like fire and lightning are racing up and down her limbs. Like her blood is boiling. Her legs twitch and give out from underneath her. The hand wrapped around her haladie spasms, dropping the blade to the ground with a harsh clatter.

Her knees bark against the marble. She barely feels it against the all-consuming agony that ravages her entire being. Distantly, Telium understands that it is this Fae, with her black and yellow armband, causing this torture. That she should try to fight her off. But she cannot string together coherent thought.

Another wave of anguish racks her body and she screeches, all but collapsing in the female's grip. Muscles convulsing in pain as she screams herself hoarse. The pain suddenly subsides, drawing back just a touch. Telium can feel the Fae readying to hurl another onslaught at her. She chokes back a whimper, blood coating her tongue. Her eyes roll back in her head, but not before she sees a shadow-falkir hurl itself at Jiah. The brave female barely twitches as the falkir smashes against her shield and dissipates in a burst of black wind.

Struck by inspiration, Telium scrambles to rally her Gifts, power building in the air around her like a storm. She reaches down deep, hauling up every last dreg she has in her.

Next to the smaller Fae gripping Telium, the *Ohic'a* cries out fearfully. Her eyes turn completely blue, the irises swallowing her pupils whole. They dart about, unseeing. '*Niya!*' she cries. '*Sak!* Stop! Stop her!'

The *Dolomae* crashes her brutal Power into Telium. When the next wave of suffering hits, she is ready. She blasts every final drop of Gifts she has left in her, just as the *Dolomae* pushes the torturous fire into her body again. The force of her next scream tears at her throat. She tastes blood even as her Gifts shatter out of her. Right into the circular wall of arches.

They force their way into every nook and crevice they can find: between bricks and the minuscule cracks in the mortar. The cracks expand and her Gifts chase them, pushing and widening. Causing a domino effect until the entire bottom half of the inner wall is spider-webbed with fissures. The Fae gripping Telium's arm gapes at the walls around her, before turning back to Telium with a snarl, rage burning in her grey eyes.

The moment hangs, suspended in time. The large columned wall defies gravity for a breath; slowly, so slowly, it bows. Inward in some places and leaning to the outer wall in others.

Time snaps back into focus, with a shuddering groan and puff of dust, it comes toppling down on top of all of them. Jiah pales and throws out her hand to the King, her shield so thick that it warps the air around him. Hermitch drops his bow, throwing himself backward, arms curving over his head.

In front of her, the *Dolomae* snarls, jerking Telium forward by the wrist. The female wraps her small hand around Telium's throat. Telium has a moment to glance over at Mallux who is looking at her in open-mouthed astonishment. She throws her Gifts out towards him before pain like nothing she has ever felt spikes in her skull. Like a thousand blades being driven into her head. Never before has she endured such agony. It rages through her body. Bones and sinew creak under the strain. It is the worst form of torture, one she cannot escape. Her own body turning against her as it burns.

The pain is so intense, her body cannot cope. Telium's eyelids flutter and her mind flees to the safety of unconsciousness. The last thing she sees before blacking out completely are the inner arches crashing down to meet them like a giant wave. A smile ghosts her mouth and her words whisper past blood-smeared lips.

'Too late.'

CHAPTER 50

Telium groans as she swims back to consciousness. Tenebris curse her, she aches everywhere. From the crown of her head to the tips of her toes. Her shoulder throbs with each heartbeat. She cannot feel the fingers on one hand. She is sure a lump is already forming on her head. Searing pain and warmth tell her there is an open wound across her thigh.

She cracks open her eyes. Mortar dust dances in the watery rays of light and the marble floor is webbed with cracks where enormous chunks of stone have landed. Gaze widening, Telium looks around. Most of the wall has come tumbling down. In some places, part of an arch still stands, looking like jagged, broken bones in the queer lighting.

She sits up, breathing deeply, and coughs from the dust. Her forehead spikes in pain and she grips either side of her head. It feels like her brain is about to burst out from the confines of her skull.

Goddess, when this is over, she will never complain about a regular headache again. She will have to find some more of the bitter root that helps with pain. She gave the last of her stash to Mallux when—

Alarm makes Telium's heart stutter. Her limbs tingle with adrenaline as she shoots to her feet and looks around, pain temporarily forgotten. Her eyes scan the rubble frantically. *There.* From between the pieces of rubble, Mallux appears, his muscular body uncoiling like a snake.

When his piercing blue eyes meet hers, a sob escapes her throat. The adrenaline drains from her so fast her legs fold. She slips to the ground, suddenly weak and giddy with relief, as her head spins violently.

He is there in an instant. Strong arms coming around her as he holds her to his chest, making comforting sounds. She groans, causing Mallux to pull back to look her over.

I must look like death, she thinks. She can feel the dust and chips of stone tangled in her hair. She is cut and bruised all over, her clothing ripped. Blood coats her hands and shirt, and is splattered on her face and boots.

She sits still as Mallux runs his hands over her body efficiently. He rips the sleeve of her shirt and ties it around the wound on her leg. When his hands brush across her right shoulder she hisses in pain.

'Dislocated,' Mallux murmurs.

He grips her wrist and elbow, his touch gentle but firm. Slowly he bends her arm at the elbow. Her shoulder burns. When he has her arm in the correct position, he hesitates, looking up into her face. Telium grits her teeth and gives him a sharp nod. Mallux pushes her shoulder back into its socket in one swift movement. A pop followed by a sharp pain makes her cry out. Nearly instantly, the burning pain becomes a dull throb.

She rubs it while Mallux gently examines her hand. It looks as if two fingers have been crushed by a falling stone. The fragile bones are probably broken; possibly even parts of her hand too. The joints of her fingers are swollen and the flesh around them bruised and bloody.

'Not much we can do about this until we get you to a healer,' Mallux says.

Telium swallows. Her mouth is dry. 'I am left-handed anyway.'

Even if her powers were not depleted, she does not trust herself to set the intricate bones correctly before mending them.

Mallux flashes her a smile and pulls her to her feet. Looking around at the carnage, he whistles slowly. 'Remind me to never piss you off.'

Telium's smile is equal parts savage and proud.

Mallux's head jerks up. Turning away from her as a snarl rips from his chest. Telium looks across the room to see movement and takes off on Mallux's heels as he bolts towards the disturbance. Halfway across the room, they realise the figure is Hermitch, arm pinned to the ground by an enormous boulder. Mallux vaults over the stone and rubble, rushing to his friend's side. He throws his considerable strength into lifting the stone.

Telium moves forward to offer what little help she can but stops short on instinct. She casts out the net of her mind, forcing it past the pounding headache. The stone voids of Mallux and Hermitch part her net, but that is not what she is concentrating on. A weak fluttering consciousness sits in her net. Telium whirls to face it, scanning the room.

There, a few feet from her, the *Tia'tum*, Jiah, lies on the ground. Her body is almost completely covered by a fallen section of the wall. Her face is barely visible and one leg is bent at an ugly angle, as is her hand, still reaching out to her King and channelling the last of her strength into keeping her shield in place.

Telium flexes her jaw against a twinge of sadness, that this loyal and powerful Fae wasted her life protecting such a monster. She can feel the consciousness of the King, trapped between two huge sections of stone. Telium moves towards Jiah, her feet heavy on the cracked marble floor. She crouches next to the Fae whose face is dirty and bruised, lip cut and bleeding, one eye completely swollen shut. It is the first time she has seen a Fae look anything other than flawless. Her good eye is hazy with pain, but it sharpens when she spots Telium. Even now, Jiah is all hot Fae defiance. She snarls at Telium, her elongated canines gleaming in the dull light as she curses.

Telium does not react. Instead, she looks at the Fae solemnly as she gently removes one of the two remaining daggers from her bandolier. Jiah sees the movement. Her eye goes steely with resolution, but a shadow of confusion crosses it too.

As the enemy, Telium should leave Jiah to her fate; to live a cripple or die as the goddesses see fit. But she cannot leave this noble Fae to suffer. She is a warrior and as such, deserves to die with pride by steel or arrow or Gift.

As she leans across to place the dagger on Jiah's neck, the Fae looks at her in understanding, nodding once, accepting her death.

'May the goddesses walk the path beside you, Blade Sister,' Telium whispers, her voice strained.

She jerks the steel across the female's throat and blood spurts from the wound, splashing Telium's arms and knees. She does not wipe the blade off as she returns it to its sheath. A single shining tear tracks down Telium's cheek as she lowers her head and sends a prayer up for Tenebris to safely guide the Fae to the Gardens of Opimare, or wherever it is the Fae believe their soul resides in the afterlife.

Behind her, the stones surrounding the King shift slightly as Jiah's shield dissipates. She can feel his consciousness. With a steadying breath, she climbs slowly to her feet. Her soul exhausted from so much death.

Mallux has freed Hermitch and is tending to his comrade's wounds. With deliberate steps, she walks towards the stones. She grips the edge of the first one in both hands and heaves with all her might, fingers scraping and nails cracking. At the same time, the King pushes, and the stone moves, slowly at first, until its centre of gravity shifts. It topples away, landing with a loud crash.

Telium does not take her eyes off him. The King's gaze locks with hers and he straightens slowly to his full considerable height. His attire is filthy: dusty, rumpled and torn. Parts of the emerald-green tunic have been stained red. The golden top button has been ripped off and is hanging by a single shining thread. Another is missing entirely.

The menacing Ivory Crown has been knocked askew in the chaos. But still it stays perched on its ruler's head, as if it clings there.

She waits for rage to swamp her senses. To feel the acidic hatred rush through her veins like it did every time she thought of the Mad King. But she feels nothing except weariness down to her bones. Her energy is spent, her Gifts drained dry. She wants nothing more than to crawl back to the pile of furs in her hollow tree home in her forest and sleep for the next week.

For the Thieves, she reminds herself. *For people like the slave woman in the pass. For every child who suffered at the hand of this male's experiments. For my Queen … For me.*

Telium hardens her heart and draws the dagger from its place at her thigh, holding it loosely at her side. Waiting to see what the Mad Fae King will do.

He looks around, that stupid crown still perched on his head, the expression on his face switching from astonishment at the chaos to sadness as his eyes alight on Jiah. Finally settling in a look of blank stoicism as he watches Telium.

He begins speaking in Old Fae, gesturing about him.

'I don't understand you.' Telium cuts him off, her voice flat.

'Is all this worth it?' he asks in the Common Tongue, brow crinkling into a confused frown. His voice is harmonic, his Fae accent making the words musical. When she does not answer him, he tries again. 'How could you do this to our people? Our children? Our country is dying.'

Telium does not reply. Merely tucks her hair behind one ear, revealing the rounded tip and his mistaken assumption. Then she lunges. The King focuses on her human ears and frowns as he backs away from her, keeping his palms turned outwards as he dodges her with Fae swiftness.

'Why?' he asks, voice pained.

He has no blade, no weapon with which to defend himself. She swipes at him again. When he dodges out of the way once more, a snarl rips from her throat. His fallen sword lies at her feet. She kicks it over to him in a skid of rasping metal.

'Pick it up,' she intones, her voice dead.

The King glances between her and the blade.

'Pick. It. Up,' she repeats, a snarl entering her voice.

Slowly, the King of Thresiel crouches down and grasps the gilded hilt of his blade, before standing back to his full height. He does not raise his sword. Instead, it hangs uselessly in his grip. He searches her face intently as they stand facing each other; again, Telium feels that odd flare of recognition. He looks exhausted. A cut bleeds at his shoulder and a bruise is forming across his head. Even Jiah, with all her Power, had not been able to stop the King from escaping completely unscathed.

'Why?' he asks again.

This time, she feels her rage deep down in her soul. Like a giant ancient beast, it cracks open an eye and gazes at the King.

'What could he have possibly offered you, that I could not? Why would your people not want trade and prosperity? Peace. To unite our kingdoms?' he asks. 'I have never had any quarrel with Alkoria.'

With each word, Telium's wrath builds. At last, she snaps. She knows *exactly* what type of unity he means – a Fae on the throne of Alkoria so he can have full access to Thieves and their children. To torture and experiment on them as he saw fit. All for his own selfish desires. Is it not enough that he is Fae, that he is blessed with beauty and grace and strength, with long life?

Drive a blade through his heart.

Her bitterness and fury rise with startling ferocity. She throws herself at the King, screaming her rage and heartache.

'Because you are a MONSTER!' she screeches. 'A selfish, greedy, brutal bastard!'

Her breath is coming in hard pants, and Telium – Tenebris Kin – fights the Mad Fae King in his palace with nothing but a dagger and pure wrath.

She continues hurling abuse at him the entire time. Screaming herself hoarse, unable to contain the emotions that threaten to drown her. This male is responsible for her ruin. He is responsible for her Queen's paranoia, the depression and darkness that consumed Selenia. He enslaves humans, tortures innocents.

His actions inadvertently led to Trigg's death, the only mother she had ever known. He caused the rift between their peoples. He is corrupt and vile and cruel. He does not deserve to rule.

Her fury puts him on the back foot. He blocks and parries Telium as she rages against him like a wild beast. One moment, she is throwing herself at the King and the next, her blade is dripping with his blood from a nick on his cheek.

The King makes his first mistake. He glances at Mallux, still crouching beside Hermitch. Telium slashes her blade in a sweeping arch. It leaves a gaping wound across the King's chest. He jumps back with a startled cry, hand splaying across his injury. Blood instantly pools between his fingers.

'Torturing, filthy, raping *snake!*' the words burn Telium's throat.

The King's eyebrows shoot up into his hairline. Likely no-one has ever spoken to him like this. To hear such insults thrown at him must shock him to the core. Nobody is the villain of their own story.

Again, the Fae King considers Mallux. 'What has he told you?'

The King's words are strained as Telium attacks him again and again. He struggles to defend himself with one hand staunching the bleeding wound on his chest.

Telium ignores his words, refusing to let his poison seep into her ears. Ignoring the trickle of doubt that creeps in, she continues to strike at the King, covering him in wounds. Draining his energy as his body works to heal him. He stumbles, and Telium reaches in boldly to grip the wrist that holds his sword, then pivots her body, using her momentum to bring her elbow down onto his straight arm, hard.

The King cries out in pain. In one smooth motion, Telium relieves him of his sword and spins around to face him again, the blade touching his chest. Right over his black heart.

The King holds out a hand in supplication. He pulls back his lips and bares his teeth at her in a snarl.

'Fool,' he rumbles. 'You have doomed your people. What do you think he will do when he assumes the throne? Whatever he has promised you, it is baseless. He is just like our—'

Telium cuts him off, whipping his own blade up to his throat and settling the tip just under his chin. He swallows thickly, the motion causing the sword to prick his skin. A bead of blood rolls down his throat. Yet he does not flinch. His brown eyes blaze with hate and disgust.

Disgust. Something in Telium falters.

Gritting her teeth, she holds the image of Selenia's beautiful face, the sound of Trigg's brassy laugh, close to her heart as she returns his gaze with a hard look of her own.

Drive a blade through his heart.

She is breathing hard when she draws the King's sword back. And rams it into his chest. Angling it upwards, the force of her blow pushes the tip of the blade out the other side.

She stands so close that she can feel his breath on her as he gasps in surprise and pain. As if he did not expect her to follow through. Telium forces herself to stand and watch his face. Determined to watch his soul flee his body.

The King looks down at her. Then at the place where his own sword has pierced his body. 'Why?' he asks again, his voice reedy and fading.

'For Trigg and Alkoria,' she says, her voice barely a whisper. 'For all the children you experimented on. For my Queen you raped and pushed into madness.'

Confusion crosses his face again. Followed by an unfathomable sadness. He glances over at Mallux who watches them intently while the final guards lay dying at his feet.

'Oh, you cunning bastard,' the King rasps at him. He

laughs a harsh, empty sound and sways on his feet. He reaches out unconsciously to grip Telium as his heart fails and his eyes begin to dim. Still, he does not look away from Mallux, who is watching them with his jaw clenched so hard the tendons stand out in sharp relief.

'It looks like you win after all.' The words sigh out of the King. His brown eyes find Telium's again. He frowns down at her.

Recognition hits her like a slap. From this angle, standing as close as lovers, she realises who the King looks like. It is right there in the strong line of his jaw and wide, piercing eyes. *Mallux.* The King looks like Mallux. Her mouth drops open in shock, air hitching in her lungs. The King merely looks at her with a smile full of heartbreak and pity.

'You poor soul, I ...' He is about to say more, but his heart finally gives out. His body unable to heal the grievous wound. His eyes dull as he sways to the side. His broad hands slip off Telium's arms.

Hands numb with shock, she lets him fall to the floor without protest. She continues staring into the space where the King had stood. Her mind moves sluggishly, trying and failing to wrap her head around the understanding hovering just at the edges of her mind. The room is as silent as a tomb. The only noise is the gentle patter of a light rain on the glass roof as the clouds finally release their burden and weep.

The quiet is broken by the sharp clip of boots on the floor. Mallux appears in her peripheral vision. He does not reach for her, does not so much as glance in her direction as he sinks onto his haunches and gazes at the fallen King.

Telium watches as Mallux reaches out to press two fingers against the dead male's neck. He holds his breath as if he can barely believe what is happening. Telium stares at the top of

Mallux's head, crowned in a tumble of golden locks, that is disturbingly similar to—

No. She pushes the thought away. There is an explanation. There *has* to be. It is all just a trick; the last drop of poison left behind by a mad king.

She continues to stare at Mallux detachedly. Praying that he will look up at her with that heated smile. His piercing blue eyes will swallow her whole, his essence will wrap itself around her like it always does. He will pick her up and spin her around before setting her down and kissing her soundly. Then tonight, they would rest and celebrate their victory. He would lay his love over her with his hands and teeth and tongue.

Telium's fingers twitch as they ache to reach for him. She forces them still. Forces herself to stand without moving as she watches him, barely breathing.

Mallux reaches out and closes the King's eyes reverently. He twists his hand against his chest in that strange sign of their faith. He murmurs something in ancient lyrical Fae that sounds strangely like a prayer. He rests his hand atop the King's chest. Right on top of the gaping wound.

'Threal, brother. It looks like I do win after all.'

Telium staggers back a step as if he has hit her, hand flying to her throat. She stares at Mallux in rising horror. Her heart rebelling at what her mind is just beginning to fathom.

The scrape of her boots makes Mallux look up. His eyes seem unfocused, turned inward at first, then they blaze with a pure male possessiveness that makes her heart stutter. In a flash, he stands before her, arms encircling her. His essence pours over her in waves.

'Telium,' he says, his voice a low baritone. *'Upa.* My brilliant, powerful Telium.' He squeezes her arms as he draws back to look down at her, triumph lighting his features.

'What …' The words do not come. Telium clears her throat and tries again. Forcing life into her voice. 'What did he mean? And why did you call him "brother"?'

He looks at her a moment, gazing down at her in his arms. How had she not seen it before – the resemblance between the two?

Mallux does not answer her immediately. His lips are set into a grim line, like a disappointed parent. Her heart begins to race as her limbs tremble, but she forces herself to ask again.

'That is not the King, is it?'

A muscle feathers in his jaw and he shifts his eyes to the side. 'He was *a* king, *vel.*'

A king, not *the* King – the Mad Fae King – the one she had come to kill. She feels like she is standing at the edge of a precipice, toes hovering over the edge of a deadly drop.

'Mallux,' she says slowly, her voice surprisingly steady. She points to the dead male. 'Who is that?'

His eyes harden; Fae arrogance in every line of his body. 'He was my brother – Malakai IV. Up until a moment ago, the King of Thresiel.'

'The Mad King's name is Erthrius. Not Malakai.' Her mind cannot register what he is telling her.

Hermitch struggles to his feet, a devious grin spread across his face as he limps over to them, his eyes hard. Mallux throws his friend a dark look.

Telium steps back from the circle of Mallux's arms. Her pulse ratcheting up another notch.

'Just get it over with,' Hermitch snaps. He gestures at Telium dismissively. 'She has served her purpose.'

Mallux snarls at the other male, canines flashing. 'You will not touch her,' he growls.

When Hermitch does not respond, Mallux snarls again. 'She is mine. I want her, and I will have her.'

Hermitch's face darkens in anger, but he says nothing, instead turning to Telium and pointing at the fallen King.

'That,' Hermitch says with deliberate slowness, 'is Malakai. Spineless, soft-hearted, mortal-loving—'

'Shut up,' Mallux growls threateningly at his friend. Then to Telium, more gently, 'He was the firstborn son of King Erthrius. Or as you Alkorian's so kindly call him, the Mad Fae King. Erthrius ... suddenly passed near one winter ago. The time of mourning had passed; it was time for *Ramaeris* – a coronation – time for someone else to carry the Ivory Crown.'

Hermitch takes no notice of Mallux's anger. Continuing as if he has not been interrupted, waving a hand at his friend. 'His second-born son, and now the rightful King of Thresiel, who will continue his father's perfect vision, stands before you.'

Her stomach bottoms out so fast she thinks she might be sick. She stares at Hermitch in horror, revulsion clawing its way up her throat. *Lies*, she tells herself. She drags her eyes away from Hermitch to look at Mallux, who is staring at her with shining eyes. She sees pride in his conquest there. He does not refute Hermitch's claims. He does not need to. She can see the truth in his face.

Oh Goddess, what has she done?

CHAPTER
51

Hate and pain and shock swirl around her; emotions so thick and hard she can barely breathe around them. But overlaying it all, like a thick, suffocating blanket, is betrayal. Raw, visceral betrayal. With her Queen, the shock had numbed almost everything. This pain nearly brings her to her knees.

She looks up at Mallux, her stupid fickle heart still beating for him. He has betrayed her. Used her as his dark weapon. And with her black powers, she snuffed out the spark of this country that could have turned into a burning flame. How could she have been so foolish? So blind?

No, her heart cries, *it cannot be true*. The pain in her chest feels like it is cleaving her apart as she looks up into his handsome face.

Her mind is so clouded it cannot come up with coherent thought. Bile rises, acidic and harsh. Her chest tightens, making it hard to draw air into her lungs around the emotion squeezing her throat.

She stands rooted to the spot. Mallux is speaking, trying to *explain* himself to her. But she barely registers the words. They swim in and out of focus.

'I planned this from the beginning ... always knew who you were ... but then you ... knew from the start what you could do ...'

A word squeezes past the lump in her throat: 'No.'

Hermitch laughs, swaggering over to Mallux and clapping him on the shoulder. His hateful brown eyes bore into Telium as he responds for Mallux.

'Vel,' he says, smirking. 'You single-handedly destroyed the one male who would have reconnected ties with Alkoria, opened trade routes, and offered you the hand of peace.' His show of teeth is a harsh facade of a smile, all menace and cruelty.

'Be silent, Hermitch,' Mallux says as he gazes at Telium with pleading eyes. Yet he shows no remorse. 'This does not change anything. You will still be mine. You will be behind me as I create a new world for the Fae. I will protect you. You will not be harmed.'

Telium just stares at him dumbly. He cannot be serious. All her feelings are muted. Her mind unable to process the change of events. She stands wooden as Mallux speaks to her, his voice reaching her as if from a great distance. He tells her about his father's great plans to gift males with Power to unite Alkoria and Thresiel under one rule: his.

Hermitch fills in the blanks that Mallux leaves out, delighting in Telium's distress. 'Once he captured her, Erthrius stripped her naked. Draped her in chains and lead her back to his kingdom. Shaming the woman who had dared oppose him. There, he wore down her defences. Bit by bit. Drawing out her agony for as long as possible.'

'No.' The word barely more than a whisper of air as it passes her lips. Pain lashes her senses, head spinning, even as her chest severs in two.

Hermitch laughs. 'Yes. Even as she tried to push at the minds of those gathered, she screamed. Her so-called *Gifts* were useless. Her greatest power abandoned her when she needed it most.'

He nudges Mallux whose mouth cocks up at the side, looking at Hermitch in friendly reproach. As if the story were some great joke. Like an innocent tale of when they were young and foolish, getting themselves into trouble.

A new feeling begins to build in Telium, pushing aside the all-encompassing pain of Mallux's betrayal – rage. The surge of power that comes with it makes her gasp and drop to her knees. She thought bringing down the walls had drained her dry, but her rage has opened up another door inside her. Suffusing her soul with her dark Gifts. She covers her ears in an attempt to block out their poisoned words.

Mallux tells her how the Queen tried to sway his father with her Gifts. As punishment, he had tossed her to the floor of his throne room and let his guards have their way with her. Beaten and bloody, she could do nothing to fend them off.

Hermitch laughs again and licks his lips with a smacking sound. 'Her cries were particularly delicious.'

'No,' Telium croaks. She can feel the tenuous hold she keeps on her power slipping, her grip frayed to a thread.

'Telium, my *upa*, you have to understand.' Mallux crouches in front of her, removing her hands from her ears gently. 'Did you not wonder what it was between us? Why you lusted for me so?'

She stares at him, her mind gone to eerie stillness. Her heart breaking in two after hearing his silken voice paint a picture of the horror her Queen had endured. Even now, his eyes burn with desire. As if he has not just pulled her world out from under her, shoved a knife between her ribs and ripped out her heart. Her emotions swing so wildly she feels bile rise in her throat.

Mallux is speaking again.

'My father finally, *finally*, worked out how to syphon power. That was the only thing that kept his attention all those long years after the war. But it was finally worth it. All those experiments and trials were no longer for naught.'

Telium squeezes her eyes shut at the images of Fae children and Thieves, the too-small skull that had toppled to the bottom of that pit – the results of the King's 'trials'.

'He only wanted to level the playing field. Why should females be the only ones to bear Power? Why should males not share in the Power? When test after test failed, he tried a different tack; turned his sights to Alkorian Thieves … and the Freedom-Thief ruling there. Imagine his delight when he was invited for an audience with the Queen, only to find out she was willing to bargain with him, to spare her people. A bargain was struck, one that would allow our kingdoms to unite, for a Fae to sit on an Alkorian throne.'

Telium tries to block out his words. She does not need to hear this. She knows what would have happened after that. Once the Siren Queen gave birth to her half-Fae child, the Mad Fae King would have unlimited access to the Thief children of his neighbouring land. He was old, one of the oldest Fae in the land. Twenty-one winters was but a moment to his existence. He could wait.

But then something happened that he had not expected – the child did not come. He marched his armies on Alkoria, and when he claimed his prize, he took her straight to his private area of the palace. There, after years of failed attempts, he was able to pull the power from one and transfer it to another.

'Selenia was but the first. There will be more. After all, once

Father worked out how to syphon her power, he passed the siren Gifts onto his son. Not his firstborn, who was a useless soft-hearted thing, too much like our mother, too cowardly to offer up his body for the greater good. But to—'

'*You.*' Telium finds her voice at last. The sound of her Queen's name has snapped the world around her back into focus. Mallux is looking at her with mingling pride and triumph. Horror and revulsion war in her as she realises what he is. Whose power he carries.

'Yes,' Mallux proclaims proudly. 'Me.' He steps forward, crowding into her space. Telium is too numb to react.

Hermitch's mouth twists into a sneer.

'He was able to infuse her Gifts of compulsion within me. Not to my weak older brother – who you have so obediently disposed of – but to the true ruler of Thresiel. Father never planned to give Malakai the throne, anyway. It took me a long while to master the Gifts until I learned that I could not influence people with my words like your Freedom-Thieves, but if I concentrated hard enough, I could stir the feelings within a person: lust, want, loyalty.'

That is why he is telling her all of this. He thinks that with his stolen Gifts, he will be able to compel her to stay with him, to forgive his heinous deeds.

Weakly, she grips his shirt front. Wanting to strangle him. He smiles down at her fondly, as if she is his favourite pet come to lie at his feet. Another realisation crashes into her, one that shatters her already broken heart. It is not love she sees in his eyes; it is possession. She is a conquest. A wild creature that he has tamed. A savage beast that he has brought to heel.

A commotion sounds outside one of the many doors, but no-one pays it any heed. Mallux's blue eyes shine as his gaze searches her face. Blue ... not brown like his brother's, but

blue like the sea. Like the shore on the clearest day. Blue ...
like her Siren Queen's because ... Telium can feel it now; the
waves of compulsion wrapping around her body.

He is trying to compel her to forgive him, to wipe away her
thoughts with a wave of lust like he has so many times before.
She struggles to her feet. Begins backing away from him as he
follows her with a smooth, sinuous gait. Fury coats her tongue
like ash and the threads of her mind whip about her like angry
snakes.

Mallux does not seem to know that a Freedom-Thief's
Gifts do not work on someone whose heart is spoken for. That
is why a Freedom-Thief cannot work their Gifts of compulsion
on the Fae, who are each born with a *Wai'tinate* somewhere.
The perfect other half of their heart and soul. And there is a
part of her, no matter how small, that is Fae. She can fight this.

Images flash in her mind in quick succession: her dream
of Tenebris trying to wire Mallux's mouth shut, as if trying to
protect her from his poisonous words, and Lotte's prophecy
about her heart betraying her.

... *He drained her dry* ...

They certainly had drained her Queen dry. Poured every
last drop of her power into the male standing before her. How
had she not noticed before? How had she not seen it? Mallux
had said the words, delusional from smoke inhalation after
outrunning the fire. *Vortas*. King.

'Together, we will finish what my father started. We will
take Alkoria and infuse Fae males with Power, starting with
more for myself, of course.'

Thunder rumbles in her mind as lightning cracks overhead, momentarily blocking out the sound of the rain. Her
limbs begin to tremble. Across the room, a door rattles from
the force of a blow.

'All this time, you were lusting after the male who had your Queen's Gifts. Ironic, isn't it? Though you showed extraordinary resistance to my power. Do not worry, my *upa*, you will not suffer the same fate. You will stay at my side and serve me. Imagine it, Telium! What powerful beings our children will be. As soon as I saw your powers, I knew you would bear my children. We are both *more* than the rest: better, faster, stronger. Elite. Our children will rule akin to gods. You will forgive me—'

A high-pitched whine sounds in Telium's head. From the corner of her eye, she sees one of the doors crash open. Paxium and Lillian hurtle through the door, both coming up short to gape at the carnage surrounding them.

Too late, Telium thinks bitterly. *I have already doomed us all.*

Lillian runs and drops to her knees beside the fallen King. Her hands run over Malakai, tears falling from her eyes.

Something about the sight breaks her.

Mallux is still talking, telling her how she will serve him – in all ways. But all she can see is the hand Lillian holds, pale and lifeless. The hand of a king who would have united their kingdoms, who had been moments away from making a speech to free human slaves and write off his father's unjust laws. The male she struck down would have ushered this land into a time of hope and prosperity. In her chest, her heart shatters yet again. Shame fills her, along with hot, molten rage. Enhanced by the Life-Thief Gifts that have slipped through her grasp.

Drive a blade through his heart. Her Queen's words whisper to her. She has failed ... Or has she? She may have killed Malakai, but Mallux is still here. A reincarnation of the Mad Fae King and his ideals.

Paxium's face is a picture of barely contained wrath as

he looks down at the King. His head snaps up and he stares at Mallux. A growl rumbles in his chest, the sound sending goosebumps skittering across Telium's skin. He draws his blade and stalks towards them.

Hermitch draws his sword. 'I never trusted you,' he growls at Pax. 'You should have gone back to your lands when you had the chance.'

Telium turns to Mallux, eyes blank. His face lights up in triumph and he holds a hand out to her imperiously. High above them, through the multifaceted glass roof, thunder rumbles and lightning splits the sky.

His voice is layered with possession. *'Telium.'*

CHAPTER
52

Black Gifts detonate out of her. The chains and cages she keeps them in turn to ash on the wind. Mallux and Hermitch are blasted off their feet. Paxium falls to his knees as Lillian cries out and throws herself over Malakai's body.

The force of Telium's Gifts whip out of her in a black wind, rattling doors and shattering the glass roof far above them. Glass rains down around her, flashing like diamonds in the light. The shards so tiny they could have been raindrops, the sound of them hitting the floor like a million silver bells.

One of the few remaining doors bangs open. A handful of rebel soldiers run into the room but hesitate at the scene in front of them. Unsure how to proceed.

Grey clouds far above them flash with lightning and rain begins to fall in earnest; big, fat drops of water pelting through the now-open roof. A dark gale swirls around Telium, whipping her hair about her face and catching up burnt bits of banner and debris.

Free of their tethers, her Gifts run wild, howling in wicked delight. Claws tip her fingers and fangs gleam as she snarls. Shadows condense from the wind and take shape into creatures of the dark. Falkir and other beasts from her forest rage around her. Devouring the soldiers who try to run to Mallux's defence; they give up their lives for the male they had hoped to crown as their King. The rest hesitate, grouping together and facing outwards. Hoping to ward off the shadows with sword and spear. Telium's beasts consume them in a heartbeat.

Mallux throws his hand up to protect his face as he struggles to his feet. Behind him, Hermitch gapes at the chaos. Telium, dyed black hair snapping in the unnatural wind, turns her merciless gaze upon him. He pales. Scrambling to his feet, he flees. Bolting straight past Pax who has not risen from his knees. A mere thought has a trio of shadow wolves chasing after Hermitch's retreating form.

'Telium!' Mallux's cry is snatched away by the wind.

Overhead, clouds gather and thunder rumbles, the force of it shaking free more glass. Power, the likes she has not felt since her madness in the forest, tingles up and down her arms. But this is better, so much better. Oh, the sweet feeling of strength coursing through her; the way her Gifts dance with wild abandon.

The air is tight and heavy with power.

She turns her gaze back to Mallux and whips the threads of her mind out. Wrapping them around him and squeezing with bruising force. His hand flies to his chest and he stumbles. Instead of ripping his life-force from him, Telium *pushes*, throwing out the net of her mind to encompass his consciousness. Letting her Gifts guide her, she adds the weight of her mind to the attack. When she feels it flowing around his stone walls, she doubles back, swirling around his shield with a black wind. A thought has a dark glittering storm smashing against his walls. They shake as stones rain down.

Mallux grabs his head and falls to his knees, moaning.

Encouraged, Telium attacks again, sending an ebony javelin spearing towards the walls of his mind. The slightest crack appears and she attacks it without hesitation. Throwing her entire being into destroying the walls surrounding Mallux's mind.

She tears at them with her bare hands, the stone ripping her nails and breaking her skin. She screams in rage and frustration, the sound demonic. In a final push, she calls up a shadow-drenched wind. Thunder rumbles overhead as she throws every last dreg of her Gifts and black soul at that wall.

With a resounding crack, it finally tumbles down, stone and rubble raining down around her. She steps over the threshold into Mallux's mind. Black Gifts pulsing at her fingertips. His thoughts hit her like a lightning strike. Full of greed and lust and envy. His true character exposed. Twisted and warped by the attentions of his mad father, he believes he is the rightful King of Thresiel. That every word his father had whispered to him, about Malakai being weak and how his love for peace had made him soft, was true. That power and authority is his birthright.

There are thoughts of her here too, but Telium brushes them aside, forcing the threads of her mind into his, like vines creeping around a tree. She pushes the coils into every nook and crevice she can and holds firm. Somewhere far away, she can hear Mallux screeching and someone else calling out her name.

Rain pelts down on them. Flooding the marble floors, running in little rivers off the smashed stone arches, soaking the bodies scattered on the ground. The last of the ebony dye in Telium's hair runs, causing swirls of black to run down her neck and arms, dripping off her fingertips. It mixes with the dark smoke swirling there, then splashes onto the floor. It coats her shoulders and her forearms, and pools at the collar of her shirt before bleeding into the fabric. A single obsidian drop runs from her temple to her chin, where it sits quivering for a moment, like a black jewel, before dropping to the marble.

It is like she is being washed clean. The rain soaks her hair and strips the taint of Mallux's presence from her soul. She lets all of it wash out of her and run in black rivulets to the floor where it pools beneath her feet like oil.

Within moments, her jet-black hair has returned to its natural bone-white colour. The remains of the black dye running in dark rivers from neck to fingertips make her look other-worldly; a dark angel standing amongst them. Black mist swirls at her fingertips and her startling eyes are blank, turned inwards, as she delves deeper into Mallux's mind.

She has wandered so far into his mind, she is not sure if she can find her way back. Killing him could well destroy her in the process. Her entire being is wrapped around his so wholly, he cannot escape. So she can feel every part of his life draining away. She takes a deep breath, revelling in the bedlam she has wreaked in his mind. Delighting in his ruined plan, shattered by her chaos. Her body now stands above his. *You will die here,* she thinks. He twitches and she knows he can hear her thoughts as she whispers them into his mind.

You will die and your father's legacy with you. You thought you could control me? Enslave me after you used me like some dark pawn? Fool. Tenebris will take your soul from your cold corpse and you will spend eternity in suffering, learning again and again why they call me her Kin.

He begs with her on his knees.

'Don't do this, Telium. *Upa, stop.* Stop!' He continues pleading for his life.

She does not heed him.

Telium closes her eyes and again calls that black wind from within her, sending it tumbling through his mind, shredding everything in its path. Violently squeezing the threads of her mind, she feels his consciousness start to crack. In another heartbeat, it will shatter completely.

Suddenly, Telium becomes weak. Her energy drains rapidly. She blinks as the threads snap and her black gust peters out to nothing. Her head spins dizzily and her legs collapse under her, teeth singing as she hits the marble floor.

It is deathly quiet in her mind as if her head is packed with cotton. The only sound is Mallux's ragged breathing. She feels the emptiness like the loss of a limb. Telium gasps, blinking rapidly as she tries to orientate herself, grasping for her Gifts. For the first time since she found herself in the Siren Queen's prison, she cannot feel them. There is no power prowling under her skin. No violent Gifts to keep caged or to curl up in her bones. Nothing. She is empty. Mortal.

A pair of shoes step into her vision and she attempts to rise, swaying so violently she falls. She looks up into the tanned face of a female. Though she remains unmarked by time, there is something ageless in the fathomless abyss of her black eyes. The colour of her irises is startling against the white. Her long grey hair hangs in a rope down her back. A depthless black ribbon is tried about her arm. Her mouth is bracketed with lines of pain.

'What a tempest your powers are, girl. So hard to contain.' The female grimaces, 'Nevertheless, I shall hold them until my King tells me to return them to you.'

Telium feels a snarl in her throat but only manages to twitch her lips. Weak. She is so weak. She feels like her body has been beaten, drowned, then wrung dry. Telium's limbs are too heavy as she struggles to her hands and knees, arms trembling. The female, who must be a *Ka'hine,* watches her for a moment longer, before glancing around the area. Tutting at the sight of the fallen King.

'Such a mess,' she admonishes before turning to Mallux. 'Get up.'

Mallux gingerly climbs to his feet, ignoring Telium completely. Like she had not been a mere moment away from shattering his entire being from the inside out.

'Ka'hine Tak'nis, vel thruik.' Mallux greets the newcomer with stiff formality.

Telium watches in dismay as Mallux surveys the area around him. His eyes light up with satisfaction when they land on his brother.

Lillian has disappeared. Paxium is nowhere to be seen. There is an odd feeling in Telium's chest like someone has tied a string around her stripped, raw soul and is now tugging on it. Her eyes wander around the great hall unseeing. Mallux's conversation with the *Tak'nis* falling on deaf ears.

She thinks of Trigg and her Siren Queen, of her quiet, hollow home. All the people in Alkoria who will now fall before the blight of Mallux. The young boy and his mother on the farm. Kya and her lover Lucy. Derik the teller. Their future will be bleak and dark. She has failed them. Her hope to bring light with her dark Gifts has fallen short. She can never go back to burn that woman's body in the pass, her soul never to reach the Gardens of Opimare.

She looks up at Mallux from her knees, his words blurring into focus.

'… We will need to mobilise the troops as soon as possible, crush any resistance quickly so we can move into Alkoria.'

Resistance? The word sticks, as if pleading for Telium to understand. There must be others who will stand against

Mallux. Telium recalls all the Fae celebrating in the streets on what was meant to be Malakai's coronation day.

The *Tak'nis* nods at Mallux; at her side, her fist clenches and unclenches. Mallux notes the female's seeming discomfort. He enquires about it sharply, as if she is a grave inconvenience for interrupting his monologue.

'The girl's powers … they are unlike anything I have taken on before. They fight me like a living thing inside my breast.'

'Well, can you hold them or not?' Mallux asks irritably. 'It is not forever. Just until she agrees to serve me.'

'I can, *Vortas.*'

He turns his head in Telium's direction, his eyes roving over her possessively. Like she is a horse he wishes to buy or a wild thing he thought he had broken, only to be bitten.

'And the courtiers?' the *Tak'nis* enquires, her voice strained as she holds onto the weight of Telium's Gifts.

Mallux snorts in derision. 'If they are not loyal to me, get rid of them. Even those who claim to be will have to earn their salt.'

Earn their salt. Though the pain and betrayal fogs her senses, the words trigger something. Trigg had used similar words when Telium got the first of her *Ta Vir.*

One day, your name will echo throughout the realm of Tenebris and blow through the Gardens of Opimare. Earn your salt and ink, Telium.

Telium blinks and the memory fades. *Earn your salt and ink.* She is more than just her Gifts. Before her powers had started to manifest, she was still the Siren Queen's assassin. Her greatest weapon, her most trusted advisor. At twenty winters, she was the most feared and notorious assassin in Alkoria. They called her Tenebris Kin long before her Gifts. Bloodless Maiden, too.

Her resolve hardens. She had promised Tenebris a soul. Had promised herself to mark the life of the Mad Fae King on her skin before she died. Well, she will die before she becomes Mallux's plaything or broodmare, and he is already well on his way to following in his father's footsteps.

She grits her teeth. Forcing her head up, she eyes Mallux. She creeps her hand slowly towards her chest and the bandolier that holds her last two remaining daggers, one still covered in Jiah's blood.

Without warning, the *Tak'nis* stumbles, pressing a hand to her chest where Telium's Gifts are contained. *'Fe'ta,'* she gasps.

Mallux reaches forward to aid her, leaving himself wide open. From behind the pair, out of Telium's sight, comes the sound of a sword being drawn. Mallux turns his head toward the noise. Seeing her chance, Telium lunges. She explodes up from her knees, crashing into Mallux whose eyes bulge in surprise. Recovering quickly, he wraps his arms around her and smirks down at her. That smile she once thought sexy and charming now fills her with disgust.

She pulls her lips back, baring her straight, human teeth at him. Warmth pools between their bodies. Mallux's smile falters. He looks down between them to where Telium has buried a blade to the hilt under his ribs.

With a savage snarl, she twists the blade into his heart. Blood gushes from the wound with startling speed. She clenches her jaw at the sight, dragging her eyes up to his face. Mallux is looking at her with such betrayal she cannot decide whether to laugh or cry. He looks down, touching his wound wondrously. His fingers come away red with blood.

Blue eyes meet hers, and despite her knowing that for him it was all false – all the trick of a siren's Gifts – her broken, shattered heart cries out when he reaches his fingers to her lips and breathes her name for the last time. Their position mirrors that of Telium and Malakai's only moments ago when she struck him down.

Was it only moments? It feels like a lifetime.

Against her will, she leans into his touch. His fingers are wet with his blood where they touch her lips. A muscle feathers in her jaw as she fights a sob. Her throat closes up. Telium wonders if it is possible to die of heartache. Does not think she cares anymore.

They stand that way for the briefest of moments, wrapped in a lover's embrace. She forces herself to keep staring into his eyes as he sways sideways slightly before his knees give way under him. She keeps her grip on the blade as he falls. It makes a grisly scraping sound against his ribs on the way out.

A pained whimper escapes her. She stares at him as his breath comes in wet, rattling gasps. In her peripheral vision, she sees a pair of black boots come to a stop behind Mallux and the tip of a sword as the owner lowers the blade.

Still, she cannot take her eyes off the male dying at her feet. On his knees, Mallux watches his life-blood drain out of him as if in a trance. It pools in his lap and runs to the floor. Too much, it is too much blood. He will not survive this.

His eyes move lethargically over the area, passing the body of his brother and that of his fallen soldiers. He watches the *Tak'nis* clutch her chest and sway violently, sweat beading her brow as she attempts to wrangle Telium's stolen Gifts into submission. His heartbeat gives a final weak flutter in his chest as he slumps over to the ground, looking up at Telium one last time. Dead.

Mallux is dead.

Dead.

The thundering of feet announces Malakai's soldiers have

finally made it past the last of the rebels. They reach the circular room and see their fallen King, the carnage and dead guards. Then they spot Telium in the middle of it all, blood coating her hands. The sound of a dozen swords being drawn rings through the air. As one, the soldiers move towards her, naked steel at the ready to strike her down in revenge for their King.

She pays them no heed, still gazing at Mallux. She swallows thickly. Tears running unchecked down her face.

'*Tenebris claim you*,' she curses, her voice a cracked whisper.

Telium works her jaw, looking down at him, breathing sharply through her nose as her chest rises and falls with emotion. Her blade clatters to the floor.

Through the haze of pain and dimming rage, there's that tug on her soul again. More insistent this time, followed by an emotion running down the tether – surprise.

A startled noise nearby makes her look up. Wide brown eyes set in a handsome face that is framed by dark hair meet hers. A familiar rain and eucalyptus scent. Paxium. His sword hangs uselessly at his side and he stares at Telium as if she were the sun, the moon and all the stars.

'*Wai'tine*,' he breathes. *Beloved*. '*Keth rel amrath thro'sul*.' *My soul recognises yours*.

EPILOGUE

BEFORE THE WAR

Telium stands on a fallen trunk, looking down on the aftermath of a battle.

Bodies litter the ground, most of them men: soldiers sent to destroy her. The state of their bodies makes it hard to tell how many had fallen to her beasts. Some creatures have been slaughtered as well but countless men lay dead or dying around them, a testament to how many the beasts felled before succumbing to their own injuries.

She jumps down from her perch and walks through the churned-up mud to the closest animal, the squelch of her bare feet in the mud the only sound. The creature's black eyes are glazed, multiple arrows stick out from its body and blood crusts its scaly hide. The ground beneath it looks like a pool of liquid rubies.

The metallic smell of blood lingers in the air, mixing with the woody scent of the forest. She crouches next to the man closest to her, one of the few remaining survivors, his shallow breaths wet and gurgling. An enormous bite wound covers half his chest, blood trickling from it in a steady pulse. The edge of his armour is shredded and dented, revealing mauled flesh beneath.

Telium cocks her head to examine the wound and the single sharp tooth lodged in the armour. Her movement is predatory and animalistic. She glances over her shoulder and notes missing and cracked teeth on the nearby beast – damaged, she assumes, from biting through so many shields and armoured bodies. A sound from the injured man causes her to whip her head back around, the movement unnaturally fast; enhanced by what she has ripped from Thieves.

'Please,' he whispers, his voice barely audible.

Telium gently lays a hand on his chest, armour cool against her fingertips. She pauses and flicks her eyes over his face. Hope lights the man's eyes for a moment until she leans hard against him and savagely rips the embedded tooth free.

The man screams in pain as fresh blood gushes from the wound, coating her hand in a warm, scarlet glove. He reaches for her face, but Telium bats his hand away as she would a fly and stands, leaving the man to bleed out in the dirt.

She surveys the area through bloodshot eyes before walking to the fallen beast and pulling out the teeth loosened by trauma. She works methodically, moving back and forth, removing teeth and claws, each sweep adding to her small, gruesome pile.

⁘

She stalks through the trees in her court clothing, now ripped and stained with dirt and blood. Her bone-white hair is unbound and tangled with sticks and leaves; the ends stained red. Upon her head rests a crown of teeth and claws – a tribute to those creatures who had fought and died for her.

Up ahead, she can hear the screams of those men too wounded to keep up with the furious pace of the retreat. Her beasts have caught up to them. A feral smile splits her face as she reaches them. They cry for help or mercy. Like she has any of either to give.

With her enhanced vision stolen from a Mind-Thief, she can just make out the flicker of movement between the trees in the distance. All discipline has gone as the men break rank and flee before her. She launches into a run, fuelling herself with the swiftness of a Blood-Thief, her beasts letting out excited yowls as they join her in the chase.

The first soldier she comes across dies instantly from a dagger to the back. Not even stopping to remove her blade, Telium carries on. She has no need for blades anyway, not when she can call upon claws and fangs as weapons. She becomes a storm of deadly fury. Anyone who gets within her reach dies or is left with mortal wounds in the undergrowth. Blood and gore crusts under her Thief's talons and dries in her hair.

What feels like moments, but could have been lifetimes, later, Telium stands on the edge of the forest, watching the retreating backs of the men who had come to kill her. The sun is just beginning to stain the sky, black shifting to deep blue. Behind her, the creatures retreat into the depths of the forest to find refuge from the rising sun in their holes and hollows.

At her feet, a young soldier struggles weakly against her grip. A long slash from her talons has left his ear in tatters and a wound streaking across his cheek. Hefting him up by the shirt front so he can look at her, Telium snarls in his face, her fangs gleaming in the growing light. His breath hitches in fear, but he does not beg. With a laugh, she plants a kiss right over his wound, leaving her lips smeared with red blood, before tossing him on the grass at her bare feet.

'Tenebris claim you, should any of you ever return,' she curses, her voice a low, dangerous growl.

She looks down her nose at him, her grotesque crown digging into her brow. As he scrambles to his feet, Telium laughs again and licks the blood from her lips while she watches him back away.

Once he is a few paces from her, he turns tail and flees, stumbling in his haste. She stands for a moment longer, running her tongue along her teeth smeared with the copper tang of blood, before turning her back on the plains and stalking back into the shadows of her forest.

ACKNOWLEDGEMENTS

It's a really bizarre feeling writing acknowledgements for your first novel – like everything has suddenly become very real and I'm a real-life author. When I sat down to start writing, I never imagined I'd actually be here. So many people have helped shape this book from the jumble of scenes it started as to what you read now. So, I'll do my best not to miss anyone, but if I do, just know I appreciate you.

Firstly, of course, a huge thank you to the amazing team at New Dawn. Without whom none of this would be possible. They say having good editors makes all the difference, and I believe in that with every fibre of my being. They have taken my dream to a reality with more excitement and determination than I could have ever dreamed possible – you are all amazing!

Thank you to Dylan and Chelsea, my editors and the head honchos at New Dawn. Thank you for taking a chance on me and believing in *The Assassin Thief* when it still needed so much polishing. You guys have been so gentle with me and my work since we met. Your feedback and hard work has been invaluable in making this book what it is today. Your patience and insight are worth more than I can say. I'm so excited to see what the future brings for New Dawn.

To Ellie and Jen, for your proofreads, excitement and feedback – thank you for being here on this journey with me. I love having fellow readers to get completely side-tracked with during book meetings!

To my lovely marketing agent, Tilly, whose enthusiasm and drive to get this book out into the world is infectious. Thank you for pushing me to write characters I may have otherwise been too scared to without your encouragement.

To my husband, Joey, who has been a constant and steadfast supporter since *The Assassin Thief* was just a vague idea in my head. Thank you for being my sounding board, my ideas-prompter, my snack-bringer, tea-maker and number-one believer from day one. This journey wouldn't have been possible without your love and support. I love you to the moon and back. And back again.

Thank you to Andrew for catching the essence of *The Assassin Thief* with this insanely beautiful cover (it seriously blew me away) and Francesca for bringing the world of Alkoria and Thresiel to life with your gorgeous map.

Thank you to my friends, who have known about my writing journey from very early on and never once told me my dream was too big or far-fetched – especially Jorja, Missy, Katie and Jodie, I love you all. Also to all my friends (online and in real life) that I have found since starting this journey – I am so glad to have met you.

A special shout-out to my brother Ethan and Nanna Alma who kept *The Assassin Thief* a secret from Mum until I couldn't possibly keep it a secret anymore (sorry, Mum, that dream of surprising you with a finished copy of *The Assassin Thief* would have never worked!).

And of course, to my mum, who read me stories as a young girl and nurtured my love for books. Who knew that one day I would be writing acknowledgements for my very own! Thank you for everything.

Writing a book is a hugely personal journey, but one we share with so many people. If I have missed anyone, I'm deeply sorry. But know that everyone in my life influenced this book in some small way.

To my readers, I hope you'll forgive me for that ending! There is more love, fighting and heartache to come. See you all in book two.

Wishing you all good books, swift edits, a comfy armchair and hot tea (or coffee).

Love,
Maddy

RECOGNITION

Dylan Ingram: Publisher, structural editor and typesetter.
Chelsea Wilcox: Copyeditor.
Eleanor Narey: Proofreader.
Matylda Bejger: PR and marketer.
Jennifer Edwards: Publishing assistant.

COLLABORATORS

Andrew Davis: Cover designer (www.andrewdavisdesigns.co.uk).
Francesca Baerald: Map illustrator (www.francescabaerald.com).

PRONUNCIATIONS & TRANSLATIONS

A'gnis	(Ahh g-nis) Flame (gifted Fae)
Altum	(Al-tum) Water (gifted Fae)
Bonai	(Bor-nigh) Good
Cirrus	(Sirrus) Wind (gifted Fae)
De ves tor mesisil?	(Deh ves tore mess-iss-ill) Did you get my message?
Dolomae	(Door-lor-may) Pain (gifted Fae)
Eluth	(E-looth) East
Fe'ta	(Fe tar) An exclamation, like 'oh my!'
Gari de sethta	(Gaa-ri de seth-tah) You may call me
Ha'lau	(Ha lor) Stone (gifted Fae)
Ka'hine	(Car hin-eh) Gifted females. Fae blessed by the All-Mother with Power
Kah	(Caar) Guard/solider
Keth rel amrath thro'sul	(Keth rel am-rath throw sol) My soul recognises yours. What is spoken when a soulmate finds their beloved
Kia'ra	(Key-ah rah) Teacher. Directly translates to 'learned'
La'ne	(Lah neh) Sir/male
Lei'kah	(Lee caar) The royal guard

Lei'sidio	(Leh Si-dee-oh) Meaning 'the guard'. A set of large, carved stone pillars scattered throughout Thresiel
Li'ne	(Li neh) Lady/female
Lotos	(Luo-tos) Grandfather/elderly male
Meannthe	(Me-anne-thee) The Fae capital of Thresiel
Na'tai	(Nah tie) Seed (gifted Fae)
Nai vel'e	(Nai vel eh) Farewell
Neuth	(Nee ooth) North
Niya	(Ni-ya) No
Ohic'a	(Or-hic-ahh) Eye (gifted Fae)
Pae'ri	(Pay ree) Sorry/forgive me
Pito	(Pit-or) Rum
Ra'sito	(Rah sit-oh) Distorter (gifted Fae)
Rai'na	(Rye-nah) Dye, commonly for the hair, can also refer to dye for the skin or clothes
Ramaeris	(Ra-meh-ah-ris) Fae festival
Rel sekta	(Rel sec-tah) I am ready
Sak	(A as in back) Stop
Sek lith ses de mo'ra	(Sec lith ses deh mo rah) I will see you again
Sekta	(Sec-taa) I am
Sen	Silver coin
Seuth	(Se-ooth) South
Sk'ril	(Sk rill) Oaf/brute
Tak'nis	(Tah-k nis) Void (gifted Fae)
Tanu de rel'ak	(Tah-new deh rell ack) You are mine
Telith	(Tell-ith) Really
Threal	(Three-al) Peace
Thresiel	(Three-sea-el) The Fae Lands
Thril'ra	(Thrill-rah) Thank you
Thro'sul	(Throw sol) Soul
Tia'tum	(Tee-ah tum) Shield (gifted Fae)

To'a kep	(Tow a kep) Scouts/spys
Upa	(Oo-pa) Pet
Vel	(Like bell) Yes/okay
Vel Thruik	(Vel trough-ick) Well met. A Fae greeting
Wai'tan	(Why taan) Beloved/soulmate (masculine)
Wai'tina	(Why tin-uh) Beloved/soulmate (gender neutral)
Wai'tinate	(Why tin-ahh-the) The Bond between Fae. Literally translates to 'the tether'
Wai'tine	(Why tin-ehh) Beloved/soulmate (feminine)
We'ng	(Wey-ing) West

CONTENT GUIDANCE

This book is recomended for mature audiences. It contains themes that may not be appropriate for some readers. These include, but are not limited to, the following:

- Violence (including weapon violence).
- Death.
- Rape.
- Miscarriage.
- Sexual content.
- Coarse language.

For more information about content guidance in this book, please visit the product page on our website.

www.newdawnpublishing.com.au/the-assassin-thief

Madeline Te Whiu is a veterinary nurse based in Perth, Western Australia. She lives with her husband, dog, two cats and small flock of chickens.

Her passion for books began when she was growing up in rural South Australia. She has always had an avidity for reading, with her favourite authors being Victoria Aveyard, Sarah J Maas and Peter V Brett, just to name a few.

For more information on Madeline check out her socials:

@madelinetewhiu